Dispatches from the Cold

a novel

Leonard Chang

T0164325

BLACK
HERON
PRESS

ISBN 978-0-930773-93-9

Black Heron Press
Post Office Box 13396
Mill Creek, Washington 98082
www.blackheronpress.com

For
Joseph Strauss

ACKNOWLEDGEMENTS

The author wishes to thank the following people for their help with this book: Jerry Gold, Judith Grossman, Walter Lew, Ben Pham, and Art Sousa.

A special thanks to Cara, again, for everything.

Dispatches
from the Cold

Part I
Presidents' Day Sale

1

Everything I learned about Farrel Gorden I learned from reading his letters, and although I knew reading someone else's mail was illegal, the letters that came to my apartment that year I was living in Marnole, Long Island, that year I lost my job, and my money was running out, and in my naive way I thought that my life was ending at the young age of twenty-nine, the letters helped distract me from my problems, helped me become concerned about something, anything other than myself.

I was living in an old apartment on Sunrise Highway, about two hundred feet from the Long Island Railroad tracks, the hourly rumbling and shaking of the earth first driving me mad, but then becoming a punctual, rhythmic reminder of movement, of life. The rent for this apartment was cheap, since I was in an old building right in front of a busy, noisy highway and railroad, and directly below my studio was Lucky's, a three-tabled, six-stooled bar where it seemed only Led Zeppelin and The Charlie Daniels Band pulsed and whined through the jukebox and through my floor. The trains shaking by every hour, the cars honking and speeding by my window, the high-pitched screeching of Heaven and Hell—I learned to like it there, eventually.

Recently laid off from my high school teaching job, I was living off my savings until the summer arrived, when I would have a three-month teaching job at the community college extension, a job I had set up long before I knew I was about to be let go. I was too depressed to look for another job—too depressed to do anything, really—so I stayed in bed until the mail came at around one, read newspapers, watched my portable black and white television set, and stared out the window, hypnotized by the cars driving by in the brown and grey slush.

I am sure that Farrel Gorden, the letter writer, during this time could have stared at less mundane things. Semi-rural New Hampshire in January: sun blinding white snow, tall green pines, the smell of burning firewood, and cold, Canadian air. Maybe four-wheel drives or cars with chains churned down unplowed roads. I had never been to Yanack, New Hampshire, but from his letters I pictured his house, his street, his town. So much of his life was vivid to me, and even now after all this time I can still imagine Gorden's full, reddish brown hair, his freshly-shaven face with small acne scars near his sideburns, and his white shirt and blue tie he wore to work every day. I can still imagine him lowering the hunting rifle slowly, the long, black barrel coming to rest on warm, perspiring skin, pressing lightly, indenting, aiming.

The day the first letter arrived, I thought nothing of it. It was addressed to a Ms. Mona Gorden, and this former tenant received advertisements or bills here often, which I either threw out or left on the counter beneath the mailboxes, and the mailman, the landlord, or someone would usually take them away. In a business envelope with the return address of "Jakeson's Sporting Goods," Mona Gorden's name and my address were handwritten neatly on the front in small block letters, and this particular letter seemed important, though now I am not sure why I thought so, but I brought it upstairs with me, making a mental note to write "Return to Sender—No Forwarding Address" on the front and drop it in the mailbox on the corner. I was normally not this considerate, but I had always had bad luck with the Post Office—lost mail, insufficient postage—so I thought I would give the sender a break. I threw the envelope on my kitchen counter, along with other "To Do" items; I still had to fill out a few job applications, write my adoptive mother in Chicago, and read the Kendal-Marnole School District Newsletter, which I knew would have more news about budget cuts and layoffs.

I did not know at the time that Mona Gorden was dead, and that Farrel Gorden was her brother, and this letter was the beginning of a long, strange, one-way correspondence to the buried. All I knew was that the letter happened to be some misdirected mail, and I had other things to think about.

Often, when I felt suffocated and I was sick of looking at my room, the grungy mattress on the floor, the unused desk with old grade booklets still scattered on my blotter, I would walk outside and across the highway to the railroad platform. The Long Island Railroad company had constructed elevated tracks that lay on huge concrete Y-shaped blocks about fifty feet off the ground, the base of the blocks at least twenty feet thick. Below the tracks were ticket windows and a newspaper stand, and this concrete area was kept clean, shoveled and swept by an old hunched-over man who lived nearby, whom I would see at the diner down the street. That night, after I threw the letter onto the other piles, I walked outside into the cold, sharp air, waited at the corner as cars roared and splashed by in the sickly yellow streetlights, and I hurried across the muddy highway. The station downstairs was empty, and as I climbed the stairs of the train platform, hearing the winter wind echo in the stairwell, smelling oily, freezing air, I thought only of how eerie this place was. During the morning and evening rush hours, I could see packs of bundled-up commuters huddled at spots where they knew the train doors would stop, hoping to get a seat. But now it was too cold, too late. When I reached the top, I stood behind the blue divider which shielded me from the wind, advertisements for Broadway shows and movies on the thick rippled plastic. I saw my three-story red-brick building, with Lucky's on the ground floor, a few cars parked in the small parking lot. There was a Mobil station across the street, a clothing store one block over. Marnole was a residential suburb, with ten times as many privately owned homes as apartment buildings, and slowly the buildings were being bought out, knocked down, and two or three small houses put up. My building on the corner of Sunrise and Harold Street was the only apartment building in view from the railroad platform. I stayed up here, wondering what was happening to me, why I felt so lousy, and I thought, It's the weather, the snow. The wind was becoming too much for me, swirling around the divider and freezing my bare ears, and after the New York train came and went, I walked back to my apartment, my face stinging with cold.

When the second letter came less than a week later, I stared at the envelope and asked myself what was so important that required two letters within five days. Both envelopes were thin, and when I held one up to a light bulb, I saw beneath the overlapping pages small, dot matrix print. I became curious, but resisted the temptation to open the letters. Instead, I put the second letter with the first, and reminded myself again to send these off. It crossed my mind that Jakeson's might have been waiting for a reply, so I told myself to send them out tomorrow.

But each day seemed like the last; they blurred together in my mind, and I stopped looking at my calendar. Time, not just dragging by but hitting an impenetrable wall, halted. I was always so tired and stayed in bed longer and longer, not bothering to wash, drinking coffee and Kahlua; I lost track of the days, staring at the waves of hot air quivering from my heater towards my window.

By the time the third letter arrived, I had been unwashed for days, unshaven for longer, and I had come to depend on the wincing sweetness of Kahlua in my coffee. The third letter to Ms. Mona Gorden was in my hand as I trudged upstairs with my newspapers, my bills, and coffee mug, throwing this mysterious addition onto my pile on the kitchen counter. I stared at the mess of papers and crumbs, wondering what was so urgent about these letters, and in a fit of irrational annoyance (Who the hell is writing me all the time? I thought) I opened the third letter.

I won't quote the entire two-page, single-spaced, small-font letter, but as I skimmed the paragraphs, looking for an explanation, I ran across this:

> ..but I already wrote that to you Mona. In my last letter I think I told you about my goddamn cocksucking boss, and how he made me shave off my beard and said I had to clean up my act and I told him I worked here longer than you and he said yeah, but Im the boss. Fucking christ I want to knock his damn teeth out. But hell I wrote all of this before. Sorry for the ramblin. I feel better writing this all out so dont mind me, big sis, and Shari is probably drunk as shit right now so I cant talk to her. I dont know what to do with her, that dumb bitch. I didnt hear from you yet but thats ok. I dont mind writing to a listening audience. Its even easier knowing youre listening and all I gotta do is write this. I can sorta picture you sitting there reading this and shaking your head like you do and saying, that kid is running off at the mouth again. But that goddamn guy is driving me nuts...

A listening audience. This partially answered my question as to why he would continue writing without any replies, though I felt uneasy that I, not Ms. Mona Gorden, was the audience. But Farrel Gorden's enterprise was still viable—that is, for him to have someone to read about his problems, and, at this stage of our one-way relationship, Farrel Gorden seemed less concerned about receiving answers than with just mouthing off. Anyway, I made myself another cup of coffee after re-reading his letter carefully, not fully understanding some of the references. Who was Shari? This letter went on and on about his boss, and about this woman, Shari, whom he was living with, or married to, though I couldn't tell.

Re-reading the letter now, I wonder if I have adopted this purpose of having a listening audience, needing to review and consider everything through writing, if this is one of the things prompting me to write about Gorden. Perhaps because I too need a Mona Gorden I write this to an unseen, receptive audience. Perhaps it took me this long to assimilate and understand Gorden, and it has taken me this long to reveal this material, finally, completely, and maybe even in the clichéd fashion of the writing cure—therapeutically?

After reading that letter back then, I knew I couldn't return the opened envelope, and I figured that since I had already read the third one, opening the first and second ones was only logical. As I ripped open the first envelope, I felt a vague sense of moral impropriety. Would *I* want some person to open my letters sent to an old address? Well, I probably wouldn't send letters to someone who did not respond, that was certain, because how could I know that the person had indeed received the letters? Might not there be another dangerously curious reader, like myself, lurking by mail-boxes? Of course this would not happen to *me*. As for Gorden, well, I could pretend to be his sister, and read his letters with a detached, analytical eye. Why not? Besides, Gorden wouldn't know the difference. I pushed aside my doubts and began reading. Perhaps as an introduction I ought to quote the opening passages of Farrel Gorden's first letter to his sister.

> Sis, its been years since I last wrote you and I was wondering how you are and whats life been like, since things here are getting bad and I thought I could talk to you about things. Im at the department store still working at Jakesons and I was promoted as head of sales half a year ago. Not bad for a dumb shit, heh? I get to stay

late to close up and take care of receipts and all that, and Im learning how to use this computer. Im not supposed to use it, alls I do is record the sales in a book and the assistant manager takes care of the computer records. But shit, Im here anyway and this thing is sitting here and whats the problem with playing around with it? I aint heard from you in a while, and ever since ma died we dont get to see each other anymore. I was going to call but I hate using the fucking phone and besides, I dont know your number. Did you ever give it to me? I hear you getting into some heavy shit down there in NY and dont expect me to give you any money again. You still owe me about four hundred, remember?...

I had some trouble getting used to his writing, because I had the impulse to add punctuation and apostrophes, but then I thought about the biology papers I used to receive, the pseudo-scientific, ungrammatical jargon from students trying to impress me, and I didn't care so much anymore.

To ease my conscience, I thought I should at least find out where Ms. Mona Gorden lived now, and perhaps redirect the mail, even though I wanted to continue receiving the letters. I had to at least try. This was when I learned from the landlord that Mona Gorden had been evicted. She was a heroin addict and everyone in the building knew it. The landlord, a small compact man who came by on Wednesdays told me that she was a basket case (his words) and after she got sick all over the front stairs one night and had some kind of fit, he gave her an ultimatum. He demanded the last two months rent, which she didn't have, so he promptly threw her out. "She was a fuckin' pain in the ass," he told me. "And I was sick of her. And for all I know she's ten feet under the dirt right now."

I realized I had become Mona Gorden, the drug-addicted letter reader who lived alone in a cramped studio, tired and sick.

The letters continued regularly. Once a week, I would find in my mailbox a letter for a missing woman, from a stranger. Farrel

Gorden told me every detail of his life for the next six months, but before the stream of letters began, I wanted to know more about him. Although I tried unsuccessfully to research him in the library, not even finding his number in a New Hampshire telephone book, I learned that Jakeson's Sporting Goods was a chain of stores along the east coast, concentrated in the Northeast. I remembered a Jakeson's in Boston, at Copley, I believe, though I had been in it only once, browsing for a pair of sneakers. Farrel Gorden's store, I learned, was one of three in the southern New Hampshire area, located in Yanack Hills Mall, right off I-89 on the edge of the middle-sized town of Yanack.

2

The letters became a part of my routine. Sometimes delayed a day or two, the same envelopes with the same "Jakeson's Sporting Goods" logo in which the "J" was large and bordered with silver, and the same hand-printed address for my alter-ego—these letters usually appeared in my mailbox on Fridays. I began to anticipate Fridays as I used to when I had been teaching. I held labs at the end of the week, so my lectures were condensed to ten minutes at the beginning of class, telling the students the objectives of the lab experiment (they should have read the procedures the night before) and the safety guidelines. Then, for the next forty minutes, while my students dissected frogs, played with planaria, or experimented with genetic offspring variations in *Drosophila*, I would sit at my desk and read. Although I would have biology texts all around me, I was usually reading a novel or a book of essays I had picked up at the library.

But now unemployed, I spent each day no differently from the next. The only way I knew it was a weekend was from the noise below—the jukebox, the occasional yelling and cheering; that is, until the letters started arriving. After I found the pattern that

Gorden used when writing—he began on the weekend, eventually sending the letter out on Monday or Tuesday—I became a subscriber to a serial magazine, an addict to a soap opera, awaiting the next weekly installment. Please understand that though the letters weren't always interesting or coherent—and even if they were, they often became distasteful—it was my first form of human contact for some time, and when one is starved for unencumbered distractions, no matter how trivial or how strange, one isn't very selective. My isolation was so complete that I could go days without saying a word. I often wondered if I could actually forget how to speak, if my tongue wouldn't form the words, if my larynx would atrophy from disuse.

I did see other people when I went to the grocery, or to the diner, but most of the time I stayed in my apartment, or when the weather warmed I stood on the train platform, watching the snow recede, deep green patches of Marnole's sodded lawns slowly coloring my view.

I think I identified with Farrel Gorden because his relatively solitary life resembled my own. He lived in a small one-bedroom house with a woman named Shari, actually a teenager he had become involved with four or five months before the beginning of the letters. He didn't write much about Shari or his home for a few weeks. He did however briefly mention his house in his second letter:

...you aint seen this place but because it was built small and its far from town, I got a good price and the real estate market is so bad that the bank gave me a mortgage that wont kill me. Shit I could have this place paid off in ten years and probably sell it for a profit, alls I got to do is fix it up a bit. The roof needs some better shingles, which I can do anytime, and a paint job would make it look nice, and maybe the yard once the snow melts could be fixed up. But its not bad looking dont get me wrong, I just got a nice plush carpet and old Doney a few houses down had some couches and tables he was getting rid of, and he gave them to me for free, so I got some nice furniture...

Though this wasn't a complete picture, I imagined his house to be somewhat dilapidated, the roof missing tiles, torn patches exposed to the cold New Hampshire nights, and the front of the small boxy house with two windows had paint peeling off in long jagged strips. Dirty white was the color I saw, with chipped brick steps. Though it was winter and most of the vegetation had died, brown snow-covered weeds once trying to push between the cracks of the cement walkway now reached up frozen, clawed, like fingers in rigor mortis.

I suppose that morning would be a good place to begin, since Gorden's life was fairly routine before he went to work that day when everything changed. He worked seven days a week, ten a.m. to six p.m. on weekdays, three to nine on weekends, and would wake up half an hour before his shift. He would shower, change, and climb into his old Toyota which he hated, but since he couldn't afford a new (or even a decent used) car at the moment, he tolerated the ugly brown rusting body, the seats ripped in dozens of places from carrying equipment, and the stiff steering wheel. The turn signal had stopped blinking a few months ago, so whenever he signalled, he had to push the lever up and down and few times, manually making the lights blink. He would drive onto I-89 (although the mall was in Yanack and he could use the local streets, it was faster to take the freeway) and after ten minutes he would arrive at the Yanack Hills Mall.

That morning when his routine would be broken, he was shivering in his car driving as fast as he could since the heater wasn't working right. I saw him hunched over his steering wheel, thinking about how Shari had been hung over this morning, again, when he had left her. Her eyes were puffy and bloodshot, hair so matted and tangled that he had wanted to force a brush through it.

She had not been able to move, even lift up her head from her pillow.

He began getting angry as he thought about her downing a bottle of wine every night like it was water. Like it was fucking water, he thought. But *he* was the one paying for it. Losing her job at the steak place. How hard was it to wait on tables? Shit, he said to himself. What the hell was she gonna do now?

Gorden turned on the radio and let the news fill the car; he tried not to get angry. She was becoming more of a pain every day. Within the time he had known her, Shari had lost three jobs, the waitressing one being the last. She had been a cashier at the grocery before that, and she had been working at a fast food place in the mall when Gorden had first met her. This had been in August, not too long after his promotion.

He had been on a lunch break when he went to Leroy's Frankfurters and Grill at the other end of the mall, where most of the food places were—the Yogurt Palace, Rotolo Pizza—the smells of burgers filling the small court, and when he placed his order for a hot dog and fries at the counter, the skinny, bony girl who looked like she couldn't be more than fifteen, saw his name tag "Farrel Gorden, Head Sales" and his clean white shirt and navy blue tie, his face red-bearded with a full mustache, and she smiled. She asked him what kind of name was Farrel, and fixed her striped paper hat, pushing a lock of curly brown hair underneath the "L" in "Leroy's". Her face was mousy: a tight-angled chin, a small nose, large eyes, and her two front teeth were crooked. She had long, dark, curly hair that was tied in a thick ponytail with three rubber bands a few inches apart. He shrugged at the question, because he never knew why he had been named Farrel—he hated the name and preferred to be called Gorden—though he liked how this girl looked. He went to Leroy's more often, and eventually asked her out.

Now, turning into the Mall parking lot, he wondered if he should have done that. She was pretty damn quick to move herself into his place. But it was too late now. He pulled into an empty space, in between a Chevy Van and a Jeep, letting his engine idle, cool down, before he turned it off. He sat up and checked himself in the rear-view mirror—his bushy hair tended to stick up in the back, and he patted it down. His beard was becoming too thick, with uneven curly hairs growing out. He patted his face, reminding himself to trim this later. Zipping up his black ski jacket, he climbed out, slamming the door and rattling the whole car. He jogged to the entrance, trying not to step in the snow.

Yanack Hills Mall was shaped like a "T" with two levels. There were large department stores at each end of the "T", and a number of smaller shops in the main stretch on both the upper and lower levels. Jakeson's Sporting Goods was at the intersection on the lower level, a prime location since everyone had to pass it to get to somewhere, and Jakeson's was large enough so that Kramer's, the department store on the left, closed its own sporting goods section and expanded its home furnishings.

Not many people were here at ten o'clock on a Monday morning, except for the man in brown maintenance overalls polishing the floors, the perfumed wax smell irritating Gorden's nose, but the gentle whirring as the man pushed the soft spinning disc back and forth, back and forth, was relaxing to hear. There were a few customers wandering the halls, heading towards Kramer's. When the mall was like this—quiet, cavernous, still—Gorden liked it. He could hear his shoes tapping on the floor, hushed voices among a few people. No Muzak yet. The smells of stale cigarette smoke and mingling foods were not present, at least not for an hour or so. Instead, everything smelled clean, new.

He saw the unlit "Jakeson's Sporting Goods" sign in dark green lettering over a white background, and noticed that the metal fence had not yet been lifted, which was odd. He checked his watch: five after ten. The store should have opened by now. Walking to the side entrance next to the Cappella clothing store, he let himself in with his key, making sure the heavy metal door was securely closed. He was now in the stockroom, a large, high-ceiling storage room where boxes upon boxes of sports equipment, clothing, and sneakers were kept, some stacks twice as high as Gorden. He heard voices in the front office, a section of the stockroom with a large two-way mirror facing the showroom. His steps echoed on the cement and it became quiet inside the office. The door was open. He looked in.

"It's you. Jeez, you scared me," John, the assistant manager said. He rubbed his temple with his large hand, his arms too muscular for his shirt. A former wrestler, John still worked out and knew everything about the weight-lifting equipment.

John and the young salesman, Henry, were the only ones here—John sitting on his desk with a cup of coffee, and Henry leaning back in his chair, twirling a pencil in his fingers. "I thought it was the guy," Henry said.

"What guy?" Gorden asked.

"Shit Gord, Manny was fired." John shook his head. Manny was the head manager. "I just got a call from the Manchester office. Manny's out."

"Just like that," Henry said.

"What'd he do?"

"Nothing," John said. "That's probably why. His replacement's coming in today."

"From Boston. They're transferring someone already," Henry said.

"Probably a hot shit."

Gorden nodded, worried. Manny was the reason Gorden had become head of sales. There were a couple of times Manny had covered his ass, like when he had misdirected a new shipment of fishing gear, right before fishing season. Gorden had probably lost at least a thousand in sales, but Manny let it go. "When's he coming?"

"In the afternoon, I think," John said, looking at his watch. "We better open. I bet what's-her-name is waiting out there." What's her name, Lorraine, worked the register on weekdays. She didn't have a key.

John, Henry, and Gorden left the office and began preparing for the day. Gorden told Henry that they were putting Bauer hockey skates on sale next weekend, and left it up to him to handle the promo, and their ski jackets were moving too slowly, so he also told Henry to try to get more off the rack. Henry nodded, and walked into the showroom. Gorden sat at his desk to check his calendar. The K-2 skis were selling great, and he had to order more today, stock up before ski season ended.

So what about this fucking new guy, he thought, tapping his pen and looking out the mirror, the blinds down but the slats open. The showroom was empty and seemed darker through the glass. So, Manny's gone. Yesterday his one day off and he doesn't come back. Gorden sat up straight and looked at the desk closest to the window. Shit. His desk already cleaned off. Probably came this morning, or late last night. Didn't want to see anyone.

Gorden felt his stomach growl. He shifted uncomfortably in his seat. Manny had a goddamn kid. A wife. What the fuck. What was Manny going to do now? Gorden tapped his pen a few more times, then began filling out order forms; he checked the inventory of goods sold this week.

Job security. I think I knew how Gorden felt, especially then. I knew I should have been looking for another job, but I was so tired of it all. I wasn't even thirty but I felt like I had been teaching for decades. Teaching high school, some don't realize, is one of the most tiring jobs you could have. When I taught I was awake by six-thirty, at school by seven for homeroom, taught Intro Bio, two classes of General Bio, and two classes of Advanced Placement Bio, stayed for an hour or two after school for extra help, came home by five and graded papers, lab reports, and prepared my lesson plans for the next day. By eight or nine o'clock in the evening I didn't have enough energy to do anything except read in bed. Sometimes even that was too much, so I simply watched television. I did this for four years, and for my first year I had to stay after school even later to take care of jobs they assigned the new teachers, like detention hall or supervising the basketball courts, which kept me in school until six.

When I read how Gorden felt while at his desk, wondering about how easy it was to be fired, I thought about my lay-off. I had assumed I had some security—four years gave me some seniority—but as soon as the budget cuts began, and education spending fell, I was one of the first to go. Some older faculty members opted to retire early with their pensions, but it wasn't enough. When the rumors began spreading, my thoughts were similar to Gorden's. He wrote:

... shit I knew that I was Mannys hire and whatever they did to him they could do to me, and I was making some decent money and now some little shit from upstairs was gonna come in and fuck around? I was getting pissed about this and wanted to meet this guy who was supposed to be my new boss. What was he some kind of superman or something? Manny did a ok job and he looked out for us and tried to do the store good and this is what he gets and he got to support a wife a goddamn kid? If I got canned and had to look for another shit job I dont know what I could do except move boxes again. I got a sweet deal here and now things are screwing up. Yeah I gotta expect this since nothing goes right for me anyway...

That morning the hours went by slowly—Monday mornings were usually the worst—and he spent most of the time in the showroom, inspecting displays. Although Gorden didn't describe the store in detail, Jakeson's tried to keep their branches similar in layout and management, so I imagined the Yanack version was not much different from my recollection of the Boston outlet. I pictured a huge room, almost warehouse size, and in one corner would be the athletic shoes—tennis, basketball, walking, running, high-tops, low-tops—all lined up in neat rows against the wall, with comfortable chairs and shoe size measurers scattered on the floor, smells of new leather and foot odor. Another corner would have clothing: racks of ski jackets in bright green and orange neon stripes, then the regular sportswear like sweat suits and shirts and shorts. The rest of the showroom would have all the sports equipment you would expect: aisles devoted to fishing—rods standing cluttered to one side, springy, whip-like tips hanging high above—with tackle and lures and weights and bobbers; camping; skiing; then, a general sports aisle with bats and rackets and balls for every sport. In the center of the showroom would be the stationary bikes that kids climbed and pedalled for a few minutes until they tired; treadmills, weight benches, stair climbers, and all the accoutrements of the home exerciser, though everyone knew that most of this equipment went unused after a few months of vigorous dedication.

Gorden walked around the displays. He really didn't care how they looked, in fact he barely noticed what was in front of him. He knew his job was in trouble. He just knew it. Like Shari sometimes said in that soft, whiney voice, "Can't you just *feel* it?" Shari. What the hell was he going to do with her? Goddamn pain in the ass, he thought, frowning.

"Hey Gord, I'm going to check what One-Stop is charging for their ski jackets," Henry called to him.

Gorden looked up. Realizing what had been said, he nodded. Henry took off his name tag, grinned, and walked out of the store.

Kiss-ass wants my job, he told himself. He knew Henry would lick the new guy's butt fast. Just when things started going well for Gorden, this had to happen. Looking around and seeing the store empty, he decided to go to lunch early. He walked down the long row of stores towards the food court, glancing at the growing number of customers filling the stores, and he wondered why Jakeson's business was slow. Were sporting goods becoming unpopular? Maybe that was why Manny had been fired.

Leroy's was crowded, the lines at the counter long, and he liked the smell of the various sandwiches filling the room. Through

Leroy's was known for its frankfurters, it also had burgers, chicken and fish sandwiches, and salads. Everything was bright in here, with red and yellow plastic tables and stools bolted to the floor, brown-uniformed Leroy workers sweeping and wiping. When Gorden's turn in line came up, he ordered what he always ordered and took his dog and fries outside.

Sitting on one of the benches in the food court, he watched the other employees come for their lunch, clustering in groups of three or four, the department store employees dressed better than the others. He saw men in expensive suits, looking like they worked in banks rather than Men's Clothing, and some tall, heavily made-up women who worked in the ground level, in perfumes and make-up. Gorden used to hate these people, these beautiful ugly people, but now he knew they were just nobody shits like him, but better dressed, and like him they wished they were somewhere else instead of a boonies mall. He should get out of this place. He told himself this all the time, get the fuck out of this shit hole, but he never listened. Instead he chained himself to a mortgage.

After he finished he walked slowly back to the store, feeling more relaxed than this morning, thinking, maybe the new guy will make the store better. He saw a few customers inside Jakeson's, browsing in different parts, but he didn't see Henry or any salesmen. He looked for Lorraine, and she motioned for him to come over, her bracelets jangling with each gesture. Lorraine was a middle-aged woman whose children had all left home. She had come to work here only a year ago.

"What's wrong?" he asked her.

"Gorden, the new boss's in back. Where were you?"

"At lunch."

"Everyone's in there. You better go."

"Shit," he said, walking towards the office. "Thanks." Goddamn it all, he thought, hurrying down the red-carpeted aisle, thinking of an excuse. Late already.

3

Heads turned towards him as he opened the door. Gorden saw everyone: John, Henry, and two more salespeople who usually came in at noon—Norma and Warren—and the new guy. Gorden stopped in confusion. The new guy, standing by the window, was Chinese or something. There was an awkward pause as Gorden closed the door behind him. The new guy wore a suit, the same kind as the Men's Clothing salesmen, and he had thin silver wire glasses over his smooth round face. His hair was neatly combed to one side, cut well above his ears. He was short, about five and a half feet, and stocky with extra weight around his middle.

"Mr. Gorden?" the man asked with a slight accent. Mistah Gortin. Gorden looked at John, who stared back, expressionless, but Gorden thought he noticed a slight nod.

"Yes. I didn't know we were having a meeting."

"It was a long lunch hour?" the man asked pleasantly, almost smiling. "I came here at twelve, and now it is," he checked his wristwatch, black and gold, "one-thirty?" Wan-tirty.

Fuck, Gorden thought, this bastard's gonna break my balls. "Yeah. I got held up."

"By what?"

Gorden was caught off-guard, the guy's question shot right back without warning. He paused. "The lines were long."

"Of course." He turned to the others—Gorden noticed a small bald spot on the top of his head—and said, "As I was saying, the Manchester office..." He stopped and turned around again. "Oh, my name is Shin. Roger Shin," he said to Gorden. "I understand you like to be called Gorden?"

"Yeah." What the fuck, he thought. They were talking about me when I wasn't here? What'd they say?

Roger Shin continued his speech. Gorden met John's eyes and John smirked, signalling it was okay, telling him, This guy ain't nothing. Gorden felt more at ease, but worried that he'd made a bad impression. Who the hell is this guy, he thought. Coming in here and telling you your lunch break was too long. Breaking your balls already and the guy hasn't been here two seconds. Shit, he's the boss now so stop bitching.

"...You understand, Gorden?" Gor-Ten.

He looked up, confused. Ah, hell. "What was that?"

Roger Shin smiled. "Gorden is still on his long lunch hour."

Laughter. Gorden tightened his fist, and grinned. Fucking gook. Can't fucking speak English straight and making fucking jokes. Goddamn slant-eyed son of a bitch. Gorden glanced at John, but John was staring at a folder on his desk.

"I said that I'm only acting manager until Boston finds a replacement. I am more of a consultant, a trouble-shooter."

"We have trouble?"

Shin smiled again, but this time Gorden saw his round jaw tense. "Yes. This past Christmas your profits were almost half of the year before. Also, your previous manager was very sloppy. The accounts, the reports, everything," he said. "I have to be here for a while, fixing what was done."

"Manny tried his best," Gorden said. The room was still.

Shin nodded slowly and said nothing, the silence answering Gorden. As the new manager of Jakeson's began talking again, this time outlining a three-month plan for reorganization, beginning with the next sale in a few weeks for the Presidents' Day weekend, his open hands chopping the air for emphasis, the weight of his chubby body shifting from foot to foot, Gorden hated him.

The meeting broke up and everyone went to work. Shin sat at Manny's old desk and began looking through files and reports. Gorden walked out into the showroom, angry at being made to look stupid in front of the others. He exhaled slowly, not wanting to let it bother him, and stared at the ski jacket displays. Henry came up behind him.

"One-Stop knocked a few bucks off their CB's," he said, motioning to one of the more expensive ski jackets. "They must have done it right after Christmas."

Gorden nodded.

"So what'd you think of him?" Henry asked. "That guy Roger."

"Annoying son of a bitch."

Henry laughed tentatively, a quiet, punchy laughter with his eyes still on Gorden. He said, "But he's smart. Went to business school and everything."

"Yeah?" Gorden asked. "How'd you know?"

"He told me."

Gorden was about to say something like, Getting real buddy-buddy aren't you? But he kept quiet. He knew Henry would do this, so why bother. "What else he tell you?"

"Him and his wife are living in Sunolea, near the school."

"Wife?" he asked. The guy was married?

"Wife and kid. Two-year-old, I think."

Gorden thought, A fucking family man, just like Manny. What was Shin's wife like? Then he wondered how Henry knew all this. Kiss-ass. While Gorden had been off stuffing his face with hot dogs, Henry here had been snuggling up to Shin. He stared at Henry. "We've got to move these jackets, and they're not moving yet," he said, abruptly. "Maybe the CB's can be knocked down." He was talking more to himself than to the kiss-ass. "I'll talk to John." He walked away quickly.

Opening the office door, he saw John and Shin at their desks. They both looked up. "John," Gorden said, not wanting to talk in front of Shin, but he couldn't walk out now. "One-Stop lowered their CB's by a few dollars. Should we knock ours down?"

"What?" John asked.

"No, not yet," Shin answered. "Wait and see if One-Stop does any better."

"But we overstocked—"

"I know, Gorden," he said. "I see here that you overstocked." He looked down at the records, the copies of the invoices that

Gorden had filled out. "But winter will still be here for a few months. No hurry." He looked up.

Gorden hesitated. "All right," he said, and closed the door. *I overstocked*, he thought, cursing under his breath. The guy made sure he pointed it out, that *I* was the one responsible for the CB's. The asshole. He didn't have to do that.

John and Gorden went out for a drink after work. The Camain Bar and Restaurant was a few miles away from the mall, and they met there at six-thirty. Shin, they had noticed, was staying late to go over the books. This made them nervous.

"What if he finds something wrong? My neck's in the fucking ringer," John said after they sat in one of the booths. "Jesus. They passed right over me. Didn't even consider me to take Manny's position. Gonna hire some outsider. No justice."

"The Chinese guy's leaving after a while," Gorden said.

"I think he's Korean. But yeah, after him, there'll be another. I'm just a fucking dog they kick around." He gripped his beer. "I mean, shit, it was *me* that done the books these past months." Gorden watched John's thick forearms tense on the table, and understanding that everyone, not just him, was worried made him feel better. He looked around the restaurant and saw a family sitting at one of the tables. Two kids eating hungrily, grabbing their forks like small shovels, the parents talking between themselves. The lamp above their table hung lower than the others, and lit up their faces. A waiter came over to the family, asking if everything was okay. One of the kids, the girl, lifted her fork and made designs in the air. The mother told her to stop.

"Shin's got a wife and kid, you know that?" Gorden asked.

John nodded. "Henry told me."

"Kiss-ass Henry."

"No damn justice."

Gorden said nothing, drinking his beer.

"What, they think I'm not ready for manager?" John said. "I

practically kept Manny from fucking up the place. You wouldn't believe how stupid he was."

"Manny?"

"Yeah, not caring about inventory, or keeping everything up-to-date. He didn't care."

"He had a wife and kid too."

"But no, they send some shitkicker to 'troubleshoot'—shoot me is what they mean—and then they'll send someone else to go right over my dead body. No damn justice. I work fucking hard."

Gorden kept quiet. John shook his head and muttered to himself, gripping and releasing his empty beer mug. They ordered another round, and Gorden began to feel the alcohol in his head, the nice light feeling. He began to forget about the day at work, not caring anymore if Shin gave him a hard time, if the little runt bossed him around. It was only for a few months, and though Gorden had screwed up, hadn't everyone? He shouldn't worry so much.

After their third beer, John told him that he had to leave. Gorden decided to stay for a while longer, and watched John throw a five and a couple of ones on the table. "Maybe Shin'll get hit by a car or something," Gorden said as John rose slowly.

"That'd be nice." He nodded goodbye and lumbered away.

Watching John disappear behind a row of booths, Gorden wondered where he lived. Once in a conversation, John had mentioned living outside of Concord, but hadn't been very specific. In fact, Gorden knew very little about his co-worker. This had been only the third time they had gone out for a beer together. The first time had been with Manny, when Gorden started working here. The second time was last month when they needed to talk about the upcoming Christmas sale. At that time, John had mentioned alimony, but only in passing. Gorden preferred it this way, though. The less anyone knew about him, the better. And vice versa.

It was late, but he didn't want to go home yet. He watched the restaurant fill with more customers, families and couples being led to tables, and he noticed that he was the only one at a booth by himself. He leaned back, the hard wood against his shoulder blades, and smelled the dinners cooking. Hamburgers and steaks. He should probably pick up something before he went home. Tempted to order something, he knew the prices here were high, and he didn't feel like spending more money. Camain's was expensive but it was on his way home, and it was quiet, not like that place a few miles down where the college kids liked to go, and Gorden was familiar with Camain's. That was the thing: familiar. He didn't like change. Like Shin. Screwed up everyone's life. Look at John, who's shitting rocks at the thought of being fired. And him, Gor-Tin? Was he sweating it out? No. Not anymore. He didn't care as much. Shin could go fuck himself. Why even think about it? He should just go home and get all this crap out of his mind.

Driving on I-89, Gorden cursed the heater, but the beers had warmed him a little and he stared ahead over the empty highway, his headlights filling the road, the white lines blinking and disappearing in front of him. A few cars sped by, and he felt his car shudder in their wake, their taillights blood red, shrinking away.

He turned onto his exit, Cascade Road, and headed towards his sidestreet, Wakem Place. Going west on Cascade, passing the houses built along here within the past decade, Gorden remembered when he was growing up in another part of town that there had been nothing here but a dirt road and empty fields, patches of forest scattered every mile or so. Because of the movement from Massachusetts to find cheaper and less crowded towns, development of his area had increased quickly. Further east was the Main Street intersection where the local supermarket, post office, clothing and hardware stores were. Gorden's house was about two miles from Main.

He turned on Wakem and passed a few more houses, a long stretch of land belonging to some guy named Haller whom he had never met, the land cleared for construction with mounds of dirt surrounding deep holes, stacks of lumber covered in frozen and snowed-over plastic; the project seemed to have been postponed until the spring. Maybe the ground had become too hard. Gorden finally came up to his house, pulling into his dirt driveway, the frozen puddles cracking under the tires. The lights inside the house were lit, and he wondered if Shari was still awake. Sometimes she fell asleep on the couch watching TV, and he usually liked that, not having to deal with her. As he approached his front door, he heard the wind kick up and whistle in the trees behind the house. If it weren't for the woods behind them, the cold air would speed up along the flatlands and smack into his small house, making it even colder than it was. He pushed his key into the lock and turned, but the door wouldn't open. He tried again.

"Hey," he called inside. "You bolt this?" He rattled the handle, and knocked. He listened but couldn't hear anything. "Shari?"

The bolt clicked and the door opened. Shari backed away and walked to the couch. She had been sleeping, her hair sticking out and tangled. Sitting down, straightening her black T-shirt, she ran a finger along the elastic of her panties. Her bony shoulders jutted against her shirt, and the sleeves hung loosely over her upper arms. She grabbed a glass of what was probably rum and coke, sipped it and stared at the TV.

"Why'd you bolt it?"

She shrugged. "Where've you been?" Her voice was reedy from sleeping. She cleared her throat.

"Had a drink." He looked around the living room and saw clothes all over the floor, bottles (some his) on the coffee table and on top of the TV. There was a musty, damp smell, and he said, "Why does it smell like sweat in here?"

She looked at him for a second, and shrugged. There was an infomercial on about a special car wax.

"How can you watch this shit?" he asked. The man threw mud on a car.

"I had a dream, before you woke me up," she said, not looking at him.

He turned to her.

"I dreamed I killed myself, stabbing my neck with a big knife," she said. "Pretty fucked-up, huh."

"You and your psycho dreams."

"And the knocking on the door was the police, but it was actually you, and I woke up."

Gorden hesitated. "What the hell you saying?"

"I'm not saying anything. It's a dream I had."

He was about to reply, but now it seemed stupid. She was always doing that, changing the subject right before they fought. He ignored her and walked to the bedroom. While undressing he thought about Shin, and wondered if he was still in the office, or maybe he was home now, with his wife and kid, telling her about his day with the new employees. Maybe he was even telling her about Gorden, the guy who was late, who didn't listen, who was becoming an enemy. Am I your enemy, Gorden asked Shin. Am I going to make your life hard?

He tried to picture what Shin was doing right now. Maybe he was fucking his wife. Maybe he was playing with his kid. Boy or girl? Maybe he was calling Manchester and telling them what a dump this branch was. What are you doing Shin? Why are you making my life miserable, Gorden thought. Why?

4

So, Shin was Korean. Maybe he was an immigrant, judging from his accent—coming to America as a child but still not fully ridding himself of his first language inflections. I imagine he felt self-conscious about moving into a store and taking over, and he probably had expected some resentment, some enmity. I guess he must have done this before, because he worked smoothly, coming in one afternoon and making sure everyone knew what he was going to do. I tried to picture him at the office late that first night, going over the accounting, reading through reports, and assessing his own performance so far. He was hunched over a desk with a single lamp on, the bulb lighting a small circle on his papers, casting large shadows on the wall and ceiling behind him. He rubbed his temple and took off his silver wire-frame glasses, sighing, not understanding how they could have let the place become such a mess. He was a one-man clean-up crew, assigned to pick up after the clumsy, careless children, scolding and showing them the correct way to do everything. It was exhausting. He loosened his tie, and unbuttoned the top of his shirt, rolling and stretching his neck until he felt the familiar crack on the left side. He thought about whom he would have to worry about. Not Henry—he knew Henry's type and he wouldn't have any problems with him. The two newer salespeople weren't sure what was going on, so they would listen to him. But John and Gorden. They were going to be tough. He had seen it before. John was going to listen, grudgingly, but would resent any suggestion, any command, and view Roger Shin as The Guy Who Took My Job. Shin felt sorry for the person who was going to take over after him. Although Shin could recommend John, he doubted that he would. Based on his performance, John probably should have been let go along with the other man.

He wasn't so sure about Gorden. He sensed the anger, though Shin knew he shouldn't have made fun of Gorden on the first day, but he had wanted to make it clear that any loafing that had happened before he arrived would no longer be tolerated. Make your policies clear. Be tough. Otherwise, they think they can get away with anything, as with any substitute. And Shin suspected the bigotry. He had seen it before. But this came with the territory.

It was late. Shin called his wife to let her know he was on his way home. Clicking off the lamp and locking up, Shin felt that rush he always had on a new job. I am going to turn this place around, he thought. Me. I am in control. I am the boss. He hurried out into the parking lot, the freezing wind prickling his throat, and he reminded himself to bring a scarf tomorrow.

◊

Gorden woke up with Shari standing over him. The bathroom light was on and lit the hallway outside. Shari's small, thin silhouette was motionless, her arms at her sides, head bent over, staring. He wasn't sure why he had woken up, but as he blinked his eyes open, he was startled to see her.

"Shari?" he asked, still groggy.

"You were grinding your teeth," she whispered, her words slurring. She was drunk.

Gorden sat up slowly. "What're you doing up? What time is it?"

Her head dropped to one shoulder, then straightened. "I've been standing here," she said, "wondering why you turned into such a fuck."

He lay back and groaned. "Shari, I gotta get up early tomorrow."

"What happened? When I first met you, we went out, you were nice, we did things."

He stared at her long, curly locks of hair shadowing her face. He closed his eyes, trying to ignore her. Why is she doing this now, he asked himself.

"We would come here and talk, and drink, and you were nice then. You even did things like buy me candy. Remember that?"

He remembered. And that was only a few months ago, he thought. What *did* happen to them?

"I just thought of something tonight. It was my birthday last week. You know I forgot all about it? I just didn't think of it. I don't know what happened," she said. "I just forgot."

He opened his eyes. January. That's right, he thought. She said something about that a few months ago. Her birthday. Shit. How old was she now? Seventeen? Jesus she was young. Every time he thought about it he got worried. He could get arrested for this shit. But she didn't act like a kid.

"I know my parents probably remembered, but they must think I'm dead." She sighed. "I didn't know shit from Sherlock when we started going out. And I was so into you. Isn't that funny? I was so into you. But to you I'm some kid you get drunk and fuck and then go off and do your own thing. I think I hate you now. And if I had somewhere to go, I would, you know."

"You're goddamn nuts. You're drunk and you're nuts. And I didn't force you here, you crazy bitch, you moved in here pretty quick."

She laughed quietly, which surprised him. She placed her hands on her hips. "You know, you're right. I did move in here pretty quick. Hell, it was a real house, better than my hole in the ground."

He waited, but she didn't say anything else. It was spooking him. "What the hell do you want with me? What do you want?" he asked.

She thought about this, staring off into a corner. "I don't know."

"Then, goddammit, will you let me sleep?"

Silence. Then: "I guess I will." She turned around abruptly and closed the bedroom door, leaving Gorden in darkness. He heard clinking glasses, but it soon became quiet. How the hell do I get into these things, he thought. He tried to fall back asleep. He ought to throw her out of here, tell her to go back to where she came from. But he knew she couldn't go back to her parents, somewhere in Maine, though he wasn't sure—she had run away two years ago and never intended to see them again—and he knew she had no money. Why didn't I *think* before letting her stay here? Ah hell, he thought, Happy Birthday, Shari.

At this point, Shari was still unknown to me. Why anyone would stay with someone like Gorden I didn't know, but I guessed, like she said, if she knew where else to go, she would. Although Gorden didn't write any more about this incident, it apparently kept him awake for hours, and because of that fitful night, the next day he went into work tired, in bad temper, and ready to fight with anyone who even spoke to him. Oddly enough, everyone left him alone, and he spent the morning quietly in the showroom with a clipboard, recording the inventory of ski equipment, and occasionally helping a customer. He saw Shin walking from the office into the stockroom, checking a number of items, and Gorden ignored him, trying not to wonder what he was doing. It wasn't until the afternoon, when Gorden had come back from lunch, that he had another run-in with Shin. Gorden wrote:

...so Im just sitting there checking off things and doing my job when he comes up and tells me that I dont know how to write up the commissions cause all the receipts are missing the salesmens names and he dont know who got what and how much. Im thinking this guys got to learn English cause it comes out all mixed up and I think he is angry though I dont know why. I ask, What, what are you saying? And he calms down and says it again, slowly, and I tell him not to worry, I wrote all that down separately in another file so that we can compare who got more commissions in the month and so on. Then he says like he is talking to a kid, Thats very good, but for tax purposes we need the records with the receipts otherwise it will take too long to cross check the figures. Cross check my ass, Im thinking, but I dont say anything and as he walks away I say, Tight ass, quiet-like, under my breath, and the goddamn shit hears me. He turns around and says, Im only doing what you shouldve been doing. Well fuck him. I sure as hell didnt ask you here, I say, shrugging like I dont care. He turns red, I mean really red and I feel good I got his goat, but then he says, Enough of this Gor-Tin, you clean up your act or you can go somewhere else. And I say, Ive been here longer than you, and he says, Yes, but IM THE BOSS. Then, Mona can you believe this, he says, And clean yourself up. How do you expect to sell anything when you look like you just rolled out of bed. And clean up that beard. Jesus H. Christ. Clean my beard? What the fuck? I gotta trim because my pussy boss wants me to? At least I got hair, that balding son of a bitch...

◊

Following this scene, Gorden held in his anger but wanted to take Shin's face and smash it into the wall. He wanted so badly to see his boss afraid of him, to take the little shit's neck and slam his face into the concrete, watching the blood burst from his head. How about that, Shin? Then who'd be the fucking boss? Christ, Gorden thought, this is all I need. He wondered if anything would go right for him. All he needed was some motherfucker telling him to clean his beard. It wasn't even that long, he thought, touching the curly, springy wad an inch from his chin. He watched Shin walk back into the office. He didn't know what to do about him. Fucker on a power thing.

I imagine Shin, as he returned to his desk, regretted losing his temper over such a trivial matter. But going over these books was so frustrating, and everything was in such disarray, that when he had come across the discrepancies in the commissions, he shook his head in disgust and had to find out who was responsible for this mess. Apparently the former manager was in charge of the books, though he had let John and Gorden do them for the past five months. Maybe that was why everything was so confusing. Too many cooks, Shin thought. Then Gorden had been acting so arrogant, as if he knew everything Shin did, and had already taken care of it. Shin hadn't been able to control himself, and he lost his temper, just a little bit, and maybe went too far when he made that comment about cleaning up. But he *did* look like he just rolled out of bed. Shin glanced at the two-way mirror and saw Norma showing some teenagers aerobic gear. She and Warren were doing fine, and it was because they were listening to him. Why couldn't people just accept him? If Gorden could listen to his new boss, then maybe they could get something done.

Later in the afternoon, when Gorden was demonstrating a pneumatic rowing machine to a father and son, his hands pulling on the soft rubber grips, the pumps hissing with each stroke and

Gorden feeling the strain in his lower back, but he smiled and said it was great for the lats—when he was doing this he saw an Asian woman carrying a child into the store. At first he thought nothing about it—one of the others would tend to them. He turned his attention to the adjustable tension lever, reminding the father that both he and his son could use this, simply by changing the pressure. While he lightened the tension and asked the father to give it a try, he suddenly thought of Shin and maybe the woman was Shin's wife. He helped the father sit in the machine and tuck his shoes underneath the straps. Gorden glanced at the woman, who was bending over and pointing to a bowling ball, explaining something to her little girl who stood in front of the ball and placed her hands on the smooth surface. The woman wore tight jeans over her wide hips and thighs, though she wasn't fat, and her knees seemed to point inwards, making her stooped position more awkward. When she stood up, Gorden saw that she was tall, and her white turtleneck sweater hugged her sloping shoulders and long arms, the fuzzy white material contrasting her short straight black hair, cropped at the neck. She didn't appear at ease with her body. She held her ski jacket in one hand, and tried with the other to pull her daughter away from the bowling ball. The little girl had on a maroon hooded parka with fake grey fur along the edges, blue mittens dangling from her sleeves. Both their cheeks were flushed from the January chill, and Gorden stared while the man below him rowed in place.

The father pulled himself out of the rowing machine, and told Gorden that they would think about it. Gorden smiled and held out his card, asking them to stop by any time. While the father and son walked out, Gorden watched the woman for another minute, the little girl staggered quickly to the sports clothing aisle while her mother followed slowly, her eyes fixed downwards. Gorden approached. He heard her say, "Your coat is better than those," pointing to the ski jackets on the rack.

"Be'er?" the girl asked.

"Oh, much. Yours is the best." The woman looked up and saw

Gorden. He asked if they needed any help.

"No. We're just looking," she said and smiled. She glanced at her daughter then turned back.

"Okay," he said. "Call if you need anything."

"Wait." She held up her hand. "Why don't you show us around?"

"Show you around?"

"Yes," she said, nodding. "I've never been in here before." She looked at her daughter, who was moving towards them, and asked, "Do you want to look around, honey?"

That's funny, he thought, watching the girl hide behind the woman's legs. No accent like Shin. Maybe she's not his wife.

"Helen?" Shin was walking out of the office.

"Raj, I was wondering where you were."

Raj, Gorden thought. She called him Raj?

"What are you doing here?" Shin asked.

Gorden heard a sharp tone he hadn't heard from him before. Annoyance? Not like the scolding he had directed towards Gorden, but similar.

"Just looking. This nice man," she looked at his name tag, "Farrel, he was showing us around."

"Thank you, Gorden," Shin said. "I'll take care of her. This is my wife."

Gorden nodded to Helen Shin, and walked off. Helen Shin. Helen. Helen. He wanted to remember that name.

"You call them by their last names?" he heard her ask.

"No, he likes to be called that. I'm really busy now, Helen..."

Their voices lowered. Gorden pretended to examine the rowing machine, but secretly watched them. Helen listened to her husband while her daughter wandered towards the bin of red kickballs. Then Helen spoke, her eyebrows moving up and down. The daughter poked her finger through the wire and touched one of the balls. Gorden, remembering the lacrosse balls in the other aisle, walked to the box and pulled out a neon green one. He crept towards the opposite end of the general sports aisle, away from Shin, and whispered, *pssst*. The girl turned, and he rolled the lacrosse ball down the aisle, the bright green catching her attention. "Ball," she said, reaching down as the ball stopped in front of her, her mittens scraping the ground. She had some trouble lifting the ball up, since the lacrosse ball was dense and heavy. She held it close to her, resting her chubby cheek against it. Walking unsteadily to her mother, zigzagging down the aisle, she said, "Ball ball."

"Yes, honey, a ball ball," Helen said. "Say thank you to Gorden."

But the girl wasn't paying attention to her mother anymore. She held the heavy ball out in front of her and let it drop. She chased after it as it rolled away. Gorden smiled and, not looking at either Shin or his wife, even though they were staring at him, he walked to the other side of the store, the athletic shoes section, to check on Henry who was reorganizing the display. He felt like he had done something right, though he didn't know what. And he felt good.

5

Shari wasn't home when Gorden came in at six-thirty. "Hey?" he called into the darkness. Was she asleep? "You here?" he called out, louder. No answer. For a minute he thought she had left him, and a sudden sense of relief came over him. *And if I had somewhere to go, I would, you know.* He thought, So am I finally free? But after turning on the lights he saw her clothes. The television set was still warm, so he knew she hadn't gone far. He was disappointed, and was surprised by how bad he actually felt. He wondered if he hated her, but he shook his head. No, he didn't hate her. He had simply gotten himself into this and didn't have the spine to get out. I'm a weak shiteater, he thought, throwing his coat on a chair and heading into the kitchen to find something for dinner.

◊

Picture this scene a few months ago, and everything would have been different: when Gorden drives home, he does so with Shari after picking her up at her job. They might buy some fast food, maybe pizza, and drive back to the house, talking about their day and complaining about how tired they are. Shari looks happier. Her clipped-back hair is combed tightly to her head. He can see the places where the teeth of the comb had separated rows of hair. She smiles, tells him she's glad she got rid of her apartment, and that she gets to come home with him. He likes hearing about her day, hearing things not related to sporting goods. They always have strange customer stories, and try to top each other even if it means stretching the truth, which they do eagerly. They like to touch. He reaches over and rests his hand on her leg, or she massages his neck while he drives. Sometimes she is playful and reaches towards his pants, rubbing him. They approach his house, their house, and Gorden vows to clean up the front yard that weekend, and Shari wants to help. Going inside, they fall into the couch together, throwing their food on the coffee table, and kiss. Both too tired to get up, they lie next to each other, sinking into each other's bodies, comforted, content, and Gorden becomes excited, and takes off her clip and begins stroking her hair. They like to make love while on the couch. Then they take a shower, or even a bubble bath by pouring shampoo into the stream of water, and after a half hour of soaking they dry off and sit down on the floor, in front of the TV, drinking beers, eating their pizza in Jakeson's sweatsuits. Later that evening, after they have gone to bed, they strip off their clothes and huddle under the blankets. She likes to pretend they are in the woods, lost, and have only that blanket for protection from the cold. They hear wolves, bears, the wind rustling the trees above them. We are all alone and have only each other, she says. I will protect you, he answers. She touches him, and climbs him, resting her head on his chest, her hair tickling his neck. They soon fall asleep.

◊

Gorden ate his dinner at the kitchen counter, not bothering to take the tuna fish out of the can, finishing this and two pieces of toast with a thick layer of melted butter, and a glass of milk. He felt like having a beer, but when he looked in the refrigerator, there were none left, even though he had bought a six-pack a few days ago, and had only drunk one bottle. He slammed the door and cursed. She was becoming so goddamn annoying. All I want is a beer, and of course it's not here, he said to himself. And where the hell is she?

He walked into the bedroom and looked in the closet. Her clothes were still hanging there, mixed in with his, and he saw her black evening dress, the one he had bought for her at Fashion Sense. This was the dress she had worn when they had gone to the annual Christmas party thrown by Kramer's. That night started off well, but then he had too much to drink and ended up sick in the bathroom. Shari wasn't better off either, what with her saying "I'm sixteen" to everyone he introduced her to, embarrassing him. When they made it home, they had one of their worst fights, yelling and throwing things. He didn't mean to slap her, but they were so drunk, and when she began taunting him, telling him he couldn't find a woman his own age so he had to pick up high-school girls, no woman would want him, and he had to trick little girls with candy, he lost it and slapped her hard, connecting with the side of her face and feeling his palm sting against her head. She went sprawling to the floor. He was scared then, seeing her slumped on the ground, motionless, and he thought in a drunken haze that he might have killed her. But then she began crying and he felt like shit. He stormed into his room and slammed the door. To hell with her, he had said.

Gorden felt queasy just thinking about it now, a month later. What worried him was how easy it had been. It was so simple to do, one quick movement, and it did so much. Shut her up with a smack. The feeling of the slap jolting through his hand, his arm, and seeing her head shoot back. Holy fuck, he thought. I must be going nuts.

He heard Shari at the front door. He closed the closet and met her in the living room, her arms full with grocery bags. She wore her heavy army surplus overcoat with the sergeant stripes still stitched to the shoulders, her head covered with a grey, wool scarf. She said, "There's a cab out there—he needs to be paid."

"You went shopping?"

"What do you think?" she asked, looking at the brown bags with the "Thank You" printed on them.

"Where'd you get the money?"

"The cab's waiting."

He felt the anger rise in him, but he grabbed his wallet and hurried outside. The New Hampshire AAA cab, a station wagon with the N.H. AAA logo on the side of the door, was in the driveway, its engine running. The driver was smoking, and rolled down the window when Gorden came up to him. Gorden asked how much.

"Eight fifty-five." Smoke rising out the window.

"What? From the grocery on Main to here?"

"Door to door. Eight fifty-five."

"Christ." He gave the driver nine dollars and walked away without saying anything else. He heard the cab pull out, crunching gravel and ice, then drive off. Nine bucks to go down the street. She had to go shopping tonight and take a cab. Why couldn't she wait until tomorrow?

"Why the hell you take a cab?" he asked when he walked back into the stuffy house. She was in the kitchen, putting the food away.

"What, I was going to walk there and back with all this shit?" She waved to the bags.

Gorden said, "I have a car." He noticed that she had bought pretzels and doughnuts. A few frozen dinners.

"No duh. But you weren't around, and I thought you'd be late again."

"And the money?" he asked. "Where'd you get the money?"

"I used one of your credit cards, okay?" she said, getting angry. "They take credit cards, you know."

"Who the fuck said you could do that?"

"What, you don't want to eat?"

He saw the beer and the wine. "How'd you get those?"

"I bought them."

"No," he said. "You're seventeen—they'd never let you."

"They did this time."

"Give me my credit card."

"What's your problem? You need food don't you? Why're you doing this?"

"Give it to me," he said, holding out his hand.

"You asshole!" she yelled, reaching into her purse and throwing the card at him. It flipped and arced away from him. "Asshole! *You* wanted me to do something and I did! I was doing you a *favor*! And now you give me a hard time!" She grabbed the bag of pretzels and threw it at Gorden, who ducked—the bag opened and sprayed pretzels over him. They scattered over the kitchen floor. "I hate you, sonofabitch! I hate you!" She ran past him and he heard the bathroom door slam.

He picked up the credit card and stared at it, running his fingers over his name. Shit. She was right. He had bitched about her drinking and watching TV all day. Ah, hell. And what was wrong with using his card? It wasn't like she had money, and he did need food. Gorden pocketed the card and walked quietly towards the bathroom, hearing the water running. The hallway floor creaked, and he stopped, resting his hand on the wall, waiting, examining a crack in the paint. He knocked on the bathroom door.

"Shari?"

"Go the fuck away," she said, her voice muffled by the sounds of water.

"Shit. You're right. I was pissed off, and you're right."

"I said fuck off." She turned on the shower, a squeaking followed by a low steady hum of water hitting against the bathtub.

The bathroom door didn't lock, so he turned the handle and looked in. She was naked, in front of the mirror that was fogging up, brushing her hair, her small, pale breasts moving with each brush. The shower was on full force and steam rose from behind the curtain. She turned to him, eyes narrowed. "You have trouble hearing?"

He walked in, staring at her body. The last time they had sex, two weeks ago, she had been drunk and had climbed into bed while he was asleep, taking him in her mouth, making him hard. "Leave me alone," she said now, turning back to the now foggy mirror, pinning her hair up and reaching for her shower cap. He touched her shoulders, small freckles dotting the white skin, running his hand down her side. He noticed red splotches on her arms, probably from carrying the groceries, and put his hand over them.

"I didn't mean to yell," he said.

"You're driving me goddamn crazy." She closed her eyes as his finger travelled to her breast. He circled her nipple slowly. It hardened.

"Sorry."

"I try to do something for you and you freak," she said, quietly. Her hands tucked the last bit of hair underneath the cap, and she turned towards him. "It's like nothing I do is right, and so I shouldn't do anything."

"I know." He cupped her breast, reaching over with his other hand to stroke her back, her buttocks. He moved behind her and kissed her neck, still holding her with one hand and now touching her stomach lightly, moving lower. He felt the stiff, curly hair, and began reaching further down. She pushed him away.

"No." She turned, and backed away. "Not a chance."

"What?"

"You bastard. You think I'm stupid? You shit on me and now you want to fuck?"

He moved closer. "What're you talking about?" He reached for her, but she jumped to the side, climbing quickly into the shower. She yelped and turned down the hot water.

"Forget it, Gord," she said loudly, over the sound of the water, droplets beading on her face. She closed the curtain, splashing him, and said again, "Forget it."

Gorden stared at her figure behind the curtain, a shadow rolling its head around, raising one arm. He went into the kitchen and grabbed the six-pack, bringing it into the living room. Turning on a game show, he opened a bottle and began drinking. It was cold and he finished it quickly, swallowing the bitter aftertaste. To hell with her, he thought, trying to concentrate on the TV. He opened another bottle, and began to think about Shin's wife. Did Shin have to put up with this crap? Helen Shin looked to be in her mid-twenties, maybe a little older... not some cocktease teenager, that's for sure, he thought.

The shower stopped. He put his bottle next to his groin, thinking, Shit, so fucking hard it hurts. He heard Shari walking to the bedroom, to the kitchen, but he didn't turn around. When she sat on the couch with a robe and a towel around her shoulders, he stood up and went into the bedroom. He was sick of her. With a beer in his hand, he lay on his bed, still clothed, and looked through last Sunday's paper. He had to get the newspaper to check Jakeson's advertisements. He hardly ever read anything other than the supplements and the other stores' prices, though now he glanced at the headlines, stopping at the pictures and captions. All these things were so far from him, had no effect on him. He couldn't care less if some family got killed in a fire, if some country had a revolution. Who gave a fuck?

After a half hour, the beers hit him, and he fell asleep in his clothes, the comics resting on his chest. He dreamed he saw Helen Shin in the bathroom, getting ready for a shower, through she didn't use a shower cap, and when she took off everything except her panties, she turned to him, wide-hipped and a thin layer of fat around her waist, breasts with large, dark nipples, and said, Hurry up and close the door, you're letting the steam out. He jumped in and shut the door, amazed to find her here, in his bathroom of all places. What're you doing here, he heard himself ask. Why, I'm here to thank you for the lacrosse ball—Susy loved it, she said. Gorden couldn't stop staring at her body, her adult body, with full breasts, the fat around her belly button wrinkling when she bent over to step out of her white cotton panties. She straightened and smiled. He stared at the dark patch of hair against her white skin. Well, she asked, motioning to the shower, Aren't you going to join me?

Gorden woke up. The light was still on and he had a sour taste in his mouth, his face sweaty, his body warm. What time, he wondered, squinting at the clock next to him. Three a.m. He stood up and went to the bathroom, relieved himself, brushed his teeth, thought about the dream and how Helen had been standing right here, in this spot, asking him to join her. What the hell was that about? He smiled to himself. She looked perfect.

When he walked into the living room, he saw Shari sitting on the couch, her head back, snoring. The towel had fallen off her and lay on the ground. She was still in the robe. He approached her and saw the bottle of wine, half-finished, on the table next to her. The robe was partially open, and he saw her breast. He was becoming excited. Leaning over, he checked if she were really asleep, and nudged her. She smacked her lips and turned her head to the side. He smelled the wine on her breath and thought, What the hell. Touching her breast, he felt her warm skin. She didn't move. He undid the robe and opened it, seeing her skinny body, lower ribs and pelvic bone showing. Damn, she was skinny. He lifted her up and carried her to the bed, and she mumbled something. Laying her down and pulling off her robe, he studied her. Hair covered her face, and her arms and legs were sprawled out. He touched her in between her legs. Dry. He moved her up higher on the bed so he could lie on his stomach and look into her. He touched her again— he knew she was very sensitive—and she mumbled something.

"What?" he asked, looking up.

She didn't say anything else, so he looked back down and licked her, carefully. Salty, but also he smelled soap. He pushed his tongue inside and rolled it around, up and down, and Shari pushed into him, mumbling something again. After a minute, his tongue was getting tired, and he wiped his mouth, sitting up and pulling his pants off. Not able to wait, he climbed on her and pushed himself in, Shari saying, "Oh" and lifting an arm up a few inches but letting it drop again. Gorden closed his eyes. She was so warm. He moved inside her, and it became easier after a minute and he had to stop because he was too close. Wait. Slow. He pulled out, and turned her over, making sure her arm wasn't trapped, moving it out from under her. He kneeled above her, looking at her back, smooth, white, a birthmark near her left waist, and ran his hand down to her buttock, down the line, touching her anus. Stopping. He sniffed. Musky, sweaty. Taste? A quick flutter of his tongue. Sour. He spat on the hole, running his finger around it, pushing in. She tried to move her buttocks, but he kept his finger there. Then he straddled her and spat on himself, making sure he was slick. He kneeled further down and began pushing himself inside. Slowly, slowly.

"Ow, fuck," Shari said, muffled. She moved, and he pushed her down. She turned her head into the pillow. "No—ow, that hurts," she said, her eyes still closed. He was in her, but just a little. "No, Gord, no, that hurts. I told you—oh, fuck." He stopped and kept still. After a few seconds, she relaxed. *Hng*, she said. He pushed most of the way in, feeling the tightness and then feeling nothing beyond, an emptiness or a fullness he wasn't sure which, and began to move back and forth slowly, the friction lessening but the grip around him still strong. He clutched her buttocks, feeling her bones with his fingers, and pushed further in. She stiffened for a second, then relaxed.

As he moved back and forth inside her, the tightness making him pump faster, he couldn't help it, it felt too good, shit, he closed his eyes and imagined he was on Shin's wife, Helen, and she liked this, and she said, Don't stop, and turned her head into the bed back and forth, pushing back into him, making it deeper, and finally he couldn't hold it any longer and he let himself go and thrust into

Helen, and she cried out, Ow ow, but then he held her tightly,
breathing quickly, barely moving except for down there, clutching,
goddammit, and he finally stopped and after a minute he felt
himself relaxing, and he was breathing heavily, thinking
goddammit, and then slowly leaving Helen, her hair smelling of
wine and sex, and when he left her she said, Oh, and writhed,
tensing her legs, but he held her tightly saying It's okay it's okay,
resting himself between her buttocks where it was slippery, warm,
and he thought, My Helen my Helen, it's okay, it's okay.

6

I admit that some of what I have been describing wasn't exactly
how Gorden had written it. It seemed obvious to me at the time that
this is what he had been doing, and my interpretation of his letters
may have been a bit unusual, but they seem justified if only because
I knew there was a certain amount of restraint, at least in the area
of sex, when Gorden wrote his sister. Of course he wouldn't tell her
about his sex life with Shari, and if he did, not in the same amount
of detail that I have. The actual letters read more obliquely, and re-
reading them now, I wonder about my own state of mind. For
example, regarding that evening, after Gorden woke up from that
dream, he wrote:

> ...and I was feeling really tired and sour after the drinks and
> sleeping in my clothes but Shari looked real good then and I
> couldnt help going over to her and touching her lightly, espe-
> cially after that fucked-up dream and I wanted to finish what I
> started but she was kinda drunk and also real sleepy but I just
> went ahead anyway since she dont care and she was out of it
> anyway. Ah, the fuck with it, you dont want to know this shit, but
> after that I was beat and sacked out.

◊

Perhaps reading someone else's letters in my depression led me to draw strange conclusions. Nevertheless, I remember where I was when I read this particular letter. I was at the Sunrise Diner, the roadside restaurant that was fairly cheap and only two blocks away from my apartment. When I didn't want to cook, or when I ran out of food, I would walk down there and order their hamburger special: four ninety-five for a deluxe burger, large fries, and coleslaw. It was almost ten o'clock that evening, and there were only a few customers in the booth section of the diner: a high-school couple (the boy with a green and white Marnole H.S. jersey, the girl with a large, frizzy hairdo, smoking) behind me, talking about a party; a truck driver with a Mets baseball cap at the back counter; and a middle-aged man in the booth at the far corner. Poorly lit, my section smelled of stale smoke, and from the small jukebox next to the high-school couple I heard an unfamiliar ballad. The table section at the other end of the diner, with brown carpeting and dimmed lighting, was for families and parties, and was empty.

The diner closed at eleven on weeknights. I had already finished my burger and was working on my fries while I read through the letter, getting it greasy at the corners, and Gorden ended it with "I gotta go now cause its getting late and I have to close up. Shin dont stay late on weekends so I got the place to myself, but Ill send this off as soon as I can." Although he had written more about the next few days after that evening, nothing unusual had happened, and he continued in a kind of uncertain hell.

After paying my check, I noticed a "Help Wanted: Dishwasher Needed" sign taped against the glass door as I walked out of the diner. I didn't pay that much attention to it, but I wondered when I would start searching for another job. The weeks were passing faster than I had expected, and my money was running out. I tried not to think about it.

The walk back to my apartment was something out of a Jack London story: the wind blew fiercely as I hurried down the steps of the Sunrise, zipping my jacket to my nose, shoving my hands deep inside my pockets, and hunching my shoulders to shield my neck and ears. I could hear the whistling of the wind up on the railroad platform even though I was across the highway, and my hiking boots crunched the top, frozen layer of snow. Beneath the stiff surface lay soft powder that leaked inside my cuffs and into my socks, melting and soaking my ankles. Without a hat or gloves, I felt numb. I crossed Freed Boulevard, glancing into the window of the clothing store, and continued for another block.

I saw a couple walking towards me, most likely coming from the movie theater up past the railroad station, or perhaps coming off the train from New York. They were arm in arm, the woman in a long, navy blue overcoat, a green scarf covering her neck and face, the man dressed similarly but with a blue scarf. They passed me without a glance. Their Siamese figure turned the corner, and I walked quickly through the snow towards the flickering red Lucky's sign lighting up the front sidewalk. I went upstairs to my room, and made myself some Kahlua and coffee. I sat on the bed and tried to read, but then looked around my room and felt immensely and inexplicably sad. I knew I should do something soon, otherwise I might go crazy, and I thought about that Help Wanted sign at the diner.

Farrel Gorden, although intending only to trim his beard, to "clean" it, as Shin had ordered, ended up shaving everything off about a week later. While clipping carefully along his cheek, he kept thinking how stupid this was and cut closer and closer, becoming angrier with each snip, thinking, Fuck it—he wants me to clean it up? He'll get it so fucking goddamn clean he won't know what to say. Gorden pulled out his razor, lathered his face, and began shaving everything.

After running the new blade over the last strip of shaving cream, parallel streaks of white lather over his face, he washed quickly and stared in the mirror. Although neither his beard nor his mustache had grown fully in—it had come in enough for it to feel springy, but not enough for his fingers to get lost in the hair—it had covered the small area of acne scars on his cheeks, and the beard had given him a fuller face. Now he seemed much thinner, naked, meaner. He backed up. Without the beard his jaw was more angular, and the small patches of rough skin near his sideburns made him look weathered. He remembered when he got the scars. He had broken out with a bad case of acne towards the end of high school, and used some medication that his mother had had in the cabinet, but it had been too strong. His face had stung, and even after he had washed it off, the skin had been raw. Then he had had an allergic reaction which had caused some of the scarring.

Gorden was running late, so he finished up and grabbed his coat from the bedroom, noticing that Shari hadn't moved from her curled-up position under the blankets. She had been getting worse, mixing her drinks stronger, finishing more wine, and she had begun smoking again. He didn't care about the smoke or the smell, but she left her butts everywhere, and the house was filled with dirty ashtrays along with the empty bottles. It was getting so that he hated coming home. *His* home, goddammit. Staring at her curved, lumpy figure, he tried not to let this bother him. Nothing he could do, short of kicking her out.

Outside, while trying to start his car, Gorden began to worry that he'd be really late, and Shin would give him hell. The past week he and Shin had been polite to one another, though Gorden did everything he could to avoid speaking to him. And when he had to, if Shin addressed him directly, Gorden spoke briefly and didn't stick around for small talk. Once Gorden had even slipped out the side entrance and walked back into the store through the main entrance so he wouldn't run into Shin in front of the stockroom, where Shin had been checking inventory the past few days.

The car started and Gorden sped towards work. He wondered if he would see Helen today. A few days ago she had been in the mall, though she hadn't come inside Jakeson's. He saw her and the kid on the upper level near the railing, and they were sitting on one of the benches, sharing a drink. Ever since that dream she had been popping into his mind at different times. Watching television, Gorden would suddenly wonder if Helen was watching the same show. When he was in bed, he would wonder if she was sleeping. Sometimes he wondered if Shin and she were having sex, and this made him jealous. Shin didn't deserve her. He would then mastur- bate and picture Helen on his bed, naked, playing with herself, or maybe turned over like that night. He would think of that night and feel strange that he had thought of Helen while he had been with Shari.

When he parked at the mall, Gorden hurried towards the store, checking his watch. Twenty minutes late. He almost slipped on a patch of ice and slowed down, stepping on the plowed sections of the cement and thinking of excuses in case Shin asked him. Shit, he thought, my face is cold. He rubbed his cheeks and felt the bare skin. When he entered the mall, the heat flushed his face; his cheeks burned. He cursed Shin for making him shave his beard. This would take some getting used to.

He approached Jakeson's and saw Henry in the showroom, sitting in the Helix Vertical Press home gym, a single-station gym with pulleys and cables and bars entangled around two seats, and Henry was trying the chest press on a light weight, pumping the two handles back and forth. Gorden walked inside and towards Henry, and asked him quietly, "Is Shin around?"

Henry stared, noticing the new shave but not saying anything. He motioned his head towards the office.

Gorden walked to the back, entered the stockroom, then the office. Shin was talking to John, and as Gorden went to his desk to put down his coat and check his calendar, he noticed Shin glancing at his watch, but not looking over. He's not gonna bitch, Gorden thought, surprised, and he sat at his desk trying not to look up and catch Shin's eye. Gorden tried to concentrate on what he had to do today—they were going to have a Presidents' Day sale in less than two weeks and Manchester sent them a template of a circular which they had to modify for their store. They would put certain items on sale—definitely the ski jackets—but other items they wouldn't, like the K-2's, which were selling well and were understocked.

John told Shin he'd talk to the manager of the mall, and he left the office, glancing in Gorden's direction, and raising an eyebrow, making tugging motions at an imaginary beard. Gorden nodded and went back to leafing through the store catalogs, searching for the descriptions and pictures of the items they were going to put on sale, and copied the information for the printer.

"I'd like to check that when you're done," Shin said, without looking up. His desk was next to the window, and was diagonal from Gorden's.

"Check what," he asked, staring at Shin's bald spot.

"The ad."

"Right," he said, waiting for more, but Shin was quiet. Gorden soon forgot about him as he became engrossed in arranging the new circular. It wasn't difficult work, since he used the same layout and style of previous advertisements, and all he had to do was cut and paste. Along the left border he used stencils to write, "Presidents' Day Sale" and at the top went "Jakeson's Sporting Goods". Then, within each square on the page, he pasted a picture of the item, the price and description next to it, and at the top of each box he listed the savings, calculating the percentages.

This took him some time, and when he looked up, it was almost noon. Shin was writing something at his desk, and Gorden shuffled his papers, knowing Shin would look at his work as soon as he left. Who cares, he thought. Let him. Gorden stood up and went out without saying anything. Since it was lunch time, there were more people in the mall. He moved around a family and walked towards the food court, the Muzak in the background, mingling voices around him, and he passed Fashion Sense, where bald mannequins posed in the display window. Most of their sizes were too big for Shari; she complained that she always had trouble finding things that fit her, and had to go to the junior miss departments. Fashion

Sense had a new black look, yards of black satin material hanging along the wall, and towards the back, a fluorescent light shining on luminous On Sale signs. Every store was trying to survive, and judging from the turnover rate of these smaller stores, they were losing. It seemed as if a new store set up and an old store closed down every month. People weren't shopping as much as they used to—except for Christmas, which still wasn't that busy for Jakeson's. He knew it, other store owners knew it, and no matter who Manchester sent over here, there wasn't much to be done.

Before he entered Leroy's, he saw Shin's wife. She and her daughter were sitting in Rotolo Pizza; she was leafing through a magazine while they shared a slice. He moved out of her line of sight, and watched her. She wore another turtleneck, though this one was grey, and as she bent over to cut up the pizza for her daughter, she kept pushing some hair behind her ear, using only the end of her pinky finger. He couldn't hear what she said, but occasionally she would answer a question and show a picture from the magazine. Gorden was getting hungry, but he didn't want to leave this spot. Leaning against the wall and folding his arms, he tried to look like he was waiting for someone. He concentrated on Helen. He had seen Asian women before, on television, here in the mall, but never thought them attractive. But studying Shin's wife, he thought maybe he had been wrong.

Gorden watched as she gave her daughter some juice. Helen tilted the plastic container towards her daughter's mouth, and smiled. The kid with her pudgy face looked a little like Shin, though he wasn't sure, and he wondered how Shin ever got this woman to marry him. Money, maybe. He had a good job.

After they had finished their lunch, Helen and her daughter gathered their packages from under the table, and began walking towards the center of the mall. Gorden was caught off-guard and looked for somewhere to hide. He backed into a corner. He wasn't sure if he should follow them. They stopped in front of a Radio Shack where a video camera in the display window played their images on an adjacent television. Should he approach them? He could ask her if she remembered him, or maybe he could just re-introduce himself. He heard Helen tell her daughter to wave into the camera.

Gorden approached them slowly, and thought of an excuse to speak to her. She was bending over her daughter and pointing to the camera, the kid blinking and staring at the television screen, and Gorden stood in the camera's field, noticing his naked face on the TV, surprising himself. Helen turned around.

"Oh, hey there. You're from Jakeson's."

He nodded. "How are you, Mrs. Shin."

"Great. Please call me Helen," She said. She tilted her head. "I like your new shave. Very neat-looking."

"Your husband didn't like the beard."

"Really?" she asked, raising one eyebrow. "How funny."

Gorden glanced at the little girl hiding behind Helen's leg. "I saw you here a couple of times," he said to Helen.

"Oh, no," she said, laughing. "I think I'm becoming a regular."

"Why not visit Jakeson's? Your daughter would like some of the things we have."

"Yes. She liked that ball you gave her. She wouldn't leave the store without it."

Gorden smiled. He liked the way her eyebrows jumped up and down when she spoke, giving her words more expression, as if she really was interested in talking to him. He liked how she leaned in towards him, to make sure he heard her. He wondered if Shari did that. He didn't think so.

"But Raj," she continued, "doesn't like it when we visit. Very unprofessional."

"Too bad. I like seeing you," he said, "and your daughter."

There was a pause as she smiled and then they both looked towards the girl who had lost interest in them. She was peering through the front display window, fogging it up then wiping it with her small, pudgy hand. "Don't lean too hard," Helen said to her daughter, and turned back to Gorden. He wanted to ask her out, but was afraid of what she might think. Maybe if he made it sound unplanned. "Anyway, I was going to get some lunch and I saw you. What are you two doing?"

"We just finished eating."

"Would you like to join me for some coffee, or dessert?"

Helen looked surprised. She said, "You mean right now?"

"If you have time."

"I don't know. Susy and I still have some shopping to do. Maybe some other time?"

Gorden averted his eyes, wanting to get away from there now. "Okay, well it was nice running into you," he said.

"Thanks anyway."

He walked away, his heart beating quickly, wincing when he realized what he had done. He had asked out his boss' wife. Was he crazy? Christ, he thought, shaking his head. He couldn't help it. Gorden felt her eyes on his back as he headed towards Jakeson's. The food area was in the other direction, but he didn't want to turn around and pass by her again. Damn.

Screw lunch. He wasn't that hungry anymore

When he went back into the office, he noticed that Shin hadn't moved from his desk. He was still hunched over the books, and didn't look up when Gorden sat heavily in his chair, the seat cushion hissing. Looking at his scattered papers, Gorden wondered if Shin had checked them while Gorden was out. He stared at Shin's bald spot. Did you find anything, sucker, he thought, smiling. Did you find what you were looking for?

7

Gorden sat in his car, cold, huddled in his seat, waiting for Shin to come out of the mall. It was almost ten, and he had arrived here an hour ago, checking Jakeson's secretly to make sure Shin was still in the office. Gorden had gone home and eaten, then had impulsively decided to see where Shin lived. He had driven back to the mall, and was waiting near the front entrance.

Shari had been home and hadn't been drinking, though she had apparently gone through two packs of cigarettes today. She told him she had started looking for a job, which surprised him, and that she wanted to buy a car. Just like that. One day sitting on her ass watching soaps, the next day she wants a job and a car, he thought. Christ. What the hell was she up to?

He knew he shouldn't have been so mean to her. He acted like he didn't care when she told him all this. He should have pretended it was a big deal. It was, sort of, but he had other things to think about. Shit. Now he felt guilty. Maybe tonight he should do something nice. Shari acted like a kid sometimes. He snorted. Ain't that funny, he thought. Shari acting like a kid.

Then, while warming his hands, Gorden saw Shin coming out of the mall. What does that guy do all day, he thought. He checked his watch. Shin had been there for almost twelve hours. Twelve hours. Gorden didn't think there was anything in the store that was worth twelve straight hours of work. What did Shin see that Gorden didn't? Shin tightened his overcoat, and pulled something from his pocket, pressed it, and his car alarm beeped off. Gorden sat up and watched Shin climb into a shiny black four-door sedan. Gorden didn't know why Shin needed such a big car.

"Shit," he said, as Shin sped away quickly. Gorden gunned his engine and pulled out of his spot. He didn't know if he could keep up. He followed the sedan's tail lights onto 89 south, taking a similar route Gorden used to drive home. Gorden tried to stay far enough behind as they passed the Cascade exit, Gorden's exit, and continued on the unlit parkway, a few cars and trucks ahead of them. Gorden saw black emptiness in his rear-view mirror. Absolutely nothing behind him. He had an uneasy sense of stillness, the void behind him catching up. He accelerated.

After a few minutes Shin drove onto the Sunolea exit, the town next to Yanack. Most of the Yanack kids went to school in Sunolea. This town, especially near the school, was more populated, the houses and apartments bigger and older. Gorden sped up and asked himself why he was doing this. He passed a tuft of forest before entering the town, the dense cluster of trees and brush surrounding him. Maybe he wanted to see Shin outside of work, in his home. Maybe he wanted to see Shin with Helen. He slowed his car on a curve, worried that his worn tires might not hug the pavement like Shin's car. At the end of the turn, there was a stop sign, and Shin slowed, then turned right. Gorden followed. After a mile, Shin pulled into a spot on the street, and Gorden passed him, not slowing down and not looking at him, making a right at the corner. Gorden parked and jumped out, hurrying to see where Shin went.

Shin walked directly up the stairs of a nearby building. Gorden thought this must be it. The stucco apartments had separate entrances, with stairs leading up to different doors. Shin disappeared behind a wall on the second floor, and Gorden heard a door slam. There were three floors, and the lights were on in most of the curtained windows. Shin's window, the one next to the wall, faced the street, and Gorden looked for some sign of Helen, but everything remained still. So this is where they live, he thought, checking the street. Some of the surrounding stores—the large bright grocery with its "Sunolea Supermarket" sign lit up, the "New Hamp Tavern" with its wooden door—were open, but they didn't seem to have much business.

He turned back to the apartment building. It was getting late, and he ought to be returning, but Gorden walked up the stairs to the second floor, wanting to see the apartment more closely. He ran his fingers over the stucco, the pointed surface sharp, and walked quietly to Shin's brown front door, hidden behind the wall, a small overhead light allowing him to see the number, 2B.

A security peephole. He leaned in closer, peering into the light inside, and tried to make out a magnified view of something in the apartment. Beige curtains, maybe. Movement. Withdrawing quickly, afraid someone might see him, he walked back down to his car, wondering what they were doing. What if they were fucking? That little bastard having sex with her? Gorden couldn't picture it, but felt a pang of annoyance that Shin came home to Helen. The little prick. He thought, But I know where they live now. He wondered what would happen if he dropped by when only Helen was home. Would she send him away? He wasn't sure, but the possibilities interested him. Maybe she would invite him in. Maybe she would say, We can have that dessert now, and she would bring out some cake or something, and they would sit in the living room, talking quietly so they wouldn't wake the little girl. Shin would be working late, and Gorden would know he wouldn't be back for at least two more hours.

Driving home, Gorden tried to think of a way to visit her, but everything seemed too risky. What if Shin suspected something? Would Gorden lose his job? Maybe. He better be careful. He pulled into his driveway, and saw that all the lights were on, the curtains bright with naked bulbs behind them, harsh centers with soft auras, and he thought, What the hell is she up to? He unlocked the front door and walked in, hit with the brightness of a fully lit room, warmth from the heater blowing in his face. He took off his jacket and looked around. The lamp shades were on the floor, next to the rags and the vacuum cleaner. She was cleaning? He walked into the bedroom. Shari was kneeling by the bed, dusting the bureau and night table.

Looking up, she smiled and said, "Hello. If you're wondering, I wanted to fix up the place."

"Cleaning, now? It's almost eleven."

"I had nothing else to do." She was red from working, and her small hands were dirty. Her floppy button-up shirt was rolled at the sleeves, and her hair tied back. "I was getting sick of the mess."

"But do you have to do it now?"

She stared at him, surprised by his tone.

Gorden hadn't meant to snap, and he added, "I mean, that's great, but can't this wait until tomorrow?" He realized how tired he was.

"I begin looking for a job tomorrow."

"That's right," he said.

She stared at him for a second. She scowled. "You know, you're such an asshole." She threw the rag at him and tried to hurry past him.

"Hold up," he said, grabbing her arm. "What's the matter? What're you mad at now?"

"You're such a bastard. You hate me, don't you. You hate to see me."

"What're you talking about? That's not true." He pulled her closer and tried to look at her, but she wouldn't face him. She squirmed away. He said, "Come on, let me make you a drink. I need a beer. Want one?"

She shook her head.

He led her slowly to the kitchen. "Come on, Shari. Don't be mad. You know I don't hate you." He held the back of her neck and kissed her forehead. "Have a beer with me."

He brought out two cold bottles from the fridge, and opened them quickly, handing her one. "Hey, remember when we took that walk out in the Pines? Remember that picnic?"

Shari wiped her face with her sleeve, and drank from the bottle. "Yeah," she said. "I remember."

"You were so crazy, stripping like that, right where anyone driving by could see you. You were so funny."

"I was shit-faced, Gord."

"Yeah, but we still had fun," he said. He smiled. The Pines was an area about two miles into the woods, near the lake, where the ground was padded with brown, dead pine needles. They had been at the edge of the Pines, in view of North Point Road.

"Yeah," she said. "You were fun back then."

"What do you mean? Back when?"

"You know. Back when we did things," she said. "We don't do nothing anymore."

Gorden suddenly thought of Helen, and wondered if she would ever complain like this, whine like this. He moved away from Shari. "Yeah, well." He drank his beer quickly.

"Why don't we do anything anymore?"

"Christ, do you have to grill me like this?" he asked. "Can't we just be quiet?"

Shari stared at him for a minute, studying him. "You're crazy," she said, and put her beer on the kitchen counter. "You're just fucking crazy." She left the kitchen and he heard her putting the lamp shades back onto the lamps.

Gorden stared at the refrigerator, imagining it was Helen out there instead of Shari. He felt better.

8

I started working as the evening dishwasher at the Sunrise Diner a week after I saw that sign posted on the front door. It was not very difficult to get—all I did was walk into the kitchen, ask who was in charge, and tell the kitchen manager that I wanted the job. He asked me if I had ever done this kind of work before, and when I replied no, he said, "You start in two days, five to eleven, come in at four on Monday so we can show you how to work the machine. Here, fill this out." And that was all.

I had worked at a restaurant before, actually, a fast food place, at a job not too unlike Shari's old job at Leroy's. This was when I had just entered high school, and minimum wage jobs were the only ones available to kids like me. When I worked in a lab a few years later, I did the clean-up assignment, washing beakers and test tubes, sterilizing instruments, and I didn't mind that kind of work. Though I often wondered what I was washing from the beakers, certain that I was exposing myself to diseases.

The job at the diner was more mechanized. The machine, it turned out, was very simple to use. It was a huge dishwasher that worked twice as fast as the normal household ones, and my job was to collect the dirty dishes from the dish carts, wheel them into the back of the kitchen, spray them with a steam hose which cleaned off the large chunks of food, then stack them into the dishwasher, a large aluminum box with wire trays. The machine handled large and small plates, mugs, silverware, but the delicate glassware, like wine and champagne glasses, I had to wash with a hand-held spray, since the machine usually broke them. Once the trays were full, I would add the dishwashing powder, secure the door, and turn it on. "Working the machine" required setting the size of the load—usually on "full"—and the temperature of the water ("high") and then standing back. The machine shuddered rhythmically, churning as the steaming water sprayed the dishes. Once the process was finished after about twenty minutes, I would open the door slowly, avoiding the blast of steam, and dry them quickly with a rag, not holding them for too long since they were still extremely hot, stacking them in a special cart with long padded poles that supported the plates. Then I'd wheel them to another part of the kitchen.

The kitchen was divided into a "hot" section where the cooks prepared the meals requiring the stove or oven, and a "cold" section where salads and desserts were made. Adjacent to the "cold" section were the walk-in refrigerators and freezers. The dishwashing area was next to that wall, in the corner, sectioned off by dish carts. I worked alone during my shift, though there was another dishwasher who worked the day shift, and I would meet him only once, when he brought his family to eat at the diner.

I was still receiving letters from Gorden, and occasionally I brought some to read during my break. Gorden's letters were not something to skim, so I would read each one slowly a few times, making sure I understood everything he had to say before adding it to the growing pile on my kitchen counter. I wasn't sure what to make of his trailing Shin to learn where he lived, where Helen lived. While I was sweating from pulling out the clean, hot dishes, steam rising to the ceiling, billowing and enveloping the fluorescent lights above, I thought about Gorden's plans. He had written:

> ... now that I know where they live I want to do something about it instead of sitting on my ass so I was thinking maybe I can go to Sunolea more, go eat there or something and then I can run into Helen without Shin around. In the mall its hard because of work and Shin and too much going on but if I went to her neighborhood after I get off work and before Shin comes home then maybe I can do something. Shari is acting weird like shes all different now and I dont know whats going on with her because one minute shes drinking and smoking and the next shes going job hunting and cleaning the house and I dont know what the hell shes up to. Im thinking maybe shes trying harder thats all and I shouldnt be such a shit to her. Ah hell, whats the use worrying about it. Shari is gonna do what she wants to so theres nothing I can do...

Did Gorden think that just by being there, Helen would want to be with him? I wasn't sure what he was planning, but I began to worry about her. I had no idea what Gorden was capable of, especially in view of the way he treated Shari, and what was it about Helen that he was so attracted to? Maybe it was simply the fact that she was Shin's wife. If that was the case, then she wasn't even a person to him, merely a means for revenge. This really worried me.

As I thought about this, the steam from the hot water hose completely surrounded me. I was working on some wine glasses. I liked the heat, the dampness clinging to my face, my clothes, and I inhaled the steam like Shari inhaled those cigarettes, savoring the rawness in my throat. I wanted to stay here, not go back outside, despite my tired arms and back, my hands suffocating in the rubber gloves, sweat dripping down my forehead. I stretched my back and continued washing, soaping the glasses and squirting them clean.

I didn't even know her last name, Shari's, and I realized that Gorden hardly ever wrote about her, except in the context of his coming home, or of his disgust for her. She was the same age as some of my former students, and I couldn't picture one of my students in her situation. Why had she run away from home? Why was she staying with Gorden, of all people? It was clear that at one time they enjoyed each other, maybe even cared for each other, as Shari once mentioned.

I tried to picture a seventeen-year-old, mousy face, long curly brown hair, trying hard to please Gorden, yet all I kept thinking was Gorden getting her drunk and having sex with her. She was trapped. I imagined her sitting in the house, drinking, watching television numbly, wondering when Gorden was coming home, and then cursing herself for caring, for even thinking about him. She felt dirty, sour, but was too dizzy to take a shower. As she stared at the television screen, she kept thinking, What's happening to me?

A sound outside. Gravel crunching. Gorden? Is that him?

But the sound passed and she lay back into the sofa, nausea and sadness building in her. Look at me, she thought. Goddammit look at me. Taking another gulp from her glass of rum and coke, she sniffed, feeling as if she wanted to cry or scream, but not having the energy. She knew she was a mess, but couldn't seem to do anything about it. Shifting uncomfortably, she began sitting up. She had to pee, and moved sluggishly, impeded by exhaustion and alcohol, groaning as she lifted herself up. And she was getting ugly. She could feel it. This was hell. She was going to die if she kept doing this. She knew that, but she couldn't seem to do anything. And Gorden was no help, that asshole. She knew he was sick of her, but did he try to help? No, he just bitched and moaned, giving her more to drink, to shut her up. Fuck him.

Sitting on the toilet and feeling so much pressure that she had trouble getting started, Shari pushed and concentrated. She felt the relief, and thought about Gorden when he went to the bathroom, the violent yellow piss rushing and splashing down in a loud, steady surge. It was strange how she put the same thing in her mouth, that thing which got rid of pee. She remembered laying her head on his hairy stomach once, him limp in her mouth after she had sucked him off, and he had fallen asleep. She heard digestive sounds inside him, and even his faint heartbeat. Everything came out of there.

When she was finished, she wiped herself and touched a tender spot. Sore. More careful now, she dabbed herself, and flushed the toilet, pulling up her panties and jeans. She looked in the mirror and saw her sunken eyes, pale skin, hair that was greasy and dirty; she couldn't stand this anymore. She had to get out of here. Somehow.

I thought this was probably the point when she decided to find a job, and set herself a goal—a car. With a car she could get out of that place, and maybe drive to Boston or even New York. Without one she was trapped and isolated. Leaving Gorden would be easier if she wasn't so trapped. She had very little money right now, but with a job that could change. Besides, she didn't have to pay rent or food. She could save, and maybe get enough to leave. I think that's what I want, she told herself, though she really wasn't sure of anything anymore.

A few days after he had discovered where the Shins lived, Gorden drove to Sunolea after work. Although he intended to drive home, something locked his hands on the steering wheel, kept him on the highway, and he passed the Cascade exit, knowing exactly where he was heading. "What're you fucking doing," he asked himself, his voice muffled by the over-revving of the engine. He concentrated on the cars ahead of him, three, no, four pairs of red tail lights evenly spaced, different kinds of eyes glaring at him. Slanted eyes. Chinese eyes. He thought about Shin and knew that Shin would be staying late because of the new shipments of sneakers and boots that had come in. In fact, Shin had been getting started just as Gorden had left. Preparing for the sale, Gorden could tell Shin was worried. Ha. Let him.

Although it was only six o'clock, the sky was dark and Gorden turned on his headlights, the sudden beam falling on the car ahead of him, the license plate reflecting back. *New Hampshire, Live Free or Die*, it read. What a stupid motto, he thought. He ought to scrape that off his plate. Like anyone is free. If Gorden were free, he wouldn't be in some dump of a town, freezing his balls off every day. No, Florida or California was where he'd be. If he were free. The blinkers of the car ahead of him signalled right, the same exit Gorden was going to take. Gorden also signalled, flicking the switch manually.

What the hell did he think he was going to do? He turned off Sunolea, remembering the route Shin had taken. He shouldn't be wasting his time like this, what with him being so tired. And hungry. Shari had mentioned something about cooking dinner, or had he imagined that? What was with her? Acting different and all. Today she started looking for a job, and he really hoped she found something. Maybe things could get back to regular, as long as she could keep the job. Ah hell, maybe he should go home, forget about this stupid idea. Did he think he would meet her? What did he think was going to happen?

He turned right at the stop sign, Sunolea Road. Driving slowly so he could see the apartment building, and perhaps even get a glimpse of Helen, Gorden noticed some people walking along the street—an elderly couple, a few kids—but didn't see anyone familiar. He turned right on Dorset Avenue, and found a parking spot in front of a print shop, the Printing Emporium. They were still open, and he saw people at copy machines inside. In the windows were banners announcing a sale on bulk copies. Gorden thought about the Presidents' Day sale, set for this weekend, and he reminded himself to check the newspapers for the ads.

Walking back onto Sunolea, across the street from Shin's apartment, he wasn't sure what to do now. Maybe he should wait? Or maybe he should visit? He saw a small coffee shop—there was no sign in front, but he could see the stools and a few booths inside. He entered it, sitting on a stool that let him see the street and the stairs to Helen's apartment. He was hungry anyway, Maybe he should have a small bite, and he could see what happened. No rush. He ordered a doughnut and coffee, and stared out of the window, watching people returning home from work in their suits and briefcases, probably driving in from Nashua, Concord, or Manchester. Maybe even Massachusetts. He hoped Shari wasn't waiting for him. He'd stay here a while to unwind. No rush, he told himself. Just drink your goddamn coffee and eat your goddamn doughnut. No rush.

9

Gorden waited in the coffee shop for almost two hours before he saw Helen. He had been staring out and absently sipping a cold coffee, the sugary layer at the bottom of his cup oozing down his tongue, his throat. His mind leaped easily from topic to topic without any real transition—Helen, Shari, Shin, Jakeson's, Presidents' Day sale, Shin—and occasionally he would see a passerby on the street and sit up, trying to see who it was. Bundled under mufflers and ski masks, the people were hurrying in and out of stores, avoiding the evening cold. A man with a ski mask, the area around his mouth flaked with ice, moisture from his freezing breath, walked quickly by the coffee house window, startling Gorden.

He felt sleepy in the overheated room, his head heavy, and often he had to blink and stretch to keep from dozing off. The bell attached to the front door would ring with customers entering or leaving, and he would sit up, even after the tenth time, and then relax into his stool, his body slowly melting over the counter. What was he doing here? I'm a fucking loser, he mumbled to himself. Who else would do something as stupid as this? He wanted to go home, get some real food, have a drink, relax, but no, he had to sit here for hours and stare out at nothing. He looked into his empty cup and swirled the large coffee granules stuck at the bottom. Very thick coffee. Shari had once told him his fortune using coffee grinds. He covered the top of his mug with his plate, the doughnut long gone, then turned the plate and mug upside down, letting the coffee grinds fall onto the plate. He kept the mug upside down for a few minutes, remembering what Shari had done—the designs of the coffee grinds would tell his fortune.

When he lifted his cup he saw some of the liquid run off the side of the plate, but the grinds had formed tiny mountains, small peaks and valleys in a semicircle. He tried to see what this looked like. He grinned. Actually, it looked like shit. Did this mean he was headed into deep shit? No, he thought. He saw breasts. No, actually they were little craters on a moon. Ah, hell. He didn't know what they were. He rubbed the image away with his finger. It was all Shari's stupid stuff anyway.

Then he saw Helen getting into her car, a white Volkswagen, her daughter already in the passenger seat. He cursed and hurried to pay the cashier. He ran outside, throwing on his coat, struck by a biting wind. The car drove off and he cursed again, thinking, What a dumb shit I am. He watched the car continue for a block, then, to his surprise, it turned into the parking lot of the Sunolea Supermarket. She drove two blocks to go shopping? Hurrying towards the small grocery, he realized that it made sense, that if she had too many bags to carry with her daughter, especially in this cold, she would need the car. He jogged down the street, his cheeks stinging, his ears freezing, and although he wasn't sure what was going to happen, he knew he wanted to meet her again.

Gorden passed the New Hamp Tavern, and a bank, the front walkway lit up, and entered the parking lot of the supermarket. About a dozen cars were parked diagonally in their stalls, and he saw Helen's dirty white Rabbit near the front. Out of breath and wheezing night air which hurt his throat, Gorden walked through the automatic doors shushing open. He heard the familiar background Muzak playing above him. Yellow and white harsh lights made him squint for a second. Vegetable smells. He stood for a moment, getting his bearings, looking up and down the aisles. He picked up a blue plastic basket. The store wasn't very busy, with only two cashiers at the parallel islands of conveyors and registers. Gorden walked slowly up the first aisle, not wanting to bump into her right away, choosing to see what she did first. Maybe she didn't want to see anyone. Maybe she was in a bad mood. He wanted to be careful. The first aisle was the milk and diary products, and he tried to think of things to say when he ran into her. He needed a story, an excuse, and had to seem genuinely surprised. At the end of the aisle, Gorden saw her by the deli counter towards the back wall, and she was peering through the glass display, her daughter in the seat of the cart. Helen was wearing the same blue and pink ski jacket, though this time she had a thick light blue v-neck sweater on underneath. Gorden took off his coat and held it in the crook of his arm, putting some cheese and a box of crackers in his basket. He walked slowly towards her cart, attracting Susy's attention. Susy looked uncomfortable, trapped in the cart, her parka restricting her arms.

"Hello, Helen," he said. She whirled around, her ski jacket swishing, her short hair hitting her eyes then falling to the sides.

"Gorden?" she said. "I didn't know you lived around here." A small smile, her lips barely moving. Little wrinkles near her eyes.

"I was visiting a friend. Thought I'd do a little shopping." He turned to Susy and waved. Susy's eyes widened, her mouth slightly open.

"Where does your friend live?"

Gorden thought quickly. "Just a few blocks from here." He tried to remember the name of the street where he had parked his car, but couldn't.

"And you're done with work for the day?"

He nodded. "Your husband is probably staying late. For the

sale."

"Yes." She moved towards Susy and freed her arms from her coat, letting it hang over the child seat. "He's always working late." She began pushing her cart, and Gorden followed. "Since college, he's been like that."

"So you two met in college?"

"In his last year," she answered, turning to him, her eyebrows raising up and down again. "He works very hard."

"I know."

"Have you been working there long?" she asked. "At Jakeson's, I mean."

"Not long." He pretended to examine a can of soup. "Your husband been with Jakeson's ever since?"

"College? No. He worked for a consulting firm before Jakeson's hired him on."

Gorden felt strange. This woman seemed so different from him. She shrugged off her jacket and threw it over the edge of the cart. He noticed her bare neck and couldn't stop staring at the smooth pale skin running down under the sweater, prickly wool fibers touching her throat. He followed the contours of the sweater over her breasts, and he thought about his dream of her showering in his bathroom.

Helen glanced at him and caught him staring. He looked quickly towards his basket and flushed. Christ.

She asked, "What did you do before Jakeson's?"

"Lots of things. Worked in a mill," he said. He remembered his first job after high school as part of a clean-up crew. "Delivered beer, worked as a cashier, clerk... lots of things. Never went to college, though," he added, thinking of Shin. "Or business school."

She turned to him. "Well, I never finished. I married and dropped out."

"You didn't like it?"

"Marriage?"

"College."

"No, I did. But I thought I'd finish later."

"Ah."

She shrugged. "Now I don't have a chance to do much. We keep moving around."

"That's too bad," he said, not sure how to respond. After an awkward pause, he asked, "Would you like to go to that coffee place down the street, after you finish shopping?" he asked. Shit. Too fast. Too soon.

Helen smiled. "Thank you, Gorden," she said, "but I still have errands to run. And then I have to make some dinner."

Gorden thought about Shari, and checked his watch. Past eight. "Ah, actually, I think I should get going too."

"Okay," she said, watching him.

"I'll see you later," he said. He felt stupid again. "Bye, Susy." He walked off, trying not to hurry. When he turned a corner, he breathed. Goddamn it all, he thought. Fucked that one up, didn't I? He left his basket on the floor and hurried out the exit, wanting to be as far away from this place as possible. He felt stupid, really stupid. What was he thinking? He wasn't thinking at all, that was the problem. Had he actually thought she would say yes? She was married and had a kid, for Christ's sake.

"Shit!" he said loudly, pulling on his jacket and hurrying to his car. He turned on Dorset street, burning the name into his memory. What would have happened if she had said yes? He had no idea, but he would have worried about Shin coming home early, and maybe it was better that they didn't do anything now. Maybe Helen knew that, and gave him the lame excuse because she didn't want to tell him the real reason, that Shin could return any minute, so it was too dangerous for them. Maybe that was what she was thinking: Not now. Too dangerous. Gorden felt a small rush. Maybe, just maybe if Shin were definitely not returning back for a while, then Helen would have gone out with Gorden. And then maybe something else would have happened.

He climbed into his car and drove onto Sunolea, looking for the entrance to the freeway. He shouldn't give up so easily. Maybe some other time, she had said. Okay. He could wait.

"Where were you? I told you I was gonna cook something," Shari said as soon as Gorden walked in. She was dressed in cut-off jeans and an old Leroy's T-shirt, a faded picture of a hot dog with a smiling face on it.

"Sorry. Got held up." He felt so light, and before Shari would say anything else, he grabbed her around the waist, gripping her tightly, and nuzzled her neck, her hair tickling his cheek. She smelled musky, probably sweating from the heat of the kitchen. Also, a faint chicken and garlic smell.

"Hey, what's with you?" She pulled away from him, watching him warily. "What's going on?"

"So, did you find a job today?"

"No," she answered. "But I still have a few more places to check."

"Great. Let's fuck." He grabbed her again.

"Gor-*den*," she laughed, pushing him away. "What's wrong with you? Are you on something?"

"Come on, baby. You can't get out of this." He smiled and moved towards her.

"No way. We're eating the damn chicken I cooked."

He shrugged, and felt his stomach. "Okay, I'm starving anyway." He kissed her on the forehead. "Let me wash."

She stared at him, shaking her head. "You're screwed-up, Gord."

He shrugged again and walked to the bathroom. Why was he feeling so good? Didn't matter. So long as it lasted. He threw off his shirt and washed his face, the stubble all along his cheek and chin scraping his hand. He shaved again quickly, lathering with soap and water, and wet his hair, letting the water drip down his back and chest. The slick look. When he turned off the water he heard Shari calling him.

"What?" he called.

"Telephone!"

He pulled a towel off the rack and hung it around his neck, running to the living room. Who the hell could this be? He never got calls, and for an instant he thought that it might be Helen, but that was impossible. Why would she be calling here? Why would she call him? He wiped his ear with the towel and picked the receiver off the table. "Hello?"

"Gorden?" Gor-Tin. He tensed. It was Shin. Did Helen say something?

"Yeah?"

"Gorden, could you come in tomorrow early? For the sale? We need to set up a lot for this weekend."

"Ah, how early?" They usually stayed later the night before to set up, but if Shin wanted to start earlier, Gorden didn't care.

"Eight o'clock?"

"Yeah, sure. I'll be there."

"Okay, good night, Gorden."

He hung up. Gorden stood by the phone, wondering how Shin knew his number. Probably from the records. Hearing his boss while he was at home was unnerving. Why didn't Shin tell him today at work? Was this a warning about something? Did Shin know about tonight? Shit, that'd be all he needed now. No, he was jumping the gun. Gorden hadn't done anything. What the hell. He dried his hair and walked slowly into the kitchen, smelling the burnt chicken and melting butter. He wasn't in such a good mood now.

10

Sis, its been one hell of a tough weekend but I gotta tell you what happened during the middle of the day yesterday when we were having the sale and Helen came to visit the store. The sale was for the three-day weekend and it was what, Saturday, when she came in right around lunch time when Shin was getting real nervous because there werent a lot of people and I wasnt about to tell the guy that the customers dont start coming in till after lunch, since everyones getting up late. But hell it was good to see him shitting, and I thought he aint so bad and maybe he got to worry about things too, but it was still fun to watch. I mean he kept checking the displays and the prices and the signs and he would go out to see if it was crowded somewhere else but it usually wasnt. So all of us puttered around, talking, and once in a while there was a group of customers, but nothing as big as something like the Christmas sale, so we took it easy. The store looked the same except for Presidents Day Sale signs in the front window and Prices Slashed signs over certain things, like the ski jackets. And I kept thinking about the night before and how Shari was feeling low because she couldnt find a job, not even a minimum wage one, because no one seemed to be hiring anymore. I dont know how hard she looked because I thought there gotta be a job somewhere, even if its pushing a goddamn mop, but she said no, there wasnt nothing out there. She looked real tired, and didnt want to talk, so I left her alone after dinner and watched TV. Maybe I should try to get her a job here in the mall, I dont know. Sometimes I dont know what to do with her. Im hoping that maybe this week she will be better. I just dont know what to do, is all.

So anyway I was waiting for more customers and they did begin to come in at noon, when we were supposed to be having lunch, but most of us grabbed a quick snack and ate in the office, and we began helping the customers, showing them the equip-ment, getting the right size sneakers, ringing them up, and who do you think comes in right around now? You got it. Helen and the kid. Both Shin and me notice them right off, since Im facing the entrance while talking to some kids about new arch supporting basketball sneakers, and Shin always checks the front whenever someone new comes in. As soon as I see her I look back to check if Shin sees her, and he does, though he is helping some guy with the boxing speed bag. Im thinking, Is she here to see me, and when she notices me she smiles but doesnt say nothing because Im still with the kids who are asking me about the prices. Her kid is walking behind her, not really walking but sort of rushing forward on shaky legs, and I wonder what theyre going to buy, or maybe theyre just visiting, but then I think Shin wont like this and maybe they might have a fight. Helen takes off her jacket real slow and looks around her and I see Warren walk up to her, asking if she needs any help. She must have said yes because Warren, that lanky son of a bitch, takes her to the ski clothing area. Helen scoops up her kid and looks through some ski gloves and hats, talking to Warren about something. I look at Shin and he is watching them and I think, Whats his problem? His wife cant come in here and buy something?

How much for those, one of the kids asks.

I turn and tell him that those arent one of the new kinds, and theyre $29.99, and after a few minutes they leave. I didnt think theyd buy anything, most of these kids just want to look around and tell their mothers what they want. But now Im free and I walk over to the ski section, trying to hear what Warren and Helen are talking about, but I dont want to look nosy so I make sure I look like Im doing something important, checking prices or something. Before I hear anything, though, Helen sees me and says hello. Warren turns around.

Hello, I say to her.

Thank you, she says to him. I think Ill browse for a while.

Warren looks at me, then at her, and nods, walking off. He probably thinks I stole a commission, but since Im his boss, sort of, there aint much he can do about it. Helen is wearing that same ski jacket, but now she has on a dark red sweater underneath, one of those heavy knit kinds, and she turns around to check on Susy who seems to be scared of all the people around and is holding onto Helen's leg. It doesnt hit me until I see Susy that the store is pretty crowded by now, what with every salesperson busy, with John and Shin helping out with the customers. Shit, maybe we can make some money now, I think.

Dont worry about the people, Helen tells her daughter. She bends over and touches Susy's hair.

Looking for anything, I ask.

She shakes her head and tells me, I just came to see how business is.

Your husband is over there, I say. I point to the sports equipment.

I know, she says, but he looks busy. Have you been to Sunolea recently?

No, not since I saw you.

Susy pulls on Helen's pants and says, Pee-pee. Pee-pee.

Im sorry Gorden, do you have a bathroom, Helen asks.

Yeah, its next to the office, I say. I wave my hand, telling them to follow me, and think that the bathroom is for employees only, but hell, shes Shins wife, so he wouldnt care, and I look for Shin who is now showing the heavy bag to the same guy and Shin looks funny trying to box the bag, the short pipsqueak, and he sees us walking to the stockroom, and I know he is wondering what the hell his wife is doing, but I dont give a fuck what he wonders. Who cares if he gets antsy and wonders what the hell is Gorden doing with his wife and kid, bringing them into the back room, oh no, maybe he is gonna show them around and Shin dont like that, no way, but who cares?

I take them through the back and point to the door next to the office. Thats the bathroom, I say. The stockroom is cooler than the showroom, and I want to stay here for a while, away from the rush out there, so I decide to wait for them. I hear Susy say something loud and bossy, though I cant make it out, and Helen says something sharp. Susy then says, Noooo.

Helen steps out and smiles. She wants to do it herself, she

says. I also smile because it sounds funny, and we both wait and I think, damn she is almost perfect looking. She dont even seem to know how good she looks, what with her short messy hair falling all over, like she dont care.

Seems pretty busy, she says.

Yeah, but somehow it isnt as busy as it used to be.

Is that so?

Yeah. But I run out of things to say and we stand there, waiting for her kid to come out.

Are you okay in there, Helen asks, knocking on the door.

Uh-huh, Susy says.

Helen turns to me and says, she wants to be a grown-up already. Shes looking straight at me and I feel kind of funny, not sure what to say.

Whats it like being a mother, I ask.

Its great, she says, but sometimes its tough. Helen knocks on the door and opens it. Everything okay, she asks.

Okay.

Do you need help?

Noooo.

Helen leaves the door open a crack.

And being a wife, I ask. Whats it like being a wife?

A wife?

Yeah, I say, waiting for her to tell me what I want to hear, but the toilet flushes and Helen turns around. Im done, Susy says. Helen say ok to her kid and opens the door wider, and Susy comes out.

That was beautiful, Helen tells her kid. Susy looks up at me, and I nod. Yeah, I say, great. But Im thinking of what Helen was going to say. Was she going to tell me that it sucks being a wife? Christ, I want to know so bad, but Helen picks up Susy and says, Thanks Gorden, I dont want to keep you from the customers any more.

Keep me from them? I think. Like I can give a flying fuck

about those people out there. But I say, Yeah, okay--maybe we can talk later. As we walk to the door she looks at me, trying to figure me out.

How about meeting at the coffee place on your street, I ask, on Tuesday night?

What?

Tuesday night, six-thirty, at the coffee place, I say. You interested?

We are now in the showroom, and she looks around. Shin is at the other side, near the fishing aisle. I dont know, she says.

I nod. If youre there, youre there, I say. This is when I see Shin coming and I walk slowly to the entrance, seeing some other customers. I know he is watching me but I dont care. Alls I know is I asked her out and thats that. Whats she gonna do? Tell Shin? So hell, let her. I dont give a fuck anymore. The worst that can happen? Hell, Shin can get pissed and give me a hard time, maybe even can me. But let him. And what if she doesnt say anything? What if she shows up? Then its a different story, aint it.

Gorden continued this letter for a couple more pages, telling his sister about the next day, Sunday, as the Presidents' Day Sale continued, and how it seemed to him that Shin was in a dark mood, unhappy with the turn-out and with the daily receipts. The sale would continue until Monday night, but unless there was a huge flood of buying customers, it would be an unimpressive weekend. And, as it turned out, when Gorden wrote his sister in the next letter, Monday wasn't any better. Although they seemed to have a store filled with more customers, people weren't buying anything; they were "just browsing," or "just looking," or "I don't need any help, thank you." Gorden thought the sale was fairly good, however, considering the past sales.

Perhaps you are wondering what Helen thought of all this? I know I did. At this point I knew very little about her, yet I couldn't help imagining her reaction to Gorden, filling in what I could from the little information I had. I supposed that, after being asked out by Gorden, she must have felt confused. She must have asked herself, Gorden is interested in me? Of course she knew it was blatantly a date, with who-knows-what on his mind, but she couldn't believe that it was this easy. Did this kind of thing happen to her husband, women asking him out so quickly, so effortlessly?

Helen began to feel guilty that she hadn't said no to Gorden right away. By saying she didn't know, she was giving him hope. She felt even more guilty that she was having trouble mentioning this to Raj. She hadn't told him about running into Gorden at the supermarket, and about his casual invitation afterwards. So now, if she told Raj about this most recent invitation, she would have to explain that it was the second one—or was it the third?—and that she hadn't mentioned the first one because she had thought it hadn't been important. Then it might look as if she had been hiding it, though she wasn't. Was she?

On Saturday night when Raj came home at ten, Helen thought of a way to bring it up, but whenever she mentioned the store, he became irritable, talking of how bad the turn-out was, and she didn't think talking about Gorden was a good idea. The next night was the same, and she let him bury himself in accounting figures and advertising brochures, trying to see what was going wrong.

"This store—I've seen bad ones—but this store is a mess. They were so stupid, these people."

"What do you mean?" she asked leaning over him.

"Didn't know how to keep the books. No inventory system. Not even using the computer programs we sent them to automate their sales. They still do everything by hand."

Helen thought about Gorden. "Computers scare some people."

Her husband snorted. "Those people don't stay in business long."

"Susy hasn't seen you in days. When are we going to do something together?"

"After this weekend maybe. We'll have to see."

"Raj, I thought we agreed to spend an afternoon sledding with Susy."

"After this weekend things will slow down."

Since she hadn't mentioned Gorden the previous day, bringing him up now seemed too late. Later, when Raj had gone to bed, Helen leafed through a magazine, thinking about Gorden. She asked Raj if he was staying late this whole week again. He mumbled, "Yes, sorry, but at least until Wednesday. I have to send the profit totals to Manchester."

"Fine," she said, but he didn't catch the tone of her voice. After a few minutes he fell asleep and she stared at him, his mouth half-open, his arms curled to his chest, and she tried to imagine Gorden next to her, in the same position, falling asleep after sex. Sex. How would that be with him? She couldn't see it. Though, she found herself curious. If there were a way to find out without anyone knowing, without any strings, without even Gorden knowing—was that possible?—then she might consider it. But Raj would be devastated if she tried anything like that, and Susy—she had to think about Susy. Of course Helen wouldn't do anything. But she could wonder about it, couldn't she?

What's going on, she asked herself, staring at an ad for jeans, the page itself smelling of perfume. What am I thinking?

She checked on her daughter one last time before going to sleep, pulling the covers closer to Susy's neck. She knelt down by the bed and stroked her daughter's fine hair, feeling the warmth of her scalp, listening to the quiet, quick breathing. She loved her so much, her beautiful child. But Helen was so unhappy. She hated New Hampshire, especially now with it so cold and dark and barren. Helen laid her face on the sheets next to Susy's arm. She liked feeling her daughter's elbow against her cheek.

Tomorrow night. Helen didn't know if she should simply not show up. Maybe she should call him. Or should she show up but leave after telling him she couldn't stay? Gorden didn't seem to be the smoothest guy she knew, but that didn't matter; she didn't mind the rough edges. Her husband, in his Armani jackets, Girbaud slacks, Ralph Lauren shirts, and what not... well, you began to wonder why all the nice surfaces were needed. She remembered being impressed by his ambition, his drive. She thought as they got older everything would temper, but it hadn't happened. He was still so crazy about things she could care less about.

Thinking about all this depressed her. She thought about the way her daughter often plopped down right where she was standing, not caring where it happened to be, whenever she was tired. They would be on a sidewalk looking inside a store window, and Susy would just drop onto the snow, clunk, and not get up until she was either picked up or she was rested. What a simple response to everything. Tired? Plop. No, not moving for a while. You guys go on without me. This made Helen smile, and after a few more minutes with her daughter she went back to bed and fell into a dreamless sleep.

What made her go to the coffee shop the next evening at six-thirty? Even Helen really didn't know. Gorden was surprised that she did. And I, the letter reader, tried to imagine her thoughts with little result. Perhaps there was some impulsiveness involved, some inexplicable force that pushed her to the telephone, calling a baby-sitter she had used when she and Raj had gone out to dinner two weeks ago. What compels us to do anything? Many biologists have argued for a deterministic world subject to natural forces. Perhaps it was this determinism which could be traced to a chain of causes prompting her to walk down the street quickly, fix her hair in a window reflection, and enter the nameless coffee shop. Perhaps before she even met Gorden, it was predetermined that she have an affair.

Part II
Easter Spring Sale

1

Justify. How could I justify my projected thoughts onto the players in this developing drama? How could I say with any amount of certainty what Helen was thinking and doing, what *anyone* (as a matter of fact) except Gorden was thinking and doing? Even Gorden must have dissembled and distorted himself in his letters, for who doesn't skew a self-portrait in his favor? Yet, despite all these skepticisms, I justified my machinations of character, of mind and action, to myself as necessary premises on which unknown conclusions would be based, gaps that I had to fill in order to understand. And this wasn't difficult to do, since I had so much time to myself. Time to think, imagine, concoct.

I continued my job as the evening dishwasher at the diner, my hands becoming sore and chafed from handling soapy glassware every night. Despite the rubber gloves I used, water still seemed to leak in and leave my knuckles, by the end of my shift, raw and swollen, dead white layers of skin peeling off my fingertips. One good result of this hard work was that I went home exhausted and had no trouble falling asleep. My days weren't as long and depressing now, since they had more direction, but I approached my job with ambivalence, looking forward to the different environment, the extra (but not much) money, yet also knowing it would be a physical and mental strain, standing in the hot kitchen, steam blowing in my face, the loud, rhythmic clatter of the dishwashing machine thumping in my head.

On one of these evenings while I was taking a break, about two weeks after Gorden and Helen first met in the coffee shop on Sunolea Road, I began thinking about this question of filling in the gaps, of supplementing Gorden's letters with my imagination, allowing me to see the secondary figures more clearly. For example, I wondered about Shin and how he felt about the disappointing sale. Did he feel the tightening grip around his throat, the prestige and reputation he had earned slipping away with each lost dollar? He knew he would have to send the figures to Boston, and although the store wasn't bankrupt, not yet, the sale did little to help the shrinking profit margin. Shin knew that every job was a gamble, and in the past the turnarounds he managed were lucrative, cause for bonuses, promotions, and he had yet to fail. But now? Was this becoming his first failure? No, the grip around his throat was always there, and no matter how tight it became, Shin would fight. He became determined to fix this Jakeson's.

I saw Shin at his desk, the lights off in the showroom and the office dark and shadowy from his one lamp, trying to think of a way to advertise the sale coming up in the middle of next month. His jacket and tie lay crumpled on the desk in front of him, next to old copies of circulars and newspaper advertisements. He had already decided to oversee the promotion himself, no longer leaving it to Gorden, and planned to clear out some of the extra inventory near cost, allowing Jakeson's to be more liquid. This store was cash poor and had mishandled their inventory, overstocking and underselling.

Shin realized that it was almost eleven and called home, wanting to tell his wife not to wait up for him again. He knew she would be annoyed, but what else could he do? She just didn't understand that he was doing this for her, for them. Didn't she realize that it was his working so hard that let them have Susy? Did she think they could afford her otherwise?

The answering machine picked up. She must be asleep again. That was good—at least she knew his schedule now. He wouldn't be in for at least another hour. He went through the overstocked inventory again, and began checking off things that could go.

Shin didn't suspect anything. His tunnel vision, as Helen called it, had focused on the sale and the store, and Helen's apparent acquiescence to Shin's rigorous schedule may have seemed odd at first, but Shin soon welcomed it, not even wondering why she had become so compliant. He may have seen it as her final acceptance of his way of doing things, of his arguments that all of this was necessary, at least for now, until he established his importance in the company.

However, I didn't think Shari would be so oblivious. Although Gorden focused more on Helen and his affair with her in his subsequent letters, he mentioned that Shari was still looking for a job. Poor kid. That was how I saw her, a kid, and sometimes I was tempted to send her a letter, telling her to get the hell out of there. No doubt leaving Yanack had crossed her mind too, and I knew she must have been very depressed, especially after being thwarted from her well-intentioned goals. A high-school drop-out, under-age, with a spotty employment record, Shari was working against the odds, and I could see her coming home the same evening that Shin called his wife, coming home after checking a number of stores in town with no results, again, thinking, What's wrong with me?

Gorden wasn't home yet and she wondered where he was, counting this as the fourth or fifth time he had been this late. The house was quiet, dark. She stood in the doorway, the lights off, listening to the wind outside, her feet cold and tired from the walk. The bus station was on Main, and although it wasn't that far, walking in oversized boots had made her heels burn and blister. Her nose was running from the freezing night air. She wiped her face with the sleeve of her sweat shirt, and dropped her handbag onto the floor, painfully slipping out of her boots. She winced. Another blister was forming on her right heel. She limped to the couch, and sat down heavily, still in her army overcoat. Everything was so fucked she felt like dying, but she didn't have the energy. Some maniac could come along and slash her open, and she wouldn't care. Maybe it would be for the best. Her bloody body would be here for Gorden to find, her neck slit, her mouth and eyes still open and frozen in surprise. Would he even care? Probably not. The sofa is ruined, he'd think. She ruined the fucking sofa.

But he could go to hell. She pulled herself up and wormed out of her coat. She leaned over to turn on the TV, then fell back into the cushions, resting her legs on the arm of the couch. All she had to do was walk out there into the woods, lie down, and eventually she would freeze to death. Maybe the wolves would get to her first. The cold here wasn't that bad, though, no worse than Maine, where she had lived. Whiteville Junction, Cracker Town, U.S.A. What a dump. At least she got out of that place, but then again, look where she ended up. From one dump to another.

Shari began to feel warmer and more rested, and listened to the sitcom rerun, though she didn't turn her head to watch. Fuck them all, she thought about the people at the stores.

Where was Gord? Something was going on; she was sure of it. Maybe he was pulling something, like stealing from work, or maybe he was going to be fired.

He had started talking in his sleep again. The last time he had done that was when he had screwed up at the store, and he had been worried about losing his job. Talking again, what with him staying late at the store all the time and him being so angry at everything— maybe something was up. He never really said anything in his sleep—he just mumbled for a while—but it usually woke her up.

As Shari began to fall asleep, her eyes too heavy to keep open, her body sinking away, she suddenly wondered if she talked in her sleep, and what kinds of things she would say. I have no one, she would say. I have no one and I am all alone. "You're it," she mouthed the words, her cheek pressed against the rough fabric of the couch. Don't lose it, she told herself. Hang on a little while longer.

The phone rang. A low, soft, electronic warble. Gorden and Helen kept still. "Should you get it?" Gorden asked, resting his palm lightly on her bare, warm stomach.

"No. It's just him."

After the third ring the answering machine clicked on. While they listened to the outgoing message, Gorden stared at the stucco ceiling of the living room, swirls of plaster pointing down at him, shadowed in strange angles by the dim hall light they had left on. They were lying on a thin blanket spread out over the carpet, their clothes piled next to them. They had not intended to do this— Gorden had only wanted to say goodnight, to see her one last time for the evening, even though they had eaten dinner together and had kissed and groped each other in the car like two teenagers. After Helen had left, Gorden had decided not to drive away because he couldn't take this, this quick end to the night, and had waited in the car for the baby-sitter to leave, knowing that Susy would be asleep and Helen would be undressing. He had touched himself and wanted so badly to see her. To hell with it, he had thought, climbing out of the car as soon as the baby-sitter trudged down the stairs and walked across the street. Shin would be gone for at least two more hours. Gorden had jumped up the stairs quickly, skipping steps two at a time.

Now Helen said, "Gorden, you better go. This was crazy." He sat up lazily, nodded, and touched her nipple, reaching down and kissing it. Her body, just as he had imagined, was soft and smooth and full, like some of the nude paintings and drawings he had seen in the Home Decor place on the second floor of the mall. He ran his fingers lightly over her belly—a small patch of fat pushed up by the indentation of elastic from her panties—and into the curly stiff mat of hair between her legs. *He hates my fat*, she had told him of her husband, but Gorden thought it was an important part of her, not excess, not unneeded, but... *there*, and without it she would be hard, bony, and there would be nothing to touch. To feel.

"Gorden, I mean it," she said, sitting up. "He'll be coming home soon. And what if Susy comes out?"

"I'll tell her I'm her new daddy," he said, laughing quietly. Helen rolled over and began pulling on her shirt, her arm awkwardly searching for a hole. "I'll tell her the other guy lost his place," he said.

"Very funny. Now get moving."

Gorden stared at her for a second, unable to stop smiling, feeling that pleasant dullness of his senses after sex. His limbs felt heavier, and sleep approached. If he could, he would have closed his eyes right here, right now, in her living room, and taken a nap. Instead, he dressed and bundled himself in his jacket. He turned to Helen, who was folding the blanket, wearing only a large night shirt, and he moved towards her, grabbing her waist. "I'll see you tomorrow, won't I?"

"I don't know. Maybe."

"Yeah, maybe," he said. Sometimes they couldn't meet, and Gorden felt the sudden loss, the real sense of instability between them, since anything—Susy's cold, Shin's finishing work early—could get in their way. He watched her fold the blanket on her arm carefully, smoothing the wrinkles out. He couldn't help comparing Helen with Shari, since he would see Shari only fifteen minutes after leaving here. He felt different with Helen. Shari was so angular, hard, bony, cold... Fuck that, he thought, trying to push her out of his mind, because it only made him feel sorry for himself.

"Gorden?" Helen asked, throwing the blanket into a closet.

He turned. She stood in the shadows, the hall light reaching only her toes. Her silhouette paused against the glowing curtain, light shining from a street lamp outside. Her arms hung awkwardly at her sides, knees bent slightly inwards. Again, he could not believe she was real, that he was really here.

"Gorden, don't do this again," she said. "It's too dangerous."

"I know," he replied, but he wasn't really listening. He liked the way she said his name, with a slow, heavy emphasis on the "Gor" letting the rest out slowly, carefully. "But I can't help it."

She smiled, looking down for a second. "You," she said, shaking her head, and he heard the amusement in her voice. "You."

"I had a great time tonight." He reached for the front door and Helen walked to him, grabbing his coat.

"So did I."

"You look so good."

"Give me a break," she said. He turned and kissed her, touching her lightly on her bare bottom, then squeezing the cool flesh. He smelled her dried sweat, a muskiness that reminded him for some reason of chocolate milk. She hugged him tightly and he felt her hands gripping his ski jacket. They let go, and he hurried out the door. "Be careful," she called to him quietly.

Careful, he thought. Of what? The roads, the ice, the cold, Shari, Shin, everyone. He had to be careful. They had to be careful. He still couldn't get over this. He was fucking his boss' wife? How the hell had this happened? Laughter built inside him, and he suppressed it. Look at him, sneaking around. He was a kid again, running around in the middle of the night, climbing in and out of windows, always hurrying. He remembered the time he had stolen his stepfather's car, lifting the keys from the night table while his stepfather slept, his nose inches from Gorden's hand. How easy it would have been for Gorden to punch the asshole, to slam his fist straight into the fat, sweaty face. No, all he did was lift the keys without a sound. Letting the car slide off the driveway without the emergency brake, clutch off, and then starting the engine, Gorden sped to his girlfriend's house. What was her name? Alison. After he returned, only a few hours later, the lights were on, and he knew he had been caught. What a scene—his mother screaming for the asshole to stop and Gorden protecting his head, barely. The asshole had almost kicked his teeth in. And Alison? Shit, he had dumped her a few weeks later. Or had she dumped him? So fucking long ago he couldn't remember now.

Gorden felt his car shimmy over an ice patch, and he slowed down, gripping the wheel tightly. Whoa. He hadn't been paying attention and had drifted to the shoulder. He concentrated on the road and thought about Shari waiting for him at the house. Hell. What was he going to tell her now? He couldn't believe she hadn't figured it out yet. Dumb. She was dumb.

As soon as he scratched the key into the front door, he felt his stomach sinking. He didn't want to go in there. He touched the peeling paint and ran his fingers along a long strip of exposed wood; more paint chipped away as he pressed on the bubbles. He ought to scrape and re-paint this. He leaned back and looked around. His whole house needed a paint job. Winter was ending soon, and maybe one of these weekends he would start the clean-up.

The door opened. He jumped back. Shari was standing in front of him, dressed for bed in her old T-shirt and panties, a bathrobe put hastily on. "What're you doing?" she asked.

"Nothing."

"Why are you standing out here?"

"I wasn't," he said, pulling his key out of the door. He moved quickly past her and threw his jacket on the sofa.

"Where were you?"

"At the mall."

"Still?"

He didn't reply, walking into the bathroom to clean up. Shari followed him and asked, "What's the deal with you? Why're you acting so weird?"

"Listen, just leave me alone."

She watched him. He felt her confusion, her uncertainty. "Why're you being so mean?"

"Can't you hear? I said 'Leave me alone'!"

"Jeez," she said, backing away. She turned around and left.

Gorden squeezed his eyes shut as hot water splashed into the sink, the steam rising to his face. He looked into the mirror and saw his stubble, wondering if he had scratched Helen while kissing her. He never used to think of those things, but she made him so careful. Like when they first had sex, less than a week ago, and he was worried about hurting her so he moved slowly, almost delicately, and was surprised by how it felt. *Ever since the baby, he doesn't like it anymore*, she had told him. She was open, loose, and it was an odd feeling, as if he were coming in emptiness, a warm, wet blankness. He became excited just thinking about it.

Washing his face and neck quickly, he wiped off her smell. Gorden regretting being so sharp with Shari, and thought about apologizing. But she had been all over him, pestering him, and he wanted to be alone. He didn't want to hear her whiny, mousy voice, and see her bony legs, her collar bones showing through her T-shirt. It made him angry, putting up with her when he really didn't have to. He ought to kick her out. Damn, if *her* parents could, why didn't he? Why was *he* putting up with her?

Ah, hell. He dried himself and went to get a drink. When he passed the living room Shari said, "Don't think I don't know."

He stopped. "What?"

"Don't think I don't know."

"Know what?"

"What you're up to."

He hesitated. "And what's that?"

She snorted. "Don't think it," she said, turning towards the silent TV.

Gorden stared at the back of her head for a second. No. She don't know shit, he thought. She don't know what she's talking about. Though, for a second, he hadn't been sure if she knew, and if she did, he wasn't sure how he felt. Maybe it'd be better if she knew. Then what? Would she bitch and go crazy? Would she leave? He was too tired to think about it. All he wanted right now was a drink and some sleep.

2

What exactly had happened at the coffee shop only a few weeks ago, the beginning of all this, was unclear to me, since he became less detailed about this affair as it progressed, his time and thoughts occupied by something other than letter-writing. However, I knew Gorden had been in the coffee shop on Sunolea Road at six o'clock, a half hour early, and he had been extremely tense, staring at the second hand on the wall clock. He still wore his ski jacket, since he didn't want to hang it near the door, and there was no room on the stool next to him. I imagined he felt sluggish, hot, and dizzy as he continued to watch the clock above him. Squinting, he looked around, trying to find an empty booth. When he had first walked in here, all of the four booths were taken, but it looked like two women in the back were finishing up. He stood and leaned against the stool and folded his arms. What the hell was he going to say to her? Would she even show up?

Yes, she would show up, and of the meeting Gorden wrote only this:

...she was so jittery when she came in oh man was she nervous, and I felt better because seeing her like that made me feel like I knew what I was doing even though I didnt and when I asked her to sit she looked down at the table and sat, saying that she couldnt stay long and all she wanted to do was talk for a minute then she had to go she really had to go. We ordered some coffee and I told her that we didnt have to stay here but she said real fast, No this is fine. We talked for a little while about nothing really, the store, the town, and Shin, and she seemed to be more nervous when we talked about Shin so I asked her more questions and finally I asked her if she was happy. Then something happened. She looked at me, quiet-like, and we didnt say anything for a long time, her just staring and me just staring back, and finally she said, No. Just like that. No. Then I dont know what the hell happened but it was like everything was okay then. We ended up talking about a lot of things, and I told her about me and she told me about her and Shin and man, it was great. We didnt do nothing, but it was great just talking to her, you know?

I guess I knew, though nothing like that had ever happened to me, and after reading this brief summary I couldn't help but want more. Since this letter encompassed the whole week, I read to the end, and saw what direction their relationship would follow, but it wasn't enough for me to know that they would become lovers, since I wanted to know *how* this had happened.

Gorden wrote that he took the back table, the one with the bill and the tip from the women still lying underneath a coffee cup, and I imagined he pushed the dishes and cups towards the edge of the table for the waitress to clean off, and he sat with his back to the wall, facing the front entrance. The coffee shop was small—four booths and a front counter—so Gorden could see everything going on from his vantage point. In the booth in front of him were an elderly couple, the man wearing a hunting cap, the woman wearing a plaid scarf, and they were talking quietly, sipping hot chocolate with whipped cream frothed and spilling over their mugs. An old radio near the cash register played a local oldies station, though right now a few commercials were on, an announcer competing with the low murmurs of the customers. Gorden wondered if coming to this particular place was smart, especially since the Shins lived nearby. Wouldn't someone recognize her and be suspicious? Then again, it seemed clear that both Shin and his wife kept to themselves.

Nevertheless, Gorden decided not to meet here again. That was assuming that they would ever meet more than once.

What was he going to say to her? He tried to prepare a few things to make conversation—he wanted to mention seeing her the first time at Jakeson's, his attraction, but he didn't want to come on too strong. This is tough, he thought. But hell, why was he worrying? It was just coffee.

Six-thirty. He began ripping his napkin into small pieces. The waitress came to his table and took the old dishes and the money, apologizing for the mess. He shook his head and said it didn't matter. He then told her that he'd have another coffee now, and that he was waiting for someone. The waitress, in her ketchup-stained apron over her corduroy pants that made a rubbing sound as she walked away, hummed to herself, moving carefully around the counter, dishes and cups on her tray. She disappeared behind a swinging door into a kitchen. Music from the radio came on, though Gorden didn't recognize the song. He drummed his fingers on the table to the rhythm and thought about Helen not coming. He would wait fifteen more minutes; if she didn't come by then, he'd leave and not bother himself with this. He wasn't going to act like some dumb kid. No way.

When fifteen minutes had passed, he finished his cup of coffee and continued to stare at the clock. Shit. Had he been stood up? Gorden flicked an open packet of sugar across the table, small granules spreading in an arc. Then Gorden saw Helen walk past the front window, glance in, and move towards the door. The bell jingled as she came in. A few heads turned. She was wearing her ski jacket and leather gloves, her cheeks red from the cold. Stopping at the door and looking around, she saw Gorden at the back and approached, her rubber boots, wet from the snow, squeaking on the floor.

Gorden was caught off-guard and quickly wiped the sugar from the table onto the floor, sitting up straighter. He tried to smile. "Hello," he said.

"I really can't stay long, Gorden," she said quickly, bumping her hip against the edge of the table as she sat down, wincing. "I don't know what I'm doing here."

"That's okay. I was thinking maybe we could talk a little."

"You don't understand. I don't know if this is a good idea."

"This?"

She hesitated. "Oh, and Susy had a fit when I tried to leave her with the sitter. What a day."

"How about a coffee?" he asked, holding up his mug to the waitress.

"I really can't stay long."

"Just a coffee. I'm glad you came."

She took off her gloves, tugging at her fingers one by one. "I don't know about this."

"Listen, if you don't want to stay here, we can go—"

"No no. This is fine."

There was a brief silence as the waitress came over with another cup and a coffee pot. Helen slipped off her ski jacket, the nylon rustling, and placed her gloves on the table beside her cup. The waitress asked if they needed anything else. Gorden looked at Helen, who shook her head.

They sipped their coffees, and Gorden tried to make conversation. "How do you like New Hampshire?"

"What? Oh, New Hampshire. It's so... bleak." She glanced at him, realizing she had insulted his state. "Oh, sorry, I didn't mean—"

"No, this area can be. I've been wanting to leave here for a long time."

"Why haven't you?"

He shrugged. "It's not easy," he said. "Moving all your stuff, trying to settle somewhere."

"It's too easy for Raj," she said, then tensed.

"You mean with Jakeson's."

She nodded. "Transferring and everything."

"You don't like that," he said, more as an observation than a question. He studied her as she drank her coffee, her long fingers holding the cup steadily, bringing it to her lips. Her watchband was loose and slipped up her thin forearm. When he stared at her cheeks, still flushed from the cold, he felt an impulse to reach over and warm them with his hand, and this surprised him. He wanted to touch her, just for a second, to feel her skin.

"No, I don't like it," she said after a minute. She shook her head slowly, not meeting his eyes. When she looked up she smiled. "But what about you? You live where?"

"Yanack. About ten minutes from the mall."

"Alone?"

Gorden hesitated, and she noticed this.

"Oh, I don't mean to pry," she said.

"No, you're not. I'm living with someone, sort of."

"Sort of?"

"This girl's staying with me until she finds her own place."

"I see," she said, waiting. Gorden was about to think of a story, an explanation, but he didn't know where to begin. Who cared if she knew about Shari? Maybe this was even better, putting him on similar footing with Helen. They both had someone else.

"She's a friend, more or less, and we aren't getting along, but she has nowhere to go," he said. It felt strange talking about Shari to her. "But I guess that's the way it is." He looked up and caught Helen staring. She drank her coffee. "You know?" he went on. "Sometimes you have to do something even when you're not really happy with it." Gorden found himself talking more than he had wanted to, but he couldn't seem to stop. She was listening to him. Maybe she cared. "And there really isn't much to do. Maybe everyone's got to do that, put up with something. I used to think you can do things to be better off, but I don't know anymore." He cleared his throat, embarrassed. "Are you? Happy, I mean?"

"Me?" she asked, surprised by his question.

He nodded, trying to see what she was thinking. She put down her cup and ran her index finger over the rim, circling it slowly, watching some coffee drip off the edge and leave a small stain running down the side. Gorden wished that he could know exactly what was going through her head at this moment. Was she thinking about him? About Shin? Helen pressed her finger against her napkin, leaving a stain, and looked up.

She shook her head. "No. I'm not."

Helen wondered why she was being honest with this stranger, because that's what he was—a stranger off the street. Yet she was so relieved to say this to someone, and it didn't seem to matter that this man in front of her, across the small unsteady table, was her husband's employee, a townie, and someone she probably would never have spoken to in any other situation. But now, once she admitted that she was not happy, and it must have been so obvious to this man for him to ask her so directly, that he already knew the answer long before she uttered it, but now she suddenly had an audience, someone who *listened* to what she said, really listened, and it was like breathing again. She found herself relaxing, telling him about Susy and how she loved her, but her child demanded so much from her that sometimes she couldn't think. And when she wanted to talk to Raj, well, he wasn't around. She had had Susy in part because she had thought they needed a family, a stable family, hoping that Raj would want to be there more, but in fact the opposite had happened: with more pressure to earn more money, Raj was hardly at home now. She didn't have anyone to talk to except Susy, and this was driving her crazy. Helen couldn't stop telling Gorden all this, and more.

When Gorden spoke she listened carefully, wanting to understand this man whom she found oddly interesting, and learned that the woman whom he was living with was a teenager, a runaway. This made him more intriguing. Their relationship seemed to be more than friendship, though Gorden was careful not to elaborate on this, but he was definitely tiring of her. Why was it that everyone she knew was miserable? This ought to have, in some twisted way, comforted her, since she was not alone. But it didn't.

"What's wrong?" Gorden asked.

She smiled weakly. "Nothing. But I've got to go now. I told the sitter I'd be gone for just an hour."

"Sure," he said, looking at the clock. "I can walk you back—"

"No, that's okay." She felt uneasy, wondering if Raj had come home early today. Of course not, but the thought of it soured her stomach. "It's probably not a good idea."

Gorden nodded. "You're right. Thanks for seeing me."

"I enjoyed it," she said. She had enjoyed it. And, part of her didn't want to leave. Not yet.

"Maybe some other time?"

She found herself saying, "Yes, some other time."

When she was walking back to her apartment, she moved lightly, the cold not affecting her, and she knew why. She had enjoyed herself. She had liked his company, and she wanted to see him again. Was that so terrible of her? Was it so bad to want to be around another adult, someone to talk to? She hurried across the street, unbelieving. Her heart was beating quickly. This was like the time when she was in college and had met someone in a bar, and had almost gone home with him without even knowing his last name. She had been drunk, and her girlfriend had never shown up. No, it wasn't quite like that. Still, she had to calm down. What was she doing? Did she know what she was getting herself into?

Later that evening when the sitter had long since been sent home, and Susy had fallen asleep, Raj returned from the office. Helen wondered if there was something different about her. They didn't talk much, both of them engrossed in their own thoughts, though Helen studied her husband and tried to see some sign of change—maybe her having coffee with Gorden had awakened something in her husband, a latent jealousy, an unknown possessiveness that Raj himself didn't understand, but felt. Could he sense something different had happened tonight?

"How was your day?" she asked him at the kitchen table, watching him eat some leftover chicken.

"It was all right. I don't know. I'm having trouble getting this next sale off the ground." He took off his glasses and rubbed his eyes with the back of his hand. His arms stretched his shirt at the shoulders, pulling taut the soft blue stripes and smoothening the wrinkles. Helen tried to sympathize, tried to feel the same frustration and tension that her husband felt. Instead, the thought that came into her mind, which surprised her so much she stood up to clean out her glass to mask her sudden jolt, the thought aimed at her husband which made her realize the extent of her distance was, *You need a different woman.*

3

Three weeks later, Gorden was giving Shari a ride to the mall. She seemed to have forgotten about accusing him of being "up to something." She was silent and stared straight ahead, cracking her knuckles, and dusting lint off her white blouse. She wore her hair up today, held together by a metal clip, and her long silver earrings rocked back and forth from the movements of the car. They hadn't said much to each other this morning, except when Shari knocked on the bathroom door, and walked in while Gorden was shaving. She was already dressed in her blouse and jeans, and asked him for a ride.

Gorden thought she was going to confront him about his affair with Helen, Shari's accusation still fresh in his mind. Even worse, he thought she wanted to go to the mall to tell Shin. He asked, "Why?"

When she told him she was going to try job hunting at the mall, he relaxed and said yes.

Now, as they rode in silence along 89 in the cold car, Shari pulled her army coat closer to her and shivered. Gorden said, "The heater busted a while ago."

She nodded.

He suddenly felt very sorry for her. Here was a kid trying to get her shit together, and he wasn't helping her at all. But what the hell could he do about it? "Any leads at the mall?"

"No," she said. "But I gotta check anyway. Not Leroy's though. Not that dump."

"Why were you fired?"

"Too many missed days and lates."

"Right," he said. Shari always had trouble getting up, and when they had first started going out, getting drunk and staying up late, Gorden had usually managed to wake up for work, though Shari never could. Maybe her losing the Leroy's job was partly his fault, since he assumed she'd be like him and handle the booze better. Christ, he thought. Maybe all this shit was his fault, and he was probably screwing her up even more.

"Are there any openings at Jakeson's?" she asked.

He thought about this. He could ask Shin, but he didn't want to owe him any favors. "I doubt it," he said. "We're all worried our own jobs might be cut."

"Really?" she asked. "I didn't know that."

"Yeah. Manny was fired and a new boss came in."

"Manny the guy who gave—"

"Yeah, him."

"I didn't know that. How come you didn't tell me?"

He shrugged. "Didn't think you'd be interested."

"You don't tell me nothing."

What was her problem? Gorden turned to her for a second, then looked back at the road. He pulled into the exit lane. He wondered if he'd get to see Helen tonight. Then he realized Shari would be around. "Hey, you gonna take the bus back?"

"Maybe. Can you give me a ride back if I stick around?"

"I might have to stay late again."

"I'll come by and ask you then."

He didn't reply, trying to figure out how he would get out of this. It'd be easy. She didn't know what the hell he did at the store. He'd just say that he had to help Shin with the inventory or something. He glanced at her again, and saw her staring out the window. For the rest of the ride they were both silent. Gorden thought about Helen, and how she liked taking him in her mouth. It had taken weeks to get Shari to do that, and she hated it. The only time Shari did anything was when she was drunk.

When he pulled into the parking lot, into his regular space near the entrance, they climbed out of the car and walked together into the mall, most of the stores still closed with the gates down and lights off. "What're you going to do now?" he asked.

"Look around. I haven't been here in a while."

"Good luck."

She stopped, and smiled. "Yeah, thanks." They separated as Gorden headed towards Jakeson's. Shari stopped and peered into the pizza parlor, a few uniformed employees wiping tables and mopping. He felt something gnawing inside him when he thought about Shari smiling at him. Shit, he didn't feel guilty, did he? What did he have to feel guilty about? It wasn't like they were married or anything. He didn't even know what they were anymore. They hadn't fucked in weeks and barely saw each other. She seemed to be in a better mood these days, though. Gorden tried to see what she was doing, but she had already entered Rotolo Pizza. While walking into Jakeson's, he hoped Shari found something today. Maybe he ought to give her a ride back.

By noon, Shari had checked most of the stores on the lower level, filling out applications at five places, though they all had said they didn't have any openings. The only store with prospects was the Yogurt Palace, but it was for a part-time position, and she hadn't liked the people who were working there—they seemed tight, barely saying more than a few words to her, and it looked like they really didn't want another person.

Shari stopped walking for a minute to rest her feet. Her toes were jammed together in her shoes and every time she walked she felt bones clicking. A small brick-lined garden with large leafy plants and flowers was in the middle of the mall, and she sat on the edge of it, the hard brick hurting her butt. There was a couple also resting arm-in-arm on the other side. They were watching the stream of people walking by. Directly across from Shari was a shoe store, and next to that was a clothing store for teenagers, with rock music coming from inside. Shari rubbed her calves, and felt a heaviness in her chest that kept her still. A tiredness. She couldn't do this anymore. She just couldn't.

Small patches of conversation floated by her as she closed her eyes and rubbed her legs, trying to keep them from knotting up. The rustle of shopping bags, background music, heels clicking, a child crying—sounds began to crowd Shari. When she opened her eyes, she looked up and saw the protective rails of the upper level, people leaning against it and looking down, and above them a high ceiling with long fluorescent lights, rows and rows of fake suns beaming down on her, one in the corner flickering, and the voices around her seemed to swell, startling her, and she began to feel dizzy. She gripped the brick underneath her, trying to steady herself as she swooned, sweated, and her heart began racing, and she went rigid, thinking, What's happening?

She stood up slowly, her heart still pounding, the blood rushing through her, and she began to walk quickly towards the exit—she needed air, and everything blurred around her as she felt tears well up, and people looked at her curiously when she hurried past them, and she ignored the clicking in her toes, the soreness in her heels, and she saw the glass doors ahead with the real sunlight shining through and ran faster.

When she pushed open the doors she fell forward and stumbled outside, the cold midday air hitting her face and chilling her sweaty forehead. She walked unsteadily to the side of the building, holding the wall for support, the icy cement rough under her fingers—she dragged her fingertips, wanting to scrape her skin so she could feel something solid next to her. She leaned against the building, her cheek against the cement, and she began to calm down, slowly; her breathing eased, her body relaxed. She inhaled deeply, and wondered what the hell was going on with her. She told herself to take it easy, and leaned back against the wall, blinking hard.

Shari collected herself, and bought a cold drink at Rotolo Pizza, sipping it as she walked towards the main intersection, towards Jakeson's. She hadn't seen the sporting goods store in months, not since Christmas, and she wondered about the new boss Gorden had mentioned. Gorden could be so tight-lipped. Maybe the reason why he was becoming so mean was because of this new boss. Maybe this guy was making Gorden stay late all the time, and Gord took out his anger on her. That'd explain a lot, she thought, walking in.

The showroom was filled with about a dozen customers in the various sections, a family at the athletic shoe department, some teenagers at the weights and barbells in the center, and the rest in singles or pairs scattered in the different aisles. Shari tried to find the salesmen. There were a few people in shirts and ties she thought she recognized, though she couldn't find Gorden. He must be inside.

Examining the sweatsuits on the racks by the wall, she felt the material and looked at the back office, wondering if she should try to see him. She read the signs along the wall: $16.99 - Women's Spettro Powerfit Running Tights, $19.99 - Women's Oxford Nylon Jacket, $19.99 - Women's Wind Jackets. A large red banner hung by the back wall: Easter Spring Sale! April 10-12! Ski Clearance Sale: 25% - 50% off!

Shari made her way towards the office and looked around—all the salespeople were busy. She ignored the "Employees Only" sign and pushed the swinging doors in. A radio played softly. She peered in and saw three desks on each side of the office, with

Gorden near a large window and another man hunched over in the very back.

"Gord?" she asked. Both men looked up. She was surprised to see that the man in back was Asian; an oval, tired-looking face studied her.

"Shari," Gorden said, standing up quickly. "You shouldn't be in here." He walked towards her. "Are you going home now?"

"I thought I'd stay until you leave. I can go home with you."

Gorden hesitated.

"You working late ag—"

"No. I can drive you. Meet me out there," he said, pointing to the showroom, "at six."

He seemed nervous, and she didn't want to get him in trouble. She mouthed the words "Bye" and hurried out the door. She heard papers rustling as she walked into the showroom.

As she left Jakeson's, she realized she had about five hours to kill, and decided to go to the bookstore to look at magazines. She took an escalator up, wondering if the other guy she had seen in the office was his boss, and what kind of shit he was to make Gord work so hard.

Gorden didn't look at Shin when he returned to his desk, trying not to think about Shari and Helen and what he was going to do tonight. He turned his attention to the new colored tag system Shin wanted to begin for the next sale, where red tags would indicate special items on sale. The Dynastar Eclipse and the Rossignol STS were two skis that were going to be red-tagged, in addition to the regular quarter to half-off for the Easter sale. Shin also was going to have a few coupons printed in the circular for small items—the Duofold Thermax ski underwear, Wigwam ski caps and masks—to lure people in. Gorden wasn't sure if it was a good idea, and it meant extra paperwork and they had to keep detailed records of all the different things going on different kinds of sale.

Shin called someone on the phone. Gorden glanced up, meeting his eyes. Shin then began talking and looked down at the pad of paper he was writing on. Gorden wondered if Shin was curious about Shari. Didn't he want to know who she was? It was strange that Shin seemed to care so little for anything besides his work. At first Gorden hadn't believed Helen when she told him about her husband's painful attention to his job, because he had thought no one cared *that* much about work. But maybe she was right. She told him this during their second meeting, when she hired a baby-sitter and they went to a restaurant right outside of Yanack, The Continental.

Gorden smiled to himself, remembering their conversation. They felt more comfortable with each other that night, as if some question had been answered, and they shared a bottle of wine and ate slowly, telling each other a little more about themselves.

Helen told Gorden about Shin, and how he made detailed lists every evening of what he had to do the next day, long outlines of short tasks, ordered by chronology and starred by importance. Once, when Helen had looked at one of his lists, she saw even the most unimportant tasks spelled out: "Get Gas." or "Check Messages." Once she had seen "Call H at lunch." which had made her feel like another task. Maybe this had been endearing at first, the lists, but when she saw him at his desk in the evening right before he would go to sleep, working on those damn lists, she soon felt like pulling him away and telling him to wing it for once in his life. She had been tempted on a few occasions, upon seeing the list lying on the desk, to steal it, to rip it up, and see how he functioned without it. Knowing him, Helen thought he'd immediately stop everything until he wrote up another one.

At the time, she and Gorden laughed about it, though Helen was quick to add, in Shin's defense, that the system worked, and if she had the patience and foresight, those kinds of lists would probably help her.

"Yeah, yeah," Gorden had said, grinning. "But most of us are human."

Gorden closed his eyes now, listening to Shin's voice, and resisted the urge to call Helen. He thought about the first kiss, after that night at the restaurant, when they had stood out in the parking lot, next to their cars, about to drive off in separate directions, and Helen had rubbed her arms in the cold while she had said, "I had fun, Gorden." Steam puffing from her mouth. Gorden said he had fun too, and he moved forward and kissed her, catching her by surprise. She didn't pull away. Her face felt cold, her lips cold, but he reached behind her head, feeling her short hair in his fingers, and felt the warmth there. When they pulled apart, Helen had on a small grin, as if she were thinking, Well, well, and then said, "See you soon," and climbed into her car.

He was certain that she was the best-looking woman he had ever seen. Because she didn't put that shit on her face, like those models from Kramer's, and because she just seemed more *real* than the others, like they understood each other, Gorden knew he was falling for her, and didn't care. He knew that she had Shin and Susy, but what if he ran off with Helen somewhere, and they lived like people were supposed to live, not in some shit hole with people like Shin breathing down your neck and Shari acting like a wino? Maybe they'd run off to Florida or California, and then they wouldn't have to deal with all this, with the cold, with the people, Shin and Shari. Ah, hell, he thought. He could dream, couldn't he?

As he left the store Gorden saw Shari waiting for him. There didn't seem to be a way out of this, so maybe he'd have to forget about Helen tonight. It was okay, since Helen worried that hiring a sitter for Susy all the time was bad for her. Helen wanted to spend more time with her daughter. He had thought about calling her before he left, but Shin was still in the office. Gorden had actually dialed her number on his phone, but then had hung up before it connected, not wanting to risk anything with Shin right there. But it had been a funny thought. Right now I am looking at your husband, he would have whispered, staring at Shin's balding head, small body hunched over the desk. Right now I am talking dirty to my boss' wife. What if Shin had called and had found the number busy? Gorden got a kick out of that.

Shari saw Gorden and waved. She was leaning against the wall, and he saw a small shopping bag on the ground next to her. She rubbed the back of her neck as she stood straighter and said hello.

"You spent the whole day around here?" he asked.

She shrugged. "It wasn't that bad. I went into a bunch of stores, looked around. Oh, and I got you something." She gave him the bag. It was from Charmaine, a store that carried party supplies and novelty goods. He reached in and pulled out a plastic key chain in the shape of his initials. "You just pick the letters and they connect them for you," she said.

"Hey, thanks," he said, though he wondered why she had wasted her money on something like this. He already had a mountain climber's key chain, the kind with a steel-reinforced link to hold the keys.

"You don't like it."

"No, it's great. Thanks."

She smiled, her face brightening. "Glad you like it. Ready to go?"

He nodded, and they walked out of the mall, moving against a small flow of people coming into the food court for dinner. It was dark, and the lights from the building shined on them, illuinating their breath in the cold. Shari tightened her coat around her neck and moved closer to Gorden as they approached the car.

"How was work?" she asked.

"Okay," he said, thinking about Helen. "What about the jobs— anything?"

She shook her head. "Maybe I'll try some other places tomorrow."

Gorden heard the exhaustion in her voice, and felt sorry for her. "Something will turn up."

As they drove away, she looked towards the mall. "So, who

was that guy in the office with you?"

"What?"

"That guy, when I walked in. Was he your new boss?"

Gorden said yes, but didn't elaborate. Whenever he thought about Shin outside of work it made him think of Helen, of Shin and Helen together, and it angered him. It just didn't seem like that guy deserved her.

"How come you never told me about him?" Shari asked.

"What? Oh, I don't know. I didn't think it mattered."

"He's one of those Japanese business guys?"

"No. Korean."

"What's he like?"

"Look, what's with the questions?" he said.

Shari's eyes widened for a second. "Take it easy."

He exhaled slowly.

"Gord, are you stealing from there or something? Are you pulling something?"

"What?" He turned to her.

"Are you stealing from them. Is that why you're so jumpy?"

"Stealing...?" He began laughing. Christ, was that what she thought? What the hell could he steal from that place? They had no money, and who'd want to buy sporting goods? No one, obviously, or else they'd be making money.

"What's so funny?" she asked.

"You are. No, I'm not stealing." He shook his head and reached over, touching the back of her neck. "You can be so funny sometimes," he said, noticing her cheeks turning pink. She grinned.

As they drove back to the house, Gorden thought Shari looked pretty tonight. He shook his head again. Him stealing from Jakeson's. Gorden the master thief. He snorted.

After they had eaten a quick dinner, they sat in the living room, Gorden looked through the TV listings to find something to watch, though there was nothing on. He was bored, and wanted to talk to

Helen. What was it about her that made him feel so good? He tried to figure this out, thinking of the time they had gone to a bar a few miles down 89. They had been heading to Camain Bar and Restaurant, but Gorden had worried that John or someone else from Jakeson's might show up, so they had found another place— Gorden couldn't remember the name of it, something like Marlin or Marvin—and they sat in a small booth in a corner, away from the noisy dance floor and the pinball room, and talked about summers in New Hampshire. Maybe because she had never lived up here before she seemed really interested in what he had to say. He talked about everything being green and warm, but it rarely got too hot, and when it did, the Connecticut River wasn't far and you could take a canoe out and drift downstream. He told her about the time when he and his sister rented a canoe from one of the stores along the river, and for five bucks, used the canoe all day. And if you didn't want to spend the money you could just get an inner tube and float on that, soaking your feet and butt in the cool river.

Remember that sis when we used to rent from River Rats and just hang out on those Sundays doing nothing but drinking beers and getting a tan? To tell you the truth I used to hate it when you brought one of your boyfriends along, most of them were shits except for that mechanic guy who sold me that old Chevy for cheap and fixed it whenever something happened to it, but besides him, what the hell was his name again, but besides him those other guys were shits. I dont know what you saw in them. Anyways remember when we used to do that? There was that one time when we saw those kids swinging on that rope that they strung up on that bridge, a long fucking rope that went all the way up and they were swinging from rocks and jumping into the water. That was when I screwed up my leg. What a dumb fuck I was. I remember swinging off that thing and the small string they used to pull the rope back got caught on my leg so when I let go I got all tangled up and hung upside down while it dug into me.

You screamed like I was being murdered or something. I was scared shitless too since I was heading for those rocks but I got out didnt I? You know, sometimes, if its really rainy I can still feel my left knee getting all tight and stiff. Do you think its from that time?

Gorden called Helen while Shari was in the bathroom. Maybe that was it. Maybe because Helen made him *want* to tell her things. He really didn't know, but after thinking about her for a while he really wanted to hear her voice, make sure she was real, that he wasn't fucking crazy. He dialed quickly as soon as he heard Shari close the bathroom door.

The phone rang once, twice, and he wondered where she was. She should be home. Where else would she be?

When Shin answered the phone, Gorden froze, then quickly hung up.

Shin? What the fuck was he doing home already? It wasn't even closing time. Christ, what if Gorden had gone to see Helen tonight? He sat back in the sofa, stunned, and realized that Shari had probably saved his ass today. But what the hell was Shin doing home? Gorden reached over and called Jakeson's. John answered.

"John? It's Gorden. Anyone else there?"

"Hey. It's just me and Norma tonight. What's up?"

"Where's Shin?"

"I don't know. He left early tonight. Said something about feeling tired. He's been working like a dog, getting ready for this Easter thing."

"Thanks."

"Want his home number? Got it right here."

"No. It can wait."

Gorden hung up and dug his fingers into the armrest, the rough fabric prickling his fingertips. Tired? Shin? He never got tired. Gorden tried not to think what Shin was doing now, especially with Helen there.

Shari walked into the room wearing jeans and an old Bud T-shirt, her face scrubbed free of makeup. She sat next to Gorden. "What're you watching?" she asked.

"Nothing," he said, staring at the TV. Had Shin gone home because he was horny, and wanted to fuck his wife? Maybe that was what they were doing right now, this minute. Gorden closed his eyes and pictured Helen naked, pictured her long, thin neck, and he thought of Shin on top of her and Gorden felt his face flush. Son of a fucking bitch.

"Gord, do you think I should go shopping for groceries soon?"

"What?"

"Groceries. Should I get some more?"

Gorden sighed. "What, and spend more money?"

"Well, yeah," she said, her tone uncertain.

"Christ, don't you think we ought to be *saving* money?"

"What, on food?"

Gorden gritted his teeth, trying to control his temper. Shit, she was just so *dumb*. "Look, since I'm the only one with a fucking job right now—"

"Why the hell are you getting on my case? I'm looking. It's not like I'm doing nothing."

"But you want to spend all the goddamn money we got!"

"Food, Gorden? Food? Why're you going nuts, alls I did was ask—"

"And what about this fucking thing..." he patted his pockets. Where the fuck was that—in his jacket. He stood up quickly and pulled the key chain out of the pocket. "What about this fucking thing, huh? Why'd you go and buy something like this?"

"I thought you liked it," she said.

"Liked it?" he asked, leaning forward, his hands shaking with anger. "What the fuck do I need with one of these?" He threw it against the wall and it split apart, the "F" falling straight down while the "G" rolled across the floor.

Shari stared at the broken key chain in shock. "Why..." her voice faltered. She looked at him for a second, then turned away.

Gorden watched her and felt like shit. Before he could say anything, though, Shari jumped up and ran into the bathroom, slamming the door. "Shit. Wait," he said, half-heartedly, knowing she couldn't hear him. What a fucking asshole he was. He thought he heard her crying, and he picked up the two pieces of the key chain. He hurried into the kitchen, looking for the glue, and couldn't find it. He didn't have to be such a bastard about it. He winced. "Shari, I'm sorry," he called out. "I'll glue it back." He went through the drawers and found tape, scissors, scraps of paper, coupons, but no glue. "Where's the goddamn glue," he asked himself, pulling out the drawers angrily. Why the fuck did he have to be so mean? He went through another drawer, pushing aside junk that had accumulated—rubber bands, plastic bag clips, junk mail—and became angrier. Why couldn't he find anything when he wanted it? Where the hell was the glue? After a few minutes he placed the key chain on the kitchen counter and gave up. Ah, hell. What's the use, he thought, staring at the open drawer, the rebate offers for batteries he had never sent in, the 50 cent coupon for bread, and slammed it shut. Shari, he thought, I'm sorry. It meant nothing, he knew, but he was still sorry.

4

From the connecting kitchen, Helen watched her husband play with Susy, bouncing her on his legs. Raj was on the living room sofa. "This is your horsey," he said, while Susy was laughing, pulling on his pant leg as if they were reins. Her short hair flew up and down with each bounce. Raj had to go to work in a few minutes, but this morning everyone had woken up early and had eaten breakfast together, which was unusual. They had eaten with the TV on and now, watching Susy and Raj playing, Helen found this entire morning odd: activity and noise when usually there was silence. Perhaps it was because last night everyone had gone to bed early.

Even Raj, who usually never went to bed before midnight, had fallen asleep by ten-thirty. Helen was suspicious of his sudden appearance, but after seeing how tired he was, she knew that he had come home to sleep.

"You're going to be a princess," Raj said, stroking Susy's hair awkwardly, almost petting her head. Susy grabbed his tie and tugged. He smiled. "Where would you like to go, my princess?"

Susy's head bobbed up and down. "Badum badum badum," he said quietly. Susy said "Up" and tried to crawl closer to him, but Raj then sped up his bouncing, which sent Susy into another fit of laughter.

Most mornings Helen would only hear Raj as he closed the front door, waking up to his footsteps clomping down the stairs. She would slowly ease out of bed and into the shower. She would move about softly, with only the sounds of the refrigerator humming audible. Susy would burst out of bed and into the living room, wanting to watch TV and have her cereal. Instead, today, Helen in her bathrobe, unshowered, still groggy, stared at her husband and tried to figure him out. Was this a sign that he suspected something? Could he have come home last night to try to catch her with Gorden?

Susy let out a giggle and said, "More!"

Helen dismissed this again. Even so, this was becoming dangerous. She and Gorden were taking too many risks. And for what? She certainly wasn't in love with Gorden. She tried to understand what she felt for him, but realized she didn't know.

Helen saw Raj studying her as she thought about Gorden, and she looked away, flustered, and went back to wiping the counter. He couldn't know, could he? She glanced at him. What was going on with him?

"I might be late again tonight," he said to her.

She looked up. "What?"

"I said that I might be late again. I guess it doesn't matter. You've been going to sleep early anyway, haven't you?"

She nodded slowly.

"I guess you've been tired lately."

She stopped wiping the counter. What did he mean by that?

Susy then yelled and toppled back, and Helen's throat tightened as she called out and saw Susy fall to the ground, landing squarely on her side. Susy gasped. Raj lunged forward too late and there was stunned silence as Susy sat up slowly, looking confused, her eyes wide and mouth open. "Are you okay?" Raj asked, touching her arm lightly, leaning forward.

Susy looked at her father, then turned towards her mother, unsure. She seemed to need confirmation, and when Helen rushed to Susy and cooed to her, asking if her baby was all right, Susy began wailing, her face scrunching up.

"Should we call the hospital?" Raj asked, the sound of Susy's crying filling the room. "Should we call 9-1-1?"

Helen shook her head, touching Susy's arm gingerly. "No, don't worry. It's just a bruise. She's had worse."

"She has?"

Helen looked at her husband. Concern and fear spread across his face, and she couldn't help smiling. "Yes. She'll be okay. Why don't you go to work? I'll take care of her."

He bent over Susy and said, "Poor princess. I'm sorry. I'm so sorry." He kissed her arm. Susy watched, her crying subsiding. Raj went to get his things. Helen held Susy in her arms, stroking her hair absently, thinking how frightened Raj had been. She hugged Susy tighter.

Gorden hurried up the steps to Helen's apartment, anxious to surprise her. He had left work early, knowing that Shin would stay late because he wanted to reorganize the storage room with John, as well as organize the over-inventoried items for the sale. At five, when Shin and John had been in the back room, clipboards ready and their sleeves rolled up, Gorden knew that he should go in to help, but he didn't feel like moving boxes. Besides, tomorrow he would have to continue what they started, so why begin early? Why break his damn back for Shin?

Gorden rang Helen's doorbell and moved away from the door so she could see him through the security hole. His shoes crunched on salt pellets left to melt ice. He remembered looking in this hole and seeing movement not too long ago, and thought it was funny that he had now been on the other side of that door and had seen all that Shin had seen. Gorden heard movement, and the door opened.

"Gorden? What are you doing here?" Helen asked, stepping half way out of the apartment, still holding on to the doorknob.

"Hi. Call the sitter and let's go out for a while."

"I can't. Raj might be home soon. Last night he came home—"

"I know. But tonight he'll be working late. Come on, just for a couple hours."

Helen hesitated. "I don't know about this. It's getting too risky."

Gorden felt a small jolt, her reluctance worrying him. "Hey. It'll be fun. Just for two hours."

She thought about this, then said, "Okay, but I don't know about this." She glanced back into the apartment. "Let me meet you somewhere. I've got to call the sitter."

"I can't come in?"

"No. You'd better not."

"All right," he said, lowering his voice. "Meet me in the supermarket parking lot, like that other time."

"You shouldn't show up like this. What if Raj came home?"

He shook his head. "I left him at the mall. Hey, it's been a while since I last saw you."

"Only a couple days."

"I missed you."

She looked up at him, startled, but smiled. "Give me a half hour."

Gorden returned to his car, feeling that small high he got whenever he saw her. Shit. He was acting like a kid again. He decided to drive around Sunolea to kill time, and drove up Dorset, glancing at the few stores along the street—a hardware store with the snow blower in the front window; a Bank of New Hampshire made of red brick with large, mirrored windows; the Sunolea Twin Theater, with "Closed for Renovations" on the dirty white marquee—and soon the buildings disappeared and he was on a road with woods on both sides, large deer-crossing signs posted. He passed a small lake to his left, partially frozen over with patches of white ice, and an empty parking lot. Up ahead also on the left he saw a motel, the Lakeview Inn, with its wooden sign in the shape of an oval, probably representing the lake, and the long, one-story building, extending into the woods. He stopped next to the sign, and parked.

A motel. He knew it was seedy and Helen probably had too much class for something like this, but hell, where else would they go? The sitter at her place, Shari at his... He stared at the "Vacancy" sign in the front office window, the screen ripped along the side and puffing out like a small bubble. While debating whether or not to rent a room, he wondered about Helen's, *I don't know about this.* Getting second thoughts? What'd she mean by that? Didn't know about what? Tonight, or the whole thing? He shook his head, not sure he wanted to think about it. He tried to imagine what would happen if Helen wanted out, but he couldn't see that. What the hell else did she have? Shin? And it wasn't like Gorden was really pushing her to do anything. He wasn't asking her to run away or anything like that. He was just having a good time with her. What was wrong with that?

Gorden climbed out of the car, a burst of cold wind slicing across his cheek. He slammed his door and hurried to the office, his shoes crunching the frozen dirt. He walked up the three cement steps and into the small office, and immediately felt the heat from an electric heater next to the door. An old woman looked around a doorway cluttered with old newspapers.

"Hello, need a room?" she asked, her voice scratchy. She

smiled, her face wrinkling even more, waiting for his answer.

"How much for one night?"

"Single or double?"

Gorden thought for a second. "Single."

"Thirty-eight."

"For one night?"

She nodded. "If you're looking for something cheaper, about ten miles up there's another place. But we've got cable."

"No. It's okay." He paid in cash, signed the register card, and took the key. When she told him that check-out was at noon, he nodded and knew that he wouldn't even stay the whole night there. Christ. Thirty-eight bucks.

Gorden waited in the Sunolea Superette parking lot, leaving his window open a crack for air, and listened to the metal carts rattle over the uneven cement as shoppers brought their groceries to their cars. He didn't have to wait long, since his ride to the motel and back took longer than he had expected, and in five minutes he saw Helen's white Rabbit pull in and park two cars away from him. He unlocked the passenger side door.

"Listen," she said as soon as she shut the door. Cold air mixed with perfume. "This is getting too risky."

Gorden started the car and smiled. "It makes things more fun."

"I'm serious—where are we going?—I'm serious about this."

He put his hand on her knee and said, "We'll talk about it when we get there."

"Where?"

"You'll see." He opened his hand, palm up, waiting for hers. She looked down, and then after a second placed her hand in his. "You'll see."

As they drove, Helen told him that the sitter had been annoyed by the short notice, so Helen had raised her pay to six an hour. It occurred to Gorden that having an affair was expensive. She was studying his hand. Once, while they had been driving back to

Helen's after having lunch together, she said that his hands were long, his fingers thin, compared to her husband's. Then she stopped herself and asked, "Do you mind when I talk about him?" Gorden hadn't minded. It made him feel closer to her when she talked about things like that.

"Looking at my hands again," he said now.

She looked up. "Just thinking."

"About what?"

She hesitated. "What exactly are we doing? It's been a couple of weeks now, and... I'm not sure what we're doing."

"We're having fun?"

She laughed weakly. "I don't know, Gorden. I think I'm temporarily insane."

Gorden sped up Dorset, looking for the sign on the left. "I hope you don't think this is too much."

"What? Us?"

"No. Where we're going," he said, turning to her. "I couldn't think of anywhere else."

She saw the sign. "Oh, god. A motel? Gorden, a motel?"

"Room 10A." He turned into the lot and drove past the office, into the small parking area in front of the rooms. Glancing towards the office, he wondered if the old woman would make him pay more if she saw Helen. He had the key and that was all he needed. He began to get excited, thinking about Helen and the room. They had it all to themselves.

"I can't believe this," she said.

Gorden scratched his chin. "I know, but hell, where else is there?"

Helen shook her head as he went to open his door. "Wait. We've got to talk. I don't know about this."

"What're you talking about? We're here. Come on and at least look at the place."

"No. I mean," she began, and stopped. "I mean I think you should take me back."

Gorden tensed. "What?" he asked. "Already?"

"I just don't know, Gorden. A motel is just so... all this seems really..."

"Helen, let's go inside. We can talk in there. Come on."

"Gorden, are you listening? I think I should go back now."

He stared at her, suddenly remembering the first time they had had sex, in the back seat of this car. Everything had been so strange that night. He picked her up after making a date the day before, after she told him what her husband's plans were. He hadn't meant to do anything, really, but after they went to a bar, and they were both a little drunk, they drove around Yanack. When he parked in a deserted lot, they faced each other in the front and continued talking, though he knew something was happening. They began kissing, and although she didn't want to go in the back seat, he coaxed her, soothed her, and eventually she climbed in between the seats after him, saying, Oh, I don't care anymore.

"Gorden?" she asked him now. "I'm sorry."

"Let's talk inside. Don't you think we should talk? Just for a few minutes?"

She frowned.

He touched her hand and motioned outside. "For a few minutes. Come." He opened his door.

She sighed and climbed out of the car, closing her door quietly.

Inside the motel room, which was dark even after he switched on the front lamp, the dim bulb barely allowing them to see past the bed, the TV and small table bolted together and to the floor, Gorden told Helen to sit and rest. He turned on the bathroom light, and sat next to her on the bed. He took off his jacket. "Helen, you don't mean it, do you?"

"It was just that this morning I saw Raj with Susy and I realized what I was doing. All this is so unreal, Gorden. I just drifted into it," she said. "I don't know."

Gorden reached over and touched her cheek. He couldn't help it—her cheek looked so smooth and soft, and he wanted to feel her skin. She turned to him. Before he realized what he was doing he found himself kissing her, hard, and she pulled back.

"You're not even listening to me, Gorden."

"I am. No, I am, but what do you want to do?" he asked. "Do you really want to stop this?" He leaned closer, and reached into her jacket, touching her stomach lightly.

"I don't know. Maybe we can slow it down. It's just that it's so risky."

"Okay," he said. "Maybe that's a good idea." He moved his hand up and cupped her breast, leaning forward to kiss her again. When he felt her kissing back, he pushed her slowly onto the bed, becoming more excited and wanting to touch every part of her, not caring what she had just said. It wouldn't hit him until later, much later, that Helen was trying to break it off with him, that this was the end of his affair with his boss' wife, but right now all he could think of was how soft her skin was and how he wanted nothing more than to be inside her, to be a part of her.

5

The scene didn't end there, obviously, since they went on to have sex but what interested me at this point was not their lovemaking but what happened after they finished. Gorden and Helen lay in bed, naked, the covers wrapped around them, both of them quiet, sweating. The heater was on, which made them warmer; Gorden fanned the sheets and listened to Helen's breathing, an occasional car driving by outside. Their bed creaked with every small movement. Gorden kept wondering about Shin—what did Shin have that Gorden didn't? What was it about that guy that got him everything? Wife and kid, a good job... Gorden couldn't understand it. He asked her, "Does he make you come like that?"

"What?" She blinked, shaking out of her thoughts.

"Does he make you come?"

She studied him, trying to see if he was kidding. "Sometimes."

"Are we different in the way we have sex?"

"Of course." She smiled.

"How?"

"Are you serious?"

Gorden nodded. "I want to know."

She shrugged into the pillows. "Well," she began slowly, looking up at the ceiling. "For Raj it's like another... job. Not that that's bad, but sometimes we go to bed and he wants to make love, and that's the goal, and that's what we do."

Gorden thought about this. Yeah, he could see it. Another thing on Shin's list to do. Fuck wife. "And me?"

"You play more. You know that. You tease and you're not always in a hurry, except for tonight, that is."

"You like my way better, don't you?"

"It's not liking one more than the other. You're both different."

"You'll like my way better."

"What do you mean?"

"You don't know it now, but you'll like my way better. You'll prefer me."

"Ha ha," she said.

"No, really. I mean it. You will prefer me."

Helen didn't say anything.

It was obvious to me, though I guess not to Gorden, that Helen was already thinking of her exit, of how she would get Gorden to drive her back so she could get rid of the sitter and be with her daughter. She was beginning to feel that this was out of control. If something like tonight happened again, she'd be in trouble. At least she mentioned the idea of slowing down. It was a start. Whether it had sunk in, though, was another question. She lay quietly, and felt him leak out of her. She closed her legs, but remembered that these weren't her sheets, so she opened her legs and let him drip out. She felt the slow, itchy feeling creep further down, and she shifted, letting some of the blanket rest there, absorbing him. She glanced at her watch, thinking of excuses if Raj came home early and saw the sitter. Shopping, she'd say. She needed a break from Susy. Her hair. The cleaners. Something.

She heard Gorden's breathing slow, deepen, and wasn't sure if he had fallen asleep. She should have brought her car. She'd give him a few more minutes.

Actually, Gorden wasn't asleep, but was letting his mind drift, jumping from topic to topic, following a path that went nowhere and everywhere, and then, suddenly, he began thinking about his sister. It was strange that Mona should pop into his mind at this particular moment, but he had been wondering about his parents:

> ... and I dont know why the fuck this comes into my head but it does and I think about the time pop died and how ma was all screwed up for a while, and then she met the bastard who got her to marry him. I still dont know what the hell ma was thinking, but she didnt give a shit what we thought. Christ. And then the bastard turned out to be such an asshole that even ma realized it. At least you and I stuck together, right? You REALLY hated that guy! What I never got was that he used to knock me around, but I dont think he ever hit you, did he? I remember that time you and ma were fighting about him when I got back from work. Man you two were yelling. She was screaming that you were crazy and dirty and you told her she was stupid, plain stupid, then you two saw me and stopped. Was that when you took off for the first time? I forget now. All that shit runs together. Hey, what the fucks going on? I know you hate writing but Ive been sending you a shitload of letters. Ah hell. Dont worry about it. I know how it is and I like writing these damn things.

Small moments like these showed up in Gorden's letters, and I became more curious about Mona and her relationship to her younger brother. I was an only child and often wondered about the bonds between siblings. When I was younger and growing up in a suburb outside of Chicago, I used to see brothers and sisters fighting on the playground; often the older teasing the younger, the younger getting the older in trouble with the parents, and I always thought that if I had a brother or sister, we wouldn't do any of that. Naive, yes, but normal. Perhaps Gorden and Mona's relationship was one that fit my ideal. I wanted to know.

I remember exactly where I was when this began gnawing at me. By this time I was working at the diner every evening, washing dishes with a comfortable, monotonous rhythm which began to appeal to me more than teaching ever had. There were no surprises in washing dishes. No troublesome students. No teacher politics. No administrative mazes. You went to work every evening and knew exactly what to expect. Dishes. Once in a while you broke a glass, a bowl, but you swept it up and threw it away. Very simple.

When I read Gorden's letter I was sitting at the back counter during my break—it was about eight o'clock—drinking coffee and eating an old brownie that had been sitting inside a glass cover for a few weeks. Marlene, one of the waitresses (a forty-year-old widow with short salt and pepper hair who seemed to have taken a liking to me) had slipped the brownie to me, saying that someone had to eat it soon. Marlene noticed that I kept to myself. After my first week she began asking me a few questions in passing, like what my name was, where I lived, how I liked it here. She also complimented my vigilance in keeping the dishes clean. The previous dishwasher, I soon learned, used to take his time and would often wait until the machine was completely packed before running it. The problem was that if the diner was crowded that evening, as it was on weekends, they would continually need plates and glasses, and they would often come within one or two racks of running out. Although it had never happened—running out of dishes—coming too close alarmed the busboys, the waitresses, and the manager. It seems like a small point now that I think about it, but during the busy nights when all twenty-eight tables (the twelve booths on one side and sixteen dining tables on the other) were full, and a small line in the foyer grew as the local movie theater let out, and the cooks' outgoing trays began crowding beneath the heat lamps, and waitresses were running back and forth shoving orders onto the rotating metal tree of clips, leaves of green and white orders spinning, a thin film of sweat covering their smooth foreheads, and busboys noisily clearing tables, wanting the quick turnover since they shared tips with the waitresses—with all this hurrying and yelling and movement, I could see how coming close to running out of dishes would alarm them.

So Marlene had given me a large brownie which, although the corners were hard and the nuts tasted oily, was sweet and went down smoothly with my coffee. I read through Gorden's letter slowly, keeping an eye on the busboys bringing their plastic bins of dirty dishes into the kitchen—I usually counted four or five trips and then would go and begin working—and I thought about Mona. What did she look like? Where had she gone? Perhaps I had been hasty in accepting the landlord's account of her, that she was nothing but an addict and he had kicked her out. The End. No, this was too easy, and I thought that since I, the listening audience, was appropriating her role, filling my days and thoughts with Yanack Hills and Sunolea and malls and affairs, I thought I should know more.

At this point I counted five bins of dishes, so I left the counter and went into the kitchen. I tied on my apron, pulled on my long rubber gloves, turned on the steaming hose, and began cleaning off the chunks of food the busboys had missed, stacking dishes into the machine. Being acquainted with some forms of research, albeit a different kind, I began thinking of ways to discover what had happened to Mona. Perhaps, I thought as I sprayed some smeared ketchup and french fries off a plate, perhaps I could even meet her, not letting her know who I was of course, but seeing, in person, a blood relation of this man I had been reading about for almost two months. Wouldn't that be interesting, I thought. Wouldn't that be strange?

When my shift was over I punched out my card and said goodbye to Marlene, who was sitting by the back door on a small stool, smoking a cigarette. "See you, Tiger," she said. She looked tired, with small bags under her eyes and she was stretching her legs out in front of her, pointing her toes. She relaxed and inhaled her cigarette, holding it between her index and thumb. "Hey, Tiger," she said as I walked away. For some reason she called me Tiger. I didn't know why, and I never asked.

"Yes?"

"You were on the ball tonight. I saw how fast those dishes were piling up, but you socked 'em right out."

I smiled. "It's my job."

She coughed for a few seconds, clearing her throat. "Hey, you said you live around here?"

Nodding, I replied, "Right over Lucky's, the bar down the—"

"You're kidding? That place?" She thought about this, staring at me with her head tilted. Her short black and grey hair fell onto her cheek. "The rent's cheap, I guess."

"Very." I noticed that she tended to blink very hard a few times before she spoke, making the wrinkles around her eyes deeper for a second. There was a brief pause and I said, "I'll see you tomorrow, Marlene. Have a good night."

"Yeah, you too. Have a good night." She waved her cigarette.

The evening was cold. I smelled the air—a staleness mingled with food coming from the diner—and began walking back to my apartment. But when I reached the corner, I decided to go to the train station, so I crossed the street, a staggered line of cars waiting at the light, their exhausts pumping smoke through red brake lights, and walked slowly up the concrete steps, thinking about tonight's job and how Marlene had been right—the dishes had stacked up pretty quickly—and about Farrel Gorden and his sister. When I reached the top of the steps, I moved closer to the edge of the platform, and looked out over Marnole. I saw the streetlights along Sunrise Highway, the yellow points curving to my right and left, disappearing into the distance. Brightly lit storefronts and gas stations ran parallel to the highway. Further into Marnole the residential streets with fewer street lamps became more difficult to see because the trees and the darkness hid most of the houses. This was the southern view, and there was a northern view of more stores and office buildings, but I preferred to look at my apartment and the houses extending beyond it. I liked to imagine the people moving about in those houses, watching TV, making love, eating a late supper, and I thought at this time, almost eleven-thirty, some would be preparing for bed, washing up and putting on their pajamas, lying sleepily on their couches as their spouses talked about their day and all the things they had to do tomorrow. It was comforting for me to imagine this activity, to know that there was all this life in front of me. It struck me that, like those spouses considering all they had to do tomorrow, I too had things to take care of. I had to begin my inquiry into Mona Gorden, learning what I could about the woman whose place I had taken, and perhaps this would help my understanding of Gorden, since he continued to intrigue me.

When Gorden learned that Shin had fired Warren, he was shocked. "What do you mean, 'let go'?" he asked John. They were in the front window where Gorden was setting up a new display, and John had told Gorden to keep this quiet.

"What do you think I mean?" John said. "He told him that they didn't need two part-timers, and let him go."

"Christ. Is he thinking about anyone else? Are we in trouble?"

"I don't know," John said, shaking his head. "He doesn't tell me anything. I found out this morning."

"You'd tell me if I was in trouble, right?" Gorden asked. "You'd warn me."

"Shit, yeah. But even my job might go. I don't know what he's thinking."

Gorden thanked him, turning to the pair of skis leaning against the wall. He waited until John had left before cursing to himself. Gorden didn't know whether or not to trust him. How could John, the fucking Assistant Manager, not know about that kind of shit? He and Shin worked together all the time, and it seemed suspicious that he wasn't more worried than he seemed. Gorden remembered when Shin first got here and John kept talking about how he had been passed over, and how easily Manny had been fired. Maybe John knew something now. Maybe Shin had promised him the manager job once Shin left. But what about Gorden? Staring at the fake snow on the ground—cotton that had been ripped and fluffed apart—he wondered what he could do. There was no way he'd find another job like this, that paid as well. Goddammit, he had worked his way up from the fucking stockroom and now he was going to get pissed away?

He rubbed his eyes and his temples, feeling a headache coming on. He didn't need this shit. He didn't need any of this. He wanted to see Helen, stay with her for a while. But no, even that wasn't possible right now. Her kid had gotten sick, so she hadn't been able to see him for a week. The last time was at that motel. Gorden smiled. That had been fun. After he had dropped her off at the supermarket he had gone back to the motel and had stayed there for a few hours, showering, watching the cable TV. Hell, he had paid for it.

Gorden heard Shin telling Henry to stop going to Kramer's and the other stores. Leaning towards the small door which led out of the display, Gorden listened to Shin warn Henry that they probably knew what he was doing, and that kind of spying didn't help. Once in a while is okay. Good, Gorden thought. The kiss-ass was getting in trouble. At least Gorden stayed out of everyone's way.

"No, *listen* to what I say. That's not your job. If we need to find out, John or I can go. Do you understand?" Shin said in a sterner voice.

Was he getting angry? Shin had been losing his temper. Nothing too loud or obvious, but everyone here knew that he was under pressure. The next sale, a week away, was making everyone jumpy, though Shin was showing it most. This was the second time he had gotten angry at Henry. Guess it don't pay to be a kiss-ass, Gorden thought. He looked out the door and saw Shin, arms folded, listening to Henry. Shin looked like he was losing weight, his cheeks thin, and his clothes didn't look as tight as Gorden remembered. Seeing Shin like this made Gorden feel better. And I'm fucking your wife, he thought, staring at Shin. How do you like that?

He went back to the display, trying to decide if there should be a mannequin with the ski jacket, gloves and hat, or if it looked too stupid. Where was Norma? She liked doing the displays. Gorden then wondered if Norma, who was also part-time, was going to be fired. Or had she been fired already?

He cursed and tried to concentrate on his work. He really didn't need this shit.

Roger Shin checked the advertisements in the paper for the fourth time, pretending he was a reader and seeing the sales items in the newspaper. Would he be interested? He read the "SKI CLEARANCE SALE!" at the top, and studied the row of name brand skis all lined up. He had done the layout himself, and wondered if the skis looked too crowded, if the picture implied they had to get rid of all this. The coupons with the dotted lines were on the right, and he particularly liked the coupon for free ski lessons and a one-day lift ticket for beginners at Snow Valley. This might attract families as well as first time skiers. Besides the ski listings, he had placed information on the ski boots and bindings on sale. The Raichle Elite, originally $159.99, now on sale for $89.99, was the opener, with the prices getting more expensive towards the bottom. And the Marker M-27 bindings, originally $154.99, now $69.99, led the next column. Keeping in mind that they had to get rid of some of their parkas, he had put a Columbia men's, a Fall Line women's, and an Ossi Skiwear child's parka on the front page, each 35% off, with a drawings of them next to each other. In bold letters at the bottom was "We will beat any advertised price!"

Although inside the four page advertisement were other Easter Spring Sale Items—like running and court shoes, camping tents and sleeping bags, home exercise equipment—the focus was on the ski items. Shin thought about the marketing classes he had taken in school, and realized that he had made a "tombstone" mistake, lining up two headlines right next to each other, but he didn't care. Most of what he had learned at school was worthless. When it came right down to it, like now, you had to go on instinct, and all those rules, those formulas for calculating the rate of return based on past sales and markdowns seemed irrelevant now. He couldn't depend on a formula.

This morning, he had received a call from the VP of Northeast regional sales, his boss, about the latest report. No reprimand, no comment really, just a question about the inventory. Yet he felt the implicit rebuke for the last sale. The VP usually didn't call unless something concerned him. Do you need us to take some of the inventory, the VP asked, suggesting a redistribution. Roger Shin said no, not yet. After he hung up he realized that this was getting worse by the day.

Maybe this time he had taken on too much.

And now, with his daughter sick with some kind of fever, everything seemed to be going wrong. He pushed aside the advertisement and tapped his pen on his desk, looking out into the showroom and seeing Gorden climb down from the display window, two ski poles in his hand. Gorden has been very quiet these days. Maybe he was shaping up. He wasn't giving anyone a hard time, and seemed to be doing his job. But there were other things to worry about now. With Warren gone, the books will look a little better. That probably wasn't good for morale, he knew, but something had to be done. He had no choice.

Roger Shin snapped out of his reverie, and stood up quickly—
enough of this idling, he told himself—and went to check on
Gorden's new display.

After he had finished dinner, Gorden called Helen, wondering
if she was going to give more excuses. The phone rang a few times,
and when she picked up he didn't even bother saying hello. "It's
me. Tonight?"

"I don't think so. Susy's still not well and I'd rather not leave
her."

"Even with a sitter?"

"I think it was the sitter who gave this to her."

Gorden gripped the phone harder. "What gives? It's been over
a week."

"Didn't we agree that we had to slow down anyway?"

"What?"

"Slow down. I told you about it before. Everything was happening too fast."

Gorden heard Shari moving around in the bedroom. She was
waking up from her nap. "How long before Susy gets better?" he
asked.

"I don't know. I want to spend time with her."

Shari walked into the living room, her hair tangled and sticking
out, her old T-shirt splotched with dried wine stains, and he said to
Helen, "Well, you let me know."

After he hung up, Shari asked who that was.

"The store," he said, knowing Helen was lying, that she was
trying to avoid him, and he began to get angry. He hadn't done
anything, had he? She was blowing him off and it didn't make any
sense. She had had her fun but now it was over. Bullshit. No fucking
way he bought that.

"What'd they want?"

"What?"

"The store," she said. "What did they want?"

"Nothing. It doesn't matter."

Shari looked at him for a second, then shrugged to herself as she walked into the kitchen, her bare feet shuffling across the floor. The more he thought about Helen, the more restless he became, tapping his foot and trying to figure out what the hell was going on. They had something going, didn't they? Christ, at least he had thought so. They had been having fun, acting like a couple of teenagers, but now what was happening?

Fuck it. He wasn't sitting around like a dumb shit. Gorden stood and grabbed his jacket. He wasn't sure what he was going to do, but he had to get out. He couldn't breathe in this damn place.

"Where're you going?" Shari asked, looking out from the kitchen.

"Going for a drive."

"Where?"

"What's it fucking to you?" he almost yelled, making her flinch. He checked himself and said, "Just out. I need some air."

Shari stared at him, unblinking. To hell with it all, he thought, hurrying out the door, inhaling the cold air, not looking back.

It was times like these that I really hated Gorden. I didn't know why he had to be so cruel to Shari. If I had known then what I know now, I would have tried to do something to get her the hell out of there. Couldn't Gorden see what he was doing to her? She was slowly falling into another depression, the ups and downs triggered so easily—this time by her lack of job prospects. It seemed to her that nothing she did would get her a job, and her hopes of earning some money became more ridiculous every day. Once, during the past week, she had thought about that car she wanted to buy, and she laughed, calling herself stupid for wanting something that was so clearly beyond her, and then, after dwelling on this for some time, realizing how trapped she was, she began crying. She wasn't able to stop for at least ten minutes, and it seemed that all she did lately was cry. She was disgusted with herself.

After Gorden had left without saying where he was going, Shari knew she should be insulted, angry, but she had stopped feeling anything. *Gord's going to fuck around with someone else,* she thought, *and I don't care.* And she didn't. Nothing seemed to matter. She walked back into the kitchen, and took out a beer. She rested the cold bottle against her neck, wanting to feel something, to remind her that she could. She let water from the bottle drip down her shirt, listening to the TV Gorden had left on.

She sat down on the living room floor and began reading though the newspapers scattered around her. She turned to the Help Wanted sections of the New Hampshire *Gazette,* gazing at the circles she had drawn the past few days, pointing out jobs that she might be able to get—clerical, secretarial, answering phones—but the ones she called had already filled their spots, and she hadn't bothered calling the rest. There had been no point.

She flipped through the pages and saw the obituaries, reading the small print about dozens of dead people. If anything happened to her she doubted that she'd get written up. Maybe if she was back in Maine, she might get written up—her parents would do it. But here? No one knew her. No one cared.

Thinking about Shari, I fantasized about helping her. I thought about taking a bus to New Hampshire, sneaking to Gorden's house when he was at work, and bringing Shari back to New York. I even went so far as to look up Yanack on a map, calculating distances and how much time I would need to get there and back before my shift started. I wasn't sure exactly how I would convince Shari to come with me, but how could she refuse? I pictured myself walking slowly to her front door, listening to the taxi cab's engine behind me, knowing that the meter was ticking and I had to work fast. I would knock lightly, but at first there'd be no answer, and I'd knock a few more times until I heard her yell in a tired, annoyed voice, Who is it? It would sound high-pitched, and I would be surprised since, for some reason, I had thought her voice was deeper, but of course, she was just a kid. Then she'd ask again, and I would say, Is Gorden there? She'd answer no, and I'd hear the door unlocking and she would peer out, curious.

Hey, do you know where he is? I'd ask.

At work. Who are you?

I wouldn't be able to stop staring. She would look just as Gorden had described, just as I had imagined, and I would smile. I knew him a while ago, I would say to her. I'm on my way back to New York and thought I'd drop by for a second. The cab is waiting though, I would say, pointing behind me.

New York?

Ever been there?

She would shake her head and I would say something like, I was going to ask Gorden to come with me—I have an extra ticket.

Come with you?

Sure. I have this extra ticket... but he's at work, I'd say, shaking my head. Oh well. Hey, do you want a ticket to New York? Actually to Long Island? Hey, do you want to come with me?

Her eyes would narrow. Who are you again?

I would tell her. Then I would say, The bus leaves in an hour. If you're interested, go to the Sunolea Bus Depot.

I would begin to walk away and she would say, Wait, are you kidding? Just like that?

And I would say, Sure.

I would look around the place and say, A change of scene might do you good.

She would say, Wait. Don't go yet. Let me get a bag.

Okay, I admit it was an adolescent fantasy, but there seemed to be nothing I could do, really, except read and wonder, and I was afraid to act on anything I read since with every letter I opened, the more paralyzed I became, as if my observer status became cemented, and every letter burdened me further with inaction. This would not last much longer, though, and I will get to that later.

Nevertheless, Shari was falling into another depression, and that evening, while she looked through the newspapers, drinking her beer, she tried to convince herself that everything wasn't that bad. She had a place to stay, after all. If she had been living in that apartment near the mall, she would have been kicked out months ago. She had lived with a couple, the guy had worked at Leroy's too, and his girlfriend was a cashier at a grocery, but Shari hadn't been able to stand it there, what with the two of them either fighting or fucking all the time, and they always ate Shari's food, so it got to the point where she didn't buy anything, eating out all the time, which cost more.

At least she had a place to stay and food to eat. So why was she feeling so goddamn miserable? She kicked the newspapers across the floor and leaned against the wall, finishing her beer.

6

Although I didn't have the nerve to interfere directly with Gorden's life, I knew I could begin my search for his sister, so a few days later, I went to the Marnole Public Library. The library was only a few blocks from my apartment, roughly five blocks further into the residential area, rather oddly placed in the center of suburban houses. I usually didn't venture too far south, since all I wanted to see I saw from the train platform, yet for my research I thought it important that I begin at the library. So, one early weekday morning I grabbed my notebook and pen, jotting a few notes to myself regarding things I had to look for ("telephone?", "obituary?", "jobs?"), and walked outside in the cool April air. Spring seemed to be arriving late that year, and though the snow had melted and the sun was out, trees still had not grown in their leaves, and streaks of dirt and salt were still on the roads, remnants of recent icy-road days.

I walked down Harold Avenue, looking at the houses to my left and right, satisfied with myself for doing something other than washing dishes and reading letters, and I studied my neighborhood, wondering how Mona would have looked at her surroundings. This was difficult to imagine, since I knew so little about her, but I guessed the sidewalks would have caught her attention. I am not sure why I thought this, but there was something strange about the sidewalks. First, they were uneven, with gnarled tree roots pushing up the cement, cracking it, so I often had to watch where I was walking; I could have tripped easily over one of the raised pieces. And second, many of the sidewalks were brown. I never noticed the color before, perhaps because I always walked north to the school where I had taught, and if I ever came down south, it would usually be at night. The odd brown color with an orange tint would appear in patches for a few sections of the sidewalk, then merge with the regular grey cement color. I stopped and stared. Was it a different kind of cement? I bent down and tried to see where the brown was darkest, and realized that the color was actually rust. Rusty sidewalks. After a few minutes of examining the cement I saw the sprinkler heads lined up at five-feet intervals along the edge of the grass and made the connection. Rusty pipes, rusty sprinklers, rusty sidewalks. One mystery solved.

Continuing down Harold Avenue, I looked at the mix of new and aging houses along the street, some with new paint jobs and manicured lawns, others with sagging shingles and broken gutters. Cars drove past me, kicking up dust. A woman in a blue jogging suit, a dog in tow, walked by, ignoring me.

Up ahead, I recognized the brick and glass building with "Marnole Public Library" spelled out in metal letters above the front entrance. I had checked out books from here to read during lab period. It was a small library with two levels, the basement for children's and young adult books, the ground floor for adult and reference books. I passed through the electronic theft gate, and walked on the grey carpet towards the other end, the reference section.

There were seven stacks of reference books, a long desk with the Reader's Guide to Periodical Literature, a microfilm viewer, and a wall filled with encyclopedias. I sat at one of the small tables near the encyclopedias, collecting my thoughts, and soon got to work. The details of the search were are not very interesting—I looked though old telephone books, the local Marnole Life newspaper, obituaries—and, not surprisingly, I found little of use. I discovered Mona's old phone number to my apartment, which had been disconnected with no new number given, but that was all. Her name appeared no where else, and I looked carefully at the newspapers dated around the same time I moved into the apartment, presumably the time when Mona had moved out, and although I learned some interesting things about Marnole, things which were not relevant to my search, I found nothing about Mona Gorden. I had been hoping to find something about her eviction, or perhaps she had gotten in some trouble with the law, or anything (even a death notice), but I was unsuccessful. While at the library, I picked up a few books, one by Montaigne, another by Spinoza, and one by Conrad. Eventually, after almost four hours, I decided to return home. I would think of a better approach later. I was very tired, and needed to take a short nap. Yes, I was disappointed, but in a way this was a successful trip, since it was the first time since I had been laid off that I had borrowed books for my own enjoyment.

That evening at the diner, racking the dishes into the machine, I tried to imagine Helen Shin's state of mind. She was a woman who had impulsively begun an affair, and was now regretting it. Maybe much of this became clearer to her while she was taking care of her daughter. The touch of the flu which had infected Susy, although not dangerous, was enough to give Susy a fever and keep her in bed for a few days. It pained Helen to see her daughter, red-faced, coughing, and either sleeping or crying. Never happy. Both she and Raj had been worried at the beginning, when they thought it might be pneumonia, but the doctor had assured them Susy would be fine after resting comfortably for at least a week.

Now, with the worst over, with Susy watching TV and sleeping on and off during the day, Helen had time to reevaluate her relationship with Gorden, and she didn't like what she saw. Could she really have begun an affair so carelessly? She frowned, somehow unable to be completely angry at herself, since it had been exciting. Past tense. Already she was beginning to separate herself from this affair, from Gorden. She knew he wouldn't like it. But she was *not* going to ruin her marriage, put Susy through any pain, simply because she was caught up in something new, something strange.

Over the past week, using the excuse of Susy's illness, Helen had managed to avoid Gorden, and she hoped he was getting the message. There had been times during their brief affair that she had implicitly warned him about this, that this was not going to last, that she was committed to her husband, no matter how strained their relationship might be. There was even that time she had told him exactly what her stance was. They had been together in his car, driving from one of the three restaurants they had frequented, and had been talking about what it was like to have a family.

"If I had more money, yeah, I'd definitely want to get some roots. You know? Right now I'm just running all over the place, it feels like," Gorden said.

Helen thought that he seemed wistful, and though she couldn't pin it down before, she realized then that this was what made him attractive. He acted cold, tough, sometimes even mean, but really, he wasn't very different from Helen, from anyone. Unlike Raj, Gorden seemed to need her. "You'd probably change your tune once you were saddled with all that. It isn't always so rosy."

"Yeah, well," he said, staring out onto the road. "Being with you makes me think about it. And I don't think I'd change my tune with you."

Helen tensed. "But this is just temporary, you know. Just a

fling."

He simply grinned.

Now, remembering his expression, Helen thought she should have made that clearer. He knew what the situation was, didn't he? She'd have to be more direct.

Helen sat back in her sofa and stroked Susy's hair. Though Susy's face and neck were warm, Helen knew her daughter's fever had broken and in a few days she would be running around the living room as if nothing had happened.

She stared at Susy's flushed cheeks, and felt there was nothing better than this, watching her daughter sleep.

Gorden parked his car in front of the New Hamp Tavern, and watched Helen's apartment across the street. Here he was again, just where he had started. Why was she doing this to him? When he had called before, the machine answered, and he was tempted to leave a message, but no, he hadn't since Shin could have heard it. Where the hell was she if she wasn't at home? For an instant he thought she was fucking some other guy, but Gorden couldn't picture it. When he called again an hour later, Shin answered.

So he had gone driving. This was the only place he could be alone, his car, and he liked moving around—it made him feel like he was *doing* something, even if it was just wandering across town. Now, while he stared up at their second-floor apartment, their curtained window lit up; Gorden tried not to imagine Shin and Helen together. What were they doing? He glanced at his watch— it was almost midnight—and wanted so badly to check on them. Maybe the reason why Helen wasn't going out with him anymore was because she and Shin were getting along better. Maybe Helen didn't need Gorden. Didn't want him.

Fuck it. He climbed out of his car and ran across the street, checking around him to see if anyone was watching. Everything quiet. He wasn't going to do anything stupid. Alls I'm doing is checking up, he thought.

it wasnt like I was going to do anything fucking dumb like break in there or anything, but hell I was eating away at myself just sitting there in the damn car wondering what she was doing and I kept thinking she was fucking him and I didnt know why she was cutting me out like that, with no warning, with nothing, and I was getting pissed. I mean, you just cant jerk someone around like that. You probably think I was cracked but no, I knew what I was doing and I kept thinking of the time she told me she felt like she could tell me almost anything and I began to think it was a crock of shit. But maybe I was getting worked up over nothing. Maybe because I didnt see her for so long I was getting squirrelly.

He hurried up the steps on the balls of his feet, making no noise, and walked towards their front door. He wasn't sure what he was going to do. There was a small window next to the door. Maybe he could see something. It was dark, and he tried to find a space in the curtains. Nothing. He looked through the peephole again, but couldn't make anything out of the blurry shadows. Then he crouched down behind the low wall that shielded him from the street and remained still, trying to hear any sounds. Nothing. Maybe they had gone to sleep.

It was strange, being so close to her, practically in the next room, without her knowing . He thought about her lying in bed with Shin, though Shin was probably asleep right now, and he wondered what would happen if he knocked lightly on the door. Or the window? No. But she was right there, so close. He began getting excited thinking about her lying in bed, maybe even sleeping in that big nightshirt with nothing else on. She never wore panties to bed, she had told him, since her doctor had said the air would help keep any moisture from being trapped. So she had nothing on down there. Gorden touched himself. Shit, he wanted to go in there so bad. He pictured himself breaking in and knocking out Shin, then having sex with Helen. That'd be fucked-up, he thought. Realizing that he had been rubbing himself through his pants, he stopped. What was he doing? Jerking off right in public.

He hesitated, then unzipped his pants, not caring what would happen to him if he were caught. But who would catch him? It was the middle of the night and everyone was asleep. He pulled himself out and began rubbing lightly, still crouching out of view of the street. He thought about the time Helen had sucked him off in the car, when they had parked in a lot only a few miles from here. It was the first time she had done it to him, and he was surprised. She put him in her mouth and rolled her tongue around him, then began moving up and down, guiding herself with one hand. She moved slowly, and used her other hand to grab his ass, holding him tightly. He came within minutes, not used to that. Shari had never done it like that.

Now, as he began moving faster, he felt himself about to come, and he stood and aimed at the door, arching his back and breathing quickly. He felt the short, tense spasms in his groin as he closed his eyes and pushed forward. He couldn't help laughing quietly, the release making him giddy, and after he finished, he blinked a few times, redid his pants, and looked down at the thick liquid dripping down the door and onto the ground. He was disgusted at the sight, wondering why the hell he had done that. He turned and hurried down the steps, lightheaded and tired. Crossing the street and getting into his car, he looked up at the apartment. Nothing had changed. He wondered what would happen if they noticed it. What a stupid ass thing to do. God, what a fucking idiot he was! What the hell was he thinking? He shook his head and laughed. You crack yourself up sometimes, he said to himself. You weird fuck.

When he arrived home, Shari was still up. As soon as he closed the door she asked him where he had been.

"Driving."

"Who's the girl you're fucking? Don't think I'm stupid."

He stared at her. Shari was wearing the same T-shirt she had worn for the past week and he was getting sick of it. But he didn't feel like fighting tonight. He just wanted to sleep. "What're you talking about?"

"Oh, give me a goddamn break," she said, rolling her eyes. "Just tell me who it is."

"Get off my back, Shari. I'm not in the mood." He walked behind the couch, glancing at the TV, an old sitcom on, and took off his jacket.

"Is she another school girl? Did you comb the high schools this time? Maybe the junior high schools now."

Gorden said slowly, "Not now. Why don't you go back to bed."

"Why don't you go back to bed," she mimicked, looking at the TV. "I should have known. Out with the old, in with the young."

He shut his eyes tightly, trying not to let her get to him.

She turned around and kneeled on the couch, resting her hands on the cushions. "You don't want to fuck anymore, do you. The little girl you got must keep you busy."

"Shut up."

"Come on, Gord, don't you want to fuck me?" She touched her breast and reached down and held her crotch. "If not here, how about up here?" She reached behind and grabbed her rear. "You like that, don't you."

He turned away and walked towards the bedroom.

"Maybe you got little boys this time. I wouldn't put it past you."

"You're a fucking psycho," he muttered.

She jumped off the couch and followed him. "What's the matter, truth hurt?"

He whirled around. "Get the fuck out of my face. You don't think I'll throw you out?"

"Ooooo. Talking tough. I love it when you talk tough." She moved closer to him, and he smelled the alcohol, but even more than that was her body odor.

"Christ, get the hell away from me."

"What's the matter, can't get it up anymore?"

He pushed her hard out of the bedroom and slammed the door while she was still taunting him. He didn't care. Let her mouth off. He heard her slump against the door, sliding down it slowly. "You fucking asshole," she said quietly, but he still heard her. She slid to the floor and thumped on the ground. He thought he heard her crying, but he wasn't sure. He was about to open the door but he stopped himself. What the hell, he thought, not sure what to do.

7

Shari knew it was over. Gorden didn't get angry anymore, didn't yell back or curse. She was nothing, not even worth getting annoyed about. It was a matter of time before he kicked her out and she'd have no place to go. What would she do then? Go home? She leaned back against the bedroom door, the hard wood hurting her spine. She breathed deeply, trying to keep the sickening, anxious feeling in her stomach from rising. Her heart was beating rapidly.

She remembered the night when she ran away. Her parents had grounded her after finding pot and a bottle of Southern Comfort in her dresser. Shari kicked herself for not hiding them better, but she had been in a hurry, and hadn't thought she was still under suspicion. She had been going out every night the past couple of months, hanging out with friends, drinking, smoking, and began blowing off her parents until they found out she hadn't been to school in two weeks. They began making all these rules. She told them to fuck off, and her mother slapped her. Then everything started falling apart.

The next few months became screaming matches, and Shari found herself doing things she never thought she could, breaking things, stealing their money, sleeping around. Finally, after another useless grounding—she would just sneak out anyway—she thought, This is stupid, and packed a few things and left. It was so easy. Her parents were probably relieved. Stupid jerks.

Then things got a little tougher. She slept at friends' houses, rotating every few days, but this strained everyone, especially Shari, and she was just so sick of everyone. Small arguments turned big. Her circle of friends shrunk. They were all shits, anyway. So she left, and ended up in Yanack. She could have continued south, but she had no money, and she saw the mall. How had she gotten a job so easily? It seemed unreal now.

She'd have to start all that over again. The thought of that, of having to look for jobs, of hitching rides with men eyeing her, of asking people she had known for only ten minutes if she could stay with them for a night—the thought of doing all that shit again weighed on her, suffocating her. When was this going to end? She curled up against the door and wished she could die.

Some of the information about Shari I would find out later but I mention this here not to show what I filled in myself, since my musings were more vague and unsubstantiated, although that never stopped me before, but because it seems more relevant at this juncture. Shari was falling apart, and reading Gorden's description of the sounds of her slipping to the ground affected me in a way that was unexpected. I read this and thought, Bastard! Bastard! *Do* something, you asshole! I stopped, and tried to distance myself, but it was difficult since I was fuming. I tried to analyze Gorden's reaction. Didn't he care anymore? Perhaps he had never really cared. Even when they were first going out he probably saw the age difference as a barrier, and wanted only to enjoy himself, which he did, at least until she moved in and everything became too serious for him. Or, perhaps he did care but was incapable of offering Shari the help she needed. Preoccupied with his job, and with Helen, Gorden couldn't handle too much at once, fearing a loss of control which, it seemed, was already happening. His way of dealing with this was to cut something out—someone—and to concentrate on the others. So, Shari was left adrift.

Yet there was a sense of guilt, of regret, as Gorden lay in his bed that evening, trying to sort everything out. As he fell asleep he wanted to ease some of this by forgetting, by thinking of something that made him happier, and he thought about his sister. He remembered the time when he was twelve and Mona had taught him, of all things, how to mend his ripped pants. She made him take them off, embarrassing him, and she turned them inside out, telling him how to hide the stitches. She showed him how to knot the end of the thread and sew, finally making few cross-stitches and then tying it off. You can do this yourself now, she told him, smiling. You don't need to depend on anyone.

Gorden said he could always get someone to do it, but Mona said, No, never depend on anyone. You hear me? You get yourself trapped. Like ma, she added. I'm going away soon, she told him then. Taking off. Gorden had heard her say this before, and ignored it. He wished he hadn't. He wished he had said something. Well, Gorden, she said, looking at his underwear. Looks like you're turning into a man.

Gorden turned deep red. Christ, he said. Mona laughed and laughed, telling him he had to ease up. After she threw him his pants and walked away, still laughing, he felt a strange mixture of embarrassment and pride.

I spoke to the landlord again about Mona, telling him I was curious about her. The landlord, a short fat man who came by once a week to check the building, always wore a light red and orange striped Mexican baja, a thick knit pull-on that bandits in old movies wore with sombreros and guns. This baja looked odd on a man so pale and unhealthy, always sweating and coughing, but I became used to it and never saw him without it on, even when it was ninety degrees out. When I asked him about Mona, he shook his head and told me that just because some junkie lived in my place didn't mean I'd get a cheaper rent. I reassured him that this was not my intention, and that I was curious because she had left some things behind and I thought I could send them to her.

"What things?" he asked, watching me carefully.

"A few books. A pair of shoes," I lied.

He threw his hands up and told me to chuck them out. He didn't even know she could read. He told me that she was a pain in the ass ever since she had moved in, bringing people from the city all the time, bothering the other tenants, and pretty soon her drug habit caught up with her.

I asked him what he meant.

"A fucking basket case, is what I mean. O.D.'ing, and her fucked-up friends kicking up a scene. Or hustling people downstairs for money. And she looked like a damn zombie, her place smelling like shit..." The landlord shook his head. "If it wasn't for Ray, she'd a been kicked out long ago."

"Ray."

"The bartender downstairs."

"They were friends?"

"Sort of."

I thanked him. My inquiry was beginning to lead somewhere. However, I didn't want to rush anything. Instead of walking down to the bar, I decided to wait until later, when my shift was over. I had been in Lucky's only once, when I had first moved in, and had seen instantly that it wasn't a bar I would feel comfortable in. It was small—just a counter at the rear, two booths and three small circular tables—and most people either watched the TV near the bar, played pool, or listened to the jukebox. It was usually dark except for the weak light above the pool table, and when I had gone in there it had been too loud, too dark, and too smoky for me to become a regular.

During work, I tried to think of a way to mention Mona to Ray without sounding suspicious. I could use the same story of wanting to send her what she had left behind, though this would make me seem oddly generous. I decided to improvise. It wasn't terribly important for me to find out where Mona was; rather, I viewed this as an exercise in detection, a sleuthing diversion.

While on my break, Marlene sat with me for a minute at the counter, asking me what I was reading.

"A letter," I told her.

"From who, your girlfriend?" she asked.

"No. Just a friend of mine in New Hampshire." I noticed that when she smiled the wrinkles in the corner of her eyes deepened. She sat facing me on the stool, legs crossed, leaning her elbow on the counter.

She repeated, "New Hampshire."

"He's getting into some trouble," I said, suddenly wanting to tell someone about this. "He's fooling around with his boss' wife."

"Uh-oh. Trouble with a capital 'T'," she said. "You tell your friend that Marlene says it's trouble. That Marlene knows."

"You do?"

She shrugged. "I'm no spring chicken," she said. "And lots have happened to me." She glanced at one of the tables. "Oops, six wants something. See you later."

She hurried off. I watched her tend to table six, one of the dining tables on the other side, and tried to figure out why I suddenly felt like telling her everything about Farrel Gorden. Maybe being so wrapped up in their affairs was beginning to oppress me, forcing me into an observatory role. Perhaps my search for Mona was symptomatic of a more dangerous desire to do something, to be an actor instead of a spectator.

After my shift was finished I said good night to Marlene and walked towards my apartment and Lucky's. Since it was a week-day evening there were only a few cars parked in front of the bar. I felt more comfortable with this, since Ray would not be busy and might be more inclined to talk with me. I heard the jukebox playing a quiet song. The window had a neon "Miller on Tap" sign flicker-ing in blue and red, and a plastic "Open" sign at the bottom. The front face of the bar was the same as the apartment building, old red brick, though someone had apparently tried to separate the two by painting a white border along the fringe, over the Lucky's white and brown sign, around the corner of the building, and down to the ground, setting off what seemed to be an arbitrary dividing line of Bar versus Apartment Building. The front door was made of thick wooden panelling with a small window, and I paused for a moment, studying the old-fashioned door handle, the kind that was just a gnarled piece of wrought iron metal that you pushed down. I entered the bar.

The music swelled and I walked into smoke and the strong smell of beer. A hockey game was on the TV, and the bartender glanced at me as I moved towards the bar, the acoustic guitar from the jukebox scratching out the melody. I sat on a stool and ordered a beer. The song ended and nothing else came on, so the announcer's voice on the TV filled the room. Two men were playing pool in silence, their drinks resting on a small table by the wall. The bartender wore jeans and a black button-up shirt, and seemed young, probably around my age. He needed a haircut, tufts of hair falling unevenly over his eyes and ears, and he kept watching the TV.

"Are you Ray?" I asked, deciding not to waste time.

He nodded, filling my mug at the tap.

"The landlord said you might be here."

"Who're you?"

I told him I was a friend of Farrel Gorden's looking for his sister.

"Gorden," he said, handing me my beer. "Mona?"

I said yes, becoming anxious. He knew her. I was getting close. "The landlord said she moved."

"You a friend of her brother's?" he asked.

I said I was. "It's strange. He said she was living here—"

"Not for a couple of years."

"I know. Do you know where she is?"

He studied me. "What's her brother doing now?"

"He's working at a sporting goods place. Doing okay."

"And where'd that be?"

"New Hampshire. Yanack. At the mall. You been up there?"

He shook his head. He glanced at the TV. After a minute he said, "She went to the city. She was kicked out of this apartment, you know."

"I know."

"She left me a number, but I never called. Just forgot."

I tried to act calm. "Oh, you have her number?"

"You want it?"

I said, "If it's no trouble. Gorden probably would want to know."

He nodded and reached down, pulling out a shoe box filled with pieces of paper, a handkerchief, key rings, a few keys, a small pocketknife, and placed it on the bar. "I think the number's in here somewhere."

He dumped the contents, and spread out the mess. A commercial came on the TV and Ray reached over to the register and grabbed a remote control, turning down the volume. He poked through the things on the bar and pulled out a small booklet, studying it.

"Is that it?" I asked.

"I don't remember. I think so." He flipped through it and then copied down a number onto a napkin. He pushed the napkin towards me. "Tell her I said hello. If she remembers me. Been a while."

I thanked him, leaving a two dollar tip, not even finishing my beer, and walked out. As soon as the door closed I hurried around the corner and up the steps, the napkin fluttering in my hand. That was it? So easy? I glanced at the napkin. Mona was no longer a ghost. This was her number.

I ran into my apartment and reached for my phone. But then I stopped. Wait, I asked myself. What was I going to do? Call her? I didn't plan to speak to her, but I had to find out if the number was still good. I dialed New York and waited.

The line was busy.

I hung up, thrilled. Busy. Someone was on the line! It must be

Mona on the phone. My search was over. It had been so easy. I studied the napkin and wondered what kind of relationship she had with Ray, since he never't bothered to call her. Maybe she had been a regular customer and they had talked once in a while. While I thought about this, I tried calling again, but it was still busy. Over the next thirty minutes I called a dozen times, and it was still busy. I wanted to hear her voice. I wanted to be sure.

After forty minutes of trying, I finally got through. The phone began ringing, and I prepared myself. I would ask if Mona Gorden was there, and if she was, I'd hang up. If she wasn't I'd ask when she would return, and leave no message. However, the phone kept ringing.

Someone picked it up. "Hello." A man's voice.

"Is Mona Gorden there?"

"Who?"

"Mona Gorden."

"Asshole, this is a pay phone." And he hung up. I stared at my receiver.

I was disappointed, of course. Yet all this began to make sense. If I were going someplace where I knew I wouldn't have a phone, I'd give the number of a nearby pay phone, especially if it was close to where I lived. And it was possible that once Mona had gotten her own phone, she had forgotten to tell Ray. There were a number of things I could do to continue my search, but I was tired, my hands ached from washing dishes, and it was getting late. I wrote in my notebook the things I would have to do tomorrow. A) Check "Mona Gorden" in NYC directory. B) Find pay phone. C) Get haircut.

8

The Easter Spring Sale was in progress. Other stores were also having some kind of sale so the mall was overflowing with people, many coming directly from church in their Easter Sunday clothes, jackets and ties for men, dresses for women, but the cool weather this spring kept most people in their warm winter clothes. Gorden surveyed the showroom. There were about two dozen people in the store, and he had just helped one man select a new baseball glove, directing him to the Rawlings Smith Autograph Glove, one of the higher priced mitts but with a dual H web, reinforced with leather, for $49.99. The man was going to play in a local softball league, so was willing to spend the money. Gorden saw a mother and father with a young teenage boy at the weight sets. He walked towards them, judging from the size of the broad-shouldered boy that he played sports, maybe training with weights.

He asked them if he could help, and the father pointed to the set the son was examining. "What can you tell me about this?"

"Bollinger 310-pound Olympic barbell set. High-stress chromed steel bar, the plates are enameled so they stay clean, and those are spin lock collars, to make changing the weights faster and easier." Gorden asked the boy what sport he played, and the boy answered baseball.

"This'll help your arm and shoulder strength, for throwing and batting, and with lighter weights you can do waist exercises, also your back and legs," he said. "With today's sale, you save almost ninety dollars." He pointed to the "Orig. $229.99—NOW ONLY $139.99!" sign.

The father thanked Gorden and said they'd think about it.

Gorden walked away, glancing at his watch, it was half past noon, and saw Shin helping Norma fix a display of lacrosse sticks that someone had knocked over. Shin was working the showroom, filling in as salesman for this weekend. With Warren gone, John, Henry, Norma, and Gorden's work load should have increased, at least Gorden had thought it would, but it didn't seem so. Maybe Shin had been right and they didn't need Warren.

Usually during a sale, especially one which was going well, Gorden felt jumpy, anxious, and he moved from customer to customer easily, watching their reactions and figuring out if they needed help or were just looking. There was usually a puzzled turn of the head, a looking up and around for someone which was a sure signal for him to intervene. Sometimes the customers did not want to be bothered, and they acted casual, fingering a price tag, looking bored, and Gorden stayed away. Today, though, he didn't feel any urge to work hard. He had trouble caring about this sale, even with the possible commissions on the larger purchases, and he stood by the camping aisle, straightening canteens.

Shin went to help another customer, and Gorden watched him from behind a display of Quick Dry ponchos. In his white shirt and tie, his red name tag clipped over his breast pocket, Shin was speaking to a woman about hand weights. He made jogging motions and did small curls, pointing to different points on his arm.

Gorden thought about Helen, and what Shin must have done to turn her against him. What else could have happened? Maybe Shin had noticed his wife acting differently, and he had become concerned, asking her questions, making Helen more nervous. So Helen had begun backing off from the affair. It had been almost two weeks now, and Gorden didn't know what to do. He couldn't just drop it, like Helen seemed to be doing.

Shit, he thought. He loosened his tie. He had to stop being a weak shiteater and confront her. Who the hell did she think she was jerking around? He wondered if the whole thing between him and Helen was fake, but then he thought about the time when they had eaten some burgers at a rest area off 89, a "Scenic Area" according to the sign, though it was just a view of a small valley, pines and firs growing along an incline. Gorden didn't think it was anything special, but Helen seemed to like it.

"It looks like someone sliced off half a mountain and planted trees there," she said. It was cold, but they ate outside, leaning against the front of the car, and they stared down into the valley as it began to get dark. They hadn't talked much, and Gorden watched Helen finish the last of her burger, crumpling up the foil and dropping it into the paper bag on the hood behind them, her hands then disappearing into the sleeves of her jacket. They stood shoulder to shoulder and after a few minutes Helen leaned her head against his, the sounds of a few cars rushing by, and Gorden thought he could be really happy with her—this was how it ought to be.

Had he imagined all that? Maybe she thought he was some dumb hick. Maybe she was stringing him along, making fun of him all the while she was fucking him.

so I was feeling pretty fucking low while this damn sale was going on around me and I just didnt care about this store. I was even thinking that this store could go to hell and Id lose my job but it didnt matter to me. Yeah, I was feeling fucking low. Why the fuck is she hiding from me because thats what its like, what with her not picking up the phone and if I do get to her she always says the same goddamn thing, that her kid is sick. Maybe thats the truth but hell theres something else going on and I dont know what the hell it is. I gotta do something about this. I dont know what but I gotta get to her and tell her that Im not taking this shit anymore. You never had this problem did you sis? You always had your guys by the balls and I think I know how they felt now, and let me tell you it aint very nice. And shit, Im getting tired of all of this. Not just her but Shari whos acting so fucking weird and this goddamn store with the stupid sales and I feel like theres a fucking ton of bricks on my back whenever I walk in here, wondering if today is the day I get the ax. Shit Im sick of this.

9

In the Manhattan directory, there was no "Mona Gorden." I went to the library to check the telephone books of major cities on microfiche, so it was only a matter of selecting the right fiche, and slipping it into the viewer. I had no trouble locating the name, and there were many variations. There were eight Gordan's, three Gorden's (none of them Mona), five Gordin's, eight columns worth of Gordon's, and two Gordun's. That was all. With that avenue closed, I tried to find the location of that pay phone, and it was more difficult than I had anticipated. To my surprise, the operator did not have that information. His exact words were, "I guess you're out of luck."

Then I thought I could call the phone number and ask the location of whomever answered. Every time I called, the phone rang for five to ten minutes before someone picked up. When I asked them where this phone was, they became suspicious, and either hung up or kept asking me why. I imagined them looking furtively around them, wondering if this was some kind of set-up. I began concocting elaborate stories to get this information, and finally, when a young woman answered, I told her my sister was sick, and she had given me this number with no address, and I was worried. The woman told me. A corner near Times Square, on 42nd and Ninth.

The next day I took the LIRR into New York City. This was the first time in almost a year that I had taken the train, and I felt a little apprehensive at the thought of being so far from my apartment. I had grown accustomed to the routine of my life, of spending my days in my apartment, my evenings at the diner. I had thought going to the library was a major accomplishment, yet there I was buying a round trip ticket at the lobby on the lower level, taking the narrow escalator up to the platform, and waiting with some commuters who were taking the late morning train. It was nine-thirty; had I taken an earlier train, the platform would have been packed.

When the nine thirty-five pulled into the station and hissed to a stop, the doors opened and a wave of heat fell upon the four of us waiting. The suit walked in first, and I followed, still unsure why I was doing this, why I was spending eight dollars to try to find someone I didn't know. I found a window seat on the right side, facing in the direction of New York, and stared out at the north side of Marnole as the train pulled out.

The ride was uneventful—forty-five minutes of staring out the window—and I can't remember what was going through my head at the time. I think I was lulled by the gentle rocking of the train, the rhythmic double thumps of the wheels riding over joints in the tracks, and it was only at the Jamaica stop (two stops before New York) that I blinked out of my daze. I had no idea what I was going to do once I found the pay phone. This whole trip suddenly seemed idiotic. But then it was too late. Before I knew it my train was going underground, my eardrums feeling the pressure, and the loud-speaker announced "Penn Station next and last stop. Penn Station." I stared at my reflection in the window.

The train pulled into a concrete maze of platforms, yellow lights glaring onto the brown cement, and there were crowds of people pushing towards the stairs, bottlenecking. The passengers around me stood up and worked their way to the exits, the train still slowing to a stop. I waited.

For some reason I already knew that this search would ulti-mately prove disappointing. But perhaps because I wanted to leave no avenues unexplored, I had to see this search for Mona through to the end. I am sure that there were more routes I could have pursued if I had had more money, more time, more energy. The thought of hiring a private detective even crossed my mind. Nev-ertheless, on that day I walked out of Penn Station and up Seventh Avenue, up nine blocks while looking at the bundled-up people moving past me, a few hot dog and pretzel stands along the sidewalk, steam floating out of manhole covers on the streets, yellow cabs rushing down, clustering at the lights, honking, and I walked west on 42nd, past the movie theaters, electronic shops, fast food restaurants, porn shops, and when I came upon the four pay phones lined up near the corner of Ninth and 42nd, I found the telephone I had called, and I looked around, my gaze ending on a "XXX Adult Movies and Books" store. I asked myself, What the hell am I doing here? What the hell do I think I'm doing?

I thought about having to ask around, knock on doors, act like an investigator by interviewing people, and I began doubting I could handle this. The thought of meeting all those strangers in person, of having to make up more lies to try to convince these people to help me--the thought of all this along with the fact that I had never met Mona Gorden, knew close to nothing about her, hit me. I had barely spoken to a dozen people in the last six months, and suddenly I had to interact with countless strangers? New York strangers, no less. Who the hell did I think I was—some Philip Marlowe? Some Continental Op? Who was I kidding? I was an ex-biology teacher, a dishwasher. I read other people's mail.

But I had to try.

So, I looked around and saw the XXX Adult Movies and Books store, the Camera & Electronics store, a small deli, and a nameless store that had been boarded up, the windows lined with yellowing newspapers. Above the stores were two floors of apartments, and I guessed Mona lived behind one of those windows. First I checked all of the mailboxes in the stairwells of the buildings, hoping to find her name, but many of the boxes just had numbers, and of the names I did see there were no Gordens. I knew I'd have to knock on doors. But before I did that I went into the stores and asked if they knew a Mona Gorden. The large black man in the adult shop, the two Middle Eastern men in the camera store, and the man with the white apron behind the deli counter knew nothing.

I began with the apartments above the camera store because there were intercom buttons and this was easier than going door to door. Some were not home, or perhaps asleep, and those who did answer were of no help.

Perhaps I should skip the laborious process of knocking on doors and get right to the point: Mona was dead. I learned this from the residents in an apartment above the nameless store that was boarded up. I knocked on the old wooden door with a big green zig-zag painted across the front, expecting the same response I had found with all the others: If they were home they would call through the door, Who is it?, and I would ask them if they knew a Mona Gorden because I was looking for her. Either they would say no and I'd leave, or they would open the door, the chain lock still on, and peer out at me, telling me they've never heard of her, did I have the right address? I'd then explain myself further, that she left the pay phone number downstairs and I'm trying to contact her—maybe she moved? But they'd shrug and say they didn't know.

When I knocked on the door with the green zig-zag, a man answered without opening the door and I asked him about Mona, but this time there was some whispering and a female voice asked, "Who are you?"

I became frightened, not sure if the voice answering was Mona herself, and I didn't know what to say. Finally, I just answered, "I'm a friend of her brother, Farrel."

More whispering.

The door opened and a woman with her blond hair corn-rowed looked out and said, "We don't know him, but how do you know Mona?"

I stared at her head. I could see her scalp. Her hair looked almost fake because it was so tightly braided. Her eyes were bloodshot, her face puffy.

"I'm sorry if I woke you," I said. "Her brother is looking for her and I thought I'd check here. She left the number of the pay phone downstairs."

The man appeared next to the woman. He had on no shirt and also looked like he just woke up. "She died about a year ago. She lived down the hall."

I stared at them. "How did she...?"

The woman said, "We didn't know her that well. Overdose, probably. The cops came by to ask about her."

They waited for me to say more, but I was at a loss. My search was over. I thanked them and went home.

I was very uneasy, since I had hoped, on some level, to meet Mona, yet the fact that she had died wasn't very surprising to me.

Perhaps my landlord's first comment, that she was probably ten feet under the dirt, had stayed with me and my search was just a confirmation of this. Learning the truth, of course, made what I was doing—reading her mail—all the more grisly, and my guilt was exacerbated. This was my state of mind when I returned home and found another letter from Gorden in my mailbox: depressed, ashamed of my cowardice, tired. I had to go to work in a few hours so I needed a nap, and I tried to push the day's events from my mind, push the whole letter-reading business away, since I was obviously becoming too involved, too interested in Farrel Gorden. Yet when I saw the letter, instead of throwing it away, or sending it back, I ripped it open while I hurried up the stairs to my apartment, completely forgetting my worries about this enterprise. And when I read that Shari had committed suicide, everything changed. I became more than just an observer in this operatic game. Mona Gorden and the failure in New York quickly disappeared and I became enveloped in the events in New Hampshire.

Part III
Memorial Day Sale

1

Reading Gorden's letter over and over, I tried to make sense of what had happened, of Shari's motives. I tried to imagine those last days when Shari moved closer to taking her own life. The sequence of events as related by Gorden was simple enough: he came home after work one evening and found Shari in the bathtub, the water red, her head slumped to one side, a broken bottle of vodka on the floor, a razor. There was no note. He wrote to his sister:

> When I got home I thought something was different because the TV was off and everything was quiet and usually there is something going on, the TV or the radio, so I wasnt sure if she was home and I called out her name but no one answered. I walked to the bedroom and saw the bathroom light on and I heard water dripping in the bathtub, a quick dripping, almost a small stream. I called her name again. Then I walked in and Christ, what a mess.

She was there, all bloody. What a fucking complete mess. I got sick in the sink.

Bastard, I said aloud to the letter, shaking and crumpling it. You fucking shit. I put the letter down and tried to steady myself. It was all his fault, and I wondered if he was going to acknowledge that. Of course not. I hated him. I immediately made myself some coffee and Kahlua, finishing an old bottle and opening a new one, making my drink very strong. I sat on my bed and tried to make sense of all this. The letter was deceptive—the events had taken place days ago and Gorden had the advantage of time to distance himself, to become calm and objective, or at least appear so in the letter to his sister. However, I imagined things differently. When he had found Shari, he couldn't have been so calm. I barely knew her and yet I was shaken; how could Gorden not have felt this blow? Of course he had. I pictured him right before the discovery, and saw his real reaction.

Gorden left the store after they had their post-sale clean up— the removal of the signs, of the special displays, and the tallying of the receipts. The sale had been a moderate success. Although they hadn't cleared out nearly half of the skis they had wanted to, the spring items that they put on sale—the baseball equipment, the tennis rackets, and the running shoes—had almost sold out. Most of the overstocked items had been depleted. Gross sales for the three-day weekend had exceeded $23,000. Yet there was a sense of disappointment, since they still had all that ski equipment which they would have to continue slashing for a few more weeks until they stored them for next winter, and everyone knew that one reason why the receipt total was high was because they had sold large ticket items, a home gym, an exercise bike, and not because they had had many customers. But Shin was content, and he thanked everyone for doing a great job. Compared to the last sale, they had done very well.

Tired from the long day, Gorden looked forward to kicking back with a beer, and watching TV. His throat was scratchy from talking too much, and his arms hurt from demonstrating the rowing machine and home gym a dozen times today. He liked the pneumatic hissing sound the rowing machine made when he pulled on the bar, and he thought he might get one. It was one of the machines he preferred, that and the speed bag, even though he couldn't keep up the punching rhythm for long. He was getting flabby, and a little exercise might do him good.

He drove to his house and noticed that the lights in the living room were off. She's sleeping again, he thought, knowing it was probably better, so at least he didn't have to deal with her. He entered the house and was surprised not to see Shari on the couch, since she usually fell asleep in front of the TV. Then he wondered if she had gone out. "Shari?" he said. He walked towards the bedroom, but stopped in the hallway when he saw the bathroom light on. This was when he heard the water dripping, the solitary sound filling the silent bathroom. "Shari?" he said again, unsure if she was taking a bath and ignoring him. Maybe she was still pissed.

He walked in and saw the broken vodka bottle on the floor, pieces of clear glass scattered across the tiles, and he moved forward slowly, confused. The bathtub was built into the wall, so it wasn't until he moved a few feet past the corner that he saw the reddish water and Shari's knees sticking out and leaning against the sides of the tub like small islands. The faucet was dripping quickly and rippled the water. What the fuck, he asked himself, thinking at first that it was some sort of juice, but then he noticed the razor on the floor, and he jumped forward, seeing Shari, her torso sticking out of the water, her breasts half immersed, her head leaning to the side in an unnatural angle, and he realized it was blood in the bathtub and felt his stomach lurch, thinking Fucking Christ, she fucking cut... and he felt his insides churn and he turned and threw up into the sink, the sharp, acidic bile burning his throat and mouth. He heaved and coughed, trying to breathe but he couldn't and he threw up again, emptying his stomach. He wiped his face quickly and rushed out, not sure what to think or do, everything blurring. He clutched at the wall, making his way towards the living room.

But maybe she's still alive, he thought. He knew he had to go back in there to check and he had to check *now*, before it was too late because she could have done this right before he had come in so he had to do something now, right now, *now*. He wiped his mouth and took a deep breath, determined not to lose control, not to panic. Go in there now, you fucker, he ordered himself. He walked in, avoiding the glass shards, and looked at Shari.

"Shari?" he asked, tentatively. He leaned forward and touched her cheek. Cold. He touched her neck, looking for a pulse. Nothing. Cold. A dead fish. He rushed out again, feeling his stomach tighten, and hurried towards the phone. But as he picked it up he hesitated. What if they thought *he* had done this? Could that happen? Could they pin this on him as murder? For a second he thought wildly of burying her body and not telling anyone, but he shook himself out of this, whispering, "What are you, fucking stupid?" He called 9-1-1, and told the operator his name, address, and what had happened. After that, he hung up, and walked shakily towards the couch, trying to steady himself by grabbing hold of the cushions. Take it easy, he told himself, breathing in and smelling his own vomit. He hunched over and began taking deep breaths, waiting for the police to come. What the fuck was she thinking of, he asked. He tried not to figure this out. Didn't want to picture her in his head. He just thought to himself, She was fucking nuts, a total head case.

Blame it on her, I spoke to Gorden silently. That's right, it was all her fault. I could see Gorden keeping himself free of any guilt and blaming it on her state of mind. It was interesting that he, upon finding her, would immediately worry about the consequences to himself as a possible murder suspect, rather than worrying about her situation. It's just you, I said to him. How everything affects you.

I didn't dwell on this, though, since I wanted to understand why Shari had done this. Of course she had been depressed, and drinking, but I just hadn't seen this coming. I had been as blind as Gorden, with no excuses since I was scrutinizing her actions as well as everyone else's, and yet all I could do was fantasize about meeting her, about taking her away. As I drank more coffee and Kahlua that evening, I tried to follow her actions. I tried to become Shari, and when that didn't work, I imagined her sitting on my mattress, next to me, and I asked her, Why? Tell me why you did that.

But she just shook her head slowly, staring down at her wrists.

I began to get drunk, talking to myself, to Gorden, to Shari, and I paced back and forth in my small studio, asking myself what could have been going through her mind. What was she doing the night before? "What were you doing the night before?" I asked. "Shari?" The jukebox from Lucky's thumped an answer, and I was thankful for the background noise since I didn't think I could stand silence right then. I stopped in mid-pace. Here I was, walking back and forth in a tiny room, getting drunk and talking to myself. I suddenly saw Shari doing the same thing the night before she killed herself, drink in hand, pacing in the living room. Not quite talking, but mumbling to herself. Ignoring the TV. She was trying not to get upset about Gorden, trying not to care anymore, but she was having trouble. He's fucking another woman, she said to herself. She had known it, but now it was beginning to eat away at her. Who the hell could it be? Someone at work. Someone he met at the mall. Someone nearby?

She held her head. Stop it stop it stop it, she told herself. It didn't matter anymore since she was going to be thrown out and she'd have nowhere to go and then she'd have to go crawling back to her parents. Never. So who the fuck's the woman, she thought. She tilted her head back and drank straight from the bottle, the vodka scorching her tongue, her throat, burning her stomach, her eyes watering. She shivered. She had smelled the other woman before. Men were so fucking stupid. She could smell that odd sharp smell, not perfume but some sort of soap maybe, on his clothes, even on his skin when she got close enough. Not the metallic smell of his sweat, or the warm smell when he was clean, but something else. It was so fucking obvious. But she hadn't smelled it in a while. Maybe he was getting smarter? Had he caught on? Shari ran to the bedroom and opened the plastic hamper next to the door, pulling out Gorden's clothes, inhaling his scent. Yes. That was his.

She sniffed his old shirts and underwear, trying to find that smell again. She kept smelling the alcohol along with the sweat and smoke in Gorden's clothes, which made it difficult, but she continued, and formed a small pile of dirty clothes on the floor. After a few minutes, she stopped. It wasn't there. The smell was gone. Could she have imagined it? No. That son of a bitch. Maybe he was fucking with her mind, knowing that she could recognize it, and he purposely got rid of it. That bastard.

She took another drink and staggered up, working her way back to the living room and collapsing on the couch. A commercial jingle filled the living room, "I'm gonna wash that grey right out of my hair." Shari began to cry. She hated everything, the stupid goddamn commercial and this fucking house and Gorden and everything. No fucking reason to stick around here but nowhere else to go. She put the bottle on the ground and curled up on the cushions, still crying. Get me out of this fucking place, she whispered to no one. She tried to make herself into a ball, hugging herself as tightly as possible, trying to shut everything out.

The next morning when she awoke, she thought about ending it. After drinking from the bottle to get rid of her hangover, her pounding headache and itchy eyes, she tried to stand but was dizzy. She sat back down and rested. Gorden had come and gone without waking her again, or maybe she had awakened last night but didn't remember. She was invisible to him. She didn't exist. If she died right now, no one would care or even notice.

No, Gorden would notice. He would *have* to notice, if she were dead right here on the floor. What would he do? Maybe he would feel sorry for her. Oh, if I had only been nicer, he would say. But it would be too late and he would be guilty for the rest of his life. She liked that. He would be tortured by this.

Shari stood again, this time more slowly, and walked into the kitchen. She found some plain bread and began nibbling at the crust. After finishing one slice, her head started hurting again, so she made herself a vodka and orange juice, and sat on the floor , leaning back against the kitchen counter. She thought about that dream she kept having a few months ago, the one in which she took a kitchen knife and stabbed herself in the neck. It happened so smoothly in the dream: she would reach into the drawer, pull out the long serrated-edged knife with the wooden handle, clutch it in her hand and then *ffft*, she would stab the side of her neck. In the dream she barely felt it—just a quick sharp pain and then that was it. She couldn't remember if she could turn her head, and she wasn't sure if she died in the dream. She always woke up right after she stabbed herself. She sipped her drink and closed her eyes.

When she blinked open her eyes, everything seemed to fall into place. She knew what she had to do. It was mid-afternoon already, but it didn't bother her that she had sat in one position for most of the day. Her legs were stiff. Her back ached. Her drink had turned into a warm, sticky orange fluid that tasted like metal, like Gorden's sweat, and she finished it. Where was the bottle? Still on the counter. She drank from that, cleaning her mouth with the sharp, burning vodka. She shivered.

Everything seemed so clear right now, and she walked slowly to the bathroom—even though she had never thought about this before, it was as if she had practiced this many times. She knew exactly what to do. She ran the bath, the hot water turned up high, the faucet exploding water into the tub and splashing everything.

Shari was startled by the harsh water sounds, and stared at the bottom of the tub where it was dirty with ground-in mildew. The tiles above the bathtub also had small brown patches along the white grout, and she wondered if she should have cleaned the bathroom before doing this. She smiled. Why bother?

The tub began filling, so she stood and searched through the bathroom cabinet, looking for Gorden's razor blades. She couldn't find any, so she took apart his razor on the sink, and pulled out the used blade. This was the blade that he had used to shave his beard off. Maybe he had shaved his beard to impress a woman. After shaving it off, he became worse, treating Shari like shit. It was losing the beard that changed him. Suddenly, everything made sense. Using this razor blade meant sense. It all seemed to fit, somehow.

The water in the bathtub was filling up more than halfway, so she turned the faucets off. They squeaked as she tightened them. Wisps of steam rose from the water. Shari stripped off her clothes. She wiped the fogged mirror to see her face. To her surprise, there were tears running down her cheeks, and she wiped them, sniffing. It didn't matter whether she was alive or dead; no one cared. She was better off dead. She couldn't take this anymore, any of this, and she didn't want to be here. She held the razor blade carefully and climbed into the bathtub, the water scalding her, and she tensed and continued to immerse herself, her face beginning to sweat. When she finally managed to sit in the tub, she had trouble breathing. Her skin was itching in the hot water. Where was her bottle? She reached down and had another drink. She poured Vodka into the water. Leaving the bottle on the bathtub ledge, she lay back and stared at the razor.

In one quick motion, not giving herself time to think, she slit her left wrist. There was a sharp quick pain, like someone pinching her, and that was it. A line across her skin. Then, blood oozing out. She quickly switched hands and slit her other wrist, this time deeper, and it hurt. Her pinky and ring fingers felt funny. She went to place the razor blade on the ledge, but accidentally knocked over the bottle. It crashed and echoed in the bathroom. She flinched. When she placed her wrists in the water, she felt them stinging, and slouched deeper into the tub, trying to sink most of her body. She didn't feel any different, except hotter. No. Just a hot bath. Nothing more. The water around her hands filled with red clouds. She closed her eyes, and leaned back, sighing. That commercial jingle sang in her head, and she began to feel light, tired. A sudden wave of sadness swept through her. She began crying again, but it soon subsided as she felt sleepier. Her mind wandered, and she thought about the time she and Gorden used to take showers together, right here in this bathtub, in this bathroom, and they used to soap each other slowly, and hugged while they were slippery. She smiled. That was fun. She couldn't stop thinking about that stupid commercial jingle. Couldn't get it out of her head. So tired. Head feeling light. So tired. Wash that grey. Slippery hugs in the shower. Used to be fun. Floating. Tired. So tired.

2

Helen looked up from her magazine. "Gorden? Your employee?"

Her husband nodded and said, "That's what John told me. That his girlfriend committed suicide. That's why he's taking a week off." He began undressing.

"Oh my God," she said, putting the magazine down. She sat up against the pillows. "Are you sure?"

"I think I saw her once. Very young. She was at the store, visiting him." Raj shook his head. "Why would anyone want to do that?"

"She killed herself?" Helen stared at him, still unbelieving.

"I don't know how. But it happened two nights ago. They must have been having trouble."

"Killed herself," she said, quietly. Gorden had usually avoided

talking about his friend—he had never called her his girlfriend—
and Helen wondered if this had anything to do with the girl's
instability. Maybe that was why he didn't talk about her. And
now... and now he must be completely in pieces.

"I never could understand why people do that," her husband
said, sitting on the edge of the bed.

"What?" she asked.

"Suicide. I never could understand that."

She shifted uncomfortably. "Some people aren't as lucky as
you."

Raj stopped pulling off a sock, and looked up. He shrugged.
"Maybe."

Helen pretended to read her magazine as her husband prepared for bed. She felt guilty that she had ignored Gorden, rebuffed
his attempts to talk with her all the while his friend must have been
going through hell, and Gorden himself must have also been
suffering. Maybe that was what he wanted, she thought. Someone
to talk to. And she had acted like a haughty bitch. She stared very
hard at the words on the page, and couldn't concentrate. Gorden
could be a mess right this minute, trying to pull himself together.
She should have been nicer. Tomorrow she could call him, perhaps,
and let him know how sorry she was. Gorden had listened to her
when she had been trying to adjust to life here, when she had been
feeling sorry for herself. She had used him. He probably hates me
now, she thought. No wonder he hasn't been calling here.

"Things are looking better at the store," Raj said.

"I know. You told me."

"The next sale, we'll definitely start moving into the black."

She nodded. The stupid store. The sooner he turned it around,
the sooner they could leave.

After he returned from the hospital and the police station, and
after the initial chaos had settled, Gorden cleaned. He saw the glass
all over the floor, the muddy footprints from the policemen and

ambulance workers, the bloody water that had splashed and dripped when they had taken her out. He swept the broken glass into a garbage bag, watching the red water spread with each broom stroke. He had to stop and concentrate on the job at hand. Clean the floor. He didn't want to consider what the stuff on the floor was. He needed to think of this as just another job. Clean the floor. He mopped up the water with an old towel and threw it out.

Although the bathtub had been drained, there was still a pink tint to the white porcelain. He took out an industrial strength cleaning fluid, and began scrubbing vigorously with a sponge. He began sweating, and despite the strong ammonia smell, his eyes watering, his nose burning, he forced himself to stay where he was and clean. He began coughing. Clean the motherfucking tub, he ordered himself. He tried to stifle the image of Shari in the red water, but it kept appearing in his mind, so he worked harder, rubbing the sponge into the porcelain with all his strength.

Cause of death: suicide. Suicide. Gorden still was in shock. She had killed herself. Method: self-inflicted wounds to both wrists. Using *his* razor. Christ, that must have hurt. Time of death: approximately four o'clock, two hours before Gorden had returned home. The doctor who examined her said that it couldn't have been more than a few hours. She was a minor, so her parents needed to be contacted. Did he know how to contact them, the police had asked. Somewhere in Maine? Names? Gorden didn't know. He tried to explain that she had been drinking a lot, depressed because she couldn't get a job. No inquest, probably, though the procedures would depend on the parents.

The parents. Gorden couldn't imagine Shari with parents. Who were they? What were they like? She had never spoken of them, except that they had kicked her out. What if they blamed him?

When the tub was completely white, he moved to the walls, scrubbing until his hands hurt, until his arms were sore, until pain rippled across his back. He began cleaning between the tiles, following a path around each dark blue square, working his way along the edge of the bathtub, moving up row by row until there was not one spot left. Hours passed. He stopped twice to drink some water, soothing his scratchy throat. He had to take off his shirt because it was soaked with sweat, but he liked the exhaustion which hummed through his body, pulsing in his head, tearing pain in his calves, and he knew he couldn't stop until everything was clean.

He mopped the floor. By this time it was late, almost midnight. But he wasn't planning to go to work tomorrow, wasn't planning to do anything, really, until the house was in order. He cleaned the mirror, staring at his stubbled face. His face was expressionless, completely blank. What was the matter with him? He glanced at his razor lying on the sink, the top latch left open by her. His blade missing.

The bathroom looked different now. The blue tiles that lay along the lower half of the wall and in the shower were shiny, reflecting the light of the bare bulb on the ceiling. The floor was still wet and smelled of ammonia, disinfected, the corners along the wall scrubbed out. Gorden stared at the sink counter and saw Shari's brush, strands of hair tangled and woven tight into the bristles. Her hair. Her red toothbrush. Earrings. Goddammit. Her things were all over the place. Gorden couldn't believe she was really gone. How could she be dead? Everything was still here. He sat on the edge of the bathtub and tried to collect himself. A sudden memory of him and Shari driving flashed before him. He saw her legs crossed and extended, her feet resting on the dashboard, her window open and wind blowing and fluttering her blouse. Autumn. She was talking loudly, over the noise of the car. Where had they been going? He couldn't remember.

Gorden rushed to the closet in the living room and found a cardboard box. He returned to the bathroom and began filling the box with Shari's things. From the counter: her hairbrush, lotion, jewelry, and lipstick. Underneath the sink: her Maxipads, nail polish and remover, hair spray, curlers. He cleaned out the medicine cabinet of her sleeping pills, her diet pills, her lip balm and eye makeup kit. He stood back and examined the bathroom again. All traces of her were gone. He suddenly felt very, very tired. He left the box in the bathroom, and collapsed on the couch, intending only to rest for a few minutes, but he fell asleep listening to the wind blowing against the kitchen storm window, rattling the house.

The next morning, Gorden woke up disoriented, his neck stiff and hurting, his arm cramped. He sat on the couch and looked around. When he glanced at his watch, he jumped up, late for work. But everything quickly came back to him, tumbling into his memory and he stood still, uncertain, confused. He sat back down and stared ahead of him. Shari.

He reached over to the telephone and called the store, telling John that he'd be out for a while, maybe a week. He told him that Shari had committed suicide. There was silence on the other end.

"Hello, you there?" Gorden asked.

"You okay, Gord? You doing okay?"

"Yeah. Tell Shin for me, will you?"

"No problem. Are you okay?"

"I'm okay."

"If you need anything—shit, why would she—never mind... If you need anything..."

"I'll call you."

"Okay, Gord. You just let me know."

After Gorden hung up, he rubbed his eyes and rolled his neck. Somehow none of this seemed really *here* yet. What had happened last night? Everything was a blur. He walked into the bathroom and saw the box up against the clean bathtub. The bare counter, except for his toothpaste, a comb, soap, and his razor, which he still hadn't touched, startled him. He was used to seeing all her junk there, and now... Now nothing. So, it *had* happened. So she was dead. She was really dead.

He was about to take a shower, but he looked into the clean, white bathtub, and hesitated. He couldn't go in there. Instead, he washed his face in the sink and brought the box outside, placing it in the center of the living room floor. He looked around the room, at the empty bottles and glasses on the table and floor, at the newspapers spread out by the couch and on the TV, the piles of clothes (his and hers), the mud and dirt from last night, and he felt dirty. He thought, I need to clean the house.

For the next two days all Gorden did was clean. He began with the living room, going through the same process as the bathroom—cleaning furiously until he was exhausted, then gathering all of Shari's things and piling them together—and then moved from room to room, leaving nothing untouched. He hadn't realized how much Shari actually had in this house. *His* house. Most of her things were clothes and small pieces of junk she had picked up from various places. Ashtrays from a restaurant. A roll of register receipt paper, unused, from a supermarket. A plastic hot dog from Leroy's. A "God is Love" key chain. He wasn't sure why he was cleaning all this now. He just had to clean. He moved almost mechanically, focusing on small decisions such as which box to put the shoes in, how to clean out the dust from behind the bed, where to sleep. Every so often he would be reminded of an incident, a conversation, an image of Shari, triggered by the cleaning. The clothes, for instance. That black dress which he had bought her for the Christmas party. He had trouble putting this away, trouble even touching it, because he remembered how she had felt when he had grabbed her thin waist, his hands holding the small of her back while they had danced, the rough knit fabric scratching his wrists. He didn't think about what had happened later that evening, after they had both drunk too much and fought, but instead remembered how nervous she had been while they were driving to the party. She kept biting her lower lip, asking three or four times if she looked all right, smiling when he had said yes, she looked sexy. When he opened her drawers, he saw her bras and panties, her shirts and socks. It was so strange to touch these cold pieces of clothing, knowing that they had once been on her body. Her body. He could picture her naked body on the bed, spread out and awkwardly posing for him as he came home from work. She'd smile and say, Surprise. Welcome home. Christ, what had happened to them? Everything seemed to fall apart after only a couple of months. Had it been his fault? He hurried and threw the clothes into the box, emptying the cabinets. He counted the clothes to keep his mind busy.

Slowly, the house began to change. Floors scrubbed. Windows cleaned. Rugs shaken out. All of Shari's belongings fit into three middle-sized boxes. Not that much just looking at it, but Gorden thought it was way too much, each item there digging a little more at him. He taped up the boxes and put them next to the door. He then began throwing away things he no longer needed. His high school yearbook, the model car collection he had started as a child. His sister used to buy him small plastic kits and he had spent days alone in his room by the window, cutting off the pieces from a plastic frame, gluing them together with model cement, blowing carefully. At one point, he had had over a dozen model cars lined up on his desk and windowsill, a testament to his patience and work, until his stepfather, drunk one evening, had come in when Gorden was out and knocked them onto the floor, crushing most of them. It had probably been an accident, but Gorden remembered the horror he had felt when he had walked into his room, pieces of plastic scattered everywhere. He had only been thirteen or so, but had felt this was the worst thing that he would ever experience.

I was bawling like someone shot me in the gut or something and man that guy was sorry. You werent there but he kept saying he would buy me more and that if I didnt say anything he would get me the biggest model car there was. It was all bullshit because he changed his mind a week later but hell it was good seeing him so sorry assed. So I got rid of all that kid junk because I want everything clean. It was strange looking at the pile of her stuff and then my pile of old junk and then looking at the house since it looked like a different house what with everything clean and almost new and nothing messing it up but I was still feeling real shitty. I dont know. The house seems real empty now. Real quiet like. I dont know if I like it so much.

Of course you don't like it, I said to him while I read this again at the diner. I was having trouble deciphering his letter for his genuine reactions. Was he just putting on a calm facade for his sister? Or maybe this was really how he felt. Some shock, blankness, numbness. It was only through work that he was able to deal with Shari's death. Or maybe he really didn't care, and concocted a reaction to fit the situation. Maybe what he really had done was to clean the bathtub and then clean out Shari's things, telling himself Thank God she's out of here. It was possible.

But that was unfair. I saw no reason for him to lie to his sister, especially since he seemed to have been honest about most things. At least it seemed so. True, he may have given minimal details where more would have helped, skimped on important points, but the jist of the message was there. Yet this didn't mean he was absolved. I still blamed him for her suicide, and no matter what he did I wouldn't forgive him. I thought about Shari in her last minutes, sitting in the tub, bleeding to death, and I felt a futile, resigned depression that weighed heavily in my limbs, in my stomach, and made me slump over the counter, hunched over the letter. She is dead, I told myself. She shouldn't have died, and I, somehow, felt responsible. My spectator status did not completely free me from responsibility, did it? I thought about Claude Bernard, the 19th-century physiologist and his experimental method. If the people whom I had been observing were part of a scientific experiment, then I could not, in order to keep the experiment pure, interfere. Yet was this really an experiment? An ant farm?

"Hey, why the long face?" Marlene asked, approaching me.

I looked up, and debated whether or not to tell her. She was smiling and resting a hand on her waist. In any other situation I probably would have pretended nothing was wrong, but I couldn't bring myself to lie. I had to tell someone. "A friend of mine committed suicide."

She stopped, surprised. "That's terrible. Your friend?"

I nodded slowly. "I feel responsible. I could have done something."

"Come on, don't talk like that," she said. She sat next to me. I covered Gorden's letter with my hand, which she noticed but chose to ignore. "It's always like that. You always think that, but unless you told her to do it, how can you blame yourself?"

I told her I knew she was right, but I still didn't feel comforted. She clucked her tongue and kept quiet. We listened to the clatter of utensils coming from the kitchen, the cash register, the low mumbling of voices. I suddenly liked this feeling of being listened to, of having an audience. I turned to her. "You feel like going for a drink after work?"

She studied me. "Sure. I have to stick around for a few minutes, for splitting the tips, but sure."

"You don't mind?"

She shook her head. "It'll be nice," she said, glancing towards the tables. "So, we'll meet after work. I have to go now. See ya."

Watching her walk away, I was surprised by how easily I had asked her out. A few months ago, I would have frozen at the thought of talking to someone, yet a minute ago I had told someone I hardly knew how I was feeling, and went so far as to ask for more. But this made me feel better, and I went back to the dishes, Gorden's letter folded in my back pocket.

Although there was no way of knowing this for sure, at the very moment I asked Marlene out for a drink, Helen called Gorden. I learned this in the next letter; while Gorden had been wandering around his house, restless, uneasy, looking for something to do, the phone had rung. He froze, still not completely certain if the police thought he had somehow caused the suicide, if he was going to be charged with murder, and he stared at the telephone. It continued to ring. He tried to imagine the worst. Maybe it was the coroner calling for him to testify at an inquest. Then he had a wild idea that it might be Shari, calling from the dead. He shook his head at this stupid thought. But maybe she wasn't really dead. Maybe he had imagined all that. Finally, he picked up the receiver.

"Hello?" said a woman's voice. Gorden recognized it but had trouble thinking clearly. "Hello?" she asked again.

"Yeah," he answered.

"Gorden? It's me. Helen."

"Helen!" He straightened. Then he thought, She knows. John had told Shin, who had told Helen. "Hello. How's Susy?"

"Susy's fine," she said, her voice softening. "How are you? You know, I heard the awful news."

"Yeah, well."

"I'm very sorry, Gorden. I really am."

He was silent. What was he supposed to say? She had ignored him for this long, and now she called. What did she want?

"Gorden?"

"Yeah, I'm here. I'm surprised you called," he said.

"Why?"

"Because you were trying to get rid of me."

"What? No, it wasn't that. It's, well, things were getting so—"

"Forget about it. Thanks for calling," he said.

"Gorden, wait. I'm sorry. I know it was unfair."

He paused.

"Gorden?"

"Come over," he said.

"What?"

"I want you to come over. Just for a while."

"I don't know," she said. "I still have—"

"Never mind." He didn't want to beg for company. Fuck her. She had called out of guilt. Fine. He didn't need this now.

"Wait, Gorden. I'll come over. But not tonight. I can't."

He wanted to set a date, to test her. "How about tomorrow night," he said.

She hesitated. She cleared her throat, and said, "Okay, tomorrow night."

3

I waited for Marlene while she and a busboy calculated and divided the tips. Another one of the busboys was pushing a hairy dust mop across the floor, under the tables, while on the carpeted side of the diner, one of the waitresses ran a vacuum around the tables. The whirring vacuum was the only sound, a soothing mechanical counterpoint to the crowded voices of customers just a half hour ago. I had never stayed longer than my shift, so I watched curiously as they closed down the diner, calculating receipts, storing food, wiping tables, most everyone so tired that they spoke in short, quiet sentences, or spoke not at all, simply nodding and shrugging to each other. Apparently, the waitresses and busboys took turns cleaning the floors and vacuuming the carpets, and Marlene had done this yesterday evening, so after she had split her tips, she approached me and asked if I was ready.

I told her I was. "Where would you like to go?" I asked.

"Is that bar down the street open?"

I nodded and worried about the bartender who might remember me. Then I considered all that had happened recently, and I wasn't sure if going out with Marlene tonight was a good idea. I didn't think I'd be very good company.

But Marlene didn't give me a chance to change my mind, because she was already walking towards the door, her tan raincoat tied tightly at her waist, her small black handbag hanging in the crook of her arm. She turned to me and gave me a questioning look. I stood up and followed, zipping up my own jacket as she held open the door for me. She smiled as we walked down the steps of the diner, the wind blowing small wisps of hair across her forehead.

"I'll have to call my son when we get there," she said.

"Your son?"

She nodded. "He might worry if I'm late," she said. "He usually comes home after I do. He takes evening classes at New York Tech."

I hadn't known she had a son, and it made me feel younger. I hadn't been married, hadn't even had a serious relationship except for that one woman in my last year of college, Jackie, who had gone to France and had ended up living there—she's still there for all I know—and yet here was Marlene, in her forties, already a widow, with a son, and she wasn't *that* much older than I was. What was wrong with me? I thought about my brief stint in graduate school, my tenure at the high school, and wondered why I hadn't been married yet. Why I hadn't even really dated.

"You look so serious," Marlene said as we left the parking lot. "That's my car." She pointed to an old rusting station wagon. "I think I'll just leave it here."

"It's big," I said, unable to think of anything else.

When we arrived at Lucky's, I saw that Ray wasn't working tonight. Instead, an older man with a graying beard sat behind the bar and looked up from a newspaper when we came in. Marlene and I sat at the small table near the door. There was only one other man in the bar, and he was sitting by the pool table, half asleep. Marlene draped her raincoat over her chair, stuffing most of it behind her back. She was wearing her light brown waitress uniform; it seemed oddly appropriate here. She fit in this bar better than I did, relaxing back against her coat, her legs crossed. She pulled out a cigarette. I offered to buy her a beer, and she thanked me.

I walked to the bar and ordered two Millers, looking around quickly as the man filled the mugs from the tap. I noticed the jukebox, and realized that this was why everything was different tonight—no music. I got change from the bartender and walked to the jukebox, which looked banged-up from years of misuse. I put a quarter in and chose "Angie," since this was what I always heard coming from this bar, and I had begun to like the song. Marlene and I drank our beers, resting quietly. I asked her about her son, and she told me that he was learning about computers, hoping to get a good job once he graduated. She described him as lazy but good-hearted. "He really looks out for me," she said. We continued talking, and when she learned how old I was, she was surprised. "Really? You seem younger."

"I feel younger," I said.

"So do I," she said. "I always feel young. Even when I've been on my feet all day and I have bill collectors hassling me and my son loafs around the house, I still feel young. I keep thinking it's a mistake, my age."

"Well, you look young," I said.

"Bless you, but you don't have to lie."

"I'm not." And I wasn't, but before I could say anything else she put her beer down and asked, "So are you going to tell me about your friend?"

"My friend?" Then I realized she was talking about Shari. "My friend. She's—she was the girlfriend of that man I told you about, the man writing the letters."

Marlene's head tilted a little more.

I realized how removed it sounded, how these permutations of relationships made little sense when I said them aloud, and I didn't want to talk about it. "It's all too complicated," I said. "I'd rather try to forget about it."

"All right," she said. "It's okay."

We stopped talking as the song on the jukebox ended. I glanced up at Marlene and she was staring at me. I became embarrassed and looked down at my drink, wondering what to say. She said, "I have to call my son. Can you wait a sec?"

She went to the pay phone by the bathroom doors, I watched her back; her uniform hugged her shoulders and her waist, the zipper on the back of her blouse sticking out. Her skirt was wrinkled. I wondered what Gorden would have thought if he had been in this bar with Marlene. Would he have thought she was some old, washed-out waitress? Would he have found her attractive? From across the room she seemed tall and languorous; she leaned with one shoulder against the wall, then she rested her head as well, so her body stood at an angle to the ground, the arm against the wall hanging lifelessly, the other supporting the telephone receiver. Her calves under her light brown stockings were large, muscular, and she crossed her legs at her ankles, one leg supporting the body, the other bent and resting on a toe. She nodded into the wall. I found myself wanting to confide in her, wanting to tell her about the letters, about Gorden and Helen and Shari. I wanted to tell her that I felt connected with Shari and that her death frightened me because it was too real, too close. I had never known anyone who had committed suicide, and there had been times when I had wondered if I could do it. After seeing Shari die in that bathtub, I thought I could.

When Marlene returned she smiled and dropped into her chair. "Sorry about that. He wanted to know who you were. Can you believe that? Eighteen and already he's my father."

"What'd you tell him?"

"I said you were a millionaire who picked me up at the diner. We're at your mansion right now."

"What did he say?"

"He told me to marry you." She laughed. "But I said I was just in it for the sex."

I smiled, trying not to read too much into the remark. She watched me, waiting for my reaction. I had none. I said, "I'm surprised he isn't coming here right now to rescue you."

"Who needs rescuing?"

Later that evening, after Marlene left the bar and drove home, I walked upstairs to my apartment and collapsed on my bed. I hadn't talked with anyone like that in years, and I was exhausted. I had forgotten how much conversation drained me. It required an effort to listen and be listened to. I became anxious if the conversation lulled, and would think furiously for something to start it up again. I remembered when I had to go to faculty meetings, and I tried to talk with the other teachers. I couldn't seem to find anything in common with them, except for griping about the students, which I didn't like. Inevitably, when I ran out of things to say, I'd ask, "Got any interesting students?" and then they'd go off and talk about a smart one, a stupid one, a troublemaker, a sweetie. Although I hated listening to this, it gave me the semblance of being friendly. Maybe it was best that I had stopped teaching.

I pulled off my pants and shirt and lay on my mattress, my thoughts reeling from too many beers, and tried to run through some of the things Marlene had said, but I was losing them. She had talked about how she had worked at that diner for five years, and had worked as a waitress for almost ten, beginning right after her divorce. Before that, she had tried various part-time jobs—working at a gift shop, a movie theater—but mostly stayed at home. She liked the diner since it paid well and she got along with the others, and intended to stay there for a while.

She asked me questions too, and I told her about growing up in Illinois with my adopted parents, my becoming a latch-key child, raised on afternoon television and comic books. I skipped over my high-school and college years, telling her about my plan to be a doctor, but was rejected from all the medical schools I had applied to. My big disappointment. Instead, I enrolled in a small graduate program in biology with a part-time teaching assistantship, hoping to save some money and reapply to medical school, but somehow lost my ambition and ended up teaching high school kids about photosynthesis. She seemed surprised that I had taught at the local high school, and wondered why I wasn't looking for another teaching job. I shook my head and told her that I didn't know. I was just tired of it all.

I noticed while we were sitting at the table that she kept crossing and uncrossing her legs, and I couldn't stop glancing down whenever she did that, staring at her calves which arced smoothly underneath her stockings. At one point she caught me looking, and grinned, but didn't say anything. After it passed midnight, she said she had to go, and I walked her back to her car. She told me that I was very sweet and kissed me on my cheek, then climbed into her car and revved the engine to life, sending huge clouds of white smoke from the tailpipe. As she drove loudly away, the muffler apparently not working, I watched her turn onto Sunrise Highway and followed her tail lights until she disappeared among a cluster of other cars. The parking lot was empty; parking lanes painted over an uneven surface warped the lot, giving the illusion in the moonlight that the surface was moving. I watched puffs of breath rise above me in the cold.

Now, while I lay half asleep, the heaviness descended on me like a thick blanket eased slowly over my body. Marlene came to me in my semi-conscious state, asking me if I thought she was too old. I said no. Her hair, instead of being tied back, fell to her neck and onto her cheek and she mussed up her hair on top, a childish gesture, so that it became tangled. She disappeared, and I eventually fell into a deep, dreamless sleep.

Roger Shin was hopeful. He began thinking about buying advertising time on local radio stations for the Memorial Day sale. It seemed that adding incentives, like coupons and free gifts, worked, and he would do this again, but on a larger scale. Maybe he would print up an entire page of coupons. Even if the discounts weren't that valuable, customers would come in thinking they had a good deal in their hands, since their doing the work of cutting along the dotted line somehow meant they were earning their discounts. That was it, he thought. When they worked for it, they felt more entitled, and this brought them in. He had never had to resort to coupons before, but they worked, so why stop? This was a chance to clean the store out and begin restocking with newer goods more likely to sell. Clothing moved faster than equipment. Smaller items faster than larger. They had to balance this out. Expand the running shoes, the aerobic gear, and cut down on the big-ticket exercise equipment.

Shin walked out of the office and into the showroom. Empty. It was dinner time so most of the shoppers were eating, and only John and Henry were in today. Norma had today off and Gorden was gone for another few days. Shin hadn't spoken to Gorden. John had filled him in. As much as Shin tried, he couldn't recall the face of the girl who had visited Gorden here weeks ago. He remembered brown hair, but that was all. She hadn't seemed suicidal, as far as he could tell, and he was curious why she had done it. Everyone here was curious, but who could they ask?

But it didn't really matter, Shin thought. Office gossip. There was no way *he* would ever do something like that. He remembered that someone in upper level management at Jakeson's had committed suicide some years ago, before he arrived. He didn't know the details but he could not imagine anything being so bad that you would kill yourself. There was always a way out. Even if it meant dropping everything and leaving, there was always a way out. The only thing he could think was that Gorden's friend had been crazy, otherwise why else would she do that? He knew his wife wouldn't agree, many people wouldn't, but he had always believed in taking charge. He controlled his life. Destroying it was unthinkable. A complete waste.

He viewed the stores he worked in as a part of his life. He controlled them, redirected them, and now they were thriving. He would do the same with this one. It was a part of him, and once he put it back in the black, he would begin thinking of some long term plans. He felt that small rush of power whenever he began moving things forward. He liked being able to shape the future of a store. It was more than money, than control, but a feeling of doing something, of completing and finishing an important job. That was why he came to Jakeson's, giving up the consulting firm, since at the firm there were always too many people on one project, and they often simply gave recommendations, and left it at that. Here, he jumped into a job and became a part of the store.

Returning to his desk, he began searching for local advertising companies who could, under a limited budget, help produce some commercials. He glanced at the clock and decided to call his wife to tell her he'd be late again.

"Hello?" someone answered. Not his wife.

"Hello? Who is this?"

"Well, who is this?"

"I'm calling for my wife, Helen."

"Oh, I'm the baby-sitter. Your wife went out for a short while."

"Baby-sitter?" he asked. Since when did they use a baby-sitter?

"Yeah. Can I take a message?"

"No," he said. When he hung up he wondered what his wife was doing. Why hadn't she taken Susy along, as she usually did? He shrugged and went back to the business yellow pages. For a second, it occurred to him that she was acting strange lately—this baby-sitter, her long silences, thinking about things she refused to talk about, a restlessness—but he dismissed this, connecting it with Susy's recent fever. Being stuck in the apartment with a sick child probably made her restless. He thought about Gorden's friend and if his wife would ever do anything like that. Kill herself. Helen? No, not her. Too much to live for.

After shaving and washing with a soapy washcloth by the sink (he had not been able to use the shower yet), Gorden dressed quickly and began pacing around his living room. He stopped at the boxes by the door, wondering if he should hide them somewhere. He shook his head. Too much trouble. But he wanted to get rid of them soon. He rubbed his cheek and chin and felt no stubble. Clean. His hair was greasy. Last night he had washed in the sink, and kept bumping his head into the faucet until he gave up and simply washed out what little soap there was. It was stupid not to use the shower, he knew, but after not using it for the first few days, it had become harder and harder to step in there. Even going near the damn thing made him nervous. What the hell was he worried about? It was just a hunk of plastic—not even porcelain but a light plastic substitute—and he had scrubbed it clean a number of times. But he couldn't use it. He was acting like an idiot.

He checked his watch. Helen would be coming any minute, and he was getting antsy. How did the house look? He surveyed the living room, trying to see it through her eyes, eyes that had never seen this place. It was a little too neat, the lamp squarely in the center of the end table, the cushions lined up neatly in a row, the newspapers stacked on the coffee table. Now that he thought about it, everything looked so strange.

He heard the gravel crunching outside—a car parking out front—and he cleared his throat. He tried to relax. It had been three weeks since he had last seen her, since that time at the motel, and his heart began beating faster. He wasn't sure what he would say to her. He didn't want to talk about Shari, didn't even want to think about her, so he'd have to make sure they stayed away from that. What was taking so long?

Gorden looked through the curtains and saw Helen's car parked in front, but she was still inside. Was she chickening out? What was she thinking? Not wanting her to drive off, he turned on the front light, and opened the front door. Cool air hit his face and neck. Helen saw him and climbed out.

"Hello," she said as she closed her door. She was wearing a new coat, a navy blue wool overcoat, and her hair was cut shorter than usual, cut above her ears, her bangs higher.

"I'm glad you came."

She approached, looking around the yard, at the house. "Nice place."

"When it warms up I've got to re-paint it." He moved aside to let her in, watching her reaction when she saw the room. She glanced quickly at the sofa, the table, then her eyes moved to the bare walls, the hallway leading to the bathroom, the kitchen entrance. She nodded slowly. He asked her if she wanted a drink or something. She shook her head.

"I can't stay that long. I don't want to leave Susy for too long."

Gorden motioned her to the couch and took her coat, hanging it in the front closet, which was practically empty now, except for his coat and some old sweaters he stored there. Helen wore jeans and a grey flannel shirt, and she left her blue scarf hanging loosely around her neck. She sat down carefully, leaning back against one of the cushions.

"It's been a while," he said, sitting next to her.

She nodded. "How are things?"

"Okay. I missed you."

She didn't say anything. She took off her scarf and laid it next to her. "I mean, how are things after..." She let the words trail away.

"They're okay. I'm doing okay." He moved closer to her and put his hand on her leg. "How are you?"

She shifted her position and moved his hand away. "I'm fine. Susy's all recovered now." She folded her scarf while she continued talking. "Everything is fine now. Raj is happy that the store is doing better. Susy's active and full of energy. It was scary seeing her so sick. I don't think I've ever seen her so sick. It's this weather, I think. The cold won't break."

Gorden watched her mouth as she spoke. She was so pretty, the way the corner of her mouth drooped on some words. He told her this.

She shook her head. "No, Gorden. That's not why I'm here. I'm here because I thought you were sad. Because you needed someone to talk to."

"I am sad," he said. "But I also missed you."

Helen sighed and shook her head again. "I also came here to tell you in person—"

He moved closer and grabbed her hand. "Helen, it's been so

long." He put his hand on her waist.

She pulled away. "Stop that. I told you to stop." She stood. "This was a bad idea. I came because you asked me to, because I thought you were upset."

Gorden also stood. "Come on, Helen. I really needed to see you." He took her hand again, lightly. He pulled her closer. "Don't you want to stay?"

"You don't get it," she said. "You just don't get it." She shook her head and pulled away. "Goodbye, Gorden."

"Wait," he said, gripping her shoulder hard, feeling her softness between his fingers. "Not yet."

"You're hurting me," she said in a low voice, staring ahead. "Let go of me."

Gorden felt the anger rising in him, but he let go. "I'm sorry," he said as she walked towards the closet. "I just... ah, Christ. Forget it. You don't give a fuck."

She stopped. "I'm married, Gorden," she said. "I have a family. I can't do this anymore."

"We did it before, and it didn't bother you."

"It did."

"And you're married? To who? Shin's married to Jakeson's, you know that as well as I do."

She was silent.

"I'm not asking you to give anything up. Shit, all I want is some company." He suddenly felt very tired, and he sat back down on the couch, heavily. "I don't know what the fuck's happening to me."

Helen turned around and watched him.

Gorden continued. "You know what I mean. You feel so fucking... alone. You know what I mean." He rubbed his temple and shut his eyes, feeling the pressure in the middle of his head pushing outwards. A dull pain. What the hell, he thought. He was becoming a goddamn basket case. Whining to Helen. Acting like a little damn kid.

She sat next to him. "I know," she said quietly.

"It was the bathtub. She did it in the bathtub," he said, not opening his eyes. He wanted to be in darkness. He pictured her slumped body in the reddish water. "All that blood."

Helen didn't say anything.

"You know I spent the past few days doing nothing but cleaning?" he told her. He opened his eyes and looked at her. He was surprised to see that her eyes were teary. She didn't even know Shari and she felt this bad. "I must have scrubbed that bathroom twenty times."

"Why... Can I ask why she did it?"

"A lot of reasons. She was drinking too much. She couldn't find a job. I was being an asshole," he said. "Christ. She was only seventeen."

Helen drew back in surprise.

"Yeah," he said. "She was only fucking seventeen." Gorden tried to remember what he did when he was seventeen. He graduated from high school. He loved cars. All kinds of cars. He even thought about becoming a mechanic, but that required more training and he wanted to get a job, earn some real money.

"Seventeen?" Helen said.

"And I just made it worse by treating her like shit. What with her drinking and all, I didn't want to deal with it, with her." Gorden tried not to think about it, but he couldn't help it. Shari just kept appearing in his head. He wished she'd stop that. But at least Helen was here. It wasn't as bad when she was here.

"I'm really sorry," she said. "I wish I knew what to say."

There really wasn't anything she *could* say, but he didn't care. He felt her hand on his shoulder, the warmth coming from her palm, passing through his shirt and on his skin. He wanted to touch her, to be a part of her, and he knew everything would go away if he were with her, and he turned to her. Helen wavered for a moment, and when he leaned back on the cushions pulling her hand off his shoulder and placing it on his cheek, he closed his eyes, feeling the warmth of her hand passing to his face. He heard Helen say quietly, to herself. "I don't know, Gorden."

What happened next was difficult for me to understand. Gorden wrote it and I read it, but I still could not believe it. This was a painful scene for me to witness, since I could not, like Gorden, stop thinking about Shari, and when Gorden grabbed Helen by the shoulder I felt a small jolt of fear, of anxiety for Helen, because I did not know what Gorden was capable of at that moment. He was a wild card, a frightening unknown. I raced to the end of the letter, and when I saw what was to happen, I went back and read more carefully, trying to understand their motives. They slept together, and this confused me.

Perhaps this was my own naivete and lack of comprehension in the games two people can play, but it seemed to me that Helen was firmly set against that course of action, and yet after her quiet and sad statement to herself and to Gorden, they moved closer to each other and kissed. I might have underestimated their short but concentrated history together, and underestimated the uneasy attraction they had for each other, since *something* seemed to draw them together. It might have been pity on Helen's part, seeing Gorden so distraught and needy, and although she could have stood up and walked out at that moment, she chose not to out of compassion. She knew what it was like to feel so alone and to reach out for something, and she weighed this against her original intentions: to sever the relationship for good. I imagine she saw this as a final gesture of comfort, of thanks, since he too offered some solace when she felt confused and alone. I am certain that after all this had happened, after she had dressed quickly and had left Gorden in his bed, asleep, while she was starting her car and hurrying home, she regretted it. She cursed and called herself cheap and stupid and how could she have done that? Why was she acting so weak, and how did she get manipulated so easily? She felt sorry for him, but she shouldn't have let it go this far. Never again, she vowed to herself. This was the last time. She promised herself this.

Compassion. Seeing him like that on the sofa, her hand resting against his cheek, his eyes closed and the weight of guilt and sorrow filling her, she had felt truly sorry for Gorden. And Gorden knew this.

...then she said real quiet and almost to herself, I dont know, Gorden, and I felt her hand get soft and I knew she still liked me and that it wasnt really over and everything was okay so I opened my eyes and I saw her looking right at me, and I couldnt stop myself so I kissed her slowly, not wanting to scare her off and at first she froze for a second but then when I touched her cheek and touched her ear I told her it was okay and I just wanted to be with her for a while and she let me kiss her and then I pushed a little harder and wanted to get close to her to feel her next to me and then everything was okay and it was just like before, just like nothing happened and everything was okay. She kissed me back and I didnt want to let go of her. I wanted to stay there with her.

4

"Hello. Mr. Gorden? I'm Mrs. McCann. Shari's mother." Gorden stared at the woman with the same kind of brown curly hair Shari had had but it was rolled up in a bun on the back of her head with small curls poking out and falling down her temple and cheek. A few grey hairs streaked the sides. Gorden stared for a second, then stood up, extending his hand. Her face was full with a small extra chin, and when he shook her pudgy hand, he wondered if Shari would have looked like this in twenty years.

"Nice to meet you."

"I'm glad you could make it."

Gorden nodded and motioned to the seat across from him. They were at Rotolo Pizza, and Gorden had chosen this place because there were private booths. He hadn't wanted to meet her at Jakeson's. Actually, he hadn't wanted to meet her at all, but when he received her call yesterday evening right after his first day of work, she sounded like she would have cried if he had refused to see her. The police had given her his name and phone number. It wasn't until the body had been shipped to a funeral home in Maine, and Mr. and Mrs. McCann had *seen* the body, that they finally believed that their only daughter had died—not just died but had, according to the report, killed herself.

This was why Mrs. McCann had had to see Gorden. I have questions, she had said, and surely there are some... things of hers. Gorden said he could send them by mail, but no, she wanted to get them in person. Rather than meet at his house—he had been very definite about that—they agreed to meet at the mall. He would bring her daughter's things there.

"I don't understand why she was there," Mrs. McCann began, after Gorden told her that Shari had been staying with him. "Were you her boyfriend?"

"No. I met her here and she needed a place to stay. I own a house. I had an extra room."

"You don't look like one of her usual friends," she said. Gorden was wearing his shirt and tie, and had combed his hair back this morning. Clean-shaven.

"I don't," he said, not sure if that was a question or a reply. He stared at her clean navy blue blazer that hugged her stocky body, a white blouse with a curled collar underneath. This woman looked like a real estate broker or a bank teller. Somehow he had not expected this. He had been expecting a Shari twenty years older, dressed similarly, just more wrinkles.

"She had terrible friends. That's why we became strict, but she couldn't accept our terms. She wouldn't listen to us."

"You kicked her out."

"Is *that* what she told you? She ran away! We gave her choices. All she had to do was go back to school. Stop doing all those things with her friends."

"Things?"

"Drugs," she said, lowering her voice. "She went to all kinds of parties. She never went to school. My husband and I were going crazy. She just wouldn't listen."

Gorden began to hate her. He didn't know why he was reacting this way, but he suddenly became defensive for Shari. This woman was making it seem like it was all Shari's fault. "She tried to get a job. She tried to shape up."

"But then why did she—but why did this happen?"

"She had nowhere to go. No one would hire her. She became depressed," he said. "She wanted to go home, but she said she couldn't."

Mrs. McCann's face whitened. "Th-that's not true. We would've—"

"You drove her to this."

"No," she said, bringing her hand to her mouth. "We gave her so much. She just didn't—"

"She said you hated her. She said she had no one in this world."

"What about you? She stayed with you for..." She became confused, trying to calculate time but was having trouble.

"Seven, eight months. There wasn't much I could do but put her up and give her food, money. I bought her clothes. But I wasn't her parent. I was just a poor shit she latched on to."

She flinched when he cursed. He added, "She felt like she had fucking no one."

Mrs. McCann was shaken. She moved her unsteady hands into her lap. She said in a wavering voice, "Maybe I should get her things now."

While they walked out into the parking lot to his car, Gorden couldn't understand why he was being an asshole, why he was making this harder for her. He felt like apologizing and telling her that it wasn't really like he had said, but seeing this fat woman walking next to him, he imagined her stuffing her face at every meal, talking with her mouth full to her fat husband, and he imagined that she'd put on a big crying show in front of others to show what a grieving mother she was when, in fact, if she had really given a fuck she would have sent Shari money, or tried to find her, but no, she hadn't. She had let Shari go. And die.

They came to his car, and he opened the trunk, lifting out the three boxes of Shari's things. He placed them on the ground and asked where her car was. She said, "Just in the next row, near that lamp." She pointed. "I can carry one."

He gave her the heaviest box, the one with clothes packed tightly in, and he took the other two, one stacked on top of the other. He followed her through a number of parked cars, weaving carefully behind her. She took short, hurried steps. They were silent. She stopped behind a dirty black Jeep Cherokee, the rear fender dented. She opened the back and shoved the box in. Gorden followed her example. After she slammed the back shut, she asked, "Is there anything else I should know?"

"What?"

"About Shari. Anything I should know?"

He thought for a second, then shook his head.

"Then let me tell you this, Mr. Gorden. You are a vile, vile man."

"What?"

"A vile man. I know you were lying about my daughter and you probably took drugs with her and are just like the rest. Don't think I can't tell when you're lying. No, don't say anything else. I've heard enough from you. You think I don't know your kind? You take some girl in and give her drugs and make her so dependent on you that—I know your kind. Goodbye, and someday it's going to strike you what you did—"

"You fucking fat hag," he said, moving closer to her. "You ugly fat bitch. You think you can come here and tell—"

"Goodbye, Mr. Gorden," she said, moving towards her door.

"Goodbye my fucking ass. Your daughter slit her fucking wrists because of you."

"No you don't. I know what happened! You probably killed

her! You probably killed her and it only looked like suicide!" She jumped into the car and slammed the door shut, locking it.

"You bitch," he said, amazed. She started the car, and gave him a dirty look. "You fucking bitch!" He raised his leg and kicked the front door as she backed out, the side view mirror coming within inches of his arm. She said something which he couldn't hear, and drove away quickly.

He stared at her car as it sped out of the parking lot, and then shook his head. What the hell just happened? That crazy... He shook his head again. He knew meeting her would be a mistake. Christ. Now she was going to tell her husband about the psycho their daughter had been shacked up with.

He walked back into the mall. His lunch break was over and he wanted to get back to work. He didn't kill her, he thought, so why had the mother said that? Did he look like a killer? A drug addict? What the hell was that woman's problem? Gorden clenched and unclenched his fists, wondering if maybe she was right. No. What the hell. He just wished everyone would leave him alone.

When he went back to work—they were beginning to store some of the winter sporting goods and bring out the spring and summer items—he concentrated only on moving boxes from the storage room and into the showroom. He could have asked John to help, but he wanted to do this himself. He liked the feeling of pushing himself, of lifting and moving things. For a few of the boxes, he had to use the dolly, but he carried most by himself, feeling his arms and back strain. The harder he worked, the better he felt. Gorden began to forget about that woman and about Shari. All her things were gone. It was as if she had never existed. Could he do that—erase her from his mind? He could try. And tonight he would try to see Helen. He needed to see her.

Helen checked her birth control pill dispenser for the fifth time today. She kept forgetting whether or not she had taken the pill this morning. She had forgotten before, usually missing only one day, and she would just double up the next day, not really knowing if it would work or not (sometimes, when she did this, she would bleed a little). Once, she had lost her pill dispenser about half-way through her cycle, and had stopped taking the pills. That completely threw her rhythm off, and her period came three weeks earlier than normal.

Now, satisfied again that she had taken the pill today, she went back to watching television with her daughter. Susy loved the Woody Woodpecker cartoons, and sometimes if Helen had nothing else to do, which seemed to be quite often, she would watch them with her daughter. Susy sat on the floor with her legs crossed and her hands in her lap, her head pulled upwards towards the screen, mesmerized. Helen sat back in the recliner, trying to read a paperback she had picked up at the supermarket. But she couldn't concentrate. She heard the woodpecker's laugh, and looked up. Her daughter sat almost perfectly still, and Helen decided to take her out once the show ended. They could use some air. Also, she didn't want to be home if Gorden called. Ever since last week he had been doing it again: calling, wanting to meet. Of course it was her own fault for letting things happen. You're so stupid, she told herself. She wanted to punish herself for allowing it to happen, but now she realized that she was already being punished.

She couldn't for the life of her figure out why she had so much trouble ending this thing. She wondered how other women did it. Maybe she should be stronger. Helen noticed Susy yawning, blinking out the sleepiness.

She left the recliner and sat behind Susy, wrapping her arms around her. Her baby. Her little baby. She felt Susy's warm scalp under her chin, and after a few seconds, Susy struggled to free herself. Helen laughed and let her go, but then her daughter lay back against her and continued to watch, her head resting on Helen's lap. Helen began stroking Susy's head, running her fingers through soft, fine hair.

◊

Alone in the house after working late again, Gorden became restless. He wasn't very tired even after putting in over ten hours today, and wasn't sure what this meant. But he liked the fact that he was making some overtime and keeping busy. The only problem was that when he came home he needed something to do. He would watch a few minutes of TV, then go make himself something to eat, then flip through a newspaper, then go back to the TV. He paced, and tried calling Helen a few times, but he only got the answering machine.

He tried to think back to when he had lived alone, before Shari, and what he had done then. Working in the stockroom and having more moving and cleaning jobs tired him out faster, so he had come home exhausted.

Yeah, I remember now. I was breaking my balls doing all the grunt work for Manny and John like helping the trucks unload equipment, moving around displays and cleaning the place. Now Lorraine the cashier helps with the cleaning and everyone else does the moving. Anyway now that I think about it it wasnt that bad because I got to check out all the new things that came in and even test them to make sure they were working or all the pieces were there. I worked like a dog and came home real tired and took a long shower for almost forty minutes then Id eat and watch TV. What a boring life. And then I got promoted and then I met Shari. Is it like those seven months never happened? I mean I remember a lot of things but now it seems so fake, like it wasnt really me but some other guy. I remember when me and Shari used to make dinner together. We both couldnt cook for shit but we just turned on the TV loud so we could hear it and stayed in the kitchen and began throwing things together. Damn we made some godawful things in there. There was once this stew that smelled like rotting fish for some reason, but it tasted okay. There was another time when Shari saw a recipe in the newspaper and tried making some kind of meatloaf but she did something wrong and it was just real hard pieces of meat that crunched when you bit it.

Gorden had to get out. Every time he was alone in the house he kept thinking about her and it was beginning to get him angry. He didn't want to remember. He wanted to pretend she never existed. Grabbing his jacket, he hurried out the door and into his car. As he drove down Wakem and turned onto Cascade he noticed for the first time in the moonlight that the snow had melted, and the muddy season was beginning. New Hampshire in the spring meant that all the hardened ground softened into mud, and the rains would begin soon. At least it would be warming up.

He stared at some of the houses along Cascade, their windows lit up and he thought he saw movement behind curtains and blinds, even the bluish light of a television in the background. Activity. A car headed towards him in the opposite lane, its headlights in his eyes for an instant as the car climbed an incline. There were no street lamps on this road. A large white satellite dish stood in the yard of a two-story house on his right, the curved surface glowing.

He thought about visiting Helen, but decided not to pester her tonight. There was no reason to rush things, and he knew she would want to see him again later, probably in a few days. Lately, he had been having wild thoughts about her, that maybe they could run away together, to Boston, or even New York. He knew he was just dreaming but wouldn't it be nice? He'd finally have a family, a real family, and maybe they'd have a kid together, a boy, and Susy and their son would play and Gorden would teach him things, sports maybe, and it'd be the kind of family he had always sort of wanted.

Look at me, he said to himself. A fucking sap. Gorden turned onto 89, speeding up and turning on his brights. No cars out tonight. He liked having the road to himself and he let his mind wander as he headed towards the scenic stop a few miles past Sunolea. Nothing else to do, he thought. If it looked nice enough at night, he'd tell Helen about it. They could come here when it warmed up more.

5

One morning when I was half-asleep in my bed, trying to remember what I had just dreamed, watching a ray of sunlight travel across my room, I received a call from the community college where I was supposed to be working next month. It was the director of the Extension school, and he wanted to know if I could come in next week to meet with the other science teachers. They wanted to talk about a syllabus and this was an opportunity for me to ask questions. I also had to fill out the tax and employment forms. It took me a few minutes to sort this out, since I had forgotten about this job, and when I realized that I had to teach biology again, my body suddenly seemed twenty pounds heavier. I fell back into the mattress with the receiver against my ear, and sighed.

"Is everything all right?" he asked.

I hesitated. That I could use the money from this job was not the question. They were going to pay me $35.00 an hour for four to five hours of teaching a week. But I couldn't imagine opening those textbooks and preparing lectures, standing up there in front of a class and explaining nucleotides and mitochondria, grading papers, running labs. I hadn't realized how tired I was of teaching until I was away from it, a safe distance from those chores. Finally, I asked the director if he had alternates to teach this course, if something were to happen to me.

"If you had a better offer somewhere else?" he asked.

"Something like that," I answered.

He paused and then said that this happens and that it made things more difficult for them, but they could find someone. Was I resigning this teaching job?

I knew that once I turned this down I would never teach at this community college again, but that didn't bother me. I actually felt better at the thought of this. I told him yes, I was resigning this post, and I apologized.

When I hung up, I lay back down and considered what I had just done. I had turned down $175.00 a week for a few hours worth of work. I probably could have used my old notes and I also could have kept my job at the diner, rearranging my hours. Yet I was glad not to have to worry about that anymore. Perhaps I acted foolishly, but at the time I didn't think so. I didn't want to have anything to do with teaching or with biology if I could help it.

Then I remembered my dream. I had dreamed about Shari again. My dreams of Shari weren't nightmares, but they were frightening because of the clarity with which I saw her. She had seemed so real to me, even though I had never met her, and I remembered that in my dream I had watched Shari climb out of her bedroom window to see her friends. I was standing unnoticed in her room, watching her dig through her drawer full of underwear and pull out her bag of marijuana and the small flask of Southern Comfort. She pocketed the marijuana and took a sip from the flask, sealing it tightly and shoving the bottle back deep into her clothes. She tip-toed across the room and opened the window quietly, stopping every few seconds when there was a sound. I was invisible because she looked right at me but didn't seem to notice. She climbed out. I saw a boy standing outside waiting for her, and it turned out to be me. Then, I think, I woke up.

Shari McCann. Like Gorden, I couldn't get the image of her in that bathtub out of my head. I wondered if she had hit the radial artery when she had cut her right wrist, since she had gone deep and perhaps even severed the tendons to her fingers. Those red clouds of blood in the steaming bath water, contrasting the white tub, had been permanently imprinted in my mind. Even now I can see those clouds of blood, swirling and expanding around her wrists, encircling her hands. She had closed her eyes. She felt the hot water, the sweat on her brow, the sound of the water dripping. Her heartbeat.

I thought about my fantasy of helping her get away from

Yanack, from Gorden, and wondered if it would have worked. If Shari had been desperate enough to commit suicide, then she certainly would have considered leaving with a stranger. In fact, had I acted on my adolescent desire to save Shari, she might have been sitting right next to me that very second, in my room.

There she was, sitting on the corner of my mattress, her hair cut short—one of the very first things she had done when she arrived here. She had wanted to start over fresh and even wanted to look different. In fact, she had let me cut her hair, giving me a pair of scissors to use on her long brown curls, telling me, Make it real short. She sat in my chair in the center of the floor, newspapers spread around her, wearing an old T-shirt. I snipped away. Long locks of hair fell to the ground, curling and bouncing off the newspapers. Cut it all off, she said. All of it. Make me into a different person.

The ghostly image of Shari in short hair, thanking me, faded as the sun filled my room with a bright yellow light. My Shari.

Gorden must have put four hundred miles on his odometer within the past week. And he hadn't really gone anywhere. He drove around Yanack, visiting his old hangouts. He drove past the site where the junkyard used to be, two miles up North Point Road, past the lake, where he had spent hours on the weekends just sorting through piles of car parts that he could use for his old Chevy. A few years ago the man who owned the yard sold the land, and developers had cleared the junk to build more homes there. Gorden liked the area though, with the dense woods nearby, and the highway far enough away so that people rarely drove through here.

He also visited his mother's old home. They had sold it a while ago, and now a young family was living there—they had converted the attached garage into another room and had built a small unattached garage in the side yard. The house was now white, instead of beige, and Gorden had parked across the street. It was a small split level with maroon shutters, an old oak tree in front. He had hated that tree, the roots that humped out of the ground near the base making it so difficult to mow the lawn. He had never been nostalgic for this house before, but seeing it now after all these years made him wish that he were a teenager, having only to worry about passing his classes and staying away from his stepfather.

I dont know if you remember this but we were real young and playing some screwed up game called Five Minutes with some other kids where we spun a stick and whoever it pointed to would go into the woods with the person next to him for five minutes. We sat boy-girl and you had some guy named Bobby and someone else on your other side and the stick pointed to you and Bobby. Remember that? I got all pissed when you came out of the woods zipping up your jeans and I almost started a fight with Bobby but you told me that you were kidding and you guys didnt do anything, just pretending to the others. For some reason I thought of that when I saw the old house. I never told you this but when the stick pointed to your friend Janine I think her name was and she picked me and we went into the woods, she really made me pull down my pants and she sucked on me, though I was too young to know what the fuck was going on. Thats why I got all pissed when you came back from the woods zipping your pants. I thought everyone was doing it and when you said you were kidding I felt real stupid.

Early evening. Rain. Gorden had finished work and had driven around Yanack and Sunolea, not really sure where to go, watching the grey, wet world from his car. He had decided to see Helen. Right now he was parked on Dorset, sitting in his car and debating whether or not this was a good idea. He knew she wouldn't like his surprise visit, but he couldn't go much longer without seeing her. She was never home, or she never answered the phone, and he *had* to see her. He wasn't sure how late Shin was staying, but since the sale was less than two weeks away, Shin would probably be working tonight. Gorden would have to chance it.

He watched the rain splatter his windshield, drumming the hood. He climbed out of the car and hurried across the street, turning the corner onto Sunolea Road. There were more cars out tonight than usual. Gorden stood under an awning for a second and saw the cars splash through deep puddles, spraying the sidewalks. He scratched his head, his scalp itching. He was getting better at washing his hair in the sink, but sometimes it still itched up there. Maybe it was the rain. He ran his fingers through his wet hair.

Just to be certain, he looked up and down the street for Shin's black sedan, and didn't see it. Walking towards Helen's building, he ducked his head as the rain came down harder, drops of water trickling into his collar, down his neck.

By the time he reached Helen's door, he was soaked. He shook some of the rain out of his hair, off his jacket, and knocked. He heard movement, and stood back so she could see him in the peephole. Bolts unlocked. She opened the door but blocked the entrance.

"Gorden? What're you doing here?" She asked, annoyed. She was in jeans and her plaid flannel shirt. Her hair was messy.

"Hi, Helen. I thought I'd surprise you."

"Now? Are you crazy?" she said. "Raj could come home any second, and Susy's awake."

He stared at her, not expecting this reaction. Although he knew she would be surprised, he thought she would be glad to at least see him, if only for a second. "I just wanted to say hello."

Helen shook her head. "I told you I didn't want you showing up here like this. Remember what I said?"

"Don't get mad," he said.

"I'm not mad. But I think you should go." She turned her head inside and said something to her daughter.

Gorden wanted to go inside. He was cold and wet, and he didn't want to return to his car to drive in circles for the next few hours. What was the matter with her? It wasn't like he was going to stay the night or anything. All he wanted to do was say hello and talk for a little bit. Gorden saw Susy poking through Helen's legs. "Hey there, Susy. Remember me?"

"Gorden," Helen said. "You should go."

"Susy, I gave you the lacrosse ball?" he said, crouching down. "The ball ball?"

Susy stared back at Gorden with wide, unblinking eyes. She pulled on her smooth black hair, and smiled shyly. Her mother pushed her back slowly. "Gorden," Helen said again. "You should go."

"Let me stay for a minute." He stood and faced her. "Just to warm up."

"I told you Raj could be home soon." She turned around and said something to Susy, moving away from the door. Gorden, seeing this opening and not wanting to stand out there, pushed his way in. "Gorden!" Helen said as he entered the apartment. "What are you doing?"

"Just for a second. I'm freezing." He checked his shoes to make sure he wasn't tracking any mud on her carpet. "Look at this. My socks are completely wet."

"Gorden. This isn't funny. I want you to go."

He studied the apartment. Everything was exactly the same. In the kitchen area, on the counter, Helen seemed to have been making a snack. Chips and dip. The TV was on low, and Susy had wandered back into the living room area, sitting on the floor. He turned back to Helen, who had folded her arms and was glaring at him, shaking her head. "Let's go out tonight," he said.

"No." Her lips tightened.

"You're mad," he said.

"Who the hell do you think you are?" she whispered fiercely.

"What?" He realized that he had gone too far.

"I want you to leave. Now." She held open the door. "Get out."

"Helen..."

"Out."

He paused. "Don't be mad. It's been so long. I just wanted to see you."

She didn't say anything while he backed out. She just shook her head and closed the door. He heard her bolting it. Gorden stood there for a few minutes, worried, and considered knocking again to apologize. But it hadn't been like he had really done anything wrong. He could understand why she had been like that—Shin could come home any minute—but he didn't care.

He watched his steps on the wet stairs. Maybe he didn't care because he *wanted* Shin to know. Then what would happen? There'd be a scene and then maybe Helen and Shin would divorce. How about that?

Gorden knew that probably wouldn't happen, but he liked to think of the possibilities. Now what, he thought as he headed back towards his car. Now where the hell would he go? Christ, this weather sucked.

Helen, after she closed the door and heard him leave, thought, He is going to be trouble. She *knew* it had been a mistake to sleep with him that last time, to let him think that they still had something, and now this was what happened. He thought he had some right to barge in here. This was going to be a problem, she just knew it, and she had to end it before it became worse. He would be getting more careless, and eventually Raj would find out. She had to end it, now, completely, once and for all. She would have to be definite otherwise Gorden would not get it. He had to get it.

Gorden looked through the new advertisement that Shin had made. Although it looked snappy, with the reds and blues, the "Jakeson's Sporting Goods" in bold black letters at the top, Gorden didn't understand why Shin had highlighted the golf clubs. The Wilson Prestige metal woods and irons for $199.99. The pictures of the clubs also looked nice, with the small descriptions of the items, but he didn't think golfing was very big up here. Gorden didn't even know what the descriptions meant. "Metal woods (1, 3, 5) of 17-4 stainless steel are very forgiving on mis-hits. Irons (3-PW) are perimeter-weighted for added control." What the hell was that all about? Shin must know what he was doing. That back page full of coupons, for instance, seemed kind of dumb to Gorden, but during the last sale a bunch of people came in with the few coupons from the newspapers, so it seemed to work. But to Gorden, coupons were too much like a grocery. The second page of the advertisement showed the fishing gear on sale, the things Gorden had expected to appear on the first page. The reels (Daiwa Apollo XB, $19.94; Mitchell 750 Series Long Shots, $44.94), Freshwater rods (Fenwicks, Rodcos, Berkeleys), and all kinds of lures, hooks, and lines. The rubber waders were also on sale, the lowest priced one starting at $49.97. These should sell well.

Gorden watched Shin at his desk, hunched over some books, the radio on. He was checking the commercials that played on the local AM news station, WNHN. "News You Can Use, All The Time," was its motto. Gorden had already heard the commercial—just a fifteen-second spot with a woman announcer telling listeners about the Memorial Day Sale, listing a few of the big savings, asking them to look for the newspaper ads—and liked the low-key style. Gorden had been worried that Shin would put on something loud and annoying. The radio ads were a good idea, and he wondered why they had never done that before.

It was almost noon and Gorden wanted to call Helen to apologize for last night. What a stupid move. The last thing he wanted to do was piss her off, but what did she expect when she didn't call him or talk to him for such a long time? Of course he'd want to see her.

Gorden picked up the phone while keeping his eye on Shin. I'm calling your wife now, he told Shin mentally. How do you like that? Gorden smiled.

When Helen answered he said in a quiet voice, "Hey. It's me."

"Gorden?"

"Yeah. I wanted to call to say I was sorry about last night," he said. He watched Shin, and wondered how much Shin could hear, but Shin continued to study the books.

"Gorden," she said evenly. "I don't want you to call here ever again."

"What?"

"And I don't want you to come around either. It's over. I don't want to see you. Do you understand?"

"Listen, if it's about last—"

"No, it's more than that. You don't seem to understand the word 'no'."

"What're you talking about," he said, becoming angry. "You can't really mean it."

"Goodbye, and I'm sorry if this seems rude, and I know you're going through a lot, but this is ending right now. Right now." She hung up.

"What?" The other end was dead, and he couldn't believe what had just happened. He kept the phone to his ear, waiting for her to pick up again. That bitch, he thought, when the dial tone came on. He slammed down the phone, and Shin turned towards him, curious, but then looked away after Gorden tensed his jaw and stared back. So that was it? He made a little fucking mistake and now she never wanted to see him again? That just didn't make any sense.

He stood up abruptly and walked out through the stockroom, wanting to get out of Jakeson's. He left through the side door, and headed for the food court. All of this shit confused him. What was her problem? How could this be over when it had barely got started? She was fucking around with him, and he didn't like it. Was he just going to lie down and get kicked around? He didn't think so. He had to do something, and no fucking away was he going to just take it.

Maybe theres something else going on that I cant see or know about and thats why she talked to me the way she did, like Shin putting pressure on her or shes getting second thoughts because of I was an asshole when I showed up at her place. Im not just going to take it and forget I ever met her goddammit. Helen and I got something good going and I didnt want to just forget about it. No fucking way. I tried calling her a few times, but she never picked it up, so I know what I got to do. I got to see her in person and figure this shit out. And Im not going to do it like last time. I want to make sure everything is okay before I show up.

6

Marlene and I were on top of the train platform. She thought it was odd that I liked to spend time up here, but as we sat on top of the small, waist-high concrete wall protecting the stairwell, we lapsed into silence as we looked out over Marnole. We had left work together again, and I decided to take her here because she mentioned that she had a headache. This was better than going to the bar. She smoked a cigarette while the cars below us sped along Sunrise Highway, and though it was chilly, neither of us wanted to go.

I was thinking about Gorden's last call to Helen, and what had gone through Helen's mind. I admired her for being so tough, but I pictured her, right after hanging up, standing by the phone, shaken, trying to catch her breath. She had done it. She had told him to go away, and it was frightening. Not that she didn't want him to go away, but telling him directly not to call and not to visit had seemed harsh. There hadn't been any other way. Had she done the right thing? Doing this over the phone? He wouldn't have listened if she had been anything but direct. What a horrible mistake, she thought. She took a deep breath, steadying herself, and went back to her daughter.

◊

"I've never been up here this late," Marlene said. I turned to her and asked her how she liked it.

"It's nice. It'll be better when its warmer though. The wind is kind of cold." She pulled her raincoat tighter around her body. "What do you think of when you're up here?"

"Everything," I said. "Sometimes nothing. Sometimes I try to imagine what people are doing in the houses below." I nodded to the neighborhood.

She looked down Harold Street, "What is the house next to your building doing?"

I turned and stared. "It's a family," I said. "The kids are asleep. The parents have gone to bed after another fight. They're sulking."

"How about the one next to that?"

"No one's home. They went away for the weekend."

"How boring. I think... I think in the next house they're drinking and fooling around."

I grinned. "You're good at this."

She shrugged as if to say, Of course.

After a few minutes we decided to leave. She flicked her cigarette onto the train tracks, the red ember bouncing and leaving dying sparks in its wake, and we descended the stairs slowly, our footsteps in rhythm. She asked me about Shari, though she didn't use the name, and I paused before telling her that there was nothing more about her. We waited at the light on Harold and I mentioned that the boss' wife had ended the affair.

"Really?" she asked. "Did the boss find out?"

I shook my head. "My friend, the letter-writer, the one having the affair, is a little crazy. He was being... indiscreet." The Walk sign flashed and we crossed Sunrise, the music from the bar becoming louder. It was another Led Zeppelin song, "Ramble On." The wind raced across the highway, pushing Marlene's raincoat against her legs. I asked, "Do you want to go into Lucky's?"

"I don't know," she said. "It seems kind of noisy in there."

I looked at the four cars parked in front. Maybe she was right.

I wasn't in the mood for noisy people and loud music either. Marlene waited, her hair being blown across her face, and I asked, "Would you like to go to my room?"

"Sure," she said.

I didn't know whether or not my invitation was simply a friendly offer with the purpose of showing Marlene where I lived, or if this was a proposition of something more than coffee. I was anxious as we walked up the brick steps into the small foyer with the mailboxes, and then up the wooden steps to my apartment. The steps groaned under our weight, and I noticed Marlene looking around her, taking this in. The old, peeling hallways seemed even more dirty than I remembered, and I was embarrassed that she would see me living in conditions like these. And my room, I thought as we walked down the hall towards my door.

"It's a mess," I said as I pulled out my key.

"I don't care." When I looked at her, it struck me that she really *didn't* care. I felt less self-conscious about my apartment now and opened my door. I let her walk in first.

She saw what I had seen for months: old clothes scattered on the floor by my mattress, the blankets unmade and balled up by the wall; old, dried-out mugs with coffee and Kahlua stains lined up on my windowsill, by my sink, on the floor; crumpled newspapers and junk mail piled up on my small, unsteady kitchen table alongside a plate of half-eaten bread; the walls bare except for a few full-page newspaper ads of clothing or cars I had hung up to cover odd stains and cracks. It was too warm—my heater acting up again—and I immediately went to the window and opened it. I kicked aside much of the mess.

I offered to make her some coffee, and she agreed. She took off her raincoat and sat at the kitchen table, watching me pour the grinds into the coffee filter. The music downstairs began, and we felt the beat through the floor. I couldn't recognize the song. Marlene continued to look around the small studio, and as I prepared the coffee, I sneaked glances at her, trying to guess her thoughts. I couldn't. She fanned her neck and said, "Warm."

I told her about the broken heater which either didn't work or didn't turn off. I sat on the mattress as the coffee maker gurgled. Marlene's perfume travelled past me and out the window, a flowery smell that made my nose itch. She stood, walked to the mattress and sat next to me.

"So what do you *do* with your time?" she asked.

I thought about Gorden's letters, and worried for a minute that the envelopes with Mona's name might be discovered. They were stacked on the counter, under a dish. No, they were fine. The letters themselves were piled by my bed, underneath a half-filled coffee mug. "I read. Sometimes I take walks," I said.

"Don't you get lonely?"

"Lonely?"

She waited for my answer. Lonely. I could not imagine my life any differently, and the thought of being someone like Roger Shin—with a family, an important job, responsibility—frightened me. Though at another extreme, Gorden, who was now completely alone, frightened me even more since the absences in his life were now significant, acute. "Not really," I finally said to her, standing up to get the coffee.

"Everybody gets lonely," she said as I cleaned out two mugs, trying to scrape off some dried bits of soup in one.

I nodded while I poured the coffee.

"Black is fine," she said.

I told her about the Kahlua.

"I'd like that."

When I finally sat down next to her, I asked her if she had to call her son, to let him know where she was.

"No. It's okay," she said. She sipped her coffee and looked at me from behind the mug. "Did you know that some of the people at the diner are talking about us?" she asked.

"About us?"

"Yeah. They think we're an item."

I smiled. "An item."

I am not sure how this happened, but it seemed right. We put our coffee mugs down on the floor, and while the music below us continued to thump out a steady beat, we leaned towards each other slowly. Both of us knew what was happening. The mattress creaked as we leaned forward to kiss, her lips warm from the coffee, and I smelled the Kahlua on my breath as well as hers. I was sensitive to everything around me at that precise moment: the noise downstairs, the squeaking mattress springs as our weights shifted, perfume and coffee and Kahlua mingling around us, cars speeding by outside, an occasional swelling of music whenever the door of Lucky's was open, sounds drifting through my window, the feel of her rough hand against mine, the slight taste of cigarettes. I wanted to be closer to Marlene, and I felt, for the first time in a while, despite all that had happened and was happening in my life and in Gorden's life, despite the depression that had been hovering over me for the past five months, I felt within me a sense of everything falling into place and my life not being so confusing and frightening; I felt content.

7

Gorden used a bowie knife he had borrowed from the camping section to puncture Shin's tires. He had to be very careful since he wanted a slow leak. He didn't know if the car alarm would go off if the tire went flat right away, the shift in the position in the car could trigger something, so he planned to make small but damaging holes. It was ten-thirty and the Memorial Day sale had just ended. Shin and John would be working for at least two more hours, calculating receipts, checking inventory, but Gorden wanted to be sure that Shin wouldn't be home soon. Of course Shin would call a tow truck or a cab, but these kinds of delays were necessary if Gorden was going to see Helen tonight, alone.

A few people were approaching, so Gorden left the knife hidden behind a tire and stood up, walking away, acting like he was looking for his own car. Most of the parking lot had cleared, but a few stragglers from the food court were now leaving as the mall closed. Gorden waited until the cars had driven away before approaching Shin's sedan. He knelt back down and began pushing the tip of the knife in between the treads, moving slowly until he felt the rubber give. He hoped a few small holes would do the job.

Gorden's hands still hurt from setting up the tent this evening. Shin wanted everyone to begin the preparations for camping season. The Memorial Day sale wasn't even finished and Shin was thinking ahead to the next one. The tent Gorden had set up was a new Greatland 10 x 14 feet Sierra with an 84 inch center height, not one of those easy pup tents Gorden was used to constructing. Shin wanted a big tent this time, and the Sierra, which sleeps nine, was the one he chose. The whole damn thing took Gorden two hours to put up because the poles kept slipping on the carpet. He had to tape the ends and even dig them into the carpet, probably leaving small holes but he didn't care since it was Shin's idea to put up the fucking thing anyway. Now Gorden's hands hurt from all the gripping and pulling.

Moving to the other tire—the right one seemed to be leaking slowly—Gorden hurried and pushed the blade into the rubber. He didn't want to waste any more time here. Just finish this and go, he told himself, not quite sure what he was going to say to Helen, but he had to meet her and talk. He had to know why she was doing this.

There. He went a little too deep and he heard the faint hissing. He sheathed the knife and hurried to his car, not wanting to be around if Shin's alarm went off. Ten forty-five. Susy would be asleep. Helen would be alone. Driving out of the Yanack Hills Mall parking lot, Gorden took a deep breath and prepared himself.

The light over the door flickered on as Gorden knocked again. He stood back to let Helen see him. "What do you want?" he heard her say through the closed door.

"It's me. I want to talk."

"I told you not to come here," she said.

"Please open the door. I can't hear you."

Silence, then she knocked on the side window as she opened the curtains a few inches. "Gorden," she said through the closed window, her voice muffled. She leaned forward. "I told you never to come here again." She was in a white robe.

"I just want to talk," he said. "Let me in and—"

"No. Raj will be back soon."

Gorden shook his head. "The sale just ended. He'll be there for at least another hour and half."

"I'm going to bed. Please go." She closed the curtain.

"Okay," he said loudly, and continued knocking on the door. "I'll just stay here," he raised his voice even more, "and wait until you see me. I might even YELL a little."

"Gorden!" she said, back at the window. "Be quiet! The neighbors."

"I'm not LEAVING until you LET me—"

"Okay! Stop it. Wait a second." She disappeared behind the curtains and unlocked the bolts. When she opened the door a few inches she said, "Gorden. I'm getting very angry. I told you to leave me alone."

"Just let me in."

"I can call the police, you know."

"You can. And then I'll tell them why I'm here."

Her face hardened. "Okay, Gorden. What do you want?"

"Let me in."

"No."

"I'll raise my voice," he said.

"Damn it. Just tell me what you—"

Gorden pushed open the door, surprising Helen, and he slipped in. She stepped back, her eyes wider and her hands gripping the lapels of her robe.

"What the hell do you think you're doing?" she asked.

Gorden felt his throat tighten, his neck becoming warm. He was in. He looked around.

"What is it?" she asked. "What do you want?"

He walked into the living room and sat on the couch. Helen watched him, and after a minute she closed the front door and followed.

"Why are you acting like this?" he asked. "What's going on?"

"Gorden, are you stupid? Can't you see? I can't do this anymore. I don't want to."

"You can't just jerk me around like that."

"Who do you think you are? You can't come in like this. Don't you understand? It's over. No more. I can't see you anymore."

"Why?"

"Look at you! You show up here all the time, you're careless and you don't think. It's not worth it."

"So if I'm more careful?"

"No." She shook her head. "I don't want to do this anymore. Please go, Gorden. I'm very tired."

Gorden stared at her, not really listening, not concentrating. How could she just drop it like that? He stood up. "I miss you," he said.

"Please go."

He walked towards her and she held her hand up, backing away. "Stop. I'm not doing anything. Do you hear me?" she said, her voice rising. "You better go."

For the first time, Gorden thought he heard fear. She was afraid of him? He studied her, and she blinked hard a few times, her forehead wrinkling each time she squeezed her eyes closed. He said, looking down. "I really miss you."

She didn't say anything.

Gorden sat back down on the couch. "Come on, Helen. I promise to be more careful."

"I won't say this again," she said, her voice wavering. "I want you to go."

"Not until you promise to see me again."

She pushed her fingers into the center of her forehead. Gorden stood up and took her hand, pulling her towards the couch. She resisted.

"Just sit down," he said. She did.

"We can still see each other," he said, touching her arm. She drew back. "No. All I want is for us to be like before."

She stared at him.

"Just like we used to be." He touched her leg.

Helen moved away and rubbed her eyes. "Don't do this, Gorden."

He couldn't help himself—he moved next to her and started touching her arms lightly, running his fingers up and down them. He wouldn't let her pull away, and he stared at her smooth skin, her neck, her face.

She began crying silently. "Please go."

Gorden stopped and stared at her, horrified. Crying? Wait. Nothing was working the way he had wanted it to. He had thought she would see things his way, that he would convince her, but now everything was wrong, completely wrong.

Then the phone rang, startling them both. She jumped up, sniffed, and answered the phone. "Hello... What?..." She glanced at Gorden. "No, I'm fine... Right now?... Oh, okay... I will..." She hung up and stared at the phone. "I have to pick up Raj. His tires are flat."

It hadn't occurred to him that Shin would call her.

She turned to him, her eyes red, her face flushed. "You did that, didn't you," she said.

He was silent.

"Get the hell out of here."

Gorden shook his head. "All right. I didn't mean anything. It's only that—"

"Just get out of here."

He sighed and walked towards the door, not sure why everything was going wrong. He turned and said, "Helen..."

She shook her head, not looking in his direction. As Gorden left the apartment, he knew he had fucked up. There was nothing he could do right now except drive around for a while, and then go back to his house. He would go back to his empty house and be alone.

Part IV
Father's Day Sale

1

She picked up her sleeping daughter, who writhed and tried to struggle out of her arms, Susy's small chubby cheeks avoiding a kiss. Helen shushed her, and said they were going for a short ride, to pick up Daddy. Helen had washed her face and dressed quickly, but only after checking out the window to be certain that Gorden had left. She was sure of something else too: he was crazy. She had had an affair with a man who was crazy, and now he was threatening her, trying to use her. But there was a way out of this.

Susy fought being dressed and carried outside, and her soft whine grated Helen's frayed nerves. Please, Helen thought as she patted Susy's back, Be good. She walked carefully down the stairs to her car, the late evening air cool against her damp face, and she held Susy tighter, hoping to keep her warm. She looked up and down the street, checking to see if Gorden was around—she was expecting anything at this point. Except for a few cars driving by, the streets were quiet. This is a nightmare, she said to herself, walking towards her Rabbit. I am in a nightmare.

After strapping her daughter into the safety seat, Helen climbed into the front, and started the engine, unsure of what she was going to say to Raj. She had to be direct and wanted to make sure he understood that it had meant nothing. It had been a terrible mistake. But she knew Raj wouldn't care. All this meant to him was that she had cheated on him, that she had lied and had snuck around behind his back. And the fact that it had been Gorden... well, she had no idea how Raj would react to that.

Helen began pulling out of her parking space when suddenly there was a loud honk, and a car swerved around her, still honking. She slammed on the brakes and lurched forward. Susy gasped, then began crying. The car that had swerved around her drove on, honking again angrily. Helen's heart thumped as she realized she had pulled out without looking behind her. Her hands shook as she put the car in park and turned to check on Susy. Her daughter was all right, just startled by the sudden movements, though Helen herself was still rattled, having to sit quietly for a few minutes to calm herself. Susy quieted down. Helen checked her mirrors and looked behind her a few times before tentatively pulling out and heading towards the highway. Raj was at a gas station right next to the mall. She exhaled slowly.

I have something important to tell you, she practiced, not sure whether to wait until they returned home or to tell him right away. What was he going to say to her? She began to feel queasy. How could she have done that, have an affair? It wasn't *really* her, but someone else. An unthinking, bored housewife. On 89 heading south, she began thinking about that girl who had killed herself. Maybe Gorden had driven her to it, and now that she was dead, Gorden was beginning to work on Helen. Work on Helen? Gorden was some kind of devil. He wanted to kill her. He wanted her to kill herself, like the girl, and wouldn't stop until she did.

Helen stared at the empty road, feeling her stomach sinking

with every mile closer she came to Raj.

Gorden stormed into his house and flung his jacket across the room, watching it turn and tumble until it hit the far wall, swishing onto the floor into a small heap. He began pacing the floor, and shook his head. He had fucked up. He knew it as soon as he saw her face. She didn't want to see him anymore, and if he had had a chance to change her mind, he had ruined it by showing up like that again. Goddamn it all. He went into the kitchen and grabbed a beer from the refrigerator. Now what the fuck was he going to do? She hated his guts.

Gorden sat on the couch and began watching TV, not bothering to change the channel when he saw a nature show on. He noticed it was a public television station on the UHF dial. Then he realized that the last person to watch the TV probably had been Shari, and maybe she had been watching something like this that night...

"Fucking stop it," he said aloud, shaking his head. Christ. He couldn't go two seconds in this fucking house without thinking about her. What would he be doing if she were home? Maybe he would bitch to her about work—his hands still ached—and then they'd drink together. Maybe they'd even fool around. He remembered the times he had come home and yelled at her for no reason except that he had been in a shitty mood. What an asshole I was, he thought. She'd done nothing and he'd been a mean bastard. The broken key chain, he thought, suddenly. Now he couldn't remember where he had put it. Why did he have to break it like that? Why was he so mean?

He put the beer bottle on his forehead, rolling it back and forth. Shit. He missed Shari. He never thought he'd hear himself say this, but he really missed her. Gorden felt self-pity weighing on him, and he gulped his beer down. You miserable piece of shit, he said to himself, staring at a porcupine waddling across a field on the TV show. He finished the beer and dropped the bottle; it bounced off the cushion and fell onto the floor, breaking. He jumped away.

"Fucking great," he said. He stared at the broken pieces of brown glass on the floor. Sharp jagged points stuck up, and he pushed one with his foot. He kicked off his right shoe and pressed a piece of glass with his toe, the brown sock protecting his skin. What did it feel like? Gorden reached down and picked up a jagged piece. He pressed the tip against the back of his hand. Sharp. He dragged the glass across his skin and saw the white trail. He drew some curvy lines. What had it felt like for Shari? He dragged the glass further up his arm until it was against his forearm. He pressed harder, watching the tip indent his skin. He heard Shari's voice ask, Can you just *feel* it? But no he couldn't, not yet. He pressed harder until the tip of the glass broke through his skin, and a small dot of blood appeared at the puncture. He pressed again and dragged the glass against the skin, opening it. A pinch. He lifted the glass and examined the cut: blood began seeping out of the one-inch wound, small droplets forming at the edges. He stared. So this is what it feels like, he thought. It didn't even hurt. Gorden realized how easy it was. How easy it had been for her.

When Helen put Susy back to bed, she heard Raj in the kitchen fixing himself something to eat. She hadn't been able to tell him in the car, and simply listened to him complain about some vandals who had slashed his tires. He continued talking about the sale, and how well they had done, and it looked like, if things continued, they could leave this place by mid-summer, probably after July 4th. Helen had wondered if she could somehow avoid this whole mess until then, until they left, and then she would never have to worry about it again. But no, it wasn't that easy. They still had over a month to go, and who knew what would happen by then? Maybe she could take Susy and move to Boston first, setting up for when Raj would follow. He wouldn't like that though. He'd want to know why, and dismiss it as unnecessary.

Helen kissed Susy again, and walked into the kitchen, sitting with Raj while he ate leftover chicken. "I can re-heat that for you," she said.

"It's fine," he said. He had taken off his tie and unbuttoned the top of his shirt. There was a thin film of sweat on his forehead.

"You look warm," she said.

"All this running around."

God, how was she going to tell him? She stood and went to the sink for a glass of water. What would happen if she just didn't say anything? Maybe Gorden had gotten the message and he wouldn't do anything, wouldn't bother her anymore. Maybe all that had happened was now forgotten.

Right. She ran her index finger around the rim of the wet glass, mentally composing a small speech. Raj said something which she hadn't heard. "What?" she asked, turning around.

"It's really late. Sorry for dragging you out."

She shook her head absently and smiled. Sorry? He was apologizing to her? It was almost comical, and she was glad she at least still had her sense of humor. Her husband wiped some grease off his lips and drank his milk, which reminded her of a little boy after a big meal. In fact she could picture Raj as a child, even more than the pictures she had seen of him when he had first come over from Korea, wearing green polyester pants and a white button-up shirt. She almost expected Raj to have a milk mustache after he finished his glass, but he wiped his mouth again and stood up with the dish and empty glass, pushing the chair back as he rose.

"I should get some sleep," he said.

"Raj..." she began, watching him shake the chicken bones into the garbage and place the dish and glass into the sink slowly, deliberately, so as not to clink the dishes together.

He looked up.

"I think we have to talk."

You can imagine for yourselves the scene that followed— Helen wavering as she prefaced her revelation with apologies and regrets, then crying as she told him what she had done; the disbelief of her husband slowly turning into anger. Since this was the first time anything like this had happened to the Shins, I imagined they followed a familiar script of distress and shock, repentance and anger, defensiveness and threats. By no means do I intend to trivialize their conflict, but what interested me was not their fight but what was to follow. In this script Helen exited stage left, retiring to her room while her husband lay down on the sofa, unable to understand any of this. It was a strange feeling being cuckolded, and more than anything else at this point, after his anger had been exhausted, he felt foolish. How could he have missed all the clues? Of course *now* he saw the signs, the changes in behavior, schedules, the phone callers hanging up, the empty messages on the machine, the baby-sitter. He became queasy as he thought about the baby-sitter—he had called here once, speaking to her, and had thought nothing of it. He'd been so blind! Why hadn't he *seen* this?

Gorden. Now it made sense, he thought. At first Gorden had been difficult but there had been a change. The reason was clear: he had been having sex with his wife. How Gorden must have been laughing behind his back! And the others... did they know? Were they also making fun of him?

Gorden. Shin knew exactly what he was going to do with him. How could Helen have fallen for *him*? It was unbelievable. And wasn't it obvious that Gorden had done it to get back at his boss? That she had been used? Was Shin the only person who saw this? He tried not to stay angry at her but he couldn't help it. Maybe *he* should sleep with other women to get back at her, to show her what it felt like, but he really didn't want to. This was what angered him, that she would want to sleep with someone else. He wanted only to be with her, but she didn't feel the same way. He could get a divorce—he knew some of the best lawyers in Boston—and destroy her. It'd be so easy. She had cheated on him. She had left Susy with a baby-sitter. She had let Susy get sick. She was an unfit mother. Didn't she know that? But he didn't want to do that. But didn't she know that he could?

He wasn't sure what to do next. Maybe they should see someone about this, a counselor, a minister. Maybe they should separate for a while. He didn't know if he should get back at her, or if he should try to forgive her. But he wanted to stay angry for a while. He heard Helen crying in the bedroom and he felt like his heart was being squeezed. But he didn't want her to stop crying.

2

Marlene smiled when I saw her the next evening at the diner. She didn't say anything as she passed me, her hands filled with a tray of food, hamburger smells lingering around her, and our eyes met. She winked. So it *did* happen, I thought as I went into the kitchen. I wasn't sure because when I had awakened this morning, she had been gone. Last night was very unclear. I actually found myself searching the bed sheets for stains, and when I couldn't find any, I thought perhaps I had dreamed the entire evening. There was no note, no lipstick on the coffee mugs... nothing. I had slept with a ghost.

But the wink seemed to confirm the previous evening, and a few very distinct things became more real: We had turned off the lights, but the street lamps outside filled the room with a yellow tint. Odd shadows formed on our faces and bodies, our contours heightened and distorted, and I couldn't recognize her in this darkness, noses and cheekbones elongated. I saw her bare arms, skin slightly wrinkled with some birth marks. Her hands were strong and thin with hard knuckles and gold rings on her index and middle fingers. Her nails were long and I could feel them when she held my shoulder. She massaged me, kneading my arms slowly until I relaxed. She undressed me.

Because I had been washing dishes for almost seven hours, I had trouble concentrating. I remembered Marlene slowing me down, telling me that there was no hurry, to take it easy. I became nervous. I tried too hard, and needed a few gentle reminders from her. The last thing I remembered was listening to Marlene's heart beating loudly and steadily, lulling me. That must have put me to sleep.

Thinking about it now, while I was stacking dishes in the machine and hosing down the glasses, I began to get aroused, and busied myself. I was embarrassed, though no one saw me. Everything seemed to remind me of sex. The noises of the dishwasher, the hose, the sudsy water, the wine glasses, and I shook my head, telling myself to stop that. Think about other things. I concentrated on arranging the plates so that they would not strike each other when the cycle began, and I became engrossed in alternating the large and small dishes along the rack, maintaining a sufficient buffer between the tops of the large dishes, the area where there seemed to be the most breakage. The inside of the dish-washing machine was cavernous, dripping with water from the top, a few splattered pieces of food stuck on the bottom filter, dark, damp, and warm. I wondered what it was like to be in here when the machine was on, the furious jets of steaming water from the tentacle-like arms with small holes, arms placed at the bottom and center of the cavern, rotating relentlessly throughout the cycle.

While I ran the machine, I finished the glasses, stacked them, and leaned against the sink. It was a busy evening with the cooks sweating by the ovens and grills, their white aprons and small paper hats looking like shower caps. Only the head chef wore the tall billowing white kind I had seen on television shows, the kind that mushroomed above the head. The cooks on the cold side were also hurrying, chopping up lettuce and a myriad of vegetables for the salads, scooping bowls of macaroni and tortellini and dumping them on large green leaves. Next to the salads a cook was preparing a dessert, spraying whipped cream designs on a large chocolate cake, adding cherries in symmetrical patterns. Sounds of chopping, frying, pots and pans clanging, my dishwasher thumping—soothing sounds of the kitchen.

My thoughts traveled to Gorden. I thought he was getting what he deserved, yet at the same time I couldn't help feeling mixed emotions. Picturing him at his empty house, I saw him cutting himself with that piece of glass and then finding a napkin to stop the bleeding. He wasn't alarmed at what he had done, rather, he accepted his actions as logical connections to Shari, feeling what she had felt, at least physically. It seemed that with each day, instead of distancing himself from Shari, he wound up closer to her, perhaps more than he had ever been. It was her absence that triggered this, and he viewed his previous behavior towards her with shock. Had he really been that shitty to her, he thought. Had that been him? Yeah, it had been him, and he had been more than shitty; he had probably driven her to kill herself.

Later in the evening, Marlene walked into the kitchen to place an order on the wheel, calling out for two cheeseburgers. She saw me stacking dishes into the cart and walked towards me. I stood up and smiled. She said to me, "Let's meet at Lucky's after work, okay?"

I nodded, but before I could say anything, she turned and walked back out. I wasn't sure if she was being curt with me, or if she was simply in a hurry. Did she regret our evening together? We had known each other for only a short time, and perhaps we had rushed into this. Although I didn't expect anything more after last night, I wondered if this would change everything, if she would no longer wish to spend time with me, or, if she would want me to become a part of her life. I was so unused to this that I began to have such wild thoughts as, What if I have to meet her son, who was only a few years younger than me? Or, What if she considered last night a terrible mistake and never wanted to see me again?

I tried not to let my anxiety grow, but as the night progressed I became more nervous with this impending meeting. I thought she would tell me, Look, Last night was a mistake. Let's forget it happened.

With my imagined scenarios running through my head, I almost came to accept the fact that Marlene and I would no longer be friends and what had happened was an aberration in my solitary life. A glitch in my otherwise continuous monotony. I began to think of our relationship in the past tense—it was nice while it lasted—and after my shift was over and I couldn't find Marlene anywhere (Had she left without me?) I used this fact to confirm my theory. This was the end.

I left the diner and walked in the cool night air, wondering why it still hadn't warmed up yet. I remembered that last year by this time it had been hot, especially in the classrooms where I opened all the windows and left the door ajar, though I had not liked the open door, since other teachers and students could surreptitiously hear me teaching. This year winter extended into spring, and spring bled into summer. Trees turned green later. Hot, sweltering days had not yet arrived. Perhaps it was my own disconcerting sense of time, since I was no longer teaching and lived not by the calendar of holidays, or, like Gorden and Shin, from sale to sale.

There were more people out later now, and the diner usually stayed crowded until closing time, with customers lingering at their tables, by the front foyer, in the parking lot, talking, trying to prolong the evening, and I watched a few cars drive off the lot before I began walking towards my building. There was a group of teenagers in front of a car, some sitting on the hood, others standing, and they were all talking at once, laughing.

When I arrived, I saw the cars parked in front of Lucky's, a big crowd tonight, and walked in, scanning the tables filled with customers. Marlene was at the bar, sitting with her legs crossed, her foot resting on the horizontal peg of the stool, and she was looking up at the TV, a cigarette in her fingers. The jukebox was playing Clapton's "Layla" and the noise from the voices and music filled the bar.

I went to her, and when she turned to me, I saw her smile and wink—another amused, conspiratorial wink with a small tilt of her head. Everything that I had been worrying about before seemed stupid and foolish, and I knew then as I sat down next to her and her foot touched my shin and she offered her beer to me, which I drank gratefully, and through the noise and music and TV and yelling and laughing I heard her say, "Hey there, Tiger," and I grinned—I knew everything was all right and that we were going to spend another night together.

Roger Shin sat with his wife at the kitchen table while he finished his breakfast. It looked like she hadn't slept much, her eyes puffy and red, her face sagging and her body moving painfully slow as she got some toast and coffee. She had come to the kitchen and prepared breakfast while he had been taking his shower, which was unusual since she liked to sleep in. They hadn't said a word yet, and Shin knew she was waiting for him to say something first. But there was no hurry—he wanted to make sure what he said was understood, so he prepared his words carefully.

Shin had also slept fitfully, and had often stifled impulses to run into the bedroom and yell at Helen, especially whenever he thought about her actually having sex with Gorden. How many times had it been? It must have been many, many times. And he couldn't avoid the image of Gorden inside Helen, giving her pleasure. This sickened him. Even as the thought passed through him now, he realized his stomach was tightening and he couldn't eat. Helen still hadn't looked directly at him. He considered keeping silent for a while more, but then he cleared his throat and she looked up.

Their eyes met, and she looked away. He finished his coffee, and finally said, "First." His voice startled them both. She stared at the plate in front of him. "First, you do not speak to him or see him ever again. Not even on the phone. Not one word."

She nodded. "Of course," she said quietly. She rubbed her eyes and nodded again. They heard Susy getting up in her room.

"He's not to know anything. Do you understand? He cannot

know that I know."

She looked up, surprised, and tightened her bathrobe. "Why?"
He shook his head and said, "That doesn't matter. Do you
understand what I'm saying? Not one word."

She nodded slowly, watching him now. Susy walked into the
bathroom, and they heard her trying to use the toilet.

"Second, you are to stay here with Susy until we can talk. I don't
want you to leave Susy with any," he paused, letting the word
sound distasteful, "baby-sitter." He heard his taxicab outside. He
finished his coffee quickly. "Finally, I want you to know that I'm not
sure I can forget this, forgive you. Ever. I'm not sure yet." He stood
up, not waiting for a response, and grabbed his coat. Walking into
the bathroom and seeing Susy on the toilet bowl too big for her, legs
dangling and her body balanced forward, he smiled and said hello.
He kissed her on the top of her head and told her he would see her
tonight. "Okay, daddy," she replied with an adult-like clarity that
surprised him.

"Do you need help?"

She shook her head defiantly.

Not even glancing at his wife as he grabbed his briefcase and
left the apartment, he knew she was staring at him. He tensed his
jaw, closing the front door quickly. He really didn't know what he
was going to do or say to her tonight, and the only thing he wanted
to make clear was for her not to have any contact with Gorden. The
thought of them exchanging just one word angered him. He hurried down the stairs and waved to the cab driver. He'd have to pick
up his car later. Then he wondered if his tires being slashed had
anything to do with Gorden. There couldn't have been vandals in
the mall lot, could there? Shin climbed into the cab, throwing his
briefcase on the seat next to him, and tried not to get too angry. He'd
get his, Shin thought of Gorden. He'd get what was coming.

Gorden walked into Jakeson's showroom tired and hung over.
He had finished a six-pack last night because he had been restless

and wanted to relax. Now, while he checked the clock and saw that he was ten minutes early, Gorden tried to ignore the dull ache in his temples and the heaviness in his limbs. The cut on his forearm was bandaged, but hurt a little whenever he made a fist.

The Memorial Day Sale signs had already been taken down, and Gorden knew that today they would begin reorganizing, restocking, and deciding which things to leave on display. He saw the fishing poles in disarray, some out of their racks, tangled; tackle boxes left open, the arrangement of weights, bobbers, lures, and hooks lying on the bottom of the case. Next to the fishing poles was the tent he had put up, and today he had to furnish it with a cot, a small collapsible table, maybe a sleeping bag, lanterns, and other camping equipment. He didn't mind that part; it was just setting it up that was a pain. John walked out of the stockroom with a large box and nodded to Gorden.

Gorden asked if there was anything planned today.

"Just the clean-up. Maybe more setting up."

"Shin wants to do that already?"

John shrugged and continued walking, carrying baseballs. Gorden saw the labels: Rawlings National and American League Balls ($7.97) and Official League Balls ($3.97). "Did the sale do well?" Gorden asked.

John turned. "Real well. Cleared thirty this weekend."

As John went to rearrange the baseball section, organizing the Louisville Slugger display and the Rawlings Signature Series mitts, Gorden looked around the store, impressed. It seemed that Shin really was doing *something* to bring in the cash. Maybe those commercials and coupons helped. Also, Gorden knew that since it was warming, sports were on people's minds more.

Gorden saw Shin at his desk, and didn't bother to say hello, since Shin always looked too busy. Right now he was on the phone, writing something. He didn't look up. Gorden went to his desk and looked through his calendar. Today was going to be a slow day— he wanted to calculate the commissions for the past weekend, and he had to check the inventory for the Father's Day Sale, coming in three weeks. They'd definitely do good business then.

Shin hung up the phone, turned, and said, "Gorden, I think we need to fix the camping aisles."

Gorden waited.

"We need to put the camping and fishing together, in a corner, for the next sale. I want it fixed up." Shin leaned back in his chair. "I want you to take the tent and the camping gear, and move it with the fishing supplies, and set up a nice display in the corner."

"Move it?"

"All of it."

"But that'll take days to—"

"If you can't, I could ask Henry or Norma."

Gorden stared at him, confused. It didn't make sense to rearrange the entire display, especially for a sale. Would they have to move it back once it was over? As it was, Gorden liked the aisle arrangement of the sporting goods. And also the tent—that goddamn tent—would have to be taken down and put up again. Shit. But not in any mood to argue, Gorden thought that maybe Shin knew what he was talking about, so Gorden nodded and said, "Okay. I'll begin in a few minutes."

Shin said, "And try to finish it today, before you leave."

"What?"

"Finish before tonight."

"You're kidding."

Shin stared at him, then shook his head.

"You want me to move all that shit in one day?" Gorden asked.

"That is what I said." He went back to his work.

Gorden stood up and walked out of the office. Maybe it wasn't as hard as he thought; he had to look at the displays and see what needed to be done. He knew how he would do this: set up the tent and arrange the camping equipment around that, and then move the fishing aisle next to it. The display stands, just long metal shelving with a green felt-lined base, could be moved by using a special dolly, so that wouldn't be too hard. Gorden looked at the two aisles of camping gear and the aisle of fishing equipment, and thought, Yeah, I could do this. He saw the corner where all this would go; right now it was filled with winter jackets that had to be stored anyway. He rolled up his sleeves, and began by moving the racks of jackets out of the way. He glanced at the wall clock. It would be a long day.

Gorden took down the tent, but only after undoing the poles and collapsing them. All he had to do was drag the tent across the floor. He put the tent back up, being careful with his fingers this time, and trying not to push the poles too deeply into the carpet. He placed in the tent the Coleman 2 Mantle Propane Lantern ($16.91) with the Wenzel sleeping bags (Cheyenne, $34.96; American Eagle, $29.94) on top of a Greatland folding bed ($29.99), a Coleman Polylite 40 quart cooler ($19.94), and a Greatland folding table ($29.99). Then he arranged a small display of camping appliances outside the tent—propane and fluorescent lanterns, butane heaters, cooksets, flashlight combinations packs. Gorden was just getting started. He inserted the special pneumatic dollies under the fishing displays and wheeled them next to the camping equipment, making sure the conventional and spinning rods were separated and shown side by side, their names and prices visible. All along this display he rearranged the lure kits by type of fish; Salmon/ Steelhead, Trout and Bass, and next to these placed Berkley, Maxima, and Stren packs of fishing lines. By the time this was finished, he had missed lunch, but ignored his rumbling stomach. He still had a lot to do.

When Gorden finally completed the new display, it was six-thirty, a half hour past quitting time. He stood near the center of the showroom, viewing the new camping and fishing corner with a customer's eye. The tent was the centerpiece and looked inviting, asking him to come in and look around. The fishing aisles were to the right of the tent, and the extra camping goods to the left, underneath the extended flap. Except for a possible problem with crowding, it was fine. Gorden was exhausted, but he didn't mind the tiredness in his arms and legs, the sweat on his back. The cut on his arm throbbed. He walked towards the office.

"I'm done," Gorden said as he opened the door, seeing Shin at his desk, drinking coffee.

"I noticed."

"In one day, like you said."

Shin nodded. "Don't go just yet. I have to tell you something."

Gorden paused and tried to remain calm, not liking the tone of his voice. Serious. It could be anything. He folded his arms and asked, "Yes?"

"Because of the way things are going, I'm going to have to let you go, like I did Warren."

Gorden stared at him and pressed his arms tighter into his chest. "But Warren was part-time."

"And now I have to let a full-time go."

"But I thought the store was doing better—"

"A few good sales won't change much. I have to overhaul many things."

Gorden began shaking his head slowly, trying to understand. "It don't make any sense. I've been doing a good job."

Shin didn't reply. He sipped his coffee and watched Gorden. Shin's shirt wrinkled along the chest whenever he brought the mug to his mouth. Gorden couldn't tell what he was thinking, the face blank.

Gorden looked out the two-way mirror and saw his display. All that work. "And Christ, you made me do that, knowing you were going to fire me?"

"I knew you could do it."

"Son of a bitch."

Shin raised his eyebrows, just like Helen did. "Don't get upset. You knew things were bad here."

But Gorden was too tired to get upset. He stared at this man in front of him, a short, balding Korean man whose wife Gorden had fucked. Ah, maybe that was it, he thought. Helen must have told him. This was the only reason he could see. He knew his work here was good, but it didn't seem to matter. Gorden couldn't help smiling. Shin looked surprised. "I know damn well this has nothing to do with the store, or my job," Gorden said, shaking his head. "You poor fucking bastard."

Shin's face reddened and he stood up quickly. "What do you mean?" he demanded.

Gorden laughed. "She told you, didn't she? Ah well, that's that. I should've known this'd happen. But I feel really sorry for you."

Shin tensed.

"She sure was nice in bed."

Shin made two fists and held them to his side. "I said you're fired. Get out."

Gorden laughed again and glanced at his desk. Nothing he wanted there. He turned to leave. Why wasn't he angry? What was going on? It seemed like nothing mattered anymore. He passed John's desk and wondered if John had known about this. Probably. And Henry. Henry would probably get his position. The kiss-ass got what he wanted. These sons of bitches had it out for him and he couldn't win. "Man," he said quietly as he headed for the door, "was she nice in bed."

Suddenly he felt a push from behind, and he fell forward, grabbing the door for support. He whirled around. Shin was facing him, shaking. "Get out now."

Amazing, Gorden thought, how easy it is to get this guy pissed. "I'm going, but do you really think it's over?" He walked out, not waiting for a response. As he left the showroom, Gorden saw Henry and John by his new camping display and John waved and said, "Nice job," but Gorden ignored him. He walked out of the store and felt a strange sense of relief as he passed beneath the Jakeson's sign, even though he knew he was in trouble. But he no longer had to come to this goddamn store, and now that he thought about it, he didn't even like sporting goods all that much. That son of a bitch Shin. Gorden couldn't have stomached working for him any longer anyway. But now what the hell was he going to do?

Gorden left the mall, feeling freer than he had ever felt, but he was exhausted and aching and all he wanted to do right now was sleep.

3

I told Marlene about Gorden being fired when she and I were walking around the neighborhood before our shift began, the weather cool and breezy, the sun falling behind large oak trees. She wanted to know more. "How did he take it?" she asked. "What about the wife?"

I didn't know if I should tell her too much, since I was still uncomfortable about reading the letters, at least uncomfortable about revealing this fact, and this was made more acute when Gorden began writing me in longhand, since he no longer had access to the store's computer. The letter writer suddenly became more real, since what I was reading was written directly by Gorden. No electronic artifice, no dot matrix intermediary. His hands had held the paper steady while he had pressed down hard with the pen, scribbling notes to his substitute sister. Though the handwriting on the envelope was always neat and legible, the writing in the letter was not, and it took me longer to read, to decipher. The letters were also lengthier, running for pages without much punctuation, and this, coupled with the handwriting, made my task more frustrating since very often I could not figure out what a word or a line was, no matter how hard I tried to trace the individual letters or words themselves, and despite the context of the sentence or paragraph, I had to give up that missing piece and hope it wasn't important. One handwriting quirk which was very annoying was his tendency to make his "a's", "o's" and "u's" similar, just small loops rising from the line with very few distinguishing features. Nevertheless, I studied these letters as if I were back in school, reading over textbooks and reams of notes by someone I had never met but whose words I had almost memorized, and when he wrote me about his last day at Jakeson's, I wasn't surprised by Shin's actions. Actually, I had expected this to happen much earlier, but Helen was more reticent than I had anticipated. Telling her husband about her affair must have been agonizing, but once she had done it, she must have felt relieved, no matter what the consequences would be. I imagined she spent that day after her revelation alone or with Susy, not leaving the apartment, as her husband had instructed. She knew Raj could be vindictive, and worried about what might happen at work. I imagine she expected something like giving Gorden a hard time and pressuring him to quit. She expected this to get messy, and there was nothing she could do except sit at home and wait it out.

Marlene asked me again while we sat on the steps of my building. She sat with her chin on her knees, looking out towards the gas station. We were both tired from staying up the night before and watching an old movie—we never found out the title since we came in a quarter of the way through—on my small black and white television set, and we had taken a short walk around the area to help wake us up for our shift which began soon. I felt sorry for her because my job didn't require running back and forth, and I apologized for keeping her up.

"It's okay," she said, turning her head towards me. "But tonight I'll probably go home."

I nodded, disappointed.

"So tell me more about this Gorden guy."

I decided to tell her the story as if Gorden had been writing me for the past few months, an old friend reviving a correspondence. I told her about his new boss, the affair, the end of the affair, and now the firing.

"And his girlfriend's suicide?" she asked when I finished.

I said yes. There were a few times when I considered writing Mr. and Mrs. McCann in Maine, just to find out more about Shari, but I knew it would become too complicated. I continued to dream about her, usually a similar dream in which I was an observer in her life at her parents' house, and after each dream I would wake up and feel an uneasy sadness for her. On one occasion I awakened with Marlene next to me. When she asked me what was wrong, I lied and said I was thirsty.

"Tell me what you're thinking about," Marlene asked me after I had not spoken for a while.

"The suicide."

"She was just a teenager?"

I nodded. "Your son's age." I looked at her, trying to see her thoughts. I couldn't. How odd that the people in Gorden's life were apparently accessible to me, yet Marlene, who was sitting right next to me, was unfathomable. I tried anyway.

"You are thinking," I said slowly. "You are thinking about your son and how he feels about you being gone these days."

She smiled and shook her head.

"You are thinking... that tonight at the diner will be very difficult."

She shook her head again.

"Okay," I said. "I give up."

"I was thinking, really, how little I know about you," she said.

"Oh." I had been way off. Perhaps when I become a part of the design, I lose my objectivity, my observer status. Rather than view the experiment, I become a part of it.

Marlene stretched her legs out and rolled her shoulders, yawning. She moved closer to me so that our arms were touching, and we sat quietly as cars turned off Sunrise onto Harold, many of them pulling into the gas station, the double bells ringing as their tires ran over a long red hose. I liked touching her.

◊

Helen tried to stay awake, waiting for Raj to come home, but it was already past eleven and she wasn't sure where he was. She had called Jakeson's and no one was in, though Raj might have been there and simply refused to answer the telephone. For an instant she wondered if he had run away, abandoned everything and had simply left. But no, he wouldn't do that. He wouldn't leave Susy, the store. Helen stood up and checked on her daughter, watching her from the doorway. Helen had been doing this all evening; she was comforting herself. You have a healthy, beautiful daughter, she kept telling herself. Susy's hair covered her face and she held her fist close to her mouth, breathing on her knuckles. A beautiful daughter.

Walking back to the living room, she stood by the window facing the street and looked out through the curtains. She remembered when she married Raj. Actually they had married twice. The first time they hadn't told anyone, and had driven to the county courthouse on a whim, getting married by the woman who had taken their application and typed it up for them. The woman was young, not more than twenty, and during the ceremony she began her speech with "Marriage is a very solemn and sacred union between a man and a woman..." and Helen tried not to laugh, these words coming from a kid, really. How did she get the authority to marry people? Then she and Raj joined hands and exchanged vows. She felt so strange at the time, not even thinking about the words she was repeating but rather of how unreal it felt to get married. Her nose itched but she didn't want to let go of his hands. She had seen dozens of marriages on TV, in the movies, but hearing those same words—"Do you, Helen, take..."—had been almost frightening. Her heart had been beating so fast.

She went back to the couch and leafed through the TV guide. Nothing on. What would she do if Raj abandoned her? She knew how dependent she was right now—no job, no money, and she hated it. Hated it. But there was Susy. Her lovely Susy. As long as she had Susy, she'd be all right. But so dependent. She couldn't live like this anymore. She lay back and closed her eyes.

When she opened them, much later, Raj was coming in. She sat up, groggy, a sour taste in her mouth, and cleared her throat. "Where were you?" she asked. She blinked, trying to focus.

He looked at her, and said, "Thinking."

Helen waited for him to say more, but he simply threw his coat on a chair and walked towards the bedroom. She stood up and followed. Thinking about what? He couldn't think here? "I thought we were going to talk tonight," she said quietly, not wanting to wake Susy.

"Not tonight," he said. He looked down at his shoes. "I don't feel like it now."

"Okay." She walked into the bedroom, but before she could sit down, he stopped undressing.

"Am I going to sleep outside, or are you?"

She stared at him in surprise, but then nodded. "I guess I will tonight." She left the room and heard him closing the door behind her. She paused, feeling a small pain in her stomach as Raj locked himself in. "I will *not* feel sorry for myself," she whispered. "I will *not*." But it looked liked she had really messed up. She turned off all the lights and lay on the sofa, curling herself up in the corner of the cushions. She knew that Raj would take a long time getting over this, and she better not expect things to improve for a while.

Helen listened to the refrigerator click on and begin humming, rattling something inside, but she didn't want to get up again. She just stared at the soft shadows on the wall, listening to the humming.

Gorden woke up abruptly the next morning, looking wildly around the living room. Christ, he was late. He jumped from the sofa and began dressing, wondering why he had overslept, when he suddenly stopped. He'd been fired. Had that been real? Gorden went back to the couch and sat down heavily, not sure what he should do next. This wasn't the worst that had happened to him. He had lost jobs before—the one that came to mind was his first one, at the sawmill when he had been part of clean-up. There were a bunch of lay-offs and almost fifty employees were gone in one day. Of course, he was just out of high school back then, and didn't have any bills to pay except for car insurance.

He walked into the bedroom and opened his checkbook: Nine hundred left. He pulled out his credit card statements: He owed almost three hundred. Then the mortgage, insurance, utilities, food... He felt a fluttery sense of panic and threw the bills across the table; they scattered and fell on the floor. Now what the fuck to do, he thought. He stood and stared at the unmade bed. When he touched his cheek with his palm, he felt the stubble growing in, and he knew he wanted his beard back.

The sun shone through the bedroom window, lighting the curtains, and Gorden realized that he had never watched the sun fill his bedroom. He had always had to go somewhere—he didn't like staying in bed because he felt like he was wasting time. He opened the curtains and was hit by direct sunlight. Sitting on the bed, he let the sun travel over his body, onto the floor and towards the window. He fell back asleep. For the rest of the morning he drifted in and out of sleep, until he finally pulled himself up and shuffled to the bathroom. He stripped and climbed into the shower, letting the hot water blast his body.

He cursed and jumped out, staring at the tub. This was the first time he had taken a shower since Shari's suicide, and he had completely forgotten about it. As he stood there, dripping on the floor, he realized how stupid he was being and climbed slowly back in. He had become skilled at washing himself from the sink, and had even figured out how to wash his hair (he used a pitcher of warm water). Now, standing in the tub, he knew Shari was becoming more and more unreal. That was why he had forgotten. Looking down at the tub, he could see Shari there again, in the red water, and he quickly soaped and washed himself.

The first thing he did when he dried off and dressed was to call Helen. The answering machine came on and he said, "Helen, this is Gorden. I know you're there. Please pick up." He waited. "Okay. Well, your husband fired me, I'm sure you know, and now I have nothing to lose by calling. Why'd you tell him? Why'd you get me fired? I want to know. I want to talk to you. Call me back." He hung up. She'd never call him, he knew, but he wanted her to know what had happened. Funny how fucked up things get, he thought.

...this day was real strange because I didnt know what the hell to do with myself, you know? I just couldnt pick up a paper and begin looking for another job. I knew then how Shari felt. Damn. Shari again. Fucking stop it! Im sitting around all day watching stupid shows on the TV and I *[illegible]* with nothing to do and its like Im half asleep all day, just doing nothing and feeling nothing. Yeah, I feel like a fucking loser and I should get off my ass but hell, I dont feel like doing anything.

I thought Gorden was taking this very well. He seemed bewildered by this freedom, but I knew what it was like, and I think I did the exact same thing at first—checking my accounts, my bills—when I had been laid off. While reading his handwritten letter, I pictured him lying on the floor for some reason, rather than the couch, blank sheets of paper littered around him, watching television, and when a commercial came on he would go back to writing me. He liked this, in a way, though whenever he thought about why he was here and what he ought to be doing, he felt that familiar unsteadiness in his stomach. It was better that he not worry about it now, and just try to take it easy. This was to be, I would soon learn, a self-deceptive calm, since what really seemed to be going on was his attempt not to lose control.

Shin is nothing but a fucking coward and he shouldnt be with Helen because he dont realize what he got and ~~if it were to me Id~~

I just gotta stop thinking about him because I begin to get mad. I ~~want to kill that goddamn~~ Sometimes I think about me and Helen being together with the kid and what itd be like and that makes me feel better and then I think about how things with Shari couldve been different but its too late now so I try not to think about her. Christ mighty Im going batty doing nothing. I ought to go to the store and knock the hell out of Shin. That fuckhead. I ~~even thought abo~~ Anyway thats whats going on right now.

When I told Marlene about Gorden, about his facade of stability, she didn't seem surprised. "Everyone's a little crazy," she said. "Just that some are better at hiding it than others."

I laughed when she told me this, but it struck me a few days later as true. I tried to think of the sanest person I knew, my adoptive father, but even then I realized that he was just a passing shadow in my life, that I saw him late in the evening in his favorite chair with a newspaper, and on the weekends outside taking care of the lawn. He was steady, trustworthy, and ultimately boring. Yet for a man to work as an amortization specialist for an insurance company for forty years before dying in his sleep from a heart attack, forty years of analyzing intangible assets—he had to be a little crazy to do that. I never knew if he enjoyed the job, since he rarely talked about it, but my mother once said that he had accepted his lot in life and wouldn't complain, which she advised me to do as well. The more I thought about it, the more crazy my father seemed. Maybe he had been an expert at hiding it.

And Shari? I couldn't help but think of her. But she seemed completely sane to me. What people like Shin couldn't understand was that sometimes there was no way out. And, like Gorden, thinking about Shari saddened me, but rather than supress it I chose to imagine all that I could about her. I wondered if there would ever be a point when she would be completely forgotten. Once everyone who had known her died, there would be nothing to continue her memory.

Marlene, if she heard me go on like this, would have told me to lighten up, and I was grateful to be with her during the warming months of approaching summer. I looked forward to seeing her at work, and often when, for various reasons, she couldn't stay with me after our shift ended, I felt her absence and would go down to Lucky's to hear other voices around me, even though I kept to myself and made friends with no one. To this day I am not really sure how I felt about her—if she was just a friend who had come by at a time when I needed one, if she was someone with whom a lasting relationship could have developed if the events that would soon come hadn't occurred. But I know that the sight of her in that light brown waitress uniform always pleased me, and that being physically close to her, feeling the warmth from her hands, touching her hair which, though it looked stringy and rough, was actually very soft, and listening to her talk to me in a low voice almost as if she were talking to herself made me happy. What a sap, Gorden would say, and I would have freely admitted it.

4

Gorden woke up that third morning and decided it was time to see Helen. He took a shower, ignoring the uncomfortable feeling as soon as he stepped in the tub, combed his hair neatly, and checked the beginning of his beard which had grown in about an eighth of an inch. This was the worst time for the beard, when the hair grew straight out and didn't curl much, so he felt like he had to keep patting it down. He noticed in the mirror that he looked different—not just because of his returning beard, but a kind of blankness had taken over his face. A dullness. This was what happened after two days of lying around. He blinked a few times and stretched his mouth open. Wake up, he told himself, slapping himself on the cheek a few times.

"You're an asshole," he said, pointing into the mirror. His

cheek stung. "A fucking asshole." He leaned forward. "A screw-up." He pressed his index finger against the mirror and touched the finger of the man in front of him. "Yes, you. Fucking A. Goddammit. What's next? What else do you have planned?"

He liked how his voice sounded in the bathroom—deeper, stronger. He shaved his neck and clipped a few long hairs from his sideburns. When he finished, he went outside, looking up at the sky. A clear day. Warm. His watch read nine-thirty, so Shin had left his apartment already. Maybe if everything looked all right, he would try to talk with her. He wanted to see how she was doing. Nothing wrong with that, is there, he thought.

When he drove up to Sunolea and parked down the street from Helen's apartment, he saw that her car was still there. She was probably home. Good. He climbed out and looked up and down the street. There was a lot of activity this morning: people walking, stores opening, more traffic than usual. Gorden decided to linger along the street, looking into the stores, waiting for Helen to come out. He was in no hurry. He had all the time he could ever want. He put his hands in his pockets, and moved towards the store near him, the printing shop, and watched a young woman making copies at a large machine. All the time in the world.

By noon, Gorden was no longer sure if Helen was home. Although her car was still parked in front of the building, he thought he ought to check to see if she was there. It was pretty stupid waiting for her if she wasn't even home. Although he hadn't planned on knocking on her door, he thought he would just say hello, but not go into her apartment. The last time he had done that he had made her cry. He didn't want to make her cry. So, Gorden crossed the street and walked slowly up the stairs to the second floor, planning what to say to her.

Peering through her peep hole, he knocked lightly. Movement. Ah, so she *was* home. He knocked again. This time something blocked his view in the hole, and he thought it might be Helen looking out. He didn't move, though, and kept his eye on it. The view cleared. He knocked again. He pulled back and waited. What was she doing? Then he saw part of the curtain in the window next to him move. She must have seen him.

"Helen? I know you're in there. I just wanted to say hello."

No answer.

"Helen... I'm not going to come in or anything. Did you know that he fired me? Why'd you tell him? You didn't have to, you know."

He waited, but again she didn't answer. He knocked on the window, though he didn't mean to hit it as hard as he did, causing it to rattle noisily. "Helen?" He waited. "Okay okay, I'll go. But you didn't have to tell him," he said. "Because now I'm really in a hole." He eventually walked away.

Really in a hole. Where to now?

Helen stood still, leaning against the door, listening. Was he gone? Her head was pounding and she felt a light sweat breaking out on her forehead. Her palms were damp. Was he there? She looked through the security hole and the porch was empty. She let out her breath slowly. He was never going to leave her alone. She couldn't believe that he had come here again. Did he expect her to answer the door after what happened the last time? Please let this be the last time, she said to herself. Please.

Susy walked out of her bedroom, pressed her back to the wall, and stared at her mother. "Mommy go?" she asked. "Mommy go?"

Helen shook her head and smiled. "No. Mommy stay with you. I'm not going anywhere." She turned to check outside one last time, and then made sure the door was securely locked. She couldn't tell Raj about this—he still hadn't completely cooled off yet and this would just make it worse—but she didn't know what she would do if Gorden came by again. Why was he torturing her?

I may have imagined this scene entirely wrong, especially

Helen's reaction, though it seemed to make the most sense at the time. It was possible that Helen was not as distraught as I portrayed, but was instead angry. Perhaps she was standing by the door with her arms folded, shaking her head not out of anxiety or fear, but out of disgust. That stupid man, she could have thought, frowning, listening to him knocking on her door, her window. Who the hell did he think he was? She was tempted to open the door and yell at him, then slam the door in his face, but she didn't want to give him the opportunity to push his way in. No, she'd just let him go away. He had no hold on her anymore, and she could call the police if she wanted to, but she wasn't going to make any more trouble for him. Just go away, she told him silently, and eventually, he did.

Either way, Helen was no longer having anything to do with Gorden, though he told himself that she was upset and now wasn't a good time. He knew he wasn't being honest with himself, that things were becoming more screwed up all the time, but he needed to believe that not everything had gone to hell. His job, yes. But he tried to assure himself that not everything was lost. It was as if he had shut out any opposing voices in his head, and what he wanted to believe became the truth.

He drove into the mall parking lot, finding it fairly crowded. It was strange coming here after a few days away. Everything seemed new. His usual spot had been taken, so he parked a few cars down, and casually made his way towards Jakeson's, stopping at store windows and looking around him to make sure he avoided anyone familiar. The new season brought new displays at Radio Shack— "VCR Clearance!" the sign read—and new styles in the clothing store. Gorden stared at one bald female mannequin with white summer pants and a light blue sailor shirt. Bathing suits hung from wires attached to the ceiling. He walked around the corner, keeping his distance from Jakeson's, and stared into shoe stores, a guitar and keyboard store, more clothing stores, and when he was sure he didn't see anyone he knew, he moved across the floor and stood at Capella's, the women's fashion store right next to Jakeson's.

He looked around the corner, and saw that nothing in the store had changed. To his surprise, he was disappointed. Then again, it'd only been three days. He saw his tent and camping display in the far corner, and thought, Yeah, *my* handiwork. He saw Norma working by the athletic shoes, bringing out an armful of Puma boxes. Shin came out of the stock room with a clipboard, asking Henry to wait a second. Gorden stared. His bastard of a boss. Ex-boss. He wondered what it would be like to have the power to fire people so easily. Did you think you were important? Did you let it get to your head? Shin had rolled up his sleeves and loosened his tie. Gorden watched him as he pushed his pen behind his ear. He rearranged his glasses.

A man Gorden hadn't seen before walked out of the stockroom and spoke to Shin. Gorden tensed as he saw the small rectangular name tag stuck to the man's pocket, and he squinted, trying to get a better view of the stranger. Short curly hair, clean-shaven, a few inches taller than Shin. Who the hell?... Shin pointed to the exercise machines in the center of the showroom and the man nodded. This couldn't be a replacement, could it? Just three days later? Gorden felt the calm that had been with him all morning dissolve. Replaced already, he thought. Body's not even cold.

He realized how much he hated Shin, really hated him, for everything.

"Gord?" a voice behind him asked.

Gorden turned around quickly. It was John. Shit. "Oh, hey."

"Hey," John said, watching him carefully. "How're you?"

Gorden shrugged. "Who's that guy with Shin?" He pointed over his shoulder.

"Yeah, I know. That was fast. I'm sorry about you being... let go."

"So who is he?"

"Some guy Shin hired."

"To take my place."

"Uh, no. To take Henry's place."

"So Henry..."

John nodded and cleared his throat.

"You know," Gorden said, after a pause, "I was fucking Shin's wife."

John looked up. "You were... Was *that* why he—"

"Oh, yeah."

"No wonder. We thought—Norma and me thought something was wrong. You doing good work and all."

"I was fucking his wife and he couldn't handle it. That spineless piece of shit." Gorden made a fist and held it to his side. The cut on his arm hurt, but he didn't care.

John didn't say anything for a few seconds then asked, "So what're you going to do?"

"Beats the hell out of me. Any ideas?"

"Maybe some other place—"

"No one is hiring. It's the fucking worst time to get fired."

John nodded and looked around him. "Well, I gotta get back in there."

"Yeah, you do that."

He glanced at Gorden and waved, then walked into the showroom. Gorden turned and hurried out of the mall, cursing to himself. He had to get out of this fucking place because it was driving him crazy and all he wanted to do was to take Shin outside and beat the shit out of him and tell him what a goddamn slant-eyed bastard he was before he smashed his face into the ground. Yeah, he would love doing that to him, just making the bastard fucking beg to live. Then what kind of smart fuck would he think he was? Shin was nothing, just a dumb fuck manager.

When Gorden returned home, he brought with him two six-packs and a bottle of Jack Daniel's. He didn't give a fuck right now how much this cost him and when he saw another credit card bill and an electric bill in his mailbox he tore them up and threw them on the ground, saying, "Screw you all." He had cooled off by driving around, but maybe it was seeing that new guy there, or maybe it was talking to John, but everything hit him and he just couldn't take it right now. He had to do something to get his mind off all these fucking problems. What the hell had happened? Just a few months ago it seemed like everything was okay, but now nothing was right and it looked like he was in deep shit. Go fucking looking for another job? He thought about Shari. There was no goddamn way he was going to end up like that. He suddenly felt lousy, thinking, Christ, I should've seen it better, but hell it was too late now and he had to take care of himself, number one right now. But man he should've known how she felt. He was just too wrapped up in his own shit. Mother fucker Shin.

Smokes. He should've gotten smokes. He didn't care what the hell was going to happen to him because tonight he was going to get fucked and not think about anything or anyone and goddamn them all. Opening a can of beer, liking the hiss from the flip top and the twang as he ripped the piece off, he felt the cold metal in his hands and drank two fast gulps while he kicked off his shoes. The beer was cold and sharp and he swallowed it while it was still fizzing in his mouth. He knew it would take a lot more before he would feel anything so he continued drinking, and wandered around his small house, moving from room to room but not really paying attention as he held the beer tightly. When he came into the bathroom he looked at himself in the mirror and saw that his eyes were red. "You got fucked," he said aloud. "Fucked over." He finished the beer and stared into the mirror. "You should knock him around." He punched the mirror and it cracked down the center. He jumped back in surprise, and cursed. He hadn't even hit it that hard. He looked at his fist, but it was okay. In his reflection his face was split and distorted, his right side higher and off-center.

5

Sis, alls I did this fucking week was drink my ass off and Im feeling pretty shitty right now but I dont really care anymore because Im just waiting for the goddamn ax to come down any second ~~ha ha~~ no really things are looking bad and I really gotta get moving for a new job but it gets me tired to even think about that ~~and Ive been real~~ I did something real stupid the other day dont ask me why but I was thinking about Shari and that fucking bathtub and I kept wondering if it was just a bad luck bathtub what with her killing herself and then when I take a shower in it bad things happen so I was thinking how do I get rid of the bad luck ~~and broken mirrors are bad luck~~ so you wont believe this but I thought well maybe I can burn the bad luck off so I squirted some of that firestarter stuff for barbeques into the tub ~~I guess I was pretty wasted~~ and lit it. Christ that thing goes up fast and all the sudden my bathtub is on fucking fire and Im staring at it wondering what the hell I just did and theres smoke and my bathroom has no *[illegible]* windows so I turn on the air vent but thats not enough and I think ok enough of this shit and turn on the shower and damn some of the firestarter stuff splashes onto the shower curtain and practically melts it. I put it all out but shit the bathrooms a mess now. ~~Its kind of funny now~~ I wasnt even scared when all of it was happening even though I shouldve been but it was like it wasnt real or something. Now its kind of funny when I think about it and you know I could use that 400 you owe me. And what the fucks with you? Sometimes I wonder if you even read these fucking things but I guess it dont matter no it does because what if I tell you something important or what if I have a secret or something, then what, huh? To hell with it. Running on empty.

I fell asleep while I was writing you but Im awake now and man this jack daniels is a fucking bitch to get down and I dont have anything to mix it with except ice water but thats better than nothing and [illegible] Ive been thinking about Helen again and how much fun we had in bed together and I keep getting pissed at Shin for screwing everything up because I cant blame her for telling him since he probably made her do it and I keep thinking that Shin dont deserve her or Susy and how he really shouldnt be running Jakesons even if he is some hot shit from Boston. He shouldve been the one to kill himself. Thatd be funny if he did, wouldnt it? Then Helen would be free and the store would be free. ~~Or maybe if~~ I You know I dont remember much about pa dying even though I wasnt that young but everything was so mixed up then and alls I could do was lock myself in my room and build my cars.

   I feel like shit right now. I had some fucked up dreams last night when I pretty much passed out and I wont even mention the one about you and me though I know youd like that kind of thing but I had another dream where I kidnapped Helen's little kid. Im not sure why I did that and what I wanted but I just drove by and grabbed her. The kid in the dream wasnt scared and the dream ended with me cooking dinner for the kid. Real weird. Though if I was going to get Shin thatd be one way. Yeah, Im still real pissed off at him and if he thinks he got the last punch at me he is plain wrong...

"So what do you think," I asked Marlene while we lay in bed one morning. "You think he'll do something stupid?" I had told her about Gorden's dream.

   She rolled onto her side so that she could look at me. "He wrote you all this? In one letter?"

   "This guy has nothing else to do."

   "I don't know about him," she said. She looked up at my ceiling.

   "What do you mean?"

   "Can I read the letter?"

"Well," I said, slowly, thinking of an excuse. "I don't think so. I wouldn't feel good about it."

"You're right, but I was just curious."

I nodded and felt guilty for deceiving her. Why couldn't I just tell her that the letters were not mine and admit what I was doing? Part of it was that I was embarrassed. What would she think if she knew I had been reading someone else's mail for the past five months? But there was also something else: I felt protective about my letters. They had become "my" letters as I became more and more immersed in Gorden's world, and perhaps I wasn't sure if I wanted to share it yet, not even with Marlene.

Ever since Marlene had been coming over, I had stored the letters in a small shoe box underneath the sink, throwing out the envelopes and sorting the letters by date. It was now a thick pile held together with a rubber band. Sometimes, if I was going to sleep alone that evening, I would take it out and read old letters. I really felt like I knew this man, yet I couldn't really figure out what he was going to do next. I had thought he would pick himself up and begin looking for another job. Like he said, he had lost jobs before and found new ones, but this time was different. His position at Jakeson's had been important, unlike his other jobs, and he made money than he ever had before. And then there was Shari.

The burning of the tub fascinated me. I viewed what he had done not as a drunken act but as an incantatory spell with Gorden as some kind of warlock, chanting and spreading a ring of fire to free himself of a curse. Shari's memory was more present with Gorden than I had previously suspected. The whole scene must have been hazy, with Gorden stumbling from the small storage shed in the back yard where he kept his barbecue and the firestarter mix. The yard was overgrown with weeds and large, leafy plants that hugged the house and spread further across the grass every day. As he carried the can of starter he must have seen the dandelion weeds choking the remaining bits of grass, and he must have been tempted to douse his yard as long as he had this stuff in his hands, but he walked back inside the house, shutting the door so he would not have to look at the messy yard. The whole house, in fact, seemed to be falling apart, with the paint peeling and the roof tiles sliding off with every storm. He used to care about how the house looked, but now he waved all this away and headed towards the bathroom. The fucking bathroom. He didn't know why even after all this time it still made him nervous to be in here, but he could still feel her here somehow. Maybe it was just him but he had to do something about it. Cleaning it hadn't been enough.

The bathroom smelled of ammonia and soap. He stopped at the doorway, holding the wall to steady himself, and said aloud, "Once and for all." He paused, listening to the echo. "Once and for all this goddamn place will be fixed." Gorden stepped into the bathroom and pushed aside the blue shower curtain quickly and turned the can of fuel upside down, squeezing. The clear gel squirted out in a heavy glob and then sputtered. He drew designs on the white porcelain—circles and figure eights—until the can felt lighter and there was gel all over the floor of the tub. He closed the lid and placed the can next to the sink.

Matches. He ran into the kitchen and found a box from the Camain Restaurant. When he returned to the bathroom, the strong gas-like smell of the starter overpowered all the other smells and made his eyes water. He lit a match and threw it in, realizing only after the match had fallen into the gel and ignited the bathtub that what he was doing might be dangerous. The flame from the match caught and spread quickly, though the flame didn't burst up like he had expected it would; rather, it stayed fairly low, letting off an odd smell, like old motor oil burning, and he began to cough, fumes filling the bathroom. He flicked on the vent switch. The fire began melting the shower curtain. Black burn marks appeared on the white tub wherever there was gel, and a thin stream of smoke rose up. He coughed again and reached over to the bathtub faucet, feeling the low heat on his arm. He turned on the shower and the water splashed the gel onto the curtain and burned holes in the plastic.

After the water doused the fire, the bathtub was streaked with black burn marks and small cracks, probably from the heat. The shower curtain was melted all along the bottom. The walls smelled of oil and smoke. Gorden kept the vent on and fanned the door back and forth. He couldn't help finding this funny, and when he closed the door to keep the smell from entering the rest of the house he leaned back and began laughing quietly to himself, shaking his head. Gord, he said to himself, you sure are fucked.

At the diner, after a flurry of customers had kept me busy washing dishes for three hours, I finally had a chance to break. I wheeled out a stack of clean dishes to be taken by the busboys. I left the kitchen, sitting at the back counter. I pulled out the latest letter from Gorden and began rereading:

> I dont know why I began taking inventory of the things in my house but I just did and it turned out to be something I should of done a long time ago because I found so much old shit that it kept me busy for hours and I cant believe how much stuff I ripped off from Jakeson's when I worked in the stockroom because in my closets there were extra sneakers, baseballs, and a whole box of things that I picked up and brought home and forgot about. So Shin can go fuck himself! ~~That goddamn~~ And Shari was fucking right. I stole things from there and I forgot all about it. So she was right. But thats not the only thing I found because when I went into the attic and it was damn hot up there but I pulled down a few things I had put there when I first moved in and I found the rabbit trap I took from the shithead and also his old Mossberg 12 gauge. I dont know if you remember that but he used to take that hunting. Its a sweet shotgun with a vent rib and an 18 inch barrel. There was also a box of Remington Sport Loads but its been so long I dont know if theyre any good. I cleaned and oiled the Mossberg and it looks and smells great. I also found one of those

old chest expanders you know those springs with handles that you pull apart to get a bigger chest and I couldnt believe I actually stole one of these from the store since it looks pretty dumb. I keep getting reminded of Shin and everytime I think of him I get pissed off and I know I should just forget about it but I cant and I dont think I will...

Gorden was beginning to spend too much time alone in the house, looking for things to do, and this only made his mood worse. Although he had lived here for almost four years, it wasn't until now that every detail of the house began to irritate him. He hated the way the floors creaked in the hallway, something he never noticed before. He hated the leaky faucets and the sticking doors. He tried not to let these small things bother him but they did and he reacted violently, often slamming the door again and again until it unstuck, or stamping the wooden floor with so much force that the walls shook. What he needed, he knew, was some contact, and after a few days of this he tried calling Helen again.

To his surprise she answered the phone, and when he heard her "Hello" he froze—he had forgotten what he was going to say.

"Hello?" she asked again.

"Hello, is this Helen?"

"Yes, who is this?"

"It's," he began, considering how he should handle this. "It's me, Gorden."

She hung up.

Gorden called back immediately but got the machine. He hung up and tried to call again, but this time the phone was busy.

About five minutes later *his* phone began ringing, and he picked it up, puzzled. Could she be calling him?

"Hello," he answered.

"Gorden, this is Roger Shin."

Gripping the phone tightly and sitting up, he said, "Yeah?"

"I want you to listen to me carefully. I don't want you to call my wife again, do you understand? I can call the police and get a restraining order if I have to. Do you understand? Don't push me, Gorden."

"Don't push *you*?" Gorden asked, standing up quickly. "You little—"

"I could've done a lot more than fire you. Just remember that." He hung up.

Gorden slammed the phone down into the cradle and pressed his palms into his eyes. That goddamn... Gorden couldn't even find the words for Shin, and he groaned as his whole body tensed with anger, shaking. No fucking way he was going to let Shin get away with all this and there was no fucking way he was just going to sit down and take this because Shin thought he was doing him a *favor* and that was... was...

His eyes began to smart and he moved his hands away; blurry patterns formed in his vision and he blinked, trying to focus. He stumbled onto the couch and punched the arm rest over and over until his fist couldn't take it anymore.

"Thank you for calling, Raj. I'm sorry this is happening."

"It's okay."

"He's very mixed up."

"He's nuts."

"God, I'm so sorry."

"I know."

"Will you be home soon?"

"Yes. Just a few things to take care of for the next sale."

"I really want to leave, Raj."

"I know, you told me. I'm already tying things up. A few more weeks after this Father's Day."

"I appreciate that."

"I have to go now, and don't pick up the phone."

"I won't. Do you want me to make anything special tonight?"

"No, that's okay. Anything is fine... Okay, I have—"

"Susy misses you."

"Tell her I said hello. I miss her too."

"Oh, Raj... I've really messed things up, haven't I?"

"Helen, we can talk about this later. I should go."

"Okay. Are you sure you don't want something special tonight?"

"No."

"Bye, Raj."

"I'll see you tonight."

"Bye."

6

Another dream: Shari looks at me and smiles. She is wearing a Marnole High sweat shirt and faded jeans with the left knee ripped, and is brushing her hair as she stares out her window. It is evening, and raining, and she can see her reflection in the glass, and uses this as a mirror. She sees me, turns, and smiles. She is not surprised by my presence, and she simply turns back towards the window and continues running her brush through her hair while her free hand follows the brush and pats the curls down. She brushes while she tilts her head left, then right, then bends at the waist and lets her hair fall forward, making sure the back is also brushed. We are not in her parents' house, but rather in a small apartment with a door to another room closed. Sounds come from behind the door.

Don't mind them, she tells me. She holds up a small mirror and purses her lips. She says, I'm going on a date tonight with a guy from the mall.

I don't say anything as I watch her pull off her sweat shirt and run her fingers underneath her bra strap, realigning it. She puts on a T-shirt and a grey sweater. She looks in the small mirror again, holding it in the palm of her hand, and carefully applies some lipstick. She grabs a tissue, folds it, and presses her upper and lower lips onto it, leaving pink smudges.

She turns to me and says, Wish me luck.

Gorden had to do something to Shin. He considered setting fire to the place; after all, he still had the key (that dumb fuck forgot to get it from Gorden) and he could slip in late one evening and just start a small fire in the showroom, letting it spread on its own. But that wouldn't really get Shin, and Gorden knew the fire insurance might actually help the store. He wanted to get Shin scared, wanted to show him that you can't fuck with people and get away with it, wanted Shin scared of *him*. Doing something to his car was another idea, but Gorden wanted something better. For a minute he considered kidnapping Susy, but that was just plain stupid. Besides, he had nothing against Helen. Gorden then wondered: If Shin were dead would Helen come back to Gorden? If Shin were to have some kind of accident, would Gorden get his old job? Suicide. What if Shin committed suicide? The store wasn't performing as well as Shin had hoped, and with all this pressure he couldn't handle it anymore. Gorden began thinking of different possibilities and stopped himself after a few minutes. Could he really kill someone?

What the fuck was happening to him? Gorden shook his head violently. After Shin had hung up on him, Gorden couldn't stop thinking about it. No one can talk to him like that and treat him like shit. Shin thought he was doing Gorden a favor? The son of a bitch thought he was a fucking saint? Just put the fucking shakes on the guy, that's all. Fired? Got to do something to show him. Show the asshole some manners.

Gorden saw the Mossberg leaning against the wall.

When I told Marlene about some of the wild thoughts Gorden was having she initially didn't believe me, suggesting that I was exaggerating. We were in bed late one evening with the window open. The cars driving by on Sunrise Highway sounded like waves.

"He'd have to be pretty sick to think about kidnapping and

arson," she said.

"I don't think he would actually do it," I answered. "But he was considering it."

"Maybe when you write him back you should straighten him out."

"Yes," I said, "I should."

"Yes, you should straighten him out, or yes you should write him?" She sat up in the bed.

"Both." I immediately knew this answer was a mistake.

"You mean you don't write him back?"

"Well..."

She leaned forward. "You mean he's been writing you all this time and you don't write back?"

I felt cornered and said, "Hey, what's with the cross-examination?"

"Nothing. But that's kind of weird."

"It's not really up to you to judge, though," I said.

We fell silent. The sounds of the cars slowed, and another muffled song from the jukebox began. I stared at her feet poking out of the covers. Her toes were long and crooked.

"Look, it's just complicated," I finally said.

She lay back down but didn't respond.

Alls Im going to do is scare the shit out of him. Thisll be the best time right before the sale since the night before he always stays late to do last minute things but everyone else goes home so alls I have to do is show up and give him a little ~~shitscaring show~~ scare with my nice little Mossberg and maybe rattle him. He thinks hes so fucking important but hes nothing and what I want to do is blow his head off but I dont think I will. Im trying to keep cool about this but everytime I think about him firing me and pretty much treating me like shit the whole time I want to *[illegibly crossed out]* Anyway, I got a week to get my shit together so...

◊

The letter rambled on about the preparations, but by this time I was worried enough about Shin to reconsider Marlene's advice. Anyone could see that this plan of Gorden's was going to backfire somehow—there were so many things that could go wrong—and I just *knew* that if I didn't do something somebody was going to be hurt, or worse. I thought about Shari and how I simply watched her disintegrate letter by letter, and I had done nothing but comment to myself what a pity it was. My inaction was despicable, and I couldn't let something like that happen again.

But Marlene's advice, to write Gorden, seemed to be out of the question. I thought about typing a letter as Mona, trying to convince Gorden to stop this plan, but then I would be endangering myself since he would be suspicious that Mona would be writing him now, and if I made any kind of mistake, he would know. I didn't want to change Gorden's perception of his sister's passivity, because what if, upon receiving the letter, Gorden decided to write back with questions? Would I have to concoct a Mona for his benefit? But obviously I could never succeed in that since I knew so little about her.

It occurred to me that maybe Gorden was testing his sister with this latest letter, that he never intended to do anything, but he wanted some kind of reaction from her. This was a possibility, though the evidence in his previous letters suggested something else, and why would he create such an elaborate trick? No, I was certain he meant to do something that night and I felt compelled to act.

What I did was this: I went to the Marnole Library and photo-copied the page of the letter in which Gorden discusses his plan to scare Shin. Although there was only one important paragraph in the middle of the page—this sandwiched between his thoughts on Helen ("I aint stupid and I know its over but hell, I can still think about her...") and by a dim memory of hunting with his father ("we didnt get anything but I liked tracking deer")—this paragraph was the only one I needed for what I planned to do. I then brought that photocopy downstairs and used their typewriter for fifty cents an hour and typed on the back of the copy:

Dear Mr. Shin,

On the reverse side you will find a copy of one page of a letter written by your former employee, Farrel Gorden. Although he means only to frighten you, I suggest you take the necessary precautions.

Signed,
a friend

I brought the photocopy home and stared at my note on the back, wondering if I was making a mistake. It was possible that I was in fact exacerbating the entire situation by informing Shin of Gorden's plan, and by asking for "necessary precautions" I was giving Shin reason to arm himself. But Shin didn't seem to me to be that kind of person, to deal with the threat of force with more force. What I hoped was that he would: a) leave early and perhaps let the police know that there might be a prowler that evening, b) change the locks, or c) show the police the letter and let them handle the situation.

Yet was it my place to interfere? My status as an observer was again questionable, and I debated for at least an hour with myself, trying to understand my role in all this. Finally, since it was almost time for my shift at the diner, I decided to let fate handle this decision. Since the Father's Day Sale began in exactly four days, I would let the mail decide what would happen. The mail took two to three days for a letter to reach Marnole from Yanack, and I assumed it would be the same in the other direction. If I sent the letter off today, right before my shift, the mailman would pick it up at five and the letter would arrive at Jakeson's either before or on Father's Day, which fell on a Saturday. So, if the mail arrived in two days, Shin would know in time. If the mail arrived in three, he would not. Also, there were other possible delays which somehow factored in the equation. However, when I thought about Gorden's letters, about when they were dated and when they had arrived, it seemed to me that they always took either two to three days, and I concluded that, truly, it was up to fate. I regretted not bringing an envelope to the library, because at my apartment I had to handwrite Roger Shin's name and "c/o Jakeson's Sporting Goods" and I worried that somehow all this would be traced to me. But I had no time—the mail would be picked up in less than a half hour—so I scribbled the address, sealed and stamped the envelope, and sent it off. I kept telling myself that it was fate deciding, the contingencies of chance. Yet regardless of how I rationalized my interference, I had still tainted the experiment, and I was no longer the observer but now an active participant, and I would soon learn what this meant.

7

I was on edge for the next two days as I continued to ask myself if I had done the right thing, trying to convince myself that everything would turn out for the best and my interference would actually prevent something terrible from happening. I think Marlene sensed my mood and stayed away from me. It also might have had something to do with that last disagreement we had in bed. To add to my worries, I thought that perhaps that incident was symptomatic of a bigger problem between us: the initial rush of attraction was wearing off, and our differences were suddenly accentuated. I didn't have the energy to worry about this as well, so Marlene and I spoke to each other tentatively, and when I told her that I wanted to be alone for the next couple of nights, she nodded slowly and said, "Are you sure? Yeah? Okay, but if you need someone to talk to..."

Normally I would have been distressed, since I liked Marlene, and she had become my only friend, but I was preoccupied with imagined scenarios of Gorden and Shin, all of them violent. Not only would I be terrible company, but I felt that having someone else around would just make me more irritable. I needed to worry about this alone. The worst imagined scenario was Gorden bursting into the office with his shotgun, and Shin already waiting for him, with his own gun, and both of them ending up dead. No, actually the worst one would be Shin not receiving the letter and bringing his wife and daughter to the office that evening. I began torturing myself with images of Helen and Susy shot with a 12 gauge, and though I had never seen a shotgun wound, that didn't stop me from imagining it.

My dreams continued: Shari raises her hand to ask a question. Yes, I say. I stop writing on the chalk board and wait for her. But she does not ask. She smiles and shrugs her shoulders, as if she forgot her question. The faceless other students laugh and I tell everyone that it's okay, maybe it will come back to her. The classroom dissolves and we are in her yard at night. There is a heavy, salty smell of sea water, and the sound of chirping crickets fill the darkness beyond our circle of grass. Shari closes her eyes and looks up, her face lit by the moonlight. She smiles as she listens to the crickets. Did you know, I ask, that from the number of chirps in a minute we can determine the temperature within a few degrees? She shakes her head and does not open her eyes. Oh yes, I say, looking up as well and seeing the quarter moon, a few stringy clouds. It's wonderful, I say.

The day before Father's Day. June 19th. I stayed in bed for most of the morning, trying to read Montaigne, but I had difficulty concentrating. It was almost noon and I thought that if the letter were to arrive at Jakeson's today, it probably would be there by now. Otherwise it was beneath a pile of other letters in some postal bin, waiting to be sorted and distributed. Today Shin would be making the final arrangements for the sale. The Father's Day Sale signs and banners would be hung along the walls and in the display window. The ads on the radio would play more frequently.

Shin considered this his penultimate sale at this branch. He was doing what he had set out to do: to turn the store around. Although he was worried about this sale, he knew that with all the publicity they were guaranteed a large turnout, and he couldn't think of anything that could go wrong at this point. Even if the receipts were lower, which was unlikely, the store had established a stronger presence in the community.

He and Helen were talking more, and though he didn't completely agree with her, he decided to slow down these location assignments. Maybe he would spend more time in Boston, or Manchester. He would decide after he returned to the Boston branch. But she was right—Susy was getting older and they needed to stay in one place, at least for a few years. Although he still hadn't completely forgiven her, they had to think about Susy. Everything for Susy.

I imagined Gorden at this point watching TV while slumped on the sofa, days of alcohol and inactivity taking its toll. He raised his arm slowly to look at his watch, and then let his limb drop lifelessly next to him. He was in three-day-old clothes, and his greasy hair and growing beard itched. Was he still going to do it tonight? He sat up and inhaled the stale air of the house. Yeah. He needed to wake up though. Everything was planned and all he had to do was wake up. His shotgun was on the table in front of him, cleaned, oiled, and tested in the back yard with the new shells. Gorden smiled. He was going to scare the fuck out of Shin.

I went to work as usual and looked forward to washing dishes; the monotony would help me stop worrying. The weather was warm enough for me to wear jeans and a T-shirt, and on my way there I had an uneasy feeling that now, almost four o'clock, *some-*

thing was happening in Yanack, though I wasn't sure what. It was very disconcerting, and I resisted the image of Gorden practicing a speech to what he hoped would be a captive Shin. Gorden would be holding the gun to Shin's head, telling him in a low voice how he had made life for everyone miserable including his wife and how he, Gorden, was doing fine until Shin showed up, and how Helen had been unhappy with her husband so of course she was going to look somewhere else.

At the diner I saw Marlene who approached me cautiously, asking me how everything was. She smiled and leaned forward, waiting, and I suddenly realized how selfish I had been, and I shook my head and said, "Much better. I missed you."

The wrinkles around her eyes deepened as she laughed quietly. "That's sweet," she said. "Do you want to get together tonight?"

I nodded.

"I have the extra late shift, though. Is that okay?"

I said it was. I watched her tie her hair back, and adjust her uniform. She checked her watch and said she had to get to work now.

The evening went slowly for me because every time I looked up at the clock I would wonder what was going on in New Hampshire. I managed to distract myself for a couple of hours when the dishwashing machine wasn't working properly—something was clogging one of the jets—so I had to wash one batch by hand and unclog the nozzle by digging into the hole with a steak knife. At one point I had an odd sense of familiarity while I was poking inside the machine, the warm, dark interior with drops of soapy water falling onto my neck. I began humming a Led Zeppelin ballad and felt like I had been working here all my life.

By the time the last shift had ended, Marlene and I walked to my apartment, Marlene limping from being on her feet all evening. I asked her if she would rather go home.

"No, that's okay. I just need to rest for a while."

It was strangely quiet along Sunrise Highway, and even Lucky's wasn't very full, with the music sounding more muted than usual. Marlene said, "How are you feeling?"

"Better, I think."

"Can I ask what's wrong?"

I shrugged. We walked in silence.

At the apartment, Marlene sat on my mattress and kicked off her shoes. She groaned. "I really need new shoes," she said to me.

I began making us some coffee, and Marlene lay down and sighed. "So, Tiger," she said quietly. "You gonna tell me what's up?"

I knew I was being unfair by brooding and not telling her why, but I just didn't feel like talking about New Hampshire. I wanted to think of something else, anything else, and I didn't answer her right away.

Soft thumping from downstairs. I was comforted by this familiar sound.

"It's officially Father's Day," I said, looking at my watch. 12:30 a.m. "My father's dead—I told you that I think—but before he died I used to send him cards every year. He loved that. Nothing fancy, just a simple 'Happy Father's Day' with a short note from me, telling him how I was."

I walked to the window and looked outside, watching the few cars waiting at the light. "I don't think he was very happy, but he did what he had to." The light turned green and the cars drove off, one with a rattling muffler lagging behind. I wiped fog off the glass.

I turned back to Marlene, but her eyes were closed. She was breathing deeply. I watched her sleep.

After a few restless hours of pacing and drinking coffee, I decided to go up to the train station, hoping it would calm me. I left a note for Marlene, and slipped outside with my jacket. I hurried across Sunrise and climbed the cement stairs. There was no one on the platform, of course, and I leaned against the wall by the stairs, near the eastbound tracks, the same place where Marlene and I had been sitting not too long ago, and looked out over Marnole. A train approached. The two lights, narrower than a car's headlights, wavered in the distance. The tracks rumbled. I moved closer to the wall because the train did not look like it was slowing down. The train honked a few times, and the platform shook even more. As the train rushed by me, the double thumps with each car vibrating beneath my feet, I saw in the lit windows a few passengers looking down and reading, sleeping, and some faces staring out blankly The cars towards the end of the train were darkened and unoccupied. A strong gust of wind blew around me, fluttering my hair and jacket, and I closed my eyes as the last car flew by, the low rumble fading. I followed the red lights on the rear car until they turned out of sight. My ears rang for a second, and eventually everything settled and I stared out over Marnole. It was as if nothing had happened. Cars still drove on Sunrise, lines still formed at the gas station, music still came from Lucky's. I was still here.

When I walked up the stairs to my studio, I heard banging in my hallway, and a voice. I thought it might be one of the drunks from Lucky's wandering upstairs. It had happened once before, but eventually the man became tired and went back down. As I reached my floor, I heard a door opening and more voices. When I looked towards my apartment, I saw a man in rumpled clothes raising his voice to Marlene. She was trying to wake up, rubbing her eyes and shaking her head, and I wasn't sure if the man was drunk. He was getting angry, but Marlene was calm.

"I don't know what you're talking about," she said. Then she saw me, and said, "Look, here's the owner. I don't know what the hell your problem is."

The man turned and our eyes met. When I saw his acne scars and his stubble, his reddish hair in the dim hall light, I stiffened, and my heart skipped. I knew who this was. We stared at each other for what seemed like an eternity. I was staring at Farrel Gorden.

**Part V
Independence Day**

1

It is the fourth of July, fifteen years later. I am on my summer vacation from the prep school at which I am teaching, and have been living and working here in California for the past seven years. Right now I am sitting at my desk in my study, overlooking an arid, uneven landscape with goldenrod blanketing the small hills, long stretches of yellow rising and falling towards the horizon. I enjoy walking out there at night, listening to the coyotes in the distance, the wind rustling the grass around me. I live alone in a small two-bedroom house near the school, and my house stands on a hill with five other houses, all faculty leased, all similar in design and layout (a split-level with a sunken living room), though mine is the only one without a family in it. I teach the Life Sciences here, which include Biology. This past year went particularly well for me since I was made acting head of the department and have more control in redesigning the curriculum.

I look around my study, and notice the books overflowing on

my shelves, the papers and notebooks all along the floor since I ran out of room on my desk, and I am reminded of my old apartment in Marnole, and how much, though the rooms don't look much different, my situation has changed. I have some money now. I have a steady, stable job. A house. The project I have undertaken—writing this account—forces me to compare my life then with my life now. I am secure. I am comfortable.

2

When I recognized Gorden at my door, I couldn't move, and became transfixed in his stare, my mind suddenly blank. I heard the soft thumping from downstairs, my heart beating in my ears, my mouth going dry, and we stared at each other for at least a full minute. I'm not sure why we stood there for so long, but with each passing second I felt myself sinking. I could only think, It's him. It's Gorden.

Marlene didn't know what was going on, and just waited for one of us to speak, but we stood there, and I soon saw a flicker in Gorden's eyes, as if he suddenly understood what all this meant. He blinked and looked up at the number on the door, and then turned back to me. He narrowed his eyes.

"You," he said. He started shaking. "My letters."

"Oh, are you the one who's been writing?" Marlene asked.

"Where's my sister?" Gorden asked me, not breaking his stare. His voice was different from what I expected: higher, with a nasal twang.

"Wait a minute," I said, beginning to collect myself. He didn't think I had done something to her? But he didn't look like he was listening to me. I had no idea how he got here or what had happened in New Hampshire, but I had to get away from him. "Just wait a minute." I backed away, my hands held up.

"What did you do with her!"

"What? Nothing! I don't know what—"

"You son of a bitch..." he said, approaching.

Marlene looked at me, startled. Without any warning, Gorden suddenly jumped towards me, and he was so quick that I didn't even have a chance to run. He grabbed my jacket and pulled me down, practically throwing me onto the floor. Marlene yelled, "What the...!" as I felt the wind knocked out of me, a heaviness falling on me, and I kept thinking, This can't be happening. This is insane. Gorden grabbed my throat and said, "Where's Mona!"

Once I felt his fingers on my throat I panicked and began lashing out, punching and kicking and scratching, and he loosened his grip on me but punched me in the face with his other hand, everything around me exploding and I cried out in pain and we began rolling in the hallway as I tried to free myself but he kept going after my throat and face. When I managed to kick him in the stomach I heard him grunt, but he didn't stop coming for me. I yelled for Marlene to help and saw her above us trying to do something but Gorden and I were rolling back and forth across the floor and she hesitated, trying to tell us apart and finally she kicked Gorden in the back, making him curse and release his grip on me. She kicked him again, and this time I freed myself and stumbled towards the apartment. I don't know why I did that, but I think I was hoping to get a weapon or something, since I probably couldn't outrun him. But before I even made it a few feet Gorden came up and slammed me into the door frame, hard, and then shoved me into the apartment, coming after me. He was frenzied, trying to reach for my face and I couldn't seem to get away from him because he kept attacking me, his hands like claws. He grabbed my hair and forced my head into the ground and everything around me jarred and blurred and I felt the pain and dizziness overcome me, but then I heard a crack and I felt him jolt back. There was another crack and he fell off me. Marlene held a Kahlua bottle in her hand and brought it down on Gorden's head one more time, this time breaking the bottle over him with a small pop, the glass bursting apart, crashing to the floor, and he slumped off me.

I was wheezing, my head and chest burning with pain, and lay there, stunned, trying to keep from moving. Marlene came to me and checked my head carefully and asked if I was okay.

I said no, but told her I had to get out of there before he woke up.

"Should I call the police? What should I do?" she asked me, her voice rising.

Then as quickly as I could, I told her what I had been doing: reading his letters. "I don't know what happened," I said. "But now he knows it was me. I have to get out of here."

"Take my car," she said, going through her bag and giving me her keys. "Call me when you're safe. We should call the police."

I looked around my apartment and grabbed my money. Then, in a surprising moment of clarity, I thought about the shoe box filled with his letters, and took that too. Marlene helped me downstairs and she went into Lucky's to call the police while I hurried to the diner parking lot to take her car. We didn't even get to say goodbye. Everything happened so fast that I don't even remember getting into her car, driving it to the Kendal Railroad Station, leaving her keys under the front seat, and taking the train into New York. I don't remember the train ride, nor do I remember checking myself into a hotel. The next thing I knew I woke up in a cheap room not far from Penn Station, my body bruised and aching. It was morning. I called Marlene at her home and learned that Gorden was gone. He had woken up and run before the police had arrived, and I too was wanted for questioning. The police thought I might have something to do with, or at least know more about Roger Shin's murder, and they wanted to know why Gorden had driven four hours straight to my place after Shin had been killed. Marlene knew nothing, and could only tell the police what she saw. But she didn't want to get involved so she didn't reveal much about our relationship. She didn't mention the letters.

I told Marlene where her car was, and then told her I might not be seeing her for a while.

"But the police? They want to see you. You'll probably be a suspect somehow."

"He's after me," I said, understanding this only after I had said it. "He's after me and I just want to get the hell away."

"I still don't understand any of this."

"I'm sorry," I told her. "None of this should have happened. It was my fault for interfering."

"What? What are you talking about?"

"Nothing," I said. "I've got to go. Sorry, Marlene."

She was quiet. "Call me if you need anything."

I said I would, though I knew that would be the last time I would speak to her. I hung up the phone. Murdered? Roger Shin had been murdered?

3

Before I started running, I tried to find out everything I could about what had happened in Yanack, New Hampshire that night, but there wasn't much. Shin's murder was first believed to be a robbery that had gone awry, but during the investigation they discovered Farrel Gorden to be missing, and soon his motives for revenge became the center of their case. Then Helen Shin told them about her affair with Gorden, and he became their prime suspect. But he had disappeared.

So what had happened? I've gone over this a number of times, and I think that Shin must have received the letter in the mail that day, but had dismissed it as some kind of prank. After all, he was very busy making preparations, and when he opened the envelope and saw the rambling page and the short note on the back, he turned it over, puzzled, reading it a few times. Who'd send him this, he wondered. Maybe it was Gorden trying to scare him? Or someone else sending it as a joke? The envelope was postmarked

New York, which made it even more strange. Then John approached him and asked him about a problem with the computer—the inventory program Shin had installed wasn't working correctly—and Shin left the letter on his desk and helped John. As the day continued, the letter was lost under inventory reports, sample advertising circulars, receipts, and an instruction manual for a stationary bicycle that had fallen out of a box, and was soon forgotten.

Later that evening, while Shin was alone in the office, estimating the costs if everyone redeemed their coupons, he checked his watch and thought about his wife. He wanted to get home before it was too late. Although he and Helen had still not fully reconciled, they agreed to have a late night snack to talk about moving to Boston. Helen wanted to live out in a suburb, perhaps near Wellesley, and Shin wanted to live closer to the city.

Shin heard a noise and looked up. The office door was opening and before he had time to react, Gorden walked through and pointed a shotgun at him.

"Hello, Shin," Gorden said, smiling. He was squinting, trying to blink sweat out of his eyes. He dragged the back of his hand across his left eye, pulling the skin back, and wiped his hand on his shirt. Shin smelled his sharp body odor, and saw his beard was growing in. "Getting ready for the big sale?" Gorden asked. He aimed the barrel at Shin's face.

Shin didn't answer, watching the gun. He felt his heart speeding up, his neck becoming warmer. He immediately thought of the letter and tried to remember what it had said... something about trying to scare him. He took a deep breath to remain calm. Gorden wouldn't really do anything. Gorden wouldn't really shoot him.

"You little shit," Gorden said. "You think you can fire me like that? You think you're important?"

What could he say to that? He just shook his head slowly, unsure if he should try to take the gun away or just sit here. This man could just pull the trigger. Was the gun loaded?

"Well, you just going to sit there like dumb fuck?" Gorden asked. "Maybe I should call your wife." He smiled.

Shin felt a flicker of anger. His wife. "What do you want?" he asked.

"Want? I want you to fucking beg me to live. I want you to fucking cry like the piece of shit you are."

"You wrote a letter," Shin said, and when he saw Gorden stiffen, he continued. "You wrote a letter about this, didn't you."

"What? What the hell you talking about? What letter?"

Shin realized that now he had the advantage. He took his time and said, "You did write a letter about this, didn't you? Telling what you planned to do."

Gorden stared at him, uncertain, lowering the gun a few inches. "How the hell you know about that?"

Shin glanced at his desk. Where was that thing? He reached towards the papers and Gorden raised the gun. Shin stopped. "It's here somewhere," he said.

"Get back. Move away." Gorden motioned the gun away from the desk. Shin pushed his chair back and watched Gorden throw aside the folders and shuffle through the papers. Then, Gorden saw it and picked it up. "What the fuck," he said. He skimmed the letter, then turned it over and read the note. He turned and raised the gun to Shin's head. "Where the hell did you get this? Tell me!"

"I don't know. I got it in the mail today. I have no idea who sent it."

Gorden pushed the barrel onto Shin's forehead. "You're lying," he said.

Shin felt his hands shaking. A chill travelled down his neck. He closed his eyes for a second, and tightened his grip on the seat.

"Where'd you get it?" Gorden asked again. "Tell me!" he yelled.

"Really, I don't know!" Shin yelled back, frightened now.

"You motherfucker! You goddamn son of a bitch!" Gorden pushed the barrel against Shin's mouth and waited for a second to see Shin's reaction. Shin stared at Gorden with wide eyes, the gun cold against his lips, the smell of oil filling him, and he choked out a quiet "Please, wait..." A click.

Helen. Susy. My Helen.

Gorden stood over the body lying on the floor, the arms twisted underneath it. Pieces of... something all over the desk and the floor. Blood dripped from the desk onto the body. Gorden didn't feel anything. Just stunned. His ears were ringing.

He looked at the letter again. His letter to Mona? That little bitch. She... that... Gorden gripped it and cursed. She fucking sent it to Shin? He looked down at the body and thought how easy it had been just to aim and shoot. Just aim and shoot. He stared at his gun and it seemed so strange in his hands. Blood splattered all over the barrel. Warm. Powder smell. He stared at the gun for a long time, not sure how something that small could have so much power.

Gorden pulled the gun away and crumpled the letter, stuffing it into his pocket. Goddamn letter. She snitched on him. She fucked him over! He looked around quickly. He had to get out of this place. He went to the cash box and took the twenties, fifties and hundreds. He then ran out of Jakeson's. He drove home in a daze, trying to figure out why Mona sent the letter to Shin.

This was when Gorden, after arriving at his house and looking for his sister's phone number but not being able to find it, called information in Marnole, asking for Mona Gorden's number. There was no Mona Gorden listed. He slammed the phone down and said, "Fuck it." He knew the police would be coming for him sooner or later, and he had to leave. He took what he could, loaded his car, and drove onto I-91, heading south. He would pay his big sister a visit.

4

I kept moving, especially for the first few years while I traveled west, truly worried that Gorden was after me. I was certain he would find out about his sister as I had, and then he would begin his search for me. I imagined this became an obsession with him, and for those first few years, out of fear, I never went by my real name. As the years passed though, the fear dissipated and now, after fifteen years, I can only guess that even if it had been true, Gorden has long since given up. I had managed to push these events from my mind, and had it not been for something insignificant that happened to me at the beginning of the past school year, I might not have begun thinking about it, and might not have written this.

I was taking roll for the first time in my Introduction to Biology course, and halfway down the list I read the name "Susan Shin." At the time I thought nothing about it, but later that night when I was preparing for class the name reverberated. It wasn't until then that I connected the name with Susy Shin, Helen's daughter. Of course the student in my class was not the Susy of New Hampshire—my student, a freshman, was too young—and there are probably many Susan Shins out there, but all it took was this name to trigger a flood of memories which I had successfully set aside for many years. Throughout these past months I began thinking more and more of that time in Marnole and I started recording on scraps of paper small incidents that I didn't want to lose. I soon turned to a spiral notebook that I always carried with me, and by the end of the school year I had enough (five and a half books) to begin writing this account. I also still had the letters stored away (Why had I even saved them? Perhaps I had always intended to write this?) and after an extended search through piles and piles of papers in my closets, I found the pack of letters held together by a brown rubber band that snapped as soon as I stretched it. I began re-reading the letters in the evenings, before I went to bed. How strange it all was, seeing them again. And I knew that I had to write about it.

Although I don't think Farrel Gorden is still after me, I am presently taking some precautions which I will not reveal, and even what I am writing now will be disguised: the name under which this book is being published is not my real name, and the picture on the back is not my real likeness, and of course, all the names in this account have been changed to protect the innocent.

I considered keeping Farrel Gorden's real name for some time, since there is a part of me that hopes he reads this *apologia* if only to understand why I did what I did, and to see that I had no malicious intent. And I never intended for someone to be killed. Never. I realize that reading someone else's mail was wrong and there really is no excuse for what I did, but now that I've shown the context and my state of mind during those months perhaps a clear, unequivocal condemnation will not be so easy.

I have also been thinking about Shari. I suppose that would be only natural, especially after re-reading Gorden's letters and reliving her suicide. It is still difficult to believe that she was the same age as most of my students now. She had done so much more than most of these students who have come to this school straight out of another private school, and whose lives centered around the beach, the top 40, and dating. At seventeen, I would not expect much else, and yet Shari was worrying about jobs and money and trying to stay sane with Gorden. She would be thirty-two now, and would probably be married, perhaps with a child or two.

I began dreaming about her again:

In my dream Shari is standing in front of the classroom and I am sitting in the back. She is a teacher, and I am one of the students listening to her lecture about the North American perennial plant, goldenrod, family Compositae. *Solidago luteus*, a hybrid of goldenrod and astor, is often cultivated in gardens. She looks the same except her face has become more angular, chin and cheekbones more prominent. Her hair is cut short at her neck and above her ears. She wears large glasses that make her face look smaller. Ms.

McCann leans against the table in the front, looking at her notes, and continues to talk about Plants We Have All Seen. She makes the class laugh when she tries to sketch a plant on the board but crosses it out and says that she never could draw. The class likes her. She turns back towards the board and we see that there are chalk marks on the back of her navy blue blouse, but no one says anything. The chalk marks form intersecting lines. We listen to her speak into the board while she writes, but we stare at her back.

4

Not too long ago I sent a card to Marlene, in care of the Sunrise Diner, hoping it would be forwarded to her. She would be in her mid-fifties by now, and I doubted she was still waiting tables. In the card I asked her if she remembered me and briefly told her about what I had been doing these past fifteen years: traveling west, picking up teaching jobs as I headed towards my destination, California. I apologized for not contacting her before, but I had been scared, and didn't want to risk anyone's safety with a letter that might be intercepted. I knew about that.

The card came back stamped, "Return to Sender. Moved. FWDG order expired." So, the Sunrise Diner was gone, too.

My story is coming to an end. I find myself staring for longer and longer periods of time out my window, wondering what the real Susy Shin is doing now, how her mother is. I look back at the pages I have written and realize that there are so many loose ends in my speculations. I do not know what anyone is really doing. I imagine Marlene is living with her son, possibly still waitressing. She lives upstairs—her son and his wife want her to live with them. There are those whom even my imagination cannot find. Mona Gorden, for example. Who knows what she had been like?

And Farrel Gorden? What happened to the man whose letters

started it all? Perhaps this is the most disturbing part of my inquiry. I have no clue as to where he is now. I often hope that after searching for a few years he grew tired, and eventually gave up. I hope that after realizing he would never find me, he drove south on I-95, past the Mason-Dixon line, with his last ten dollars and a half-dozen useless credit cards in his back pocket. He began to feel better, knowing that he never had to return to Yanack, and for the next two days he would drive until his money and then his gas ran out. He would end up in South Carolina, along the coast, and eventually would find a job at a gas station in a small town about twenty miles from Charleston, pumping gas and reading about auto repair, something he had always wanted to learn. Farrel Gorden would stay in South Carolina, first living out of his car and the back room at the garage, and eventually earning enough to rent a small apartment down the street. He would like the warmth, the sun. He would soon become part owner of the gas station, and once his partner left, own the station himself, and to this day he is still there, working behind the front desk, keeping records of car parts coming in and out, overseeing the other mechanics. Though Gorden would always wonder why I had done the things I had, he would no longer care, since that was so long ago, and he had other concerns, at least for now. He would of course think about his sister, about Shari, about Helen, but he would try to concentrate on his business, and try to forget about that time in Yanack. This is what I hope.

5

I miss that train platform in Marnole. I enjoy the life I lead now, and though I do not intend to leave this place in California, I know that I will have to return to Marnole at least once more, if only to stand again on that huge concrete station and look out over that town. I imagine that my building is no longer there, knocked down for more housing, and that the train station, now older, has become dirty with graffiti and large cracks along the walls. But that's fine with me. As long as I can climb those steps and see the houses below, imagining what the people inside are doing, and see the town at night, with the street lamps all along Sunrise Highway, the cars driving down below, the wind blowing in the stairwell and whistling around me—as long as I can see these things once again, one last time, my account will be finally resolved.

6

In my dream Shari and I are standing out in the fields near my house. It is late evening and we are listening to the coyotes yipping at the full moon. We stand completely still, staring out over the soft blue landscape, feeling the cool night air blow across the goldenrod, the rustling weeds shushing around us. Shari is seventeen again and stares up at the moon, turning her head towards me whenever the coyotes' high-pitched calls grow louder. They won't bother us, I say.

She nods and closes her eyes, her face still tilted towards the moon, and as the coyotes quiet down, the wind kicks up and Shari's long curly hair falls onto her face, covering it. She becomes cold and hugs her body, but continues to keep her face to the moon. She remains still, listening, waiting.

ABOUT THE AUTHOR

Leonard Chang's first novel, *The Fruit 'N Food,* won the Black Heron Press Award for Social Fiction. His short stories, essays, and book reviews have appeared in numerous periodicals, including *The Crescent Review, Prairie Schooner, Many Mountains Moving, MoonRabbit Review,* and *The San Francisco Bay Guardian.* He was born in New York, raised on Long Island, and attended Dartmouth College, Harvard University, and the University of California at Irvine. He currently lives in the San Francisco Bay Area, and is at work on his next novel.